A Student of Weather

BOOKS BY ELIZABETH HAY

FICTION
Crossing the Snow Line (stories, 1989)
Small Change (stories, 1997)
A Student of Weather (novel, 2000)

NON-FICTION
The Only Snow in Havana (1992)
Captivity Tales: Canadians in New York (1993)

A Student *of* Weather

ELIZABETH HAY

COUNTERPOINT
WASHINGTON, D.C.

S

Hay, Elizabeth, 1951–
    A student of weather / Elizabeth Hay
        p.   cm.
ISBN 1-58243-123-X
    1. Saskatchewan—Fiction.   2. Sibling rivalry—Fiction
3. New York (N.Y.)—Fiction.   4. Rural families—Fiction.
5. Young women—Fiction.   6. Farm life—Fiction.   7. Sisters—
Fiction.   I. Title.

PR9199.3.H3676 S78   2001
813'.54—dc21

                                                    00-064445

FIRST PRINTING

Jacket design by Amy Evans McClure

COUNTERPOINT
P.O. Box 65793
Washington, D.C. 20035-5793

Counterpoint is a member of the Perseus Books Group

10 9 8 7 6 5 4 3 2 1

*For Rhoda Barrett
and
Ben Fried*

"But when there are two sisters, one is uglier and more clumsy than the other, one is less clever, one is more promiscuous. Even when all the better qualities unite in one sister, as most often happens, she will not be happy, because the other, like a shadow, will follow her success with green eyes."

LYDIA DAVIS, *Break It Down*

A Student *of* Weather

Some nights she still goes over every detail, beginning with the weather and proceeding to the drop of blood on the old sheet – her quick wish for a man with straight white teeth and red lips – and then his arrival. His voice outside, her hand on the coin of frostbite on his cheek, his gift of an apple.

Everyone said it was eastern weather, the snow so deep and even that the carol was always in her mind, and she asked her father and sister who St. Stephen was, but as usual they didn't know. The absence of wind, a certain mildness in the air, a certain depth: instead of cutting sideways, the weather came down. People said this was the way it snowed in Ontario, and she thought, since I cannot get to Ontario, Ontario has come to me.

Everything was quiet except for the awful spoon against the awful pot. Lucinda, making porridge downstairs. It was early and the sound carried easily up to the small dark child she used to be and remembers being. She heard her father go down, she heard him speak to Lucinda, she heard the spoon start up again with the circular scrape of bad luck for which there was only

I

one antidote that she knew of. Over the side of the bed snaked her thin white arm.

Light entered the room. It came through the four-paned east-facing window packed along the edges with strips of sheet, every window in the house the same, all bandaged against the weather. It picked out the chest of drawers, the straight-backed chair, the double bed, of which one side was empty and the other occupied, but not by much, she was so little, and it changed in tone from brown to grainy white like a screen before the movie begins. In this pre-movie light her little fingers were busy.

From under the bed came her wooden box, from inside the box a small package in brown wax paper, from inside the package a heel of fruitcake so moist and rich that when she eased a bit of it away from the paper it left behind a mat of golden crumbs.

Soon she'll go downstairs and say good morning Lucinda through nearly closed lips so that her sister will not smell her breath, but in the meantime she pictures herself running away to the apple-strewn east like Claudette Colbert running lickety-split to Clark Gable.

Nineteen thirty-eight, and snow is a change from dust. There have been times when so much dust has fallen so continuously that when she rose from bed in the morning her head left behind a white oval on the pillowcase. Towns have dried out except for their names: Swift Current, Gull Lake, Maple Creek, Willow Bend. Hotel towels are so thin, a traveller's nose goes through the other side.

Here you find almost every extreme. The coldest winters and the hottest summers, the longest days and the shortest, the

richest soil and the poorest, the biggest views of the simplest
skies, the least rain, the most wind, the best light and the worst
dust in this best and worst of all worlds. Heads or tails. The wide
plain of southwestern Saskatchewan rolls away to the east forever
and away to the west, but not so far, before rising into a cold dry
Scotland. It's the sort of landscape you can run your finger over,
an apparently flat surface that's less flat than almost-even, and it's
the *almost* that makes for its beauty and the *even* that lays it open
to the wildest weather. Frosts in June, tornadoes in July, hail-
storms in August, and drought all year long.

It's a bit like Christmas. What will be in your weather stocking today? Oh joy. A plague of sawflies.

Children grew up never tasting an apple and thinking Ontario
was heaven.

At breakfast Lucinda drops a knife. Her father looks up in instant
irritation only to soften when he sees who's to blame. Of course
Norma Joyce notices.

But noticing isn't enough. She has to say, "It wasn't me this
time," in a tone of four-square insistence. A child who always has
her fists up. Who has to let everybody know she hasn't missed a
trick. Who has to make everybody uncomfortable.

She is eight years old. Afflicted by early puberty, pencilled in
by body hair, as weather-sensitive as a fish. At night she lies in
bed belting out "Good King Wenceslas" until Lucinda comes to
the foot of the stairs and says HUSH. Then there is only the
sound of the treadle going up and down under Lucinda's slippered foot. Lucinda sews and dark hairs appear on Norma Joyce.
In the morning she looks at herself and feels sewn inside out,

threads left hanging by a clumsy child or an ill-intentioned adult. She plays with the tufts of hair under her arms.

They had been reading "Rapunzel." Lucinda was perched on the side of the bed, Norma Joyce was lying back with bare arms cradled behind her head because it was summer, and Lucinda stopped in mid-word and bent over to look. Touched the shadow in her sister's armpit (skin as soft as talcum powder) and Norma Joyce's own fingers went up to feel.

Eight years old and still with all her baby teeth. Something out of season. A child leaping ahead in a kind of gulping prematurity – the aggressiveness of summer, the loss of light spring air. She was foliage in the wrong place, a jumble of weeds growing out of someone's back.

Midafternoon now, and everyone's indoors. She is at the kitchen table absorbed in *The Flopsy Bunnies*, Ernest is filling the kettle (*afloat on tea* should be the words on his gravestone), Lucinda is in the rocking chair darning socks on a wooden egg. She reaches into her ragbag and pulls out a piece of old sheet.

"Norma Joyce? Here. Make a hem."

There they are, the two of them, seated in the kitchen in this quiet time before he arrives. Beautiful, saintly Lucinda interrupting and believing she has the right to interrupt because all she sees is a tiny book in the hands of a tiny, out-of-proportion child whose forehead puts Elizabeth the First's to shame, whose earlobes could double as pillows, whose baggy eyes could sleep an army. All she sees is a child who never helps.

"I *hate* sewing," comes the plain, passionate answer, not calculated to offend, maybe, but offensive.

"Don't say hate on a Sunday," and Lucinda offers her a threaded needle.

"Oh Norma," softly, "for pity's sake," and she puts down her sock again. Both sisters watch the fat drop of blood spread across the poor old sheet. It forms a little red bird on a white background.

The sky drops. Big flakes of snow. Then wind. The first blizzard of the year puts an end to peaceful weather. For twelve hours, snow like flour blows sideways. At five o'clock they have potato soup, buttered bread, glasses of milk, bread pudding: a white meal in white weather, after which Lucinda picks up the lantern and heads for the woodshed, but not before turning to speak in that schoolteachery voice of hers.

"Don't stir until all your pudding is gone. Norma Joyce? Are you listening?"

Ernest has moved to the rocking chair and taken out his pipe. No help to be had from there, but when has Norma Joyce ever asked her father for help? This is her evening and her morning, the rotting-away looseness of milk-sodden bread that follows the slimy lumpiness of oatmeal porridge. She puts the pudding into her mouth and gags. Oh the horror.

And then, as luck sometimes has it, the salvation. She hears voices. Lucinda's voice and a man's. She slips on her coat, her mittens, and goes outside. Her sister is on the porch cradling wood (old fence posts, scavenged and split up into kindling) against her chest and holding the lantern high with her free hand so that the tall stranger is easy to see.

He comes right out of the wind and snow, his interested eyes on beautiful Lucinda, a coin of frostbite on his cheek. For a moment the two sisters look down at his relieved and smiling face, then he climbs the steps to meet them. Just before reaching the top he bends over to knock the snow off his trousers. In that moment, Norma Joyce steps forward. She slips off her mitten and puts her warm hand on his cheek.

"Most people," he says, taking in the odd little girl, "would just say, hey, you've got frostbite."

Inside, he mops the melting snow off his hair and neck, then takes an Ontario apple out of his knapsack. He polishes it against his flannel shirt, sets it on the kitchen table, says he's only sorry he doesn't have more. His name is Maurice Dove.

She will remember the hard white penny. It feels like congealed wax and turns eraser-pink in the warm kitchen. She will remember touching it a second time, when it's puffy and hot, before saying with considerable satisfaction that from now on this will be the first place to freeze. "It's going to freeze *all* the time," she says.

He wants to know if *all* little girls are so bloodthirsty. She has no answer for that. She just has the triumph of having surprised him into noticing her.

Two sisters fell down the same well, and the well was Maurice Dove. He stayed two weeks, he returned twice more the same year. Three times they were dipped into his handsome presence.

In the evenings he sat at the kitchen table with a faded red shawl over his shoulders, writing in his notebook or reading, and the others joined him one by one. Norma Joyce came first, bringing Beatrix Potter or *Hurlbut's Story of the Bible*, then Ernest came in from the barn, then Lucinda from upstairs where she had been folding sheets. The house felt warmer with him inside it; the kitchen glinted from extra sources of light: the second coal-oil lamp beside the sink, the brighter Aladdin lamp on the table, the white collar around Lucinda's neck and the tortoise-shell combs in her hair, the extra spoon beside the glazed brown teapot, and the ring on Maurice's hand, which moved across the pages of lined white paper.

"Is that a diamond?" the little girl asked, and he smiled, "You don't miss much, do you?", extending a hand she'll see again when she sees Marlon Brando in a movie, a square hand with long tapered fingers, an outdoor hand with indoor know-how.

In he came, smelling of the outside and of travel, and here she is, reaching out to touch the gold band inset with a tiny diamond star. His middle finger is calloused and ink-stained, the fingernails worn – but a diamond ring. He must be rich.

She memorizes every inch of him. Every inch of floppy, thick, brown hair, blue eyes and milky neckline, slender hips and slippered feet, and long, flat, clever fingers. No matter whether riffling through papers or pulling things out of his knapsack, he holds his fingers the way a piano player isn't supposed to.

In the morning he gets up before everyone else "to make summer," he says, by adding coal to the range and grinding coffee in the hand grinder on the wall. From his small personal supply he makes enough for everyone, pouring himself half a cup, which he sniffs long and luxuriously.

Norma Joyce says, "It's like you're sniffing flowers."

This was his greatest gift: he relaxed you into talking. He drew blood from conversational stone. And if you weren't stone, if on the contrary you were susceptible, then you were putty in his hands.

"Tell me a secret," he said to Norma Joyce.

They were alone in the kitchen. He had poured her a small cup of coffee, a demi-tasse, he called it, and added a generous amount of sugar. She was sitting in her chair, the one on the inside of the table nearest the wall so that it wasn't easy to get up and help.

She said, "I have a special room."

He was listening. He waited.

"Nobody but me goes into it."

"Here?" he asked. "Or far away?"

"I'll show it to you. If you want."

It was the room off the front hall, the study once used in the evenings by her book-loving mother, who would sit comfortably at the desk, correcting homework from the two or three students she tutored in English or Chemistry or Math. A quiet room of blues and greys. The window looked east. Its curtains were a faded blue chintz; the walls were papered in a pattern of blue and grey bands separated by white lines; her mother's desk, to the left of the window, was a well-used surface, but tidy. From the doorway Norma Joyce watched the slope of her back and the angle of her head as she worked, knowing that eventually she would turn and smile and hold out her arms. She smelled of ink and Evening of Paris, this lovely woman who every Sunday dabbed perfume behind her ears, and Norma Joyce's too. For the rest of the week they would sniff each other to see whose scent lasted longest. (Norma Joyce's, because her skin held fragrance the way it held moisture.)

Florida May was her mother's name. Florida May would take her by the hand up to the room she shared with Lucinda at the top of the stairs. Midway down the hall a ladder continued the ascent up through a trap door to the windowless attic where the thin, black, many-elbowed stovepipes rising from the kitchen range and from the Nautilus heater in the sitting room reconnected and burst through the roof into the prairie sky.

Norma Joyce began with a small blue bowl. This happened the summer after her mother died. She found it drifted up against the side of the barn and put it on the floor beside her mother's desk (A schoolteacher, Maurice said to Lucinda. That accounts for your name) and let it fill with dust. Then she moved it to the corner table and set around it the stray objects she collected in her wanderings: a small shoe; a baby's soother; pieces of wood, glass, metal, crockery; small skulls and bones; smooth stones; buttons; pieces of yarn and string. Dust fell from every direction, and over time the corner turned into a dust sculpture, a shrine of sorts. For a while a spider, as still as a little grey glove, lived in one corner of this weather room.

"I don't mind," she said when Maurice picked up the small shoe, "so long as you put it back in the very same spot."

Even a fraction of an inch off and she shared the object's sense of disturbance. There was an exactitude to her arrangements that any thief would understand.

Her sense of order was the opposite of Lucinda's. For Lucinda order was erasure, for Norma Joyce it was accumulation. Each object had its home on a shelf or table or some corner of the floor, and its biography in her secret notebook. Each bit of yarn, colourful button, broken bit of china was identified: what it was, where she had found it, and when. Her favourite stone was a smooth black one she had found in the summer of 1937 beside the Hayden well. She showed it to Maurice, whose level of interest was entirely satisfying, then put it back into its outline, wishing she could do the same thing every night with her own head; but Lucinda was always at work shaking pillows, smoothing sheets, removing dust all over the house except here. This room Lucinda never entered. By unspoken agreement it was left to Norma Joyce the way you set to one side a bit of fruit or sugar for a wasp.

"You're a natural student," he said to Norma Joyce, and it was the first compliment she had received since her mother died.

He was a student too, sent out from Ottawa to study the weather. In Willow Bend people said, *That's Ottawa for you, sending us a boy.* But they couldn't resist his charm, and so right away he heard about many things, including the Hardy farm. People said, *You came to learn about the weather, tell us why Ernest Hardy gets all the rain.*

It was a magnet for moisture, this farm to the east of Willow Bend, a spot of dew in a dry field, a small hill that attracted rain and snow when nothing fell anywhere else. Didn't Zeus once take the form of a golden shower? Maybe Lucinda's beauty captivated the rain. Or – this thought occurred to him later – maybe the small, dark, unpredictable sister was the source of all the weather.

It was the morning after he arrived. January 7, 1938, the year of a blue moon in January and again in March. Out of long habit Lucinda set the table with cups and bowls upside-down to keep out the dust. Norma Joyce began to tackle her porridge and Maurice, to her enormous disappointment, said yes, he'd have another bowl, thank you Lucinda.

And so she asked aggressively, "Who was St. Stephen?"

He turned to the little girl with the eyes that didn't let up. Blue eyes, and questions out of the blue.

"St. Stephen? They stoned him to death. He was the first Christian martyr. And do you know who held the coats of the men who stoned him?"

She shook her head.

"St. Paul. That was when he was still Saul of Tarsus, before he saw the light."

"How do you know that?"

"Because I was born on the Feast of Stephen. Maurice Stephen Dove at your service," with a smile in Lucinda's direction.

"I was born on March 29th in 1929," said Norma Joyce.

"I'll remember that," and she believed him, which was her first mistake. He added, "Now they say he suffered from migraines."

"Migraines?" Lucinda looked up quickly.

"The light that blinded him. A headache."

"I know," she said.

"You mean the light on the road to Damascus?" asked Norma Joyce, although she knew perfectly well that was what he meant. She might not know about the saints but everybody knew about the road to Damascus.

"Yup," he said, swallowing his porridge. "When he was carrying that letter he didn't deliver."

"What letter?"

"Norma."

"What letter?"

"Norma Joyce. Let our guest eat in peace." Then, raising the coffee pot over his cup, "My sister goes for days without saying a word, then all of a sudden she'll question you to death."

"I don't mind," he said. But his words weren't the comfort they might have been, because he was so busy looking at Lucinda.

He had come downstairs wondering if full daylight might reveal a flaw, but no, the more daylight the better. Glorious golden-red hair, slender shoulders, measured quickness, an apparently serene energy that seemed almost Chinese, and beyond vanity as she poured coffee, served porridge, did to her sister's hair what she took half the time to do to her own: fashioned a braid that she wound twice around her head.

Her sore, chapped hands she treated like a child who tries your patience. Thorough, quick, no-nonsense, and the lid was back on the jar of dark yellow Vaseline.

Her way with him was no different. She only glanced, then looked away from his rosebud mouth, his lanky slenderness and warm smell. Retreating in order to adjust. And so she missed the morning conversation when Norma Joyce learned so much that was surprising. He knew their Ottawa uncle. He knew exactly where Uncle Dennis lived because his street ran parallel to Uncle Dennis's street. In his notebook he sketched a series of lines, Carlyle above Fulton, and Woodbine a dotted laneway on the right, and the canal a curving line to the left.

"He knows Uncle Dennis!" Norma Joyce told her.

By the time Maurice was ready to leave, Lucinda would be interested. This was her pattern: tugging carefully at every knot, pressing the wrapping paper flat, saving everything for future use, including her own anticipation. More than any amount of having, anticipation, laced with duty, seemed to please her.

Golden Lucinda. She rose before dawn, lit one lamp and cleaned the glass chimneys of the other four before setting to work, as unflagging in her advance as the elves who toil while everyone sleeps. The weather made her job Herculean by filling every nook with dust and removing water from the scene, but she rose to the challenge, nearly as tall as Maurice and blessed with the kind of prairie eyes that can drill a speck at any distance. Nothing escaped her. Walls, shelves, ceiling, floor, shiny black stove, school map of Canada above the treadle sewing machine, table without an oilcloth because she couldn't stand the look of them, black walnut rocking chair and armchair that once furnished the reception room of dentist-uncle Dennis, who lived in semi-retired splendour near the canal, he said, and they all imagined the endless brimming water.

In the corner of the kitchen (as Norma Joyce will one day see again in tiny Manhattan apartments) was an Ernest innovation from the days when he still thought big: a bathtub shipped by crate from Eaton's in Winnipeg, enamelled white on the inside, painted dark green on the outside, with four splayed feet. A pipe attached to the plug went through the floor to the yard outside; a fitted wooden cover served as a shelf for buckets and milk pails. Every Saturday Lucinda heated water for baths and was astonished by her sister's smooth olive skin. Where did she come from, this intact child whose skin never split, whose hair never tangled, whose teeth never ached?

Her own breath smelled of cloves, an old remedy to press a clove against the aching tooth like a consoling thought, and for a moment she stopped her dusting and dropped into a chair. People said she was a wonder, no one could touch her, no one could lay a finger on her: the most beautiful woman in southwestern

Saskatchewan and the best housekeeper. The thought was a
dream suddenly remembered. She was in a large room with two
tall windows; she went to the first window and looked out at
a garden in flower, she went to the next window and the same
garden was buried under snow.

The dream was so clear, even now as she rocked back and
forth, that she dwelt on the strangeness of seeing summer from
one window and winter from the other.

"What are you thinking about?" asked Norma Joyce, surprised to see her sister seated and lost in thought.

"I had such a strange dream last night," and she went on to
describe it.

"Luce? I had the same dream!"

A coincidence that might have drawn them closer but didn't.
Lucinda felt irritated, though she couldn't have said why – competition with her sister was the farthest thing from her mind. A
common mistake of older sisters.

She stroked the arms of the rocker, running her fingers along
the grooves on either side and stirring up other images, though
these were waking ones. She thought about all the people who
had gripped these same arms in apprehension before entering her
uncle's dental chamber.

Framed by the black walnut chair, lost in thought, her sewing
forgotten in her lap, she could have been the wishful queen in the
old fairy tale. Remember the ebony frame around the snow-
white linen on which the drop of blood so tellingly falls?

The sitting-room walls are covered with flowered wallpaper white-washed by Lucinda one nervous summer. Through the white, like hairs just under the skin, you can see the faint blue of what used to be roses. Lucinda touches the wall the way she touches everything – to measure the dust – then, hand at her side, she rubs her finger-tips against her thumb like a dog scratching its ear.

She knows the pleasure of a wet cloth over a sticky table, an eraser over a blackboard, a hot iron over a wrinkled surface. The pleasure of order, routine, work.

Endless rows of knitting, endless dustings, endless buckets of water shape and soothe her days, her energy some magical jar that never empties until it's shattered. She was fifteen when the headaches began, and the pattern never varied and nor did the surprise. A sense of well-being lulled her, fooled her, opened the gates wide for the hordes of shiny zigzags that came galloping up to her eyes. The pain was always a surprise.

Ernest scrambled eggs. Norma Joyce set the table without being asked. Lucinda lay in bed facing away from the window, over which she had hung a dark blanket. After twenty-four wakeful, nauseated hours she fell into a deep sleep, then woke up refreshed, and cleaned like a fury.

Titian hair, Maurice tells Lucinda. The compliment sending her to the dictionary where she finds *Tishri, tissue, Ticino*; too shy to ask for the spelling. Years later, overhearing a docent in the National Art Gallery say *Titian*, she follows him around until the end of his tour, when he writes down the name for her. In the library she looks an especially long time at an illustration of *The Venus of Urbino*, struck by the contrast between the woman's warm nakedness and the servant's heavy garments, and reminded again of seeing summer and winter from different windows of the same dream room.

Like any good guest, Maurice is full of stories. He tells them about Cole Porter's fall the year before, and his mother's letter of condolence since she once worked as an atmosphere girl at the Shubert Theatre on Broadway. He says, "You see, I come by my love of weather naturally."

He tells warm-weather stories, describing his first hurricane when he was a boy in Florida: trees stripped of leaves and bark, rain like a milky-green wall, and afterwards, in battered branches, tropical birds blown all the way from the Caribbean. He tells about the time the Seminole Indians noticed an unseasonable blooming of sawgrass and moved north and west of the Everglades even as rabbits and rats moved in the same direction and birds stopped singing and flew that way too; a week later a wall of water swept over everything. He tells about whole civilizations lost to the weather, about a city near the Tigris and Euphrates buried under silt and uncovered after thousands of years, about mummified bodies emerging from Asian sand with shreds of silk still clinging, only to be covered once again by blowing sand.

That's why I'm here, he says. Weather catastrophes are my field and this is the nearest catastrophe.

It is?

Suddenly Norma Joyce sees herself as the star of a large-scale accident. She should be written up in the paper along with Bing Crosby's diet and Lana Turner's legs.

Not everyone finds Maurice's buoyancy so attractive. Ernest looks at him and thinks *young*. He thinks *student*. He thinks *eastern bonehead*.

Ernest Rupert Hardy. Quiet, stocky, compact, courteous to strangers, bad-tempered at home. He shares Lucinda's fair skin and hair, and abiding love of work – *He loved the work*, people will say of him – and Norma Joyce's unruly heart.

He cannot enter a room without making his presence felt, a man too wounded and ambitious to ever retreat gracefully into the background, a lucky man, but resentful, because good luck robs him of some of the sympathy he thinks he deserves. Always he needs a cup of tea, a gesture of respect, an acknowledgement of his importance, this self-indulgent man who stares out the window like General Eeyore eyeing his patch of weather. Gloomy, isolated, sorry for himself, and stubborn.

Florida May Lamb was putting flowers on her mother's grave the first time Ernest Hardy saw her. He should have taken the hint. That was in 1919, the year of the Spanish flu, when they had to tear boards off porches to keep up with the demand for coffins. Having come west to buy land and make a place for himself, and knowing a good thing when he saw it, he married Florida May within the year and he certainly loved her, though not as much as he loved his big brother Dennis. Uncle Dennis was twelve years older than Ernest and a bachelor, prosperous, wavy-haired, meticulous; he arrived for a visit in 1925, and fell in love at first sight because there wasn't any clutter, only huge sky and lifting prairie that opened so wide the dentist said *ah!*

He promised to join them in five years if Ernest would leave untilled a wide stretch of land for future orchards. We'll be the first, he said, to show it can be done. And so it happened that the

Hardy farm included a sizable portion of virgin prairie, and that made all the difference.

Four years later came the crash of 1929. In his place, Uncle Dennis sent furniture, barrels of apples, pounds of fruitcake; and then, one ill-fated winter, a small box of venison jerky.

Dust to dust, Ernest liked to mutter, staring out the window. And under his breath, *French*, when Maurice Dove had the gall to drink coffee at night rather than tea.

Maurice doesn't let it bother him. He tells himself you have to be like a cork in water, you can't let difficult people pull you down. A buoyancy inherited from his mother, the atmosphere girl whose parents left Quebec for the cotton mills in Massachusetts when she was three. She was the oldest of nine children, and another was on its way when she made her break, taking off for New York City at the age of seventeen. There she met shy Walter Dove, who was working for his father's textile company in Montreal, and from time to time came down to New York on business. He always stayed at the Ritz-Carlton, eating in the dining room and every night ordering the same dinner of fish and chips followed by a bowl of vanilla ice cream. One night, at a performance of *The Student Prince*, he saw Annette Tremblay trip over her green chiffon dress, and his eyes cleared.

Walter took home a bride whose hatred of winter gave him the excuse he needed. So long, *l'hiver. Au revoir*, suckers. Off they went to Florida, where a year later Maurice was born on the edge of the Everglades.

As a boy he spent his days looking at birds, stealing their eggs, examining plants. At nine he was so shocked that his mother didn't know the names of the weeds in her garden that he made her a book called *Dove Botany*. At ten he was reading *The Voyage of the Beagle*. At eleven his grandfather died, and at twelve he was living in Ottawa to be close, but not too close, to his old granny in Montreal. By then a mink coat had reconciled Annette to winter weather.

She told her son, "Ottawa is a lucky place because it's built where three rivers meet, and you are a lucky boy because you're one of a family of three. Don't," she told him, "don't *ever* get tied down by a big family. I mean this. Don't have children before you're fifty."

He doesn't intend to. The pitter-patter of little feet is not what he hears in his head. Rather, *Let's all clap for Maurice Dove*, and a large audience is on its feet. He can't restrain his smile. He smiles at the foolishness and at the pleasure of it.

His voice, Norma Joyce will hear again when she sees Gene Kelly in a movie. An odd, light, husky voice that excites her the way layers of tissue paper around a gift excite her. Her own voice is low.

"A whiskey tenor," he teases.

She stares at him hard, then grins such an expansive grin that he discovers her strangest characteristic: her gums are the colour of Coca-Cola. The effect is astonishing. Her face brightens while her gums darken just like Jock's, his old dog.

Night and Day, he thinks, and goes to the piano. In the sitting room, against the wall, is the Mason and Risch brought out from Ontario by Florida May's parents. He plays Cole Porter while the sisters stand on either side of him: Norma Joyce, so unabashed, so forthright in her admiration that no one takes her seriously, and Lucinda, holding back – but then, she has beauty on her side.

From his pocket Maurice pulls out the small brass barometer his mother gave him when he turned twelve. He tells his tiny audience-with-the-huge-earlobes that the barometer drops and we feel drowsy and dream more, water rises in wells, mosquitoes bite harder, fish bite less. Some people are barometers, he says. Some people are weather-sensitive; most children are.

"I'm like that," says Norma Joyce.

"Like what?" asks Lucinda.

"I know what's going to happen. I know someone is going to say something and then they say it. Or I think something is going to happen in a book and then it happens."

"You mean you look ahead to the pictures."

"I don't mean that."

Lucinda laughs, and the larger claim gets lost in the small regions of giving and taking offence.

But Norma Joyce knows what she knows. A barometer tells the weather twelve hours before it arrives, and so does she. She knows many things.

"I smell cucumbers when there aren't any," she says. "I smell them and I know the weather's going to change."

"Sometimes," she adds firmly, "I've seen my brother before a storm."

The needle goes still in Lucinda's hand, Ernest's cup of tea stops in its perpetual ascent, and Maurice waits for an explanation that doesn't come until his second visit.

The deep snow that winter of 1938 made her feel as if she were inside someone else's childhood: Hansel and Gretel coming upon the sugar house, Maurice Dove coming out of the wind and snow. She recalls how quickly he won everyone over, learning from one person about another: from Lucinda that Ernest's luck was both too much and too little, and nothing he wanted to talk about.

"He never has enough but he always has some, some crop, some feed for his stock, while most everybody else has nothing. They think we're lucky because we get twelve bushels of wheat off our summerfallow and all they get is Russian thistle. But the money doesn't even pay for the freight."

Good luck that was bad luck (as was her luck with Maurice, she thinks now). Outside was the prairie, its simple lines shifting in a way that could turn a person grey overnight, but their farm was different. Their farm was an oasis, with its hill that attracted rain, its acres that never had known the plough, its small, continuing crop of wheat, its garden that Lucinda struggled with, its deep well that never failed. In the summer, the line between green and brown was almost magical, it was so clear. Beyond the green was the kingdom of dust in which she roamed, a little girl under a dark cloud.

Neighbours asked her father how he did it, what's your secret? Unable to conceal an envy worse than bad weather, this weather in their eyes. Sometimes he cast a baleful look at his small daughter before reminding them of his own tragedies by asking about their wives and sons. Luck turns, he would say, just as the weather turns, and without rhyme or reason.

And so he welcomed the scientific men who came from the experimental farms in Ottawa, Swift Current, Medicine Hat. Let them take the credit, he thought. Let them take the heat.

"His reputation makes him testy," Lucinda said. "Don't play up his successes and don't criticize him either. Make him feel comfortable, and then he'll talk."

Maurice was deft at such things. (Norma Joyce is not. Even now, having come back to show herself capable of at least one act of loyalty, she cannot cater to her father the way Lucinda and Maurice always did.)

They were having supper. Maurice reached for the teapot and said as naturally and respectfully as if he had known Ernest all his life, "Ernie, let me fill your cup."

It was the *Ernie*. His brother called him Ernie and so had Florida May.

Norma Joyce was five when her sister pulled back the blankets of her mother's bed, smoothing the bottom sheet before her father laid down the blue-faced woman in the faded pink dressing gown. They pulled up the blankets. They fussed with those blankets. Then her father tried to close her mother's eyes, but they wouldn't close.

Lucinda took Norma Joyce downstairs. She made tea. She added two spoonfuls of sugar instead of the usual one, and stroked her head as you stroke a dog's, giving and taking comfort while your mind is somewhere else. Lucinda was fourteen. It was 1934.

That evening Mrs. Hayden suggested she put pennies on her mother's eyelids. Mrs. Hayden was English. In England they put sovereigns on the eyes of dead sovereigns. They also change their dresses, the women do, every afternoon at four o'clock. Even though Mrs. Hayden had lost one child to pneumonia and another to diphtheria, even though she hadn't been able to find her rhubarb under the drifts of dust for over three years, she still reached into her closet every afternoon to remove from a solid wooden hanger either her blue dress or her purple. The effect was like having a mailbox that produces a letter every single day.

Norma Joyce saw the pennies when she snuck back into the bedroom. Her mother's eyes looked decorative and at peace. Closer, and she could see that the penny on the right was heads and the one on the left was tails (1930, encircled by a continuous maple vine), so one eye was going to Ontario and the other was off to England. One eye would see maple trees, while the other would see the king.

She stole back a second time to press into her hungry mother's hand the piece of bread she had saved from supper. But the hand was too stiff, too cold. She slid the bread into the pocket of the dressing gown.

Her mother had choked to death on a piece of venison jerky snuck in the middle of the night. Now Norma Joyce will be watched for sneakiness, and scolded for bolting her food. She will feel sneaky. Even when she has no need, even when no one else is home, she will feel like a sneak.

Alone in the house with her feeling of release into the forbidden, she touches things, opens drawers, eats. Handfuls of raisins. Slivers of cake, edges of meat artfully sliced so as to escape her sister's notice. A pot of tea drunk in one sitting.

The quiet access to everything is what she loves. She goes into her father's room and tries on her mother's dresses, which still hang on the right side of the closet. She lies on the bed. She smiles. When she smiles, her hands feel lighter. They lift like small clouds. So does the cramp in her chest. It vanishes and many interesting thoughts move through her head.

A tiny girl satisfied with small company.

The spring she turned three, her mother took down from the shelf a marvellous little book. She drew Norma Joyce into her lap and together they rested their eyes on the delicate pictures of lettuces and lawns. L-a-w-n, spelled her mother, stroking with her forefinger the wash of light green. Outside, snow was driving sideways past the window and had been for days.

The pictures fixed her. Her eyes had been broken and now they were fixed. Two years later, soon after her mother's death, she noticed something new. Not just the odd word but whole sentences made sense; she could read the book from start to finish.

She didn't let on. Whenever her father or Lucinda looked her way, and it wasn't often, she stared emphatically at Mrs. Flopsy Bunny heading across a lawn that was bounded on the left by a stone wall, and up ahead by another low wall, beyond which lay a large farmhouse painted in tones of creamy yellow and soft grey. She walked up to the door and inside. It was dim and quiet in the long hallway. It smelled of butter. The hallway led to a carpeted sitting room, then down a step into a large kitchen where a plate of hot scones cooled on the table beside a pot of the thick cream once described to her in loving detail by a mother who was always hungry. Not a bowl of porridge in sight.

Three more years went by and Lucinda was saying to Maurice, "She doesn't read. She barely talks to us. We have no idea what will become of her."

"She talks to me."

"Everyone talks to you."

They smiled at each other. Lucinda was glad to have some-one to admire, and Maurice was glad to be admired.

"She won't go to school. I keep telling her to go, but she won't see reason."

This last uttered with a teacher's satisfaction at ranking a child at the bottom: *This one is a dead loss.* Lucinda had the manner. Capable and quick to judge; as pleased by failure as by success.

Norma Joyce overheard. She was in the sitting room curled up on the sofa, the better to hear. (She liked one thing at a time, one flavour, one texture, one attribute: voice undiluted by appearance; radio would always appeal to her more than television, though movies were another matter.) She heard Maurice say, "You shouldn't worry. I'm sure she has all her buttons."

All my buttons, she thought, are in my weather room.

In her weather room, on the desk, there was a photograph inside an oval frame. "Your mother?" asked Maurice, picking it up and looking closely at a woman with none of Norma Joyce's features except the high, wide forehead. "What was she like?"

"She was tall. She was taller than my father and she wrote a letter every day."

"I'm proud if I write a letter a *year*."

"She loved mail," taking back the photograph and polishing it with her handkerchief. "She said a letter a day was better than an apple a day, and she loved apples. They had every kind of apple when she was growing up. She told me."

"That must have been in Ontario."

"Near Barrie," agreed Norma Joyce, looking at him to see if he knew where that was. He nodded and she went on. "They had Snows," she expounded. "Spys. McIntosh Reds. Pippins. Strawberrys. Talliman Sweets. Golden Russets. There was a cider mill too. Any time you wanted to, you could turn a crank and the cider came out of a spout into a pail. One time she drank so much they found her fast asleep in the sap kettle at the end of the orchard. Another time she fell asleep in the asparagus patch. What's your favourite apple?"

"Russets, I think. Or Spys."

"You should make up your mind."

"Have you made up yours?"

"I've never tasted a Russet."

"I'll bring you one. Next time I come."

Watching her dust her mother's photograph so tenderly and possessively, he remembered the touch of her warm palm on his cheek the night he arrived. He had been taken aback by her ugliness, a word he modified to homeliness the next morning when she stood in his bedroom doorway and stared at him intently and at length; then at breakfast he thought her merely strange; and now, interesting.

Her small hand reached out to claim him. You hear about women like this, who decide within seconds they're going to marry the man they've just met. It makes you think that boldness counts for more than beauty, and persistence counts for even more.

She goes through his room and no one is the wiser – taking note of where each thing is so she can put it back exactly. The knapsack tilted to the left on the chair, its flap lowered but not fastened. The small notebook inside the right pocket, upside-down and spine pointing to the window. The handwriting as small and neat as her mother's. A star beside a café in Swift Current. *Excellent crullers.* And so he discovers that she has no trouble reading.

Looking up from her porridge, she asks him what a *crueller* is.

"Cruller," he says, "as in duller. Why?"

"I just wondered."

"A kind of doughnut. Long and twisted instead of round. I'll buy you one some day."

He tells Lucinda not to worry, your sister may know a good deal more than you think.

So transparent. She actually thinks these stealthy intrusions will draw him closer. She even quotes a phrase he has written down – "You must believe in yourself before you can accomplish anything" as if she's thought of it on her own. We have a special bond. We think the same way.

She sees *beautiful* underlined beside Lucinda's name, and in the margin pencils in her own name before erasing it poorly.

Inside the knapsack she finds three pairs of grey woollen socks, three sets of underwear, two undershirts, a second flannel shirt, a second pair of wool trousers, a leather shaving kit that contains a razor with a Sheffield blade and a black handle, the razor strop, the Yardley's shaving cup and the badger-hair shaving brush, plus a dark brown hairbrush, white toothbrush, tube of Squibb's toothpaste, and nail scissors.

Every morning she follows the even path his razor makes as he shaves at the kitchen sink, enchanted by a ritual that always concludes with his hanging the towel evenly on the rack and topping up her coffee "so we're even."

Her watchfulness is too intent for laziness, no matter what Lucinda and Ernest say, too intent, too almost-voluptuous, too fulfilled.

She watches Lucinda to see what Maurice sees, and feels reassured. Lucinda is still Lucinda. Look at her make biscuits. Out comes the square of oilcloth, the rolling pin, the bowl, the extra flour. Up go her sleeves and make way at the kitchen table. No crumb-on-the-run stands a chance. No speck of flour or fugitive morsel of dough will ever dodge those fanatical fingers. At the end, every utensil is scraped so clean, every inch of hardworking hands rubbed so briskly, palm against palm, that her astonishing sister doesn't even need to wash up. Is this a woman in love?

Lucinda slices bread in dead-even slices, dusts the crumbs off the table into a jar, scrubs potatoes in a bucket, saves the water to reuse after the dirt has settled to the bottom. Never sits without a piece of sewing in her hands. Never complains. As content to be inside as Norma Joyce is to be outside: the small girl's progress through the out-of-doors is no less intricate than Lucinda's fine stitches. Like an old dog she has her route, and faithfully she follows it, checking on the broken-toothed comb in a can at the foot of a fence post, the dog-eared New Testament under a rock, the old brown bottle under the Saskatoon bush that no longer bears fruit. And like a dog she marks her treasures, tying bits of stray wool to fence wire in winter, or to leafy caragana in summer, burying what the dog-wind unburies and possessed by a degree of guile she herself doesn't understand. She pretends she can't sew, then years later makes a perfect garment to run away in.

By hiding things, then leaving herself open to being caught, she lends a certain drama to everything she does.

A certain drama, and a certain innocence.

Lucinda makes her wear double stockings and long woollen bloomers that she hates with even more reason than most children because she doesn't feel the cold and never gets sick. The day she disobeys, she leaves evidence of her rebellion in full view on her way to bed: a soft pile of clothes on the bedroom floor. Anyone could see the summer underwear amid the winter stockings.

Lucinda saw.

She reported the misdemeanour to her father, who dealt with it the usual way. Insult followed by injury. He waited until Maurice left the house. Then, "What is your middle name?" he asked, looking at his newspaper.

"Kathleen." It was almost a whisper.

"Are you sure?" He looked up. "Are you sure it isn't Sneak?"

No answer.

"Come here."

With the first blow came the involuntary surge of pee, followed by the humiliation of washing the floor and washing her clothes. (One day she will be made to wash every dish in the house, but that comes later and for a different reason.)

It's true that Norma Joyce is sneaky. But she tells herself she can't be all bad when she is so open about what she hides.

Summer inside winter – begging to be caught, asking to be punished. So Lucinda thought. So anyone would think, except Norma Joyce, who clung to virtue by not hiding her tracks.

Lucinda removed the day-old sponge cake from her sister's reach. "A piece for someone who ate all the fruitcake? I don't think so."

This happened the day after Maurice's first visit ended. It was January 20. Dinner was over, snow was falling, Ernest was lighting his pipe.

"I didn't eat *all* the fruitcake."

"You ate all that was left."

"No."

"No?"

"Not *all* that was left."

"You mean you still have some hidden away?"

Lucinda's was a Depression-era sense of fairness about food. Stolen fruitcake cancelled out a helping of sponge cake: that's all. She said it virtuously to herself.

Out loud, "You have to learn that it's wrong to steal."

"I didn't *steal*."

"You stole."

"You have no proof."

"I have proof. I can see it in your eyes."

Norma Joyce continued to have a tiny morsel before breakfast (loving sweet things more in the morning than at any other time of day), but she took a leaf from Maurice's book and cleaned her teeth as soon as she came downstairs. The height of extravagance to brush *before* you ate as well as after. Not that she had a toothbrush. She used her finger and a glass of salt water.

"Do you *really* like porridge?" she had asked him one morning when he was finishing his second bowl.

He looked at the small, serious face willing him to say no, but he could hardly say he didn't like Lucinda's porridge. He said instead that when his little sister was born he asked his mother why she switched the baby from one breast to the other, and his mother told him because milk comes out of one breast and porridge out of the other. Ernest was in the barn when he told the joke, and Lucinda actually laughed aloud. "You have a sister?" she asked.

"I had a sister. She died when she was a baby."

"Like my brother," said Lucinda, pausing with a half-dried dish in her hand.

But Norma Joyce was not to be put off track. "What *don't* you like?" she insisted. "What food do you *hate*?"

"I'm not crazy about carrots," he said. "And I don't mind if I never see another squash. What food do *you* hate? What food do you *love*?"

"My sister loves fruitcake," Lucinda said tersely.

Maurice looked at Lucinda, but then he winked at *her*. Dear Maurice. How she loved him.

He was twenty-three, apparently at ease with himself and clearly at ease in a kitchen, where his slender, capable hands were alert to any unfinished task. This graceful bending down to domestic work endeared him to women and gave them a sense of security. It was deceptive even to himself. He didn't consider it aggressive, for instance, to have taken a discarded girlfriend out one final time so that he could watch her hands tremble. This happened during his second year at McGill when, having cut himself shaving, having nearly failed a Physics exam, having been snubbed by a young woman in third year, he recovered by looking up the high school girlfriend he had dropped as soon as he graduated. She too had moved to Montreal, and had taken a job in a pharmacy.

He phoned her. They agreed to meet the following day during her morning break; they would have coffee at the café across the street from the pharmacy.

He got there early. From his booth beside the window he watched her come out the door, wait for the light, then cross the snowy street. She was wearing the same winter coat she had worn in high school, light-grey tweed with a worn black-velvet collar, and the same black tam. She slid into his booth, blushing, then lifted her cup with hands that shook so badly the coffee spilled. Later he described her to a friend and laughed, pleased with himself and boastful.

He didn't call her again.

Now here is Lucinda with her little sister. He helps them in the house without the slightest edge of self-congratulation, a handsome young man with his fine hands and his careful, casual ways.

One evening he finds Norma Joyce at his shoulder. He's been reading *Gray's New Manual of Botany* and he shows her the small illustrations of flowering grasses. His favourite plants, he says, because they survive any weather.

"Not this weather."

"Yes. This weather too. What they can't survive is the plough."

His long fingers run from top to bottom over paper as fine as the Bible's – *gramineae* for grasses, *culm* for stem, *inflorescence* for a cluster of flowers – while he explains that grasses are the simplest, most necessary plants in the world. Nearly every cereal is a grass, also sugarcane and rice and bamboo. Yet they're the hardest plants to identify. You have to notice the smallest details; you have to have the patience of Job.

Slender wheatgrass, big bluestem, little bluestem, sweet grass, hair grass, June grass, witch grass, blue grama, fringed brome, panic grass, switch grass, Indian grass, fescue, rattlesnake grass, elephant grass, porcupine grass, spear, needle, and float grass, toothache grass, poverty grass, carpet bent, black bent, water bent.

He outlines their tough, light, flexible existence. The stems, or culms, are usually hollow with a series of solid joints from which a leaf branches out. The leaf's lower part is a split sheath wrapped tightly round the stem so it won't tear in the wind, and the stem itself slips easily out of the wind's grasp. The undersides of the leaves have very few pores; in dry weather they roll up like waterproof tubes to hold in every precious drop of water vapour. As beautifully engineered, he says with a wink, as Claudette Colbert's nifty legs. Slender-tipped, smooth, loose and open, lax at flowering time, puberulent.

"What's that?"

"From the same root as puberty. Covered with fine hairs or down."

The soft hair of the world. And here was his measured, even-grass-writing going across the page. Quaking grass, orchard grass, love grass. From the Greek *eragrostis* for *Eros*, god of love, and *agrostis*, a grass. "Often persistent after their fall," the book said prophetically, "old-world species have long been known as love grass."

"You've seen that movie?" she asks.

Maurice smiles. He likes this about her, the way her mind leaps from one thing to another, in this case back to those nifty legs.

"*It Happened One Night*? I've seen it twice."

"You liked it?"

"Sure. Have you seen it?"

"My mother took me. For my fifth birthday."

It had been Florida May's final, most perfect gift, that trip to the Eagle Theatre in Swift Current; for weeks afterwards Norma Joyce lay awake on her pillow, reliving the movie scene by scene.

In the summer, says Maurice, he hopes to collect grasses from the untilled prairie to prove how well they've survived the drought. Darwin, he says, raised eighty-two plants from a ball of mud on the leg of a partridge, and he wants to do something similar.

"You'll stay with us."

"I will?" Looking at her with the amused twinkle given out to a very few by Eros, the god of love.

She has her own memory of grasses. Five years old and lying flat on her back in the long grass behind the barn, the June sun beating down from a cloudless sky until warmth of another kind pulsed through her in waves. She lay just so for some time, smelling the hot grass and feeling the swell of two temperatures, inner and outer, conjoin in a way that even at five, especially at five, she knew to be sexual.

Yes, she would say years later, I reached my sexual peak at the age of five.

Now her finger follows his, outlining these lovely grasses and naming them. He feels her breath on his neck, she stands so close, and when he returns in May she remembers every name of every plant. A perfect student.

Blowing dust and we think of talcum powder, but it was so coarse it drew blood. Fingertips split open, cheeks ran with fissures, heels were too tender to walk upon. Any morning a grown man might have to beg a child to do up his buttons.

Immune from all this, with olive skin like an inexhaustible well, was Norma Joyce. She lay with her large, soft-as-an-egg-yolk earlobe on her pillow and counted up the drops of blood on the empty pillow beside her. That's what you get for making porridge, she thought. Lucinda was already downstairs stirring that awful spoon.

It was almost the end of March. Ahead lay the worst of the dust storm months, April and May, when dust blew the paint off cars, settled on food while you ate, landed in your mouth while you slept, choked cattle in the fields, and muffled the calls of lost children. So much dust blown so far that it landed on ships in the middle of the Atlantic.

Sometimes she helped it along. She stood with a clump of dirt in her palm and watched the wind pick at it until it was gone. So long, she said. *Arrivederci*, darling.

Inside, there were dry smells and wet smells. She parsed them as she lay in bed waiting to see if something other than porridge was in the offing. The dry smells of peeling paint, wood lifting away from itself, skin flaking into a state of permanent moonlight, and the wet smells of warm chicken fat rubbed into ankles and feet, lemon-and-glycerine-soaked cotton gloves, potent night-urine in the pot under her father's bed.

Maurice smelled like a dollar bill. Travel-softened, rich, reassuring. She had no trouble at all remembering his face and no hesitation in saying his name.

Have you written to Maurice? she asked her sister. When do you think he'll come back? What was his sister's name? Did he say? Did Maurice say?

Who do you think is more handsome? Maurice or Joel McCrea? Lucinda? Who's more handsome? Maurice or Clark Gable?

Who's richer? Lucinda, who's richer? Maurice or Uncle Dennis?

"Maurice was pretending to be rich," Lucinda said, thinking of the work-worn hands despite the ring.

"No," said Norma Joyce after a moment's thought, "pretending not to be."

Outside came inside, like some uninvited guest. Like dirty Mr. Jackson "coughing in his fat voice and sitting all over the rocking chair" in Mrs. Tittlemouse's parlour. Only Lucinda of the White Sleeves took it in stride. Without fail she rested from two until three every afternoon, sometimes reading a book, sometimes not. At the moment she was reading *Maria Chapdelaine*, all too familiar with the way weather lay the groundwork for the tragedy to come – dry sunny weather so perfect for haymaking it seemed to be a blessing, but then it continued too long.

Half an hour of reading, half an hour with her eyes closed, then up she got. Inspired by Mrs. Hayden, she took off her long brown skirt and put on a dress, skilfully resewn from one of her mother's dresses and supplemented by a sweater and heavy stockings, or free of both, depending on the weather. A sign of wealth – a sure sign – was having clothes for every season. A sure sign of poverty was having no clothes but the ones you shared. They all knew sisters who took turns going to school because they shared the same dress, and bachelor brothers who took turns at church because they shared the same coat. Mending and patching until the garment was *heavy* with how little of it was left.

As little as you have, you could have even less. That was the lesson of the thirties. The possibilities of next-to-nothing were endless.

Work was the answer. Lucinda said so aloud, and Norma Joyce pretended not to hear. She headed out the door, away from the cooking, sweeping, washing, mending, hauling water, using up, making do. At nine p.m. Lucinda slowed down and Norma Joyce always reappeared because it was time for the nightly ritual of melted fat. Into a pan on the stove Lucinda spooned a lump of chicken fat the colour of young lemons. Once it was melted, she took off her shoes and stockings and rubbed the liquid fat into her feet, legs, forearms, and elbows. Norma Joyce never tired of the look of upper and lower: lower arm shiny and moist, upper arm still flaky-white and waiting to be transformed. Her sister paid especial attention to her elbows, having heard from

Mrs. Hayden that the number of folds on a woman's elbow was absolute proof of her age.

The lotion Lucinda made from lemon juice and glycerine, she saved for her hands. It was sticky, and so sweetly tart that Norma Joyce took a swig whenever she could. Lucinda drew on the once-white cotton gloves that had belonged to her mother. She tucked her hair inside an oversized handkerchief knotted at each corner into a soft dome, and went to bed.

Early one morning at the end of March, Norma Joyce watched Indians being picked off with unerring accuracy. All the Indians were women. They stepped out of their tents into the quiet night, where they made perfect targets, adorned as they were with cloves of garlic that shone in the darkness. Surprisingly, there was no blood or pain or fear. Just these garlic necklaces shining in the darkness, and the women falling to the ground, one after the other.

Norma Joyce woke up and went to the window. On the line below, sheets were shining in the light of the full moon. It must have been full, it was so bright. She closed her eyes. *Make Maurice come. Make him come with lots of presents.* She opened her eyes and something settled on the clothesline below.

Her shoes were beside the bed. She carried them downstairs into the kitchen where she tugged them on, grabbed her coat off its peg on the wall, and went outside. A slight breeze. That smell of cucumber in the cold air. Several stones at the foot of the steps.

She was good with a snowball, good with a stone. Three birds fluttered off, but two fell and met a pair of hungry-girl hands. She carried them upside-down into the house like top-heavy bouquets, and in the bright white light of the big-globed Aladdin lamp, she drew them.

Lucinda came down.

"Good for you," patting her on the back.

Then she went outside to get the sheets off the line, and when she came in Norma Joyce stopped to help. Folding was the one domestic task she liked. After they finished, Lucinda, wonder of wonders, made biscuits for the birthday breakfast. Supper was taken care of: prairie chickens, courtesy of Norma Joyce. It was March 29. Norma Joyce was nine.

"Lucinda?" she asked. "Where do dreams come from anyway?"

"Who knows? I couldn't say," not pausing in her work.

The sheets and towels, now in a neat pile at the end of the table, smelled fresh.

"Lucinda?" Lucinda was bending over to retrieve something from beside the range. "Lucinda?"

"Now what?"

"What did you dream about last night?"

Lucinda stopped for a moment. "A yellow house," she said. "It was almost all verandah, and it had a brand new kitchen."

"I dreamt about Indians being gunned down."

"I like my dream better," shaking the towel she'd retrieved off the floor. "Yours sounds awful."

"It wasn't awful. But I wonder if it's a good sign or a bad sign."

Half an hour later Ernest came downstairs. Without a word, he went out to the barn to see to the cows. He came back, drank his first cup of tea, then his second. After that he cleared his throat and said it smelled like rain.

"I know that," said Norma Joyce.

She knows that. Every morning he faces a girl who corresponds to nothing he wants to see in himself, and a self who corresponds to nothing he wants to see either, and disappointed though he is in Ernest Hardy, he is far more disappointed in *her* for not being like him. A dud at nearly everything she does, while he can improvise the most impossible repair yet still fail, his farm as far from the experimental success he'd dreamt of as his second daughter is from his first. "If you can read you can cook, if you can read you can sew," he has said to her. "But of course you can't read, can you?"

She takes refuge in privacy. She reads secretly, she draws, she collects; she waits for something to happen other than: *Stir your stumps. Help your sister. For your dead mother's sake TRY.*

Something other than capable Lucinda venturing to ask, "Would you like to set the table?" Or, "Would you like to do the dishes?"

No, she would not *like* to set the table. She would not *like* to do the dishes. She would do them, but she would not *like* to do them.

Something other than being forced – not to be helpful, she expects to be helpful – but to say she likes it.

"I know that," and Ernest almost strikes away her notebook. What annoys him most is that she knows everything and finishes nothing. Always a mouthful of milk left in her glass, a piece of meat on her plate, a corner of bread. "Clean up your breakfast," he tells her twice, until with a whispered "Sorry" she proceeds to do so.

He thinks the sorry is meant for him. It's meant for the hungry mother hovering at her shoulder.

"My mother's skin felt like lotion," Norma Joyce will tell Maurice the next time he comes. "She used Pond's face cream. She swore by it." Then after a moment, "Do you think everybody is going to drown?"

They're in the sitting room looking at the painting of two ships about to collide on a stormy sea. "I think you can count on it. Sailors never know how to swim. Sailors or farmers."

"I wish I could swim."

"I'll teach you when you come east."

"Am I coming? Is that what you think?"

"You're sure to come some day."

"When?"

He laughs. "That I couldn't say."

"Make a guess."

"Five years?"

"And you'll teach me how to swim?"

"I'll do more than that. I'll show you around. I'll show you the Château Laurier, and the canal, and the beaver path under Parliament Hill. I'll take you canoeing on the Ottawa River. I'll give you the full tour. We'll have fun."

But for now she's alone, a birthday girl curled up under the blue-and-green afghan in the armchair near the piano, Hurlbut's bible stories open in her lap to the picture of sneaky Jacob with his sneaky mother in the background. Her father and sister are in the kitchen. "She should be in school," she hears her father say. "It's time she learned how to read."

The flare of a match, the scrape of glass chimney fitting into metal stand. A sound like a grasshopper's thighs if you've been reading the Bible.

Her sister says, "What she does around the house would fill a thimble."

"She should be in school."

"She should. She should make some friends. She's never had a friend. I wonder if she ever will."

Jacob is wearing a red belt around his light-yellow tunic, and white fleece over his shoulders and arms. He kneels before Isaac. He rests his head and arms in his father's lap. Isaac – thin old arms outstretched above his son's head – has a white beard and an old, old face. Off in the corner, crafty Rebekah smiles like a witch.

She reads: Esau was a man of the woods and very fond of hunting; and he was rough and covered with hair. Jacob was quiet and thoughtful, staying at home, dwelling in a tent, and caring for the flocks of his father. Isaac loved Esau more than Jacob, because Esau brought to his father that which he had killed in his hunting; but Rebekah liked Jacob, because she saw that he was wise and careful in his work.

Jacob was quiet and in league with his mother, who appreciated him.

The blue-and-green afghan was her mother's work. Florida May made it the year she died, always happy to set it aside and take her smallest daughter into her lap. On Norma Joyce's fifth birthday they were in the kitchen, watching it go dark in the early afternoon. They were listening to the equipment outside moaning and creaking in the wind. The lamps were lit, the butter was covered.

A hundred kinds of wind on the Prairie, her mother had told the visitor from England. It's only still if a storm is coming. Then you see a slight movement in the grass, or dust devils in the lane.

A collector, the woman from England, a botanist who claimed there were two thousand wildflowers on the Prairies. They were so abundant, so different, so many things had a faint perfume. What she saw that others missed, she said, were the flowers inside the grasses.

It went very still. She was stroking her mother's soft cheeks and thinking of a white cake with white icing on a white table-cloth. A white birthday. And a movie. Most of all she wanted to see a movie.

Her mother should have been outside helping Ernest and Lucinda and the hired man, but she stayed here instead, rocking her birthday girl and thinking about the caravans of Indians old Mrs. Beck had described crossing southern Saskatchewan fifty years ago. Now lines of displaced people were moving again, but they didn't have painted faces and feathers in their hair. No, they didn't form a line of colour like a long despairing garden. They were just washed-up farmers heading north to be among the trees, or west to be among the fruit orchards, or east to be back in Ontario again.

Florida May was wearing her pink satin slippers as a special favour to her small daughter, "and only because it's your birthday, they aren't all that comfortable you know," pushing her feet into the low-heeled slippers embroidered with tiny flowers that appeared and disappeared as they rocked back and forth. The most beautiful things in the world, "and yes, Norrie," she distinctly remembers her mother saying, "you may certainly have them when you grow up."

The kitchen door slammed to behind the others, and then the storm hit the house like something solid.

It lasted an hour.

Afterwards you could chew the dust. You could feel it in your teeth. It was in your toothbrush if you had a toothbrush.

Her mother said, "Wouldn't the Indians be glad to see what's become of us now. We must make quite a sight."

Imparting to her tiny daughter the sense that history means having to wait your turn, for what it's worth, an idea that only got reinforced when Lucinda claimed the satin slippers for herself.

⬤

Norma Joyce is nine years old plus a day. She announces her intention at breakfast and can tell without raising her head that her father and sister are exchanging looks of relief. Lucinda says, "You'll need extra porridge for the walk to school."

"No. I won't need extra porridge."

One week later: "This is what comes of not having a proper breakfast." But Lucinda looks after her, she even reads aloud to her in the middle of the night when fever keeps her awake.

What a sad story *Maria Chapdelaine* is. For Lucinda it's almost peaceful in its sadness; there's nothing to be done. But for Norma Joyce the story is unbearable.

"Will she *ever* be happy?" she asks her sister. "Will Maria ever be happy again?"

"I suppose not," says Lucinda. "Not if you mean happy the way she was before François died."

"I wish she could be happy."

And a few minutes later, "But what is there to make her happy? There's nothing to make her happy."

"There's the church," says Lucinda. "There's the land. She'll have children. She'll have to work so hard she won't have time to think.

"It's only a book," Lucinda adds. "Don't forget that. It's only a book." And then, "Norma Joyce! Stop scratching!"

Thirty-three years later, Norma Joyce still has the pock from that particular scratch. It's right between her two dark eyebrows.

She returns to school. Three weeks go by, and Lucinda is asking Ernest if he thinks it's deliberate. Norma Joyce has come home with lice.

And so the spring of 1938 is the feel of Lucinda's fingers going over her scalp, the crick in her neck from bending her head down, her sister's unendurable patience as she examines every single hair until, finally, Norma Joyce shakes her head free and won't submit. (One day she will be sitting just like this, long hair falling over her face as she dries it in the blossomy sunshine, half asleep, so only dimly aware of a humming sound that slowly gains in volume and then – this is drastic – in weight. A loud hat settles on her head and keeps settling, horrible in its dainty advance deep into her hair. Her screams bring Lucinda, who says, *Oh Lord*, and then she knows exactly how much trouble she's in.)

But right now something else intervenes. Lucinda's eyes go on the blink. They're too gritty and sore for close work of any kind. She goes to bed with *Anne of Green Gables* and weeps until her eyes feel better.

Norma Joyce is left alone to scratch and scribble. She fills the margins of her workbook with dense and complicated patterns.

"In your schoolbook?" protests Lucinda when she comes back down.

"Look," and Norma Joyce points out the letters of the alphabet inside the swirls of leaves.

That night Lucinda says to Ernest, "At least she entertains herself," relieved that something is actually going on inside her sister's oversized skull. A series of intimacies and isolations like Russian dolls: the drawing, her sister, the room, the world, the room, her sister, the drawing.

Norma Joyce has made a friend. Ginny Gallot lives a mile from the Willow Bend school. Norma Joyce lives three miles from the school and in the same direction. They walk home together, stopping at Ginny's, where Mrs. Gallot has the first volume of *Larousse du XXe siècle* on the kitchen shelf.

Huge, too heavy for children to lift, so Mrs. Gallot takes it down and shows them the arc of big gold letters worked into dark green leather, the border of golden leaves and flowers, the central cluster of three golden figures holding aloft a seashell from which pour streams of golden water.

"My inheritance," says Mrs. Gallot with a laugh almost free of bitterness.

The other five volumes went to the other five children. She got *A* to *Carl* because she was Amélie.

Inside?

Inside are smooth pages of fine black print, with every so often a splendid page in colour. These coloured pages Ginny knows by heart. First the seaweeds in marvellous lacy shapes of green, bronze, violet, and red. Then the page of acrobats creating equally surprising shapes: three brothers in yellow balance head to head, a man in white stands on a white horse and holds aloft a woman in a white dress, a violinist in a tuxedo plays atop a

ladder held upright between his elegant knees, and every config-
uration is arranged on the page like birds on a carpet, each in its
own black-bordered frame. (As a girl in Quebec, says Mrs. Gallot,
she and her brothers would swing from tree to tree all the way
around the house without once touching the ground. That's how
many trees there were! That's how nimble we used to be!) Then
most marvellous of all: two facing pages of leafy trees with
adjoining depictions of trunk, flowers, leaves, and fruit. Norma
Joyce's first forest and it's a French park of illustrated trees!

She says, "I've never seen anything so beautiful. Not even
Beatrix Potter."

The trees are so still, so unruffled by wind, so majestic and
clear.

"Are they watercolours?" she asks, knowing they can't be.

"Engravings," says Mrs. Gallot.

"*Engravings.*"

"You cut the picture into a metal plate and then you ink the
plate and press it down on paper. You won't see these trees in
Canada," says Mrs. Gallot, "even I don't recognize them."

"I wish my mother could see them."

So Mrs. Gallot passes the motherless child another ginger-
snap, and Norma Joyce loses her very first baby tooth. It's a top
front tooth.

"Make a wish!" says Ginny. "Make a wish!"

"Here." Mrs. Gallot slides over a butter plate to put her tooth
on. "Too bad. I was hoping you'd stay for supper."

"I'll stay for supper."

And down they go into the dark cellar where dozens of winter-
white cabbages hang like a string of pearls between the floor joists.
Mrs. Gallot grates the cabbage fine, adds onion and her own

mayonnaise, and Norma Joyce has three helpings. Mrs. Gallot presses her to have more, but "only if you like," because she's a woman who lets her children eat as much or as little as they want, not that she's a pushover, not at all. For instance, she wants to know what Norma Joyce intends to be when she grows up. Pleasant Ginny has no particular aspirations, and it's on her mother's mind.

Norma Joyce says she wants to be a painter, and Mrs. Gallot responds with pleasure. "Like your mother," she says. "And like me. I wanted to be a painter too."

"You did?"

Norma Joyce takes her notebook out of her schoolbag and shows Mrs. Gallot her leafy alphabet and dead birds.

"Imagine that, Ginny. A painter." And she looks from her daughter to Norma Joyce.

"Are you going to look at my pictures?" asks Norma Joyce.

"Yes, madame."

Mrs. Gallot looks for a long time, and then she says, "I'm sorry," and shakes her head. "I'm sorry, Norma Joyce. But I can't find anything the matter with these."

For which she receives a full dark-gummed grin (minus one tooth).

"Here," says Mrs. Gallot, "I know what we'll do."

She takes the tooth off the butter plate and out they go, Mrs. Gallot, Ginny and Norma Joyce, into the warm sunshine and over to the grey barn with the rusted rooster on top. Then the two girls watch as Mrs. Gallot uses her strong right arm to toss Norma Joyce's tooth high up onto the barn roof.

"The sky's the limit," says Mrs. Gallot. "I still believe that."

Drawn back to this strange household of father and two daughters, one so beautiful and diligent, the other dark and deliberately unhelpful, Maurice mounts the porch steps and enters the cleanest kitchen he has seen since leaving Ontario. Scrubbed floor, shiny dishes, a map on the wall like a soft overblown rose, and outside a sudden snowstorm.

It comes up so quickly that Lucinda, on her way home from an afternoon service given in the schoolhouse by a travelling preacher, accepts a ride from a neighbour and comes inside shaking snow off her hat. She looks up and sees Maurice at the kitchen table with Norma Joyce in full grin at his side. May 24, and he has come for the second time.

A man who never arrives without a gift. A box of cigars for Ernest, a small jar of Pond's face cream for Lucinda, a set of watercolours for Norma Joyce.

"You're a sight for sore eyes," he says to Lucinda, and the small dark sister almost doesn't mind, she's so happy to have him back.

"So are you, Maurice Dove."

"You've been to church."

Yes, she has been to church. For all the good it does. She hasn't heard an interesting sermon since the skinny boy-preacher from Toronto came on his horse. What was his name? The one who read Shakespeare in his spare time. Dad? Do you remember?

"The university boy. Yes."

"What was his name?"

Ernest shakes his head, he remembers the boy but not the name. What a strange-looking young man he was, carrying his head on a tilt as if all his brains had shifted their weight from one foot to the other. And that harsh honking eastern voice. "Not Toronto. New Brunswick." But it was all the same to a westerner. It was all the east.

"He was interesting," Lucinda says. "I thought he was. He told the story of the prodigal son, but he took the older brother's side."

"The one who stayed at home," says Maurice.

"Yes. He wanted to know what lesson we should draw from him."

"I've never really thought about him. I always identified with the prodigal son."

"And I with the older one."

The sudden snowfall has ended, leaving everything, inside and out, suspended in new light. Ernest sends Norma Joyce to the woodshed for kindling; he himself goes to the barn. Maurice and Lucinda are alone.

"Have you been busy?" he asks her. "You're always busy. Tell me anyway. What have you been doing with yourself, Lucinda?"

"I've been reading Saint Paul's letters," she answers with a pointed smile, "in the absence of any other mail."

"I'm sorry. Next time. I promise."

That evening he pulls out his battered box of watercolours and sets to work at the kitchen table. Norma Joyce watches. She could be an Indian, she's so still. She could be Robinson Crusoe deciphering the outlines of a ship.

She opens her own brand new black-japanned metal box. The hinged lid drops forward into a mixing palette for sixteen cakes of colour, a tube of Ivory Black, a tube of Chinese White. These colours all her own, and how can she not remain bound to Maurice despite all that will happen?

They work side by side for half an hour until Lucinda interrupts with cups of cocoa so hot that Norma Joyce scalds her tongue.

"How can something be *Ivory Black*?" She's mad. Her scalded tongue makes her mad.

"What?"

"Ivory Black," she points at the tube. "Ivory *Black*."

"An oxymoron," he says. "A word you'd learn if you went to school."

"I do. I go now. Tell him Lucinda."

"She goes to school now."

"I don't believe it."

"I do," she says stoutly, "I go every day," failing to rise to the twinkle in his eye.

"It's a term that contradicts itself," Maurice explains. "Like weak tyrant. Or jumbo shrimp. Or sweet sorrow."

"Or well failure," says Ernest. The first thing he has said in an hour. He's been sulking in his chair, feeling left out and annoyed with himself for feeling left out, and now he can't resist releasing his mood into the room.

"That's perfect," Lucinda says, "that's the best one yet," doing what she does every day: dusting her father's huge, wounded ego, catering to it, walking around it, patting it, humming to it. Encouraging this great turnip of an ego so that he never grows up, this man, but stands in the doorway exuding his moods until everything has the same turnip smell, the same turnip taste.

There will come a time when Norma Joyce will stand in an Ottawa doorway and give vent to her bullying mood – hurrying her son along, criticizing him for the way he is dressed – and Lucinda will say, "You're exactly like him. You don't see it, but you are."

In the morning the snow has gone. Maurice walks with both sisters to the creek bed in the coulee, where they picnic on Lucinda's lunch of cold tea, hard-boiled eggs, and fresh buttered bread. In the afternoon the wind picks up, but after dark it drops. That's when Lucinda hangs the laundry on the line. All over southwestern Saskatchewan, other women do the same. At dawn they bring the laundry in.

Norma Joyce wanders away with her paper and pencil and hard-boiled egg, so she doesn't hear Maurice ask Lucinda, "But you have to keep something in your mind, don't you? An image of something better?"

"You and Norma Joyce. The questions never end." But she's smiling.

"Don't you? You aren't satisfied with things being like this?"

"Of course not."

"Then what's your vision of happiness?"

"My vision of happiness."

And because he doesn't apologize or explain, he gets an answer.

She looks into the distance, to the eight-sided water tower several miles away, and sees a house beside a lake. It has a large garden with apple trees and roses, and a lawn. She sees herself on the lawn, and Maurice beside her.

She says, "A house beside water. An orchard full of apple trees."

"Your father's talked to me about apple trees."

"He and Uncle Dennis were going to plant orchards. Over there," and she turns and waves her hand at the gentle south-facing slope.

Lucinda is beautiful. She thinks she has all the time in the world. She thinks the only mistake she can make is to seem to be too eager.

"Apple trees would make you happy?"

"Apple trees would make me happy."

"Just apple trees? Is that all?"

Only meaning to lead her deeper into what she wants, but she takes it as a criticism and doesn't answer.

The next day little Mickey Gallot stands in the lane astonished – thunderstruck – because his shirt is sticking to his shoulders. He tears up the steps plucking at it and yelling, "*Mom! Look!*"

Mrs. Gallot, who is ironing, puts her warm hand on her son's damp shoulders. Then she follows him outside into the softly falling rain. Behind them on the porch two puppies back up in alarm and get christened on the spot. Finicky and Poop.

Two miles farther down the road, Lucinda says to Maurice, "You brought the rain."

"I thought I brought the snow."

"That too," smiling one of those slow, complete smiles that gilds the lily. They're on the porch looking east and he slides his hand into hers. "We easterners get blamed for everything." Then softly he begins to recite,

> *Whether we look, or whether we listen*
> *We hear life murmur, or see it glisten;*
> *Tis enough for us now that the leaves are green*
> *No matter how barren the past may have been.*

"What's that?" she asks.

"James Russell Lowell. 'What Is So Rare as a Day in June.'"

Lucinda is impressed. "A man who remembers verses," she says. Then a voice pipes up behind them.

> *The rain is raining all around,*
> *It falls on field and tree,*
> *It rains on the umbrellas here,*
> *and on the ships at sea.*

Maurice laughs and catches up Norma Joyce's hand. "Well done," he says.

"Do you know that one?" she asks.

"Robert Louis Stevenson," he replies to her satisfaction, and his. Now the three of them are hand in hand watching the rain fall and the grass turn green under their eyes.

"We should have a party," Lucinda says. "We should celebrate. Next Saturday. You'll still be here? I'll make my sponge cake."

"Make two," says Maurice.

The rain draws everyone to open doorways. It's like watching a movie, the way the world colours up and expressions change.

Everyone sleeps better. They rise later than usual, they dream more, they fall asleep in strange places. In the middle of the afternoon Lucinda finds her sister sound asleep on Maurice's bed, and leaves her undisturbed. She respects sleep the way she respects all forms of privacy; it would never occur to her to eavesdrop on a conversation, for instance, or to open someone's mail.

Norma Joyce sleeps on, dreaming her strange dreams. She looks out the window as a tall glass house topples forward like a woman falling flat on her face, she pushes back a blanket covered with long quills like hairs under a magnifying glass, she dreams three water dreams in a row. In the first dream she walks on water while on shore a singer laments the two wide planks in her way; next she crosses a wide river on a forbidden bridge; then she waters three very dry flowers planted in a row. She pours so much water on the first plant that it tips over; pours less on the other two and they respond well. This isn't a garden but a woods with many openings and strange cultivations, like these three apparently wild flowers planted in a row. A shady woods, a watering can in her hands.

She opens her eyes and her brother is at the foot of the bed.

He was only two, not entirely steady on his feet and much too curious that autumn Monday seven years ago. A wash day, with water heating in the copper boiler on top of the stove and in the water tank on the side of the stove. Florida May sent the twins outside to play on the porch; she heard them chattering away as she carried buckets of scalding water to the wringer washer in the corner of the kitchen. Then came a cry for help – Lucinda's voice – and she set down the pail and hurried outside.

The newspaper referred to the "farm kitchen" in which the accident happened and to the severe burns the child suffered. The paper said he must have backed up against the pail, upsetting scalding water over his back and legs. That was on a Monday. He died on Thursday in the Willow Bend hospital.

Ernest made the small coffin. Florida May sat up all night turning her satin wedding gown into a padded lining for its bottom and sides. The girl who was no longer a twin climbed into bed beside her big sister, and was still there seven years later.

The day after they buried her brother, Joyce became Norma Joyce. The dead boy had been Norman. It was her mother's idea.

Ernest remembers his son's dazzling Cheshire-cat smile as he backed out of every room; a boy who liked to keep you in his sights, and a game he must have been playing. He backed up through the screen door into the dangerous kitchen.

Ernest remembers, but his memory is clouded by suspicion and the need to blame. How could his boy have fallen all in a moment without encouragement? A dare, for instance, from his tiny jealous sister? Or a shove?

He can even see the look on her face. He can even see the tips of her tiny fingers.

Some nights he stands in the bedroom doorway and looks at her sleeping beside her sister. He looks, and feels deprived of any ability to love anything at all. His eyes shift to Lucinda, and he feels reassured.

"Twins control weather," Maurice tells her, "at least that's what the Indians think." They're painting at the kitchen table; he has asked her to tell him another secret and she has.

"I see him quite frequently," she says, "but I never see my mother."

"What does he look like?"

"Like me. Except he's handsome."

"You never know. You might be beautiful one day."

That makes her sit up.

"Do you think so?"

He doesn't think so. But he says, "My mother says the most beautiful woman she knows was a very homely baby."

She considers this. "I'm not a baby, of course."

"No."

"Although I'm very small."

"That's also true."

That rainy week he has one erotic dream after another and wakes to continuous thoughts of beautiful Lucinda. He lets her little sister do anything. She wants to brush his hair, he lets her. She asks him to read to her, he reads to her. She asks him about

Ontario and he describes air so clear and sweet it smells like maple syrup, lakes so deep they're like soup bowls, elm trees so tall and numerous they form a canopy overhead, and L-shaped farm verandahs so designed as to provide a beautiful jog of shade. He describes apple trees bent double with fruit, and hilltops covered with so many blueberries the ground itself is blue.

He says his mother and father eat outside from early May until early October, his father bare-headed, his mother in a white straw hat. A Dove tradition, he says, to eat outside until the first heavy frost.

"Is that what you do?" she asks him.

"Oh yes. That's why I'll never have a wife."

This with a wink at Lucinda who has just come into the kitchen.

Lucinda smiles. She understands. His attentions to the small girl are a tribute to herself.

Norma Joyce lies on her bed and studies her face in Lucinda's hand mirror. In this position – flat on her back and holding a mirror up in the air – her face slants back into something Asian and almond-eyed. She thinks, "This is how a man will see me when he approaches me in bed." She thinks, "Could I possibly be beautiful and not know it?"

The same slippers, but now his bare ankles draw her gaze. Now he washes and shaves without a shirt and she sees the curly brown hair on his chest, unimaginably soft, and the narrowing of his hips. When he leaves the house, she examines his soft leather slippers. The soles are as shiny and dark as black ice, the insoles worn away by his toes.

More than the weather has changed. She has dropped the pretense of not being able to read. Now she carries an open book from room to room, reading at full tilt the way women used to knit. She reads her mother's World Books and her Grammar, deriving from them the sort of settled pleasure that her sister finds in repetitive work. She learns that giraffes browse on acacia leaves, their skin smelling of honey as a consequence. They're able to go without water for long periods of time, and they're strangely silent, never uttering a sound when startled, not even moaning in pain during the agonies of death.

Every day she goes to school. She takes a jam sandwich and a raisin scone in her lard pail (other kids take onion sandwiches, garlic sandwiches, molasses sandwiches; one boy named Art takes a quart of milk and no food at all; one girl named Flora eats for two, or so the boys snicker, tormenting her because her sister Daisy had a shotgun wedding; Daisy and Lucinda were once great friends). Norma Joyce goes to see His Majesty King George the Sixth above the blackboard in his ceremonial uniform and ermine cape.

"He is so erect," she says to Maurice, "and his skin is so smooth."

She also goes to see pretty Miss Stevenson from Ontario. How lucky to have a teacher who has three attractive dresses: a navy blue alpaca, buttoned down the front and fitted tightly over her shapely figure (it has two sets of detachable collars and cuffs, one white, the other butterscotch); a maroon crepe with a round white collar and a pretty white frill that runs diagonally from the left shoulder to the waist; and a red jersey trimmed in black satin with a row of black buttons down the front. Miss Stevenson wears each dress for a full week. At the beginning of the week the dress is pristine, but by week's end it's streaked with chalk.

On the way home, Norma Joyce writes *Maurice* over and over in the road. At home she pockets the soft hair entangled in his brush. She takes one of his handkerchiefs and a few strands of his pipe tobacco. She keeps them in the cigar box inside the wooden box under her bed.

———◆———

Trees and rivers attract rain. Elusive men attract women. Fairy tales attract children. Whenever she goes for a walk, Norma Joyce takes along a piece of bread, falling into step with the old story in which stones shine in the moonlit woods and crumbs get eaten up by birds. Her wanderings take her from abandoned house to abandoned house, where she opens drawers and closets, finding stray bobby pins, lost buttons, and the occasional fancy dress useless for this weather but not every weather, not bare-shouldered or slim-waisted weather, not slipper-clad or kid-glove weather, not Ontario weather. She takes soft, rustling Ontario between her fingers, the velvet and taffeta sent west when rich Toronto cleaned out its attics for poor Saskatchewan. Mrs. Hayden in a bitter mood used to put on a gown with three built-in petticoats reeking of mothballs, then go out to the barn to milk the cows. But Mrs. Hayden has gone. They left for the Okanagan Valley because all she wanted, she said, was to reach up and pick a nice ripe peach.

Norma Joyce finds a small brass tube of lipstick behind an abandoned dresser in one of the bedrooms. This is treasure. Only half-used and dark red. She pockets it for later – infamous – use.

The barn is quiet because all the animals are gone. She likes empty barns. She likes the way light comes through the cracks up high so you're standing not in darkness but in shade, breathing in the smell of hay and animals and nothing else, except this time there is something else. Out of nowhere a hand grabs her ankle and her head hits the ground. She astonishes herself with her screams. *Now I must scream*, and out they come in a rippling tide.

He backs away. "I'm sorry I'm sorry I'm sorry," hitching up his pants and refastening his buckle. "I don't know what got into me."

"It's all right," still on her back on the floor. "Just go away."

And he does.

From the barn door she watches him scuttle down the road. Young. Skinny. Greasy black hair in need of a cut. Broken-down boots.

It's the middle of the afternoon – it's not even nighttime. But she's lucky. What happened to poor Daisy Thompson could have happened to her.

Halfway home she remembers the lipstick. She goes back, and there it is on the barn floor, in plain view.

As is he when she walks in through the kitchen door. He's at the table with a plate of beans and a cup of tea. He stops chewing when she comes in, then picks up speed. He chews with his mouth wide open and she looks away.

Maurice and Lucinda are at the kitchen table too. She sits down beside Maurice and stares at the table. He'll be gone soon, the greasy young man who eats like a pig. Maurice has been asking Lucinda if she misses school and Lucinda says, "Not much, to tell you the truth. I was good at it, though."

"Do *you* like school?" Now Maurice is speaking to her.

"I like books."

"Why?"

"They look nice."

"They *look* nice?"

"They're safe."

"You think books are safe? They're full of dangerous ideas."

"Books aren't dangerous."

The greasy young man gets up. He mumbles a hurried thank you.

And now he's gone.

"They're interesting," she says. "Today I read about giraffes. They never make a sound. Did you know that? Not even when lions are tearing them apart. People scream, but giraffes don't scream. They don't need water either. They get enough moisture just by eating leaves."

"Like kangaroo rats," says Maurice with interest. "In the Great Sand Hills?"

She nods and so does Lucinda. They know the great rolling sand dunes that lie west of Swift Current.

"As rats go," says Maurice, "they're small and bony, but their hind feet are like a kangaroo's, that's why they travel so easily over the sand."

"And they don't drink water?"

"They *never* drink water. They survive on the moisture they get from dry seeds." He nods his head. "Yes sirree. Darwin would have liked them."

"Darwin?" asks Lucinda.

"That's the second time you've mentioned Darwin," says Norma Joyce.

Maurice smiles at her. Her memory will always impress and sometimes appall him. "Is it?" And he tells them about the aimless young man whose life was changed by a letter when he was only twenty-two.

"Suppose the letter had gone astray," he says. "He wouldn't have gone on the *Beagle*; we wouldn't have his theories or his books."

"They would have written to him again," says Norma Joyce.

"Maybe."

"They would have."

"My sister." It gets said with a laugh. "Know-it-all Norma."

"Is he your favourite scientist?" she asks, ignoring Lucinda, whose nose she'd like to punch.

"One of them."

"But you like him best."

"Do I have to like somebody best?"

"Don't you like him the best?"

"All right. I like Darwin the best if it makes you happy."

It does, not that she could have explained her need to have these things spelled out and shored up.

"Twenty-two," says Maurice. "I'm already twenty-three."

"Dante was only eleven," says Norma Joyce.

"Dante?"

"He was only eleven when his life was changed by love. And Beatrice was only eight. Miss Stevenson told us."

Maurice leaves his glasses on the kitchen table in their soft cloth case. She takes them out of the case, adjusts them on her nose and stares at the banner of blur they make of the room. She drinks the last bit of tea in his cup. She plays the piano first thing in the morning. "Good King Wenceslas" or "We Wish You a Merry Christmas." Serenading Maurice.

"Subtlety is not her strong point," Lucinda says to Ernest. And to her sister, "Are you trying to make it snow?"

This time – this May-June visit – he stays three weeks. Each day he comes home with a knapsack full of tender young grasses that he draws and labels, then presses between flimsies of newsprint in his portable oak press. After mounting the grasses on cardboard, he scores the tape back and forth with his long left thumbnail.

"I see," says Norma Joyce, who had been wondering about that thumbnail.

"You have to remember," he tells her, thinking aloud while he works, trying out ideas, *pontificating*, she thinks years later, "that the west has been through bad droughts before."

"I know that."

"The 1890s were just as bad. Nine years of drought." He erases his drawing and starts again. "And it was the same sort of thing. Everybody leaving their farms. Moving away. Except for the few who were lucky, or hardy," looking at her with a quick smile. "You have to be hardy to survive here, and of course you are. Not that it's near as bad as Russia in 1921."

"Russia?"

"They ate bread made out of dirt. That's how bad it was. You can imagine how many children died."

"How many?"

"Nearly all the children under three."

He erases the upper corner of his drawing and sweeps it clean with the side of his hand.

"How do you make bread out of dirt anyway?" she wants to know.

"What they did," he says, "according to what I've read, was pound acorns and mix them with dirt and water and dried-up birch leaves."

"Ugh," she says.

His constant listener. Lucinda is too busy. (The price you pay for being helpful.)

"Does your sister ever stop?" he asks her.

"No. Not her. My father says she's a fool for work. Like him."

So Norma Joyce is the one who learns about weather while the birds return and the crops grow and the light lingers in the long evenings of early June. At Maurice's side she follows his diagrams of air masses and arrows, and what she sees is a body of warm air sliding up over a body of cold air and trapping it there against its will, or a body of cold air pushing under the skirts of warm air before thrusting up, but so clumsily, so restlessly, so *oily and cold* in its slovenly manners that there's no true mating, just a jostling for position that ends in depression, which she already knows all about, she's in one after all. Born as she was in 1929, she and the Depression have gone hand in hand from the very beginning.

She listens to him say that warm air rises and cold air flows in below, that water holds onto its heat longer than land and contrast is what sets everything in motion, and she nods, understanding that what's at play are the forces of attraction and repulsion, in other words, of love.

Hot meets cold, and what follows is wind, rain, sap, and dew. The sharper the contrast the more there is to see. The more quickly something cools off, for instance, the more dew it collects; a blade of grass gets wetter than a paved road. In the same spirit, when three freezing nights coincide with three warm spring days, buckets of sap flow down the sides of excited trees.

This has been going on forever, he says, the rising and falling of warmth and cold, and not just day to day but over time. Hot and cold alternate throughout history too. Nine hundred years ago grapes grew all over England it was so warm, then the weather turned, and by the late Middle Ages the vineyards in England were gone and the Little Ice Age had begun – the time of the great frosts when the rivers of Europe froze over, when people walked across the frozen Baltic, and Eskimos came so far south that at least one of them kayaked up the River Don near Aberdeen. Since then, it's been warming up again.

It was restful, the passage of this sort of time. Her eyes, she realized, were tired. They hurt. Those were the days, in that dust-driven part of the world, when people were always resting their eyes, rinsing them, dabbing at them with handkerchiefs. Eyes were so dry they streamed, which was an interesting contradiction. What about that, Maurice? It's curious but true, he said, and in the same way, something extremely cold burns your skin.

It was the Norwegians he admired, and the Swedes. They were light years ahead when it came to understanding the weather. Among Englishmen, only Darwin earned his admiration. His heroes were Vilhelm Bjerknes, who understood the fluidity of air; and Tor Bergeron, the truth of old folktales about endless winters; and Fridtjof Nansen, the art of travelling in snow; and Roald Amundsen, the need to move like an Indian through every weather. He had no time for Scott. No patience for his bloated overambition. A typically English failing, he thought, trying too hard to impress, worrying too much about how you come across. *You* look Scandinavian, he said to Lucinda.

"What about me?" Norma Joyce asked.

"You," he said thoughtfully, "you look Italian-Japanese, though you could be one of those dark Scots."

Her *Ontario Reader* (which she finds again in Ernest's basement in the winter of 1972, along with Lucinda's sewing machine and several pairs of old skates and many more books that haven't been opened for decades), her *Ontario Reader*, price fourteen cents and published in 1925 by the T. Eaton Company, had Captain Scott's last journey, condensed. Maurice took it out of her hands and read a paragraph, shaking his head all the while. He said if Scott were a farmer he'd still be ploughing his summerfallow fields to make them look neat. No matter that afterwards all the soil blows away.

"You need stubble to keep soil in place, I keep telling them that. Just like you need whiskers to keep your face from freezing off."

"*You* don't have whiskers."

She reached out and touched his cheek. She ran her fingers down the side of his face.

He barely noticed.

"Stubborn," he said. "So stubborn they're suicidal. They won't give in until it's too late and then they give in all at once.

"Like Hitler," he said, turning to look at Ernest in his corner of the kitchen. "Nothing's going to stop him, but in the end he won't win. He'll overstep himself."

"So everything works out?" said Ernest, dryly, but still polite. "There's justice in the world. There's fairness."

"Not fairness, maybe, but balance. Things go in and out of balance. That's what weather is all about. Heat follows cold, rain follows drought."

"And when will that be?"

"It's already happened," he said, "but the land is too damaged for the rain to do any good."

"Or maybe you're wrong," said Ernest. "After all, what do you *really* know? Not a damn thing."

Turning like that, from gallantry to abuse. A jolt, just like the Little Ice Age when the Thames froze over repeatedly and all the orange trees died in the south of France.

But there were always pockets of warmth, responded Maurice, always oases of moisture, even during the worst times. Places that seemed to escape. No doubt the little rain they received fertilized some native ingenuity and persistence, just as it has here, he said, mollifying Ernest by reacting not to his anger but to his need for flattery and respect.

But mischievous Norma Joyce has to stir the pot one more time. "You really don't like Scott?"

"I don't like the way he's lionized, that's all. And the way Amundsen gets treated."

He picks up the *Ontario Reader* again and reads out, "'Starting nearer and making a dash for it.' As if there's something criminal about not doing something the hardest way."

Ernest cannot tolerate such talk. He clamps down on his pipe before suddenly getting up and leaving the house.

Maurice looks at Lucinda. "He takes these things seriously, doesn't he?"

"He does, I'm afraid."

"I'm sorry. I didn't mean to antagonize him."

But Norma Joyce is glad. Through the window she watches her father's angry progress to the barn and hopes he falls flat on his face.

He doesn't. So she turns to a lesser pleasure. She asks Maurice what his favourite plant is, wanting to hear again what she already knows.

"Ferns," to tease her.

"You think ferns are better than grasses?"

"They're both ancient and interesting. Also economical. They use everything at their disposal, like people now. The Depression has turned everyone into economical ferns."

"But we do not flourish," says Lucinda.

"Some do," and he smiles at her.

"But which do you like best? Ferns or grass?"

"Norma Joyce Hardy," says Maurice, still smiling at Lucinda, "the girl who turns everything into a competition."

For a few minutes she's silent and deeply hurt. Then, "I wish I could go to Ottawa," she says.

"Ottawa," he muses. "Do you know what the word means?"

"Yes." Her voice is eager and definite. "It's the name of an Indian tribe."

"It means 'the city where three rivers meet.' Now. *You tell me*," winking at Lucinda, whose face has that look of complacent virtue that Norma Joyce can't stand, not even for a second, "which rivers? A nickel if you get them right."

"I thought you didn't like competitions."

He laughs, and she completes her victory by saying, "The Ottawa, the Rideau, and the Gatineau," then pocketing his nickel.

Finally it's the first Saturday in June, the night of the party in honour of the rain. The Haarings are coming, the Gallots and the Wolfes, the teacher Miss Stevenson and the postmistress Wanda Thurston. They arrive by car and on foot, bringing for the midnight lunch roast ham, roast pork, cabbage salad, pickled beets, and bread – all crowned by Lucinda's two sponge cakes and Mrs. Gallot's three lemon meringue pies. There will be cards and singing and eating and talk – lubricated by copious pots of tea, and by the easy coming and going between kitchen and porch on a night when the air is warm and the light prolonged. By two in the morning Mrs. Haaring, in the rocker next to the kitchen table, will be saying that *for the first time in fifteen years* she feels at home.

Her face has softened, her large hands are folded in her lap, her thoughts have drifted back to the day she left Holland, when it was so warm, so beautiful a day in late September that at dawn she was out in her garden cutting an armful of chrysanthemums to take on the train. Two months later she stepped out into Regina and couldn't breathe, it was so cold. The next morning, two inches of snow had drifted over the foot of her bed.

"What do they look like, chrysanthemums?" asks the whiskey tenor from her stool beside the kitchen door. Summer air comes through the mended screen and with it the weird hoot of an owl. *Listen.* They all do. A sound they haven't heard in years, or so it seems.

"Like a mop of coconut," answers Mrs. Haaring. "Mine were as white as the cuffs on your sister's dress."

"A funeral flower," explains Mrs. Gallot, "chrysanthemums. The right flower to take along if you're leaving home for the last time."

"I have one yet," says Mrs. Haaring. "In the back of the Bible. For luck."

Luck. This was the time, the 1930s, when superstition embroidered every mind, when knitting needles of worry clicked inside every skull. Taboos were many and urgent: Never boast and never overpraise or you'll draw down the jealous evil eye. Never predict a good crop. Never predict good weather. Never predict happiness of any kind. Always hedge your bets. Throw salt over your left shoulder if ever you spill any. Wait for somebody else to come along and take the bad luck if a black cat crosses your path. Never fall asleep with the full moon on your face. Turn the lucky coin in your pocket at the first sight of the new moon. Wear a red ribbon to ward off the evil eye.

"My dad always touched his collar when a hearse passed by, and my aunt wouldn't allow green in the house." Ernest, surprisingly enough. Even he has relaxed. He says the only person he ever knew who wasn't superstitious was Florida May, and maybe she should have been, but she believed in education. What a prodigious reader she was. "I used to see her in the morning, kneading bread with a book propped up behind it, and she'd still be kneading the same bread an hour later."

Mrs. Wolfe, who has just helped herself to another piece of lemon meringue pie, recalls the winter when she and Florida May read all of Jane Austen. A winter so cold she had to take the bread dough into bed with her to get it to rise. The same winter her son came home from school with ears swelled up like doughnuts. She packed them with snow, she said, against the pain.

"Why snow?" asks Norma Joyce.

"You don't want the skin to thaw out too fast. That's why."

"But why not a warm hand?"

And Maurice, seated at the kitchen table, says, "I think a warm hand is best. A warm hand for frostbite. A dark room for snowblindness. I spent three days lying in a dark room once, that's how bad my eyes were. But I was lucky. I could have been lost for good."

"Like Maria Chapdelaine's lover," says Lucinda quietly.

The word *lover*, and Norma Joyce holds her breath, amazed that Lucinda has said it.

"A reader," Maurice says with a smile.

"Not a reader," she answers, "but that was one of the books in the travelling library. I picked it up because it was short."

"Did you like it?" he asks her.

"I thought it was very sad."

"Yes," agrees Miss Stevenson, who has been listening from across the table. "Oh *yes*." She's wearing her red jersey, brushed clean of chalk, and her face is eager; her eyes shine.

"Did *you* like it?" Norma Joyce asks Maurice. She has moved away from the door and squeezed her way past Mrs. Haaring so that she can see his face, and Lucinda's.

"I did."

"Do you think," she asks so seriously that everyone looks at her, "do you think Maria will ever be happy again?"

"You mean as happy as she was before her lover died?"

Lover again, and she ducks her head. "Yes," rubbing her fingertip on the tabletop. "After the book ends."

"No," he says.

"No?"

"No. She'll have *moments* of happiness, but she'll never have *sustained* happiness."

"Oh."

And Norma Joyce sees them, moments of happiness like pearls lost in the corners of a dark room.

"That's what I think too," says Miss Stevenson.

Later on, Maurice wonders aloud how people will look back on this time, and because it's so late and everyone's in such an expansive mood, they allow themselves to be tempted into thinking they've been living not through life as it has to be, but through a "time" that's about to end.

An idle visitor's question and it's a good thing they like him so much, but he is the sort of person who can ask anything.

Miss Stevenson says, "I think they'll raise a monument to the courage of the Prairie farmer."

No one replies until Ernest says, "Nonsense."

He says, "They could care less. We might as well be invisible."

He says, "You need a flood to get people's attention, or an earthquake, or a train wreck, not a drought that starts slowly and goes on and on and on."

"That's true," agrees Maurice. "But a long drought is still a drama. I look at it that way."

"What's the drama?" demands Ernest. "To see how bad things can get?"

Testy words that hang in the air until Miriam Wolfe says it's a blessing we can't see the future and Lucinda agrees. She says something always turns up, you have to remember that. But small Norma Joyce – her father's daughter – says, "But will the something be good or bad?"

To which there is no answer.

"All I know," weighs in gruff John Haaring, "is you got to do with what you've got." From a little drawstring bag he takes enough Zig-Zag tobacco to roll a cigarette. "Remember the time," he says, rolling the tobacco, "remember the time," licking the paper shut, "do you remember the time we had all the mushrooms?" He means the warm wet June when the rangeland was speckled white with mushrooms a delicate pink under their caps, and people ate them every which way, sliced and fried with bacon or sausage, simmered in pots of mushroom soup, boiled down into quarts of mushroom ketchup. "And remember the wild strawberries?" He means the bumper crops that used to grow in the little hollows of thick moist prairie soil.

"Plenty of spring rain, that's what you need, then plenty of hot sunshine," claims his wife.

"I don't remember," says Norma Joyce.

"I remember," says Lucinda.

Miniature berries after an endless winter. It's what saves you. Something delicate and contained after endless loss. For Lucinda it was needlework, for Ernest it was the ingenious repair of broken things, for Norma Joyce it was the tiny scenes of animals-in-aprons, sweeping.

"Berries the size of my pinkie," remembers Wanda Thurston. "We'd be down on our knees for hours, my mother and I."

Her tender, amused expression; and stories of weather turn to examples of devotion. There was Neil Pratt's dog Tramp, who followed him to the train siding in 1916 and stayed right there, fed by the nearby ranchers, until Neil's return in 1919. There was the woman who every morning carried her polio-crippled husband on her back, from the house to his specially rigged tractor. There were the four Indian boys who ran away from their residential school one day in January, and were found frozen in the slush ice of Fraser Lake three-quarters of a mile from their reserve. Capless, lightly clad, their arms around each other. One boy had lost a shoe.

It was very, very late, but no one stirred until Lucinda said, "Let's have a song."

In the sitting room Maurice played "Danny Boy" and Mrs. Haaring had to wipe her eyes twice. Then Miriam Wolfe played an old sea shanty. Then Maurice played a few more old songs. At four in the morning, Lucinda found blankets for everyone. The women and girls shared the beds upstairs, the boys and men slept downstairs on the floor.

Maurice was up at seven. At the first hint of coffee, Norma Joyce and Mrs. Haaring joined him. He offered to make porridge but Mrs. Haaring said no, she'd make fritters after the others got up, and Norma Joyce looked at her with joy. It would be a lucky day.

Some of Lucinda's sponge cake was left. "Do we dare?" asked Mrs. Haaring. They dared. Mrs. Haaring said, "It tastes like angels doing pee-pee on my tongue," and she repeated the words in Dutch, and the three of them giggled.

Then Maurice asked a simple question. He asked Mrs. Haaring, who was fifty-five and had come to Willow Bend in 1912, what she thought of living in Saskatchewan. She didn't answer for a moment. She helped herself to more sugar and stirred. Then she said, "Nothing prepared me for the Prairies."

The kitchen was quiet. She kept stirring. She said, "I remember looking around and thinking, I have come to a place *beyond* beautiful and ugly, a place so new, so empty, so cold that the words beautiful and ugly don't work." People, she said, were simple and friendly, but without curiosity. They asked her not a single question about herself. Then one day, years later, a woman came to the door who was from the Royal Society in England. She was collecting wildflowers.

"She came here too," said Norma Joyce.

"And she asked so many questions, I thought, why are you asking all of these questions, what business is it of yours? And then I knew," Mrs. Haaring said with a rueful laugh, "then I knew that I was a real Canadian."

These were things she had never said to anyone, but then no one else had ever asked. All it took was Maurice. He made any question seem the most natural in the world.

Norma Joyce watched him, and while she never acquired his infinite skill with people – being too odd, too bold, being a girl – she learned that you can ask anyone anything if you do it in a straightforward way. To see someone questioned by Maurice was to watch a window as the curtains opened. He made people more interesting than they were. They rose to meet the interest he had in them, that was the point, inspired by the quality of his attention.

But when he saw Mrs. Haaring again (it was the following November on his last visit), he didn't remember her. She mentioned the long, talkative house party at the Hardys. Of course, he said, you taught me that old sea shanty. No, she said gently, that was Miriam Wolfe. He bore his mistake gracefully, without embarrassment or apology. Of course, he said. And she realized how much more he had penetrated her mind than she had penetrated his, which was natural enough, she said to herself, his charm wasn't his fault. Still, that long night had awakened in her an affection and an interest, and now a disappointment of equal proportion. Apparently he paid less attention than he appeared to, or his attention was no less intense than it appeared to be, but it was short-lived, or his interests were too varied, or his character was not of the same consistency as his manner. In any case, he trailed disappointment behind him and was unaware of it. She was only a vague face in his mind, a farmwife from Belgium, or was it Holland?

And then she realized the value of Prairie reserve. It was reliable, it did not set you up for disappointment, it let you alone, and it was balanced by steady courtesy. People never failed to recognize you, and they never pried.

Two days later it turned hot, and everyone thought, *Here we go again.* Will the summer be like last year, when the crop was gone by the end of June, and it stayed so hot that by the middle of August it was still over a hundred degrees? Or like the year previous to that, when every day was hotter than the day before and whatever grain came up burnt black in July?

Norma Joyce felt sorry for stones and moved them into the shade of the house. She felt sorry for the landlocked fish on top of the barn. She felt *really* sorry for herself when Maurice said it was time for him to leave.

She was the only one to give him a gift. A small embroidered pouch for his barometer.

Lucinda exclaimed, "You knew all along!"

She had sewn it by hand and embroidered into its front the shiniest brass button from her button collection, a piece of red ribbon, and a piece of blue satin – proof that she had the sort of imagination that can turn a few scraps into something beautiful.

"Thank you," Maurice said in his light, husky, flexible voice.

"You're welcome," she said in her whiskey tenor.

That fall, Norma Joyce practised on the dog, stealing its affections before she stole Maurice's. Or so Lucinda would think.

The dog appeared at the end of a summer ruined by millions of grasshoppers that arrived in waves to chomp their way through crops, weeds, broom handles, washing on the line, shirts on sweaty backs, and sleep. Children woke up screaming *They're coming through the window, they're coming over the bed* and older sisters would say, "It's all right, it's all right." After the hoppers came rust, hail, wireworms, and sawflies. And after that the dog, like a wolf on the heels of a long stream of choice disasters.

He fetched up at the back door one August morning just as summer turned into summer-fall. Lucinda gave him water and the porridge left over from breakfast, and at first he was content to follow her around, to push his head against the back of her hand, to wait for her while she hoed the garden, and to follow her back to the house, where he lay down on a mat inside the door while she made dinner. Then Norma Joyce came home.

"Let's call him Darwin," she said, plopping down on the floor beside the yellow-grey mutt.

She told him Darwin was a famous name and he was the first dog to have it. Her voice was soft and low, what in singers gets called a dark voice, and it seemed to bewitch the dog. After that, his ears pricked up the moment her feet touched the floor above his head and he didn't take his eyes off the doorway until she came through it. He accompanied her to school, waited hours until she came out, walked beside her to the post office, and home, and on every trek she made. She brushed his fur and he lay as if tranquilized, submitting to her attentions as willingly as Maurice had done. She gave up chairs to sit on the floor beside him.

Some mornings Lucinda found them side by side on the mat next to the kitchen door, her sister under the old Persian-lamb coat worn years ago by Florida May, and Darwin keeping guard. He would raise his head when she came into the kitchen and watch her move about, but he wouldn't stir until Norma Joyce was awake. Not for a moment would he have disturbed her sleep. He had far too much tact.

Girl and Dog. Both had a wandering foot. They knew every road and fenceline, every coulee and creek bed, every nesting place and burrow nearby. Together they found the rare berries that still appeared, the clay that, with a little water, proved supple in your hands, the various pebbles and arrowheads and occasional old pennies that Norma Joyce cherished.

And their gums were the same dark colour.

The warm weather of August continued through September and into October. A farmer in Willow Bunch claimed that the dust bowl "was" because for the first time since 1931 his crabapple tree had produced enough fruit for him to sell. Until October 14, there wasn't a touch of frost.

In early November Lucinda dreamt that her hair had gone grey. She was brushing it off the back of her neck and saw that underneath, it was as silvery as the underside of willow leaves, or the pearly interior of a peanut shell, or the dusty mildew-shine of lilac leaves in late summer. She woke up to newly fallen snow on the rooftops of the outbuildings and barn, reached for the hand mirror on the chest of drawers, and was reassured.

Maurice arrived before supper. This time he came with a jar of soap bubbles for Norma Joyce, more cigars for Ernest, a king-sized bottle of Jergens lotion for Lucinda (enough, he said, to splash around in) and, best of all, three Golden Russets.

Norma Joyce took hers and examined the yellow-brown skin that was alternately rough and smooth – and freckled with milk specks, except where large spots of pure gold appeared like bare skin through a hole in a rough stocking. *He was thinking about me. He remembered our conversation.*

In the sunlight – the sun was shining that early November day – it looked like the golden apple, this homely winter apple.

"They keep all winter," Maurice said, "but they're best at Christmas."

She couldn't wait. She cut hers in half and juice spat out. The flesh was pale green and dense; it hurt her teeth it was so tough and tart. What a lot of chewing.

Lucinda said, "I'll save mine."

But what a powerful flavour. And suddenly generous, she cut off pieces for everybody.

"Yes," said Maurice, chewing away, "Christmas," the sound of his voice reminding her of something – a tongue scalded by tea, a layer of taste buds burned off so that only light, high huskiness remained. My, she had missed it.

He said, "Now I know I've eaten an apple."

"Why?"

"I can feel it in my lips."

She looked at his lips.

"It always happens," he said, "when the apple's really tart."

His lips were a very dark red.

She followed him upstairs and helped him unpack. Inside his knapsack there was something new, a small hinged wooden box held shut by a tiny hook on a nail. He said go ahead, and she lifted the hook, opened the box, and saw ten shades of green protected by a soft cotton pillow whose underside had taken the slim shape of the ten pastels. Each pastel poked its nose into more protective cotton, lending the cotton the same progression of colour from lightest to darkest green.

Crude little jewel box of colour. She hooked it together then unhooked it, unable to resist the pleasure of seeing that row of colour so neatly at rest.

That night she lay in bed under her mother's old Persian-lamb coat. The black sheep of the family lying beside her golden sister, and thinking.

She liked the weight of a coat so heavy, hangers drooped at the sight of it. She liked its black silk lining embroidered with flowers, even in the sleeves where they couldn't be seen, drooping bell-flowers on blue-green stalks, each one (there were twenty-four) a different combination of purple, yellow, and red. The fur across the arms had cracked open in many places, which was why the coat was hers and not Lucinda's.

She fingered the tight Persian-lamb curls and thought of wily Jacob and careless Esau, and wondered why Isaac had trusted his sense of touch more than his hearing. He must have been nearly deaf as well as blind, an old, old man doing his favourite son out of his birthright.

Her own voice was already as low as Lucinda's. People said on the phone they couldn't tell the two sisters apart.

Esau took too much for granted, that was his problem. Oldest children are like that. But younger children are not.

The following day she sat on the porch blowing bubbles, and two days later she was in bed with the mumps.

"Now I'll do for you what my father did for me," said Maurice, coming into her room with a book. It was late morning and pale November light fell across the old fur coat that came up to her flushed and aching face.

She asked him, "How do you see things moving in your mind?"

"What do you see moving in your mind?"

"You think red and there it is, it's nowhere, it's just in your mind."

"Yes," he said, and he marvelled too.

"I dreamt about snakes last night."

"That was your fever."

"I hate snakes."

"I like them. You should too," he said. "Snakes know a lot. They have sharp eyes, they move fast, they know how to shed their skin and be reborn. In some cultures they guard time, or water, or treasure. I've read that in Greece they leave milk out for snakes so the snakes will protect them."

Norma Joyce was happy under her mother's coat with Maurice in a chair beside her and her mind wandering at will. He read aloud from Marco Polo's travels, and right away she liked the Tartars because they knew so much and travelled so far, restless people in light mobile tents of felt who endured the utmost privations by *moving*. For the Tartars, nine was the magical number. She was nine. Marco Polo was seventeen when he went to Cathay with his father and his uncle. It took three years to get there; they stayed seventeen years; it took three more years to get home. 17+3+17+3. That was a pattern. It made 40. The Khan wouldn't let them go and she understood why. She wouldn't have let him go either.

They got home though, despite the Khan, and nobody recognized them. The dogs barked as if they were strangers. (A homecoming you've been working towards for years and years, but it means nothing to anyone else. You stand stupidly in the street.)

"Time was so different then," said Maurice. "Can you imagine your son leaving on a trip and not coming back for twenty-three years?"

"Did he come home rich?" asked Norma Joyce.

"Filthy rich. But so shabby nobody believed it until he ripped open the seams of his clothes and let the jewels tumble out."

She touched the seam of her mother's coat, ran her fingers over the embroidered flowers.

"How do you know I'm not secretly rich?" she asked him. "I could be rich. How do you know I'm not?"

"Because you listen," he said.

With her mother's school atlas open to Persia on her lap, she followed Marco Polo's route, indefatigable yet undemanding; when Maurice wanted to stop she said, thank you Maurice. She knew how to do without, just like the Tartars. (Her doing-without was different from Lucinda's. Lucinda chain-smoked her tasks while Norma Joyce knew how to be still, solitary, lost in thought. In her own way, Norma Joyce was more economical than her economical sister.)

Maurice read to her about the beautiful plain of Hormuz, which took two days to cross, a stream-studded expanse covered with date palms and full of birds. Offshore lay an island, and on the island was the city of Hormuz, with a climate even more extreme than this one. A wind so hot that in the summer everyone headed to the river, where they constructed willow huts over the water and submerged themselves up to the chin from nine until noon, after which the suffocating land wind ceased to blow.

It was his voice as much as anything. She loved his voice. And the fact that he knew so much and wanted to know more.

It was her capacity for listening. Someone uncharitable might have said her capacity for listening to him. Had anyone accused him of flirting, dallying, arousing expectations or encouraging fond hopes, he would have been dumbfounded and hurt. But does a piece of parched ground argue about the nature of a drop of water? She sucked up whatever he said and she made it last.

He said he might follow Marco Polo's route one day. He might write a book about it.

"I wonder if I'll travel some day," she said.

"I'm sure you will."

"Why?"

"Well, you won't stay here forever."

"You said five years. In five years we'll move away."

"Did I?"

"I'll be fourteen."

"And I'll be twenty-eight. Much too old for you."

Oh, men with twinkling eyes. You should be strung up at birth.

He read to her about the fabled *arbor secco*, the dry tree that grows alone on a plain near the northern border of Persia. Its pods contain no fruit. No other trees grow within a hundred miles. They call it the tree of the sun, and the most beautiful women in the world live in its shade.

"Who is more beautiful?" she asked him. "Katherine Hepburn or Carole Lombard?"

"They're both beautiful."

"But which one is *more* beautiful?"

He smiled. "All right. Katherine Hepburn."

"Why?"

"Better bones. But I like Carole Lombard."

"Why?"

"She's more fun, she's more natural." (A distinction she tucked away for future use and comfort; Katherine Hepburn only got Spencer Tracy while Carole Lombard got Clark Gable.)

"Do you think Katherine Hepburn's more beautiful than Mrs. Simpson?"

"Mrs. Simpson isn't beautiful and she knows it. That's what makes the whole thing so puzzling."

"He loves her."

"I wonder."

"He *must*. To give up his throne."

"Or maybe she has something on him."

"You don't have to be beautiful, you know."

"Of course not," twigging finally, and mollifying her.

"But I guess *you'd* never love a woman who wasn't beautiful."

"I wouldn't say that."

"Lucinda's beautiful."

"She is."

"As beautiful as Katherine Hepburn?"

"What a girl you are," he said. "Why do you insist on comparing everything?"

"You're going to marry Lucinda, aren't you?"

"And if you're good you can come to the wedding. Now listen."

And he continued to read about the bravery, "almost to desperation," of people who could not be surpassed in fortitude, "nor show greater patience under wants of every kind." The men remained on horseback for two days and two nights at a time, sleeping while their horses grazed. They travelled for ten days at a stretch without stopping to prepare food, living on dried mare's milk and on the blood drawn from their horses, "each man opening a vein." Every morning they put some of the hard milk paste into a leather bottle with water, and by dinnertime the motion of the horse had shaken the contents into a thin porridge.

"Ugh," she said.

"Listen to this. They shot arrows backwards as accurately as forwards. Their horses were trained to turn on a dime."

He skipped over the practice of sewing up a man between two blankets and shaking him to death, but he read about their habit of marrying one dead child to another dead child. They painted pictures of horses, furniture, and gifts on pieces of paper, then consigned the papers, along with the marriage contract, to a fire whose smoke conveyed these things to the dead couple in the other world. He read to her about the musk deer of Tibet, who delight in the most intense cold, and she said, "What's musk?"

"Musk? That's the oily, waxy stuff produced by the musk glands. It says here that the musk of the male musk deer forms at the navel in a little bag that resembles a wen."

At this she took his hand and placed it on the back of her head where he felt several wens of various sizes, like small and larger eggs.

"I have nine," she said, "and I am nine."

Across her knees lay the Persian lamb, and across that the atlas open to Persia, and above both, her wide, receptive forehead.

"How do you know I'm not rich?" she asked again.

"I told you."

"What did you say?" Her eyes bright with fever.

He laughed. "Maybe I was wrong."

He began to think the over-full lips less peculiar than sensuous, the over-wide forehead not outlandish but impressive, the licorice gums not so much weird as exotic. It can happen to anyone. You see the same plain landscape day after day, and then one day, perhaps it's the play of light or the time of year, you find it beautiful and other landscapes at fault. So it must be with fashion. Ordinary judgement falls into abeyance and something else, some bewitchment, takes over. How else to explain the appeal of garments that in a few years look so ridiculous?

Bewitchment. In a land so flat, the slightest upward lift or downward slope provides a release as dramatic as a shot of whiskey. This slight shift, and Norma Joyce took on a new beauty, freshly minted and persuasive.

Something happened to allow for a shift so crucial. Men were always coming to the door in thin old suit coats looking for work, and Ernest would explain that he had no money but that his daughter would give them a plate of food. Lucinda kept a big pot of beans on the back of the stove for this purpose. Towards the middle of Maurice's third visit, when Norma Joyce had recovered enough to occupy the rocking chair in the kitchen, a tiny old man came to the door with eyes so watery they brimmed. Lucinda had to look away to keep her own eyes from watering in sympathy, but Norma Joyce didn't mind the old man's glycerine tears that neither receded nor overflowed.

The man was as brown as a nut. He patted Darwin, who licked his hand. He ate the plate of beans and bread Lucinda put in front of him. He thanked her for the food, and then he offered to read her palm. No. She didn't think so. And Maurice saw her actually stiffen.

From the rocking chair Norma Joyce held out her hand. The old man took the little hand and said, "You have a fever still?"

"My hands are always warm," said Norma Joyce.

He nudged his chair close and studied the warm little hand. He smelled of sweat, peppermints, tobacco, old coffee. Despite his accent he wasn't hard to understand – he talked so slowly and carefully. She would have a long life, he said. There would be one child. The child's life would stop, then it would start again. And so would her life. It would stop, but it would start again. You have special talents, he told her. People don't realize.

"You're a twin?" he asked her.

"He died," she said.

"That's why," he said. "Your life stops too." And he held up two crooked fingers. "One half," lowering one finger, "then the other half."

Perhaps most of us are persuaded by the sight of someone else's interest to be interested ourselves. Certainly Maurice was suggestible. He saw Norma Joyce through the old man's appreciative eyes, and in that moment ugliness passed into beauty, and curiosity into something like love.

The old man beckoned to her with a long brown forefinger so weathered it shone like wax paper. She leaned close – thinking he had something to whisper – and he kissed her cheek. An old Russian habit, he said, forgive me.

The next day they came up with their wedding game. Norma Joyce and Maurice were alone in the kitchen. Ernest was outside, Lucinda was upstairs, Darwin was asleep on the mat beside the door. Norma Joyce said, "I spy with my little eye something that is shiny."

"Okay," said Maurice. "Is it smaller than a breadbox? Is it larger than a pin? Does it burn? Does it float? Does it rust?

"Is it *all* shiny?" he wanted to know.

"Is it flat? Is it pointed? Is it dangerous? Can you put your book on it? Can you see your face in it? Can you *wear* it?"

Filling her with delight by asking questions so extensive and precise they seemed, by summoning up one thing, to summon up everything. She saw the object come into view bit by bit, and it thrilled her, it really did.

Maurice slipped off his ring. "Because you're sick," he said. "I wouldn't do this for just anyone," and let her put it on her finger.

She returned the favour by showing him her mother's recipe book, a pale green notebook of unlined pages in which her mother had divided recipes into dry ingredients on the left and wet ingredients on the right. On the back pages were various doodles of fossils and leaves and tree rings copied from books, of foliage pods, seeds, cross-sections of apples. Florida May had wanted to be a painter, "but where can you study art in Saskatchewan?" she used to say. "I should have run away to New York."

In the front of the recipe book she had written her name, Florida May Lamb, then stroked out *Lamb* and written *Hardy* above it. Maurice noticed it, leafing through a second time. "Lamb marries Hardy, that's a good match."

"Why?" asked Norma Joyce.

"Lamb needs toughening up, Hardy needs softening. Opposites attract."

"Then Jeanne Eagels should have married Maurice Dove."

"And she'd be a happy woman today," said Maurice with a smile. "But would I be a happy man?"

"Is it awful to commit suicide?" asked Norma Joyce.

"Pretty awful."

"I guess it depends how you do it. Ryatt's dad slit his throat."

"So did Robert Fitzroy," Maurice said, and she looked at him and waited. "The captain of the *Beagle*," he explained. "Remember? Darwin's ship. He was the first true weather forecaster and he ended up slitting his throat. That's what weather will do to you."

"What with?"

A Norma-Joyce question, he thought with admiration, and some alarm. "Shaving razor," he answered.

"Jeanne Eagels took pills."

"Not pills. Heroin doesn't come in pills. A needle. Into your arm."

"Oh."

"I agree," he said. "But you have to be able to adapt in this life and she couldn't. Or so I understand. She couldn't make the switch from silent movies to talkies, that's what I read some-where. Being beautiful isn't everything."

"Yes it is. I think it is."

"No you don't. You're too smart for that."

Any compliment was welcome. But then he added, "Life is hard if you're beautiful."

"*Who told you that?* Did Lucinda tell you that?"

He had to laugh. "I think it's true. Life is for the hardy."

"Then who should *I* marry?"

"Norma Joyce Hardy? Why Maurice Softie of course."

Their laughter drew Lucinda to the doorway. "What are you two up to?"

Maurice replied, "Oh, nothing. Norrie and I were just marry-ing each other off."

The icing on the cake. *Norrie.* Her mother had called her Norrie. She sat very still inside her happiness.

"George Raft and Ethel Waters," offered Norma Joyce. "Claude Rains and Louise Brooks. Luise Rainer and Orson Welles." Maurice laughed and said he liked the way her mind worked, and so she kept it up until she had nine couples. "Rudy Vallee and Gracie Fields. George Burns and Betty Furness. Stan Laurel and Judy Garland. W.C. Fields and Frances Farmer. Tallulah Bankhead and Samuel Goldwyn."

She began to do things nine times in a row. Nine pages of a book, nine swallows of tea, nine coals on the fire, his name nine times under her breath. The Tartars had entered her dreams. She saw them moving like weather across the land.

Night after night Lucinda has poured one careful drop of lotion into her palm. Maurice watches her. Will she ever use more than one drop, he wonders. Will she ever have even one ounce of her sister's recklessness?

Lucinda feels him watching and mistakes his curiosity for admiration, but it's only curiosity, and soon it isn't even that. Why is she so niggardly? What's the use of giving her a lot if she treats it like a little?

With sudden impatience he jumps up and takes the bottle out of her hands. "I'll show you how it's done!"

Norma Joyce looks up from *Hurlbut's Story of the Bible*. Ernest looks up from *The Family Herald*. They are riveted by the handsome couple standing next to the kitchen sink, Lucinda with her hands at her sides, Maurice flushed and shaking the uncooperative bottle.

Annoyance, thinks Norma Joyce. And with Lucinda.

Marriage, thinks Ernest, and grandchildren. They'll name their son Ernest. They'll name their daughter Florida May.

Norma Joyce has never seen either one of them look or sound this way before. *I'll show you how it's done* in a tone so startling that the words still ring in her head. And Lucinda looking silly.

The next moment the cherry-reeking stuff lets loose and splats through his fingers onto the kitchen floor.

"Oh," moans Lucinda.

But Maurice grabs her hands. He slops them with lotion, he tells her that big girls don't cry over spilt Jergens, and in the excess of lotion and hard laughter his ring flies off and rolls out of sight.

It's dark, of course. Nine o'clock at night. They look for the ring, even Ernest takes a gander behind the table, but it's late. They're tired. It's difficult by lamplight.

"In the morning," they say, and they prepare to go upstairs.

Lucinda can't resist. On hands and knees, and with a spatula, she carefully scrapes up the spilled lotion and puts it back into the bottle. Maurice laughs at her and so does Norma Joyce. But Lucinda doesn't laugh. She says she hates waste. Her voice is sharp and hurt. She hears the sound of her voice and tries to make amends by repeating herself even more vigorously. She hates waste of any kind. And the kitchen goes quiet.

Everyone's asleep except for the little gnome who slips out of bed and comes downstairs. She rubs Darwin's ears then goes over to the big range, lies flat on her stomach and stretches her arm all the way under. Wriggles. Stretches farther and pats the floor inch by inch. Finally, she draws out the ring. It's barely visible in the darkness, and quite cool. It spins loosely on her ring finger.

Back upstairs, she slides the ring under her pillow. There it stays until her sister is safely downstairs making porridge, then she adds it to her cigar-box collection of nail clippings, handkerchief, tobacco, and hair. Had she been able to, she would have kept the water he washed in, the skin that flaked away, the warm breath that hovered in the cold air above his head, his footprints in the snow. She would have kept the headache he got the next day, and the fever the day after that, so that for three days he was laid up in the bedroom next to hers while she read to him, his stay prolonged by another week.

What she loved (besides his extravagance, which she loved most of all) was the way he smelled of the outside and the inside, not just of the air beyond the door but of train stations, bus depots, hotel rooms, restaurants.

Besides that, the milky lower reaches of his neck and the soft flesh under his chin. Also his warm flexible voice. Also the way his tongue came down on a stamp.

Norma Joyce Dove, she used to say to herself nine times in a row.

Without asking permission, she once took his hand and traced the veins on the back and then the lines on his palm, finding his hands no less interesting than the jumble of knowledge he carried inside his head. He told them about the man in Kitchener, Ontario, who rocked fifty-five hours to take the world's rocking-chair championship. About the barber in Swift Current who no longer gave shaves because he couldn't keep an edge on his razor, so embedded with grit were the cheeks of Prairie men. About the famous year without a summer, 1816, when Ottawa lay under snow all summer long and Europe was so cold, and the skies so lurid, that Mary Shelley wrote *Frankenstein* and everyone learned the recently coined names for the clouds. Cumulus, stratus, cirrus, and nimbus.

"What did they call them before that?"

"They didn't. Hard to imagine, but they didn't. The same as Prairie winds. So many kinds but we don't have names for them. It's easy to forget that everything has a beginning and often not so long ago."

"You know everything," said Norma Joyce.

"Hardly everything," said Maurice.

"Everything that matters."

"Not even that."

"You know everything that matters to me."

He smiled. He was amused and flattered. He would be gone soon, and she would transfer her intensity to someone else.

Lucinda's thimble is on the kitchen table, a silver thimble with a border of leaves. He picks it up and twirls it on his little finger.

"You never stop," he says to her.

"I've stopped now," and indeed she has, abruptly. Embarrassed by his assessing eye and the undertone of criticism. She sits down with the dustcloth in her lap.

"You like to keep at something until it's done. That's a good quality."

But she isn't fooled. It isn't a compliment. "What is ever *done*?" she asks.

"You don't mind, though. At least you don't seem to."

He's returning her to the shelf, she can feel it. As if he knows all there is to know about her, and it isn't much.

She stands up and continues to dust.

Then she says, speaking to the wall, "I have the feeling that if I stopped I'd never start again."

She says it so simply that he relents. A few honest words of confessed weakness and he suddenly remembers who she is. He must have been very sick to have forgotten. She is the most beautiful, capable woman he has ever met.

He says, "Do you have a picture of yourself?"

She looks at him.

"Do you have one you're willing to part with?"

So it's all right then. As quickly as it was all wrong.

A few days later she's polishing silver at the kitchen table, something she always does after the light changes; by now, his third and final visit, it's almost the end of November. She polishes the salt and pepper shaker, the cruet for oil and vinegar, the large pudding spoon. Maurice is writing at the table and he feels her looking at him.

"What is it?" he asks gently, putting down his pen.

She smiles, and looks down again at the beautifully shaped spoon she's polishing with her soft cloth. The spoon comes from Ontario. *Lamb* is engraved on the long handle. Of all the things in the house, this is her favourite.

"Lucinda? Tell me."

"Norma Joyce thinks the world of you," she says without looking at him.

"I like her too. I like *every* Hardy I know."

She looks up and smiles. "You've been so good to her."

"It's nothing," he says. "It's normal."

"It's everything," she says. "It's going to be hard on her when you leave."

"I'll be back. Don't worry," and he reaches for her hand. "Don't worry, Lucinda."

"When?" she asks, looking him full in the face.

He has no idea. There's talk of a permanent job at the Dominion Experimental Farm; his supervisor hopes he will apply, and of course he will.

"In the spring? I'll come back for your birthday."

"All right," and her eyes are playful, but they also mean business. "When is my birthday?"

"April?" he guesses. "May? Not May. Definitely not May. How about June?"

This time Norma Joyce is the one drawn to the doorway by laughter.

"What are you laughing about?" she wants to know. But neither one looks at her.

"June 13th," repeats Maurice. "And don't forget the lemon icing on the sponge cake."

———◦———

On the last day of his last visit Maurice comes back from town earlier than usual; it's around three in the afternoon on November 29, a Tuesday. He has finished all of his business, spoken to the last farmer, written up the last report.

"You'll have a cup of tea?" asks Lucinda.

No, he thinks not. He has a few things to attend to. And he goes upstairs.

Half an hour later he comes back down, but not to join her in the kitchen. He stays in the sitting room with his book. She waits but he stays out there, beside the Nautilus heater, with his book.

Norma Joyce and Darwin come home. "Where's Maurice?"

Lucinda points. Her sister goes to the doorway, then across to the sofa. He is laughing to himself over P.G. Wodehouse, some exquisitely private pleasure.

"You're reading," she says.

He finishes his sentence, marks his place with his finger, looks up. "You should be reading this," he says, "instead of gloomy Thomas Hardy."

Gloomy Thomas Hardy?

He has already distanced himself, and it hurts both sisters, this facility he has for being with them and for leaving them in equal measure. He continues to read and chuckle while they make supper in the kitchen.

The next morning everyone but Norma Joyce is at the break-fast table. Maurice will be taking the mid-morning train; his knapsack is beside the kitchen door. Three heads are bent over bowls of porridge.

Lucinda's indrawn breath, and Ernest looks up to see his youngest daughter slide into her chair. Mrs. Hayden's lipstick has been applied, and not only to her lips. The trouble with small mirrors and dim bedroom light.

Ernest is so transfixed that he forgets the cup of tea in his right hand. It tips, spilling its scalding contents onto his fingers. He flings the fool thing away. Norma Joyce is in the path of the tea, but it's Ernest who yelps. Damn!

He shoves his chair back from the table. Mops his hand with his serviette. Throws the serviette in her direction. *Wipe that mess off your face!*

From his mat by the door, Darwin growls.

Maurice finds her behind the barn using hard-crusted snow to scour her face. He wipes her eyes gently with his handkerchief. "They're just worried about you," he says.

"They're not worried about me. They're ashamed."

"No," he says. "They overreact because they're worried. They don't know what to make of you. Did you get burned?"

He wipes her cheeks and lips carefully, and she says, "I love you, Maurice."

Only now is it getting light. Around them, hard stubble shows through the thin snow. Maurice looks at her unforgettable eyes, then back to the rather more manageable business of her cheek. "Oh, dear," he says. And gives her face one last wipe.

He folds his handkerchief, lipstick to the inside, and pockets it. Rubs his forehead with flattened fingers, and decides to make a joke. "How old are you again?"

"Nine."

"Well, then. Maybe in nine more years," and he gives her a lopsided grin. Turning towards the house, "Come on," he urges, "your father is taking us into town."

At school that day they read Duncan Campbell Scott's "At Gull Lake: August 1810." Mr. Scott lives in Ottawa, says Miss Stevenson. People see him walking down Wellington Street and he could be anyone at all going to an office downtown. He wears the same dark suit, the same grey hat.

"This poem is a love poem," she explains, opening the book and capturing Norma Joyce's attention. Miss Stevenson is wearing the navy blue alpaca dress with the white detachable collar and cuffs. Her voice is clear and pleasant. She reads the poem aloud and soon Norma Joyce catches its drift. A young Indian woman who loves a stealing, lowdown trader expresses her passion so openly, so recklessly, so persistently that her people punish her by putting a firebrand to her face. They leave her to wander about blind. A storm comes up – hail and wind – and then a rainbow – and then the moon.

> *But Keejigo came no more to the camps of her people;*
> *Only the midnight moon knew where she felt her way,*
> *Only the leaves of autumn, the snows of winter*
> *Knew where she lay.*

"She's Tess," Miss Stevenson says. "An Indian Tess of the d'Urbervilles. She's the Highwayman's daughter. An Indian Bess, braiding a loveknot into her long dark hair. Everything for love. Then in the end she's absolutely alone. Only the weather has any sympathy for her.

"Unrequited love," adds Miss Stevenson, "is a terrible thing."

There are rumours about Miss Stevenson. Why has she come all the way out here to teach about seals and polar bears and Eskimos who live in the dark? Why does she go on and on about Thomas Hardy and Shakespeare's sonnets and poets in Ottawa no one has ever heard of? She must have a broken heart.

Outside, snow comes down like grey feathers. After a while, the wind picks up; it blows the snow sideways and turns it into sheets of rain and lightning.

Then, on the way home, an actual rainbow.

Ginny is with Norma Joyce, and so is Darwin. They walk side by side. Ginny says rainbows are snakes coming down to drink. That's what her grandmother says. Is your grandmother Indian? Of course she's not Indian, she's from Quebec.

They go into Ginny's house for tea and cookies. Mrs. Gallot is just as nice as Miss Stevenson. She puts a cookie into Norma Joyce's pocket for the rest of the walk home.

It gets dark early now. It's the last day of November. Norma Joyce takes off her mitten and touches the places where Maurice wiped gently with his handkerchief. Already the sun has gone down behind her; the last light grazes the barbwire fence on her left and she sees something moving on the other side. Darwin growls. Shhhh, she says.

The impression of a horse and two riders. A large white horse and a small Indian woman riding in front of a man. Norma Joyce stares and they disappear.

She walks on, faster, and sees them again, out of the corner of her eye. The tall horse and two riders keeping pace with her on the other side of the fence. Darwin growls again.

She stops. Quickly, she turns her head.

There they are. The white horse and the painted woman and the dark-haired trader. The woman holds her gaze for a moment. Her face is very clear. Then horse and riders dissolve. They disappear into the dusk.

At recess the next morning she stays inside and goes up to Miss Stevenson at her desk.

"I've seen her," she says. "The Indian woman in the poem."

"Have you? Where?"

"On my way home. Just before the hill. On that stretch of unbroken prairie."

"It's a wonderful poem, isn't it?" says Miss Stevenson.

Norma Joyce nods.

"You might be a poet, Norma Joyce. Have you thought of writing poetry?"

"Miss Stevenson? Her forehead was painted with a blue half-moon. She was riding in front of him on a white horse."

"The trader."

"He was in the saddle. She was in front of him. I wanted to tell you. I think she's all right."

It was Norma Joyce who picked up the mail. Wanda Thurston was always at the wicket, and this time she said, "Here's something for your sister."

The letter was addressed to Lucinda June Hardy and to her alone. Whenever had he learned about Lucinda's middle name? Some moment when she wasn't there. And here was another.

All the way home she pictured her sister looking up from the rocker, unable to contain her happy smile, and then she had to watch it happen.

"What does he say?" she asked Lucinda.

"He says hello to you."

"What else?"

"He says Uncle Dennis looks as spry as ever, he saw him last week. He wishes us all a happy Christmas. He says he means it about coming back for my birthday."

"In June."

"He asks what I want for a present."

"What are you going to say?"

"I'm not."

"You're not going to tell him what you want for a present?"

"Of course I'm not." In a tone so prim and self-congratulatory that Norma Joyce looked at her with disgust.

Radiant Lucinda put her shining letter into the narrow uppermost drawer of their dresser. It was easily read. Norma Joyce had it memorized in a day. The letter included a poem, that was its great novelty. So many things can be read into a poem and a poem can be read so many times. Maurice had been reading Arthur Waley's *Translations from the Chinese*.

> *Peacocks shall fill your gardens; you shall rear*
> *The roc and phoenix, and red jungle-fowl,*
> *Whose cry at dawn assembles river storks*
> *To join the play of cranes and ibises;*
> *Where the wild-swan all day*
> *Pursues the glint of idle king-fishers.*
> *O Soul come back to watch the birds in flight!*

Towards the end of February another letter arrived. It was a day of cold sunshine with little wind. Norma Joyce, wearing the dark blue melton coat she would still be wearing three years later, picked up the mail and set off home with Darwin and Ginny. Beyond Ginny's, about halfway home, she took the letter out of her schoolbag and stood in the middle of the road looking at it. A small white envelope with King George in red and white in the upper right-hand corner: his nice-looking face and thick hair and worried eyes and perfect ears. To his lower left: *Miss Lucinda June Hardy*, Willow Bend, Saskatchewan. She remembers – years later when she gives her mind over to remembering – she remembers reaching into her schoolbag for the letter the way you reach for a second piece of cake if it remains on the table long enough. You do it without thinking, even though you've been thinking of nothing else.

She opened the letter. At the top was a date sufficient in itself to keep an isolated prairie mind occupied for months. *February 14, 1939*. Valentine's Day.

She read it rapidly through, searching for her own name. It didn't appear until the very end.

"Tell Norma Joyce that the man who repairs my mother's stove and washing machine is a Mr. Washburn."

She read the letter again. It followed the same pattern as the first one. It began with the weather, went on to his work, proceeded to world events, and closed with the personal thoughts she cared most about. He was working in pasture studies at the Dominion Experimental Farm, where he was picking up information about other things too, soil erosion, winter-resistant roses; he knew the war was coming, could see it was necessary, though all he wanted for himself was time to read and study. He ended with a final paragraph of fond farewells. This time he managed to say less by saying more. He said that every time he looked west she came into his mind. He would always be grateful, he said, to her and her family for their kindness and generosity. He would always remember them.

She thought, "Whenever he looks west he thinks of Lucinda, but it's her family he won't forget. That's me."

And from the ashes of Mr. Washburn she seized this faint coal.

He also said that his new job meant he was no longer his own man. He might not be able to come in June, he wasn't sure, and he urged her to write. But no poem.

And nothing about Valentine's Day, despite the date.

That night at supper – her favourite meal of chicken and dumplings, which meant luck was on her side – the letter stayed inside the pocket of her blue winter coat. At a quiet moment, when Lucinda was ironing and her back was turned, she slipped the letter out of her coat pocket and upstairs, into the box within a box under her bed.

Hers was a reverse Damascus, a shining letter she pocketed, blinding herself to the effect on her sister.

———◆———

In March they lost Miss Stevenson. Her father was sick and her mother needed her. She went back to Ontario and awful Mrs. Graviston took her place. Now Norma Joyce would learn what school was really like. Mrs. Graviston, the widow of a local farmer, had a "meanful nature," as Ginny put it, and only two dresses, one black, one brown, both shapeless; Norma Joyce did her best to look at King George instead.

But in April Mrs. Graviston's glance fell full upon her.

"What did you say, Norma Joyce?"

"I said why."

"I beg your pardon?"

And Norma Joyce went quiet.

Mrs. Graviston had got it into her head that they should take the afternoon to spring-clean the school. But what was the point of cleaning just as the dustiest weather began? There was no point in cleaning. Therefore there was no point in helping. Norma Joyce took her copy of *Tess* over to the corner and buried her nose in her book while everyone else beavered away around her. Once she helped Ginny move a table and they scrubbed that part of the floor, another time she took the mop Mrs. Graviston pointedly handed to her and made a few pokes at the floor in the cloakroom, but otherwise she lifted her feet out of the way and kept her eyes on her book.

The next day Mrs. Graviston brought in a cake. She had cut it into thirty-two pieces because there were thirty-two pupils (minus Ginny, who happened to be sick). Each student she called by name. It was a very big rectangular cake. The pieces were surprisingly generous. White cake with heavy chocolate icing. She called Norma Joyce's name last. Norma Joyce stood up. She started to walk to the front.

"Wait," said bony Mrs. Graviston in her mean black dress. "Does anyone here think that a girl who *doesn't* help should receive the same reward as those of us who do?"

Norma Joyce began to edge back to her desk, but Mrs. Graviston said: "Norma Joyce. You should remain standing."

It was the sanctimoniousness she hated most. The gloating, self-righteous, self-congratulatory, punitive virtue. Lucinda had it too, but not this bad.

"Does anyone think a girl who doesn't help should get a piece of cake? Raise your hand if you do.

"Norma Joyce. I'm afraid no one has raised a hand."

And Mrs. Graviston turned her back on Norma Joyce. Indeed, everyone seemed to turn their backs, just as men in one motion would turn their backs on the relief train when it pulled into the station. They let their wives step forward to get the apples, the cheese, and the strange salt cod.

Talk about housecleaning. These things clear your head, these acts of ostracism. You feel burnished, like a Greek baby left on a mountaintop.

After the shock was over, after her tears stopped shooting across the road (eyes like fountains, gums like rainclouds; but not – thank you, Lord – until halfway home), after Darwin licked her face so hard she had to laugh, Norma Joyce actually felt stronger. Blasted clean. An upthrust finger of rock scoured by the wind to its very core.

———◆———

Spring came late and dry. The only real rain came on the heels of a twister that did a great deal of damage, though not to the Hardy farm. May was hot. The first dust storm hit on May 6. Two weeks later, coinciding with the visit of King George and Queen Elizabeth, rain fell for two days. The king and queen came through Saskatchewan in their twelve-car blue-and-gold train, and everyone who saw them said the king raised a hand every now and then (he wasn't well, of course, unlike his tanned and feckless older brother), and the queen was a splendid, splendid woman (unlike Mrs. Simpson).

The train passed through Swift Current – they could have been there in an hour and a half – but Ernest wouldn't go. This champion of the Empire and defender of Scott wouldn't lower himself to be one of the common herd. He would not go, and his younger daughter was desolate.

After his first *No*, however, she managed to hold her tongue, waiting with enormous self-control for the right moment to ask one more time. A Sunday morning, after his third cup of tea, when he had the weekly *Herald* before him and was smiling at a joke, she passed him a note, not trusting herself to speak in the right tone or with the right words. Spelling each word very carefully, she asked him PLEASE to reconsider not just for her sake but for LUCINDA'S. It was a chance they might never have again to see THEIR MAJESTIES KING GEORGE VI AND QUEEN ELIZABETH on the first visit to Canada by a ruling British SOVEREIGN.

He looked up. "The answer is no," he said, and he handed the note back to her.

Yet he accused *her* of not stirring her stumps. How had her mother married such a man? She could have killed him with her bare hands.

Later, Lucinda said to her, "Don't be so disappointed. Maurice will be here in a few weeks. That's something to look forward to."

What could she say? Such ignorant tranquility only made her madder.

The king and queen were mentioned just once more. Ernest came back from town pleased to report that Mr. and Mrs. Salisbury had gone to Swift Current and all they had managed to see, for all their trouble, was the top of the queen's hat. The royal train had been running late; once it arrived the king and queen were whisked by automobile up main street and back in two minutes flat, followed by a second automobile containing Mackenzie King. And then they were gone. Twelve hours of waiting to see a hat.

"What did it look like?" asked Norma Joyce.

"What?"

"*What did the hat look like?*"

He hadn't even asked.

In late May a last brief letter arrived, this one with a photograph enclosed. Maurice couldn't come, but apparently he didn't want to be forgotten. This letter Norma Joyce also opened and kept.

In the photograph he didn't resemble himself. She studied it, trying to see under the face that was there to the face she remembered, but it was like trying to recapture the taste of something tart after the mistake of something too sweet. In memory, his face was either teasing or lost in thought, but always expressive, moving from amusement to thoughtfulness to melancholy to amusement. That was what she loved, the opening-up that remained in touch with, almost framed by, the old feeling.

But in the photograph he was on view and therefore – this must be why – he looked static and bland, his hair slicked back, his face wider. Where was the casual reserve, the slow twinkle and tease, the occasional sadness? Had he put on weight? Was he a thin traveller who ran to fat at home?

Who was the photographer? She examined the setting more closely. It must be Ottawa: there were trees, there was a brick house in the background, there was snow. On the back of the snapshot someone had written *January 1, 1939*. It wasn't his handwriting. He wrote in a sloping, precise, small hand. This writing seemed to have wingtips.

The letter contained a spelling mistake that made her smile. "The questions have know answers." He was saying he wasn't at all sure about his future. Will I enlist right away or finish graduate school first? What will become of all my plans? How long will the war last? He said he didn't think the war would be a short one, once it started. He said they must have been very excited about the visit by the king and queen.

She couldn't resist. She dropped hints. She wouldn't be surprised, she said. She wouldn't be surprised if Maurice had full-time work now. And if there was a war, she wouldn't be surprised if he enlisted right away. She wouldn't be surprised, she said, if the war lasted a long time.

Lucinda looked at her oddly. "Did he say he wanted full-time work? I thought he needed time to finish his degree."

"I was just thinking. He wouldn't be able to come for your birthday if he got full-time work."

"My sister, who finds a problem for every solution."

Perhaps that was the truth of the photograph. He was thinking of Lucinda when the shot was taken, and this was the result.

He should have been thinking about her.

Maybe that's all anyone wants in the end, to be remembered rather than overlooked. The thought occurs to her during the long winter of 1972, when she looks after Ernest and does little else except remember. One snowy afternoon, cooking her old dad a lunch of ground sirloin because the neighbour next door says she should be "feeding his blood," she decides that what she liked best about Maurice was his grave and flattering attentiveness. She liked him best medium-rare, the juices of sadness and gaiety mingling so that gaiety never got the upper hand.

June was hot. June 13 especially so. A day heavy with soft extravagant heat, as if a rogue furnace had been pumping all night long. A Sunday. Lucinda made the sponge cake in the morning; it was cooling by eleven. She served an early dinner; they were finished by twelve-thirty. Ernest left again for the fields and Norma Joyce went off with Darwin.

Lucinda poured several buckets of water into the bathtub in the corner of the kitchen. She bathed and dressed, and by two o'clock she was sitting on the porch. She was wearing a white cotton piqué dress with sleeves that came to her elbows, and a necklace of turquoise beads. She looked lovely, the tone of her skin even more beautiful against the white, and the dress one of her mother's, recut and resewn with great skill. She looked down the laneway to the road. There was nothing in her hands. Nothing to knit or read or mend.

Norma Joyce and Darwin were in the Wilson coulee, following the creek bed to the spring. Norma Joyce wrote her name in the dirt. She wrote her name, Darwin's name, Maurice's name, the date. They stayed down there for most of the afternoon.

It was five o'clock when they came back. Lucinda was still on the porch and her hands were idle. She rocked back and forth, nineteen years old and with that air of serenity, but she wasn't Lucinda because she wasn't doing anything with her hands.

Norma Joyce came up the steps with Darwin. Lucinda put out her hand and stroked his head. She said, "I guess he wasn't able to get away, after all."

Then she stood up and went inside and upstairs. She changed out of her dress. She came down in the long brown skirt she wore during the day.

"But it's evening," thought Norma Joyce.

A clean apron out of the apron drawer. A light supper of scrambled eggs and toast.

"It's all right, Norma Joyce," she said. "I can set the table."

She seemed perfectly composed.

But when Norma Joyce washed the dishes in the wrong order, glasses after plates instead of before, Lucinda made her wash every dish in the house.

"Who knows how many times she's done it before?" To Ernest, who couldn't think of anything to say.

Norma Joyce did the dishes in water kept scalding by Lucinda's active kettle. Her fingers rang with pain.

The next day, when she got home from school, Lucinda wasn't in the kitchen and neither was the sewing machine. But the sound of sewing came from somewhere.

Norma Joyce went to the door of her weather room and stopped still. The room had been turned inside out. The books were on the bookshelf, her mother's photograph was on the desk. But everything else, pebbles, buttons, grasses, broken curios, mounds of dust, everything else was gone. In the corner, at the sewing machine, sat her sister.

The look on Lucinda's face was hard to describe but impossible to forget. A sort of fixed stubbornness, but fixed in the wrong place, like lipstick on a tooth. Norma Joyce could only imagine the short-lived fury that had attacked her room, flushing out and scrubbing down, wilfully laying waste to the small, tender, useless things collected by a small and useless girl.

All she could think to say was, "Shall I make supper?"

"Yes. You do that." Lucinda stopped sewing and went upstairs.

Scrambled eggs two nights in a row and no dessert. Norma Joyce looked everywhere for the sponge cake. She looked again the next day, and that was the third shock after her sister's idle hands and her own lost room. She found the cake on the junk heap beside the barn.

Ernest finished his eggs. He said, "You had better check on your sister."

She went upstairs. Lucinda was lying on top of the bed looking at nothing in particular.

"Are you all right? Dad wants to know."

"I'm all right. I'm cold."

Norma Joyce took the blanket off Maurice's bed and laid it over Lucinda.

———◆———

Lucinda would remember the ledge of disappointment. The way disappointment narrowed her world to an isolated ledge on which she sat. It wasn't a matter of thinking Maurice was bound to come. She had known he might well not come, especially during the weeks before and on the day itself. But knowledge is one thing, hope another. His not coming was altogether different from the possibility of his not coming. The way it registered slowly, increasingly, all afternoon. The way it bled into her. The way it diminished her until she was only diminishment, only disappointment. Finally, she'd gone inside.

Upstairs, the emotion lifted when she changed back into her brown skirt, only to descend as she descended the stairs. The emotion lifted again while she made supper, then descended more thoroughly than ever. Those repeated floodings of disappointment left her perched on her ledge.

A very small affair. Why was it so large? Where had it come from, this flood of broken feeling?

She had thought about him all winter, that was the trouble. A quiet woman in a quiet house turning memory into a piece of embroidery until, just as in the old stories, she pricked her finger and fell into a deep and sudden sleep. She slept half of June and all of July away.

During that lost summer, Norma Joyce brought her tea and buttered toast. She drew outlines of animals in an exercise book and Lucinda coloured them in. She gently pushed a handkerchief into her sister's hand when tears ran into her hair and glided into her ears and soaked into the pillow. She turned the pillow over. She put a towel down when both sides were wet.

Once, in a puzzled, almost-mutinous voice, she said, "I didn't know you cared about him so much."

Lucinda said, "To tell you the truth, neither did I."

Norma Joyce watched her sister lie in bed from morning till evening. She thought of the *Titanic* resting on the bottom of the ocean. Evenings of summer light, and Lucinda very still at the bottom of it.

"You're so good," Lucinda said, accepting the cups of tea Norma Joyce offered. Even her father said one morning, "Thank you for looking after your sister."

"Don't thank me," said Norma Joyce, and she meant it.

What a marvellous release to have Lucinda out of the picture. How efficient and quick Norma Joyce became. She cooked, she cleaned, she even grew. A fairy tale truth, after all, that the youngest, most hapless child only comes into his own after the older brothers are out of the way.

August arrived, and with it a drop in temperature. Lucinda sat up and looked out the bedroom window at the eight-sided water tower in the distance and at the prairie in between. She saw the window frame in need of a coat of paint it wasn't going to get, and she saw herself sitting in bed with unbraided hair at ten o'clock in the morning. Winter was coming. There was work to be done.

Downstairs, Darwin and Norma Joyce were side by side on the kitchen floor. Darwin snoozed away, Norma Joyce turned a page. She looked up at the sound of footsteps, and saw her pale, tall, still-beautiful sister come through the doorway and say she felt like some gingerbread.

Two hours later, Ernest came inside to the smell of cake and the sight of his beloved daughter back on her feet. She cut big wedges and served them with butter.

Lucinda was different after that. Everyone said so. *She* said so. She joked that she had lost her love and found her sweet tooth. Her specialty became lemon meringue pie (no more sponge cakes) and her secret was spreading the meringue to touch the crust on all sides so that the meringue neither shrank nor wept.

Seven years later, when Maurice passed her in the street, he did not recognize her.

"We left the wide silence of prairie skyway, our senses stunned by the close-up to come: apple-blossomed orchards, upstanding elms by the snake fences, unknown wild flowers in the cool woods. This was Ontario – self-contained, enclosed . . ."

DOROTHY LIVESAY, *Right Hand Left Hand*

She remembers stepping outside into colour so brilliant that she had to look away to get her bearings. Nineteen forty-two, and she was taller at thirteen than she had been at eight, but not that much taller. Still small, still dark, still looking.

She tried to take in things one at a time: The shiny windows up and down the street. The flowers everywhere in shades of yellow and pink. A fat grey cat lying in the sun at the foot of a skin-red vine. Vines leafing up the sides of houses and over the tops of telephone poles and out across the wires to join the vivid trees in the deep blue sky.

So this was Ontario. These big brick houses. These rows of fine, stable, red-brick houses shaded by trees tossing their golden leaves on ground already blessed with flowers and hedges and lawns, the flowers like small trumpets or curly wigs, the hedges as tough as old lace, the lawns as warm in the sun as an old dog.

At hand was the lacquered coolness of coloured leaves, the old roughness of stone walls, the enamel smoothness of nearly new cars – and the canal, brimming like an endless horizontal well resting sumptuously on its side.

Left behind, one sad old dog. He had known from the moment they began to pack. Lying on his mat beside the kitchen door, he had watched her move from room to room, never lifting his head off the floor – a feat that only a dog could manage; his eyes revolved in his head like tragic marbles.

Ernest said, "It's better this way. He'll be on familiar ground."

Mrs. Gallot said, "Don't worry. We'll take good care of him."

Lucinda said, "Poor old Darwin."

Norma Joyce didn't say anything. She stroked Darwin's big square head and he turned away – an eloquent inch – under her hand. She could pat his head, but he would not look at her.

The day they left was sunny and cool. The sky was western-blue (lighter than eastern-blue) and the crop was good, though now because of the war there weren't enough men to bring it in; university students from Ontario would arrive by train to help with the harvest, only to have their charity cut short by an early snow. The three of them – Norma Joyce and her father and sister – crowded into the Gallots' old Ford, and Mr. and Mrs. Gallot and Ginny drove them to the station in Willow Bend. All their luggage had been sent on ahead. Partway down the lane Norma Joyce looked back.

The house was three storeys tall, if you counted the attic. On the right were the several outbuildings and the barn. Beyond that the swell of their rain-drawing hill, and beyond that the water tower which rose in the distance. Darwin was on the side porch, slowly turning around three times before collapsing in a weary heap – a carrot at the end of winter, she thought – tired beyond words. He tucked his nose into his tail and gave them his back.

Goodbye Darwin, she said nine times in her head.

An old memory floated to the surface then, and the pain of it surprised her. Maurice, happily alone in the sitting room, reading his book. His facility for leaving them before he had left. A cautionary memory. But it was gone the moment she turned around and gave herself over to excitement.

All this commotion because Uncle Dennis had died, leaving everything to Ernest, including his house on Fulton Avenue. Now the Gallots would have the farm and most of its furnishings too. Mrs. Gallot was especially pleased to have the piano, even though it hadn't been tuned in how many years?

"Not since 1938," answered Norma Joyce. "Not since Maurice Dove was here."

For Norma Joyce the next four years would pass as quickly as the previous three, a period of time like the space between two beads on a necklace. The beads were her encounters with Maurice.

She entered Hopewell Public School; it was a five minute walk from her house. Grade eight, and she had no trouble keeping up. The mean black horror had taught her a thing or two. After school she took the long way home, following Bank Street to the canal, then the pathway beside the canal. She liked to go from bench to bench reading three pages of her book at each bench: there were three benches. After the third one she crossed Colonel By and followed Seneca Street to Aylmer Avenue, walking under and beside leaves of every colour. The reds and purples were dark in tone, yet silvered, somehow; the yellows and oranges simply glowed. From high above the trees came the constant glint and drone of aircraft flown by pilots in training.

Her route home included Maurice's house on Carlyle Avenue. Number 78. No sign of Maurice, but his mother the atmosphere girl was cutting a few late roses.

"Mrs. Dove?"

The small, trim, white-haired woman looked up. Her gardening gloves matched her light-blue dress.

"I know Maurice," announced Norma Joyce. "I mean I knew him. In Saskatchewan."

"Oh, he's not in Saskatchewan now."

"I know that."

"He's in England, or he was, the last we heard. He's in the air force. You know what boys are like about letters."

She seemed fussed and out of sorts, so Norma Joyce said, "You must be proud of him." But that didn't help.

"I don't know why he had to go," she muttered. "It's England's war."

Norma Joyce stared at Mrs. Dove until she remembered that she came from Quebec. She came from Quebec and she had lived in the States. That was why. A good thing her father hadn't heard.

She bent over to adjust her socks. Mrs. Dove went back to her flowers.

"Mrs. Dove? What's the name of that vine?" Pointing to the one climbing the telephone pole. "Do you happen to know?"

"Bless you, child. I don't."

"What about that bush?"

"Which? That one? I couldn't say."

No one could. No one knew anything. She had never wanted so badly to know the names of things – she asked neighbours, she asked her teacher – but no one knew. Their ignorance was like an iron band around her heart.

"Maurice will know," she said. "Will you please say hello to him from me when you write to him?"

"Hello from who?"

"Norma Joyce Hardy. Dennis Hardy's niece."

"Oh," nodding her head. "You're the new family on Fulton."

"Number ninety-nine," said Norma Joyce.

She continued home, turning right on Woodbine and going down the sloping alley to Fulton. Berries in her pocket. Small elongated red berries, blue-black berries the size of peas (they produced tiny drops of transparent purple if you squeezed them lightly, and brown-green guts if you squeezed hard), and tiny wild grapes from the vines on the telephone poles. Inside each grape were two pellets, larger than the grape itself, it seemed, like pellet-buttocks bouncing free of a grape-skin girdle. The bit of surrounding flesh was peppery in flavour.

She remembers her first Saturday in Ontario because she found a paradise inside paradise. Early October, and having snuck outside when Lucinda's back was turned, she had the day to herself. A piece of bread in her pocket, a new direction in mind. She went to the end of her street and this time she turned left on Colonel By Drive.

The Rideau Canal was on her right, narrow, curving, up to the brim. Ahead was the Bronson Avenue swing bridge. She passed the bridge and continued around Dow's Lake, wide and glittering, to the railway bridge that also spanned the canal. She crossed the bridge and came to Eden.

A name on every tree. An illustrated page from *Larousse*. A cultivated slope arranged for truth and beauty's sake.

Close to the water were the willows, farther back the oaks and the southern cottonwood, farther back still the red, black, and sugar maples, then going up the slope, ash and linden, and at the top of these four soft levels formed by canal, lawn, wooded slope, and parkland were the eastern white pine with their long needles in clusters of five, the Canadian hemlock, and the white spruce. Then a small grove of cypresses with leaves so finely patterned that cedar leaves looked like a child's blocky printing in comparison.

She had been somewhere huge and adrift, and now she was somewhere clear and shapely. Desperate Saskatchewan, and now old Ontario.

She continued walking west under the trees until she came to a road and a sign – and then she knew where she was. On the other side were greenhouses and shaded pathways, a few fine, big houses, some wooden barns and office buildings, ornamental gardens and cultivated fields. It was the Dominion Experimental Farm. This was where Maurice had worked.

She crossed the road. The first building was a ruddy-golden shade of red brick. Rideau red, she would learn later from a builder who was a friend of her father's. She went up the steps and tried the door. It opened. Two more steps and she was walking down a pale green hallway towards the door that stood ajar at the end. A white-haired man in shirtsleeves looked up. "Where did *you* come from?" he asked. His long desk was strewn with papers; he had a pencil behind his ear, and glasses and a moustache. "Saskatchewan," she answered, and his lips twitched.

"And what can I do for a girl from Saskatchewan?"

"I was wondering," she said, "I was wondering if you knew Maurice Dove."

"Maurice who?"

"Maurice Dove." What a pleasure it was to say his name.

He shook his head. "Doesn't ring a bell."

"He worked here before the war."

"Maurice Dove." He raised his eyebrows and shook his head once again.

"That's all right," she said. "Thank you."

"Well," he said. "Carry on."

From her bedroom window she studied the back of Maurice's house. Nothing blocked her view – her uncle's garden sloped up to the grassy lane that formed the lower border of the Doves' garden, which sloped up to the three-storey house his parents occupied. She was grateful to them for the absence of a fence, and for their casualness with curtains. Many nights Mr. and Mrs. Dove moved past the kitchen window or sat in full view at the dining room table. They didn't eat outside under the elm tree as Maurice said they did, and she wondered why he had said it. Then she wondered if he had said anything else that wasn't true.

She looked up *grapeshot* in the dictionary. She looked up words she read like *sentient, expletive, incarnate*, and soon she had an exercise book crammed with definitions that she went over repeatedly, as though she had to know everything *now*. In the end, she was simply in too serious a hurry. Her forthrightness so forthright that Maurice, weary, pale, readjusting to life after the war, would take it as a joke.

Supple kid-glove smoothness of birch, as cool and moist as the powdered doughnuts she would breakfast on when she ran away to New York.

Even the light looked wet. Even the bushy twitchy growth in the way of the canal, through which she saw the canal's shining curves and, above that, the laden charcoal of the shining sky: all of it looked wet.

Frequently, she played Hot and Cold. Walking through the arboretum to the Experimental Farm she was getting warm; on the sidewalk in front of his parents' house she was hot; in her own house she was oddly cold, except in her room, where she felt peaceful. Her sister and father irritated her to the core, an endless chafing that left her raw from stem to gudgeon, she said to herself, then looked up *gudgeon* in the dictionary. There was no *traffic*, no coming and going, no *life* in the house, only her sister maintaining a steady routine of cleaning, knitting, sewing and cooking, and her father listening to the radio, reading the paper, planning out orchards, eating his meals on the dot. For the first time they didn't have to worry about money. Thanks to your uncle, Ernest would say regularly, gratefully. An unmortgaged house, a healthy bank account, some solid investments. That was what they had inherited. Ernest planned to buy farmland and turn it into the orchards he and Dennis had talked about. His plans kept him busy; the house kept Lucinda busy. Only Norma Joyce was restless.

Sometimes she would make things happen. In late November, when Lucinda was occupied in another part of the house, she commenced on a cake and not just any cake, raiding the cupboards for every sultana and currant and working fast so as to be fully committed before Lucinda appeared. What a treat to watch Lucinda stand in the doorway, wounded by the waste. To watch her survey the scene with desperation to see what could be salvaged. Then slowly approach the table.

"Norma? What are you doing?"

"We didn't have one last year."

"Would you like some help?"

"You know me," said Norma Joyce. "I don't like to help, and I don't like to *be* helped."

"What recipe are you using?"

Fanny Farmer was open to a page immaculate until this very moment. With her floured buttery finger she jabbed.

"I'm down to here."

Lucinda picked up the book, went to the sink, carefully wiped the page with a damp cloth. Then she put an apron around Norma Joyce's waist. She jerked it tight.

"Why didn't you ask? Why didn't you tell me you wanted to make Christmas cake?"

"You said I never baked."

"Suppose you tell me next time. We'll start with something less ambitious."

"You can always lock up the kitchen cupboards."

"Don't fight with me," Lucinda said.

"I'm just stating a fact."

"The fact is you're fighting with me."

"You don't like my tone of voice?"

Lucinda looked at her wasteful, homely, self-indulgent, goading sister. She said, "I don't like your tone, or your lip, or your manner. But I like *you*. What's happening to you, Norma? What's come over you? I thought you'd changed."

A few hours later Lucinda would say, "We're sisters and that means a lot, but it's not just that. I'm grateful to you and I trust you."

And outside, the sharpness of pine needles and spruce. The strange dustiness, the smokiness of certain dark fall colours.

An apple that's a Spy. She had always liked that idea even before learning that the Latin for apple was *malum*. At the arboretum all the crabapples were variations of malum. From malum comes malice and here was the word at work. She walked under the crabapples feeling livid. She walked under the cypresses feeling blessed. She understood Jacob's need to feel a parental hand smooth his brow; she would have liked such a thing. Instead she stood under never-blossoming, ever-beautiful cypresses all the way from Japan and thought, *Lucinda trusts me*. I bet she really means: Be trustworthy because you're my sister.

And having figured this out, having turned the straightforward compliment into a crooked command, she felt better about her own untrustworthiness.

The smell of lavender issued from the drawers of her sister's dresser. In the top drawer, underneath the perfectly folded slips, lay Maurice's first letter. On the shelf of Lucinda's closet, wrapped in tissue paper, were the embroidered pink slippers her mother had meant for *her*. They were too small for Lucinda but they weren't too small for her, she knew from having slipped them on when her sister was away from the house. In the narrow uppermost drawer of her father's chest of drawers (the same chest of drawers she and Lucinda had shared on the farm) was an envelope that contained money in bills.

She took one of her fruitcakes to Mrs. Dove. It would have been December. She remembers that Mrs. Dove answered the door with a duster in her hand. "I brought you something for the

Christmas season," she said, and that was enough to get her inside, into the wide hallway with the door on the left that led to the living room and the stairs on the right that led to the second floor. The hallway was papered with a geometric pattern of black and silver lines on an ivory background. "Your house is beautiful," she said. "I wonder if the rooms are like ours. I think maybe your living room is larger."

"Would you like to see it?" asked Mrs. Dove.

Oh yes.

The living room *was* larger. The wallpaper beige and salmon coloured, the furniture shiny and full of edges, the fireplace made of stone, and the mantelpiece of carved wood.

"I'll just put your lovely fruitcake in the pantry," Mrs. Dove said, and Norma Joyce followed her into the small white kitchen whose window overlooked the garden that led down to her own house. "We have three bedrooms," said Norma Joyce. "Is that what you have?"

Obligingly, Mrs. Dove took her up the narrow back stairs to see the four bedrooms, only one of which Norma Joyce cared about. To her delight, it faced west. That is, it overlooked her house. As with the other bedrooms, Mrs. Dove hung back in the hallway so that Norma Joyce would look in without entering. She saw Maurice's bed under a quilt, his desk and two tall sets of bookshelves before Mrs. Dove whisked her back downstairs.

Now she could picture him moving from room to room. She could even see him getting into bed. She imagined herself right there beside him.

Only once – as far as she can remember – did her hard-working sister step out of character. One day, after washing the dishes, Lucinda walked up to a beauty parlour at Bank and Grove and had a facial that involved steam, clay, and more and more oil until, from behind her closed eyelids, she heard the beautician call out: *Will you take a look at this!*

Lucinda loved to tell this story. I opened my eyes, she would say, to a small knot of gaping women.

"Where are you from?" the beautician asked, turning the bottle upside-down and shaking it with mild outrage and wonder.

"Saskatchewan."

"*Saskatchewan*," the beautician breathed out. *Saskatchewan*, everyone repeated. "No wonder your skin is so dry!"

It was while she was there, in the beauty parlour with the row of dryers like smooth silver beehives, the facing row of mirrors, the magazines on low tables, the buzz of relaxed talk, the smell of lipstick and shampoo cut with the sharp smell of chemicals, that Lucinda got her idea for making money. She practised first on herself, then on Norma Joyce, then on the neighbour Mrs. Hulder (or, as she was known because of her two sets of red-headed twins, Mother Hulder). By the third head of hair Lucinda was adept. Sharp scissors, sharp eyes, the same sort of unthinking confidence you need to make good pastry, and she was in business.

She worked from the house, taking customers on Monday, Wednesday, and Friday afternoons from one to four, washing and setting their hair in the kitchen. She bought two hair dryers from a beauty parlour that was going out of business and kept them in the back porch when they weren't in use. Ernest didn't object. He learned to stay out of the way, and Lucinda could do no wrong.

Her name got around. If you wanted a good cut at a good price, with tea and cookies thrown in, she was the one to go to. There was never a customer who wasn't satisfied either with the result or with the price she charged of one dollar for a cut and five dollars for a perm. Lucinda saved every cent and later bought herself a black Ford convertible with red seats. Nothing relaxed her more than going for drives in that convertible.

During the war Ernest began to buy farmland on the old Carp Road and plant fruit trees; he would come to think of himself as something of an expert pomologist, writing pamphlets during the winter months about growing fruit in a harsh climate. Norma Joyce went to school, explored the arboretum in every weather, and took in as many movies at the Mayfair as she could. After Hopewell School she moved on to Glebe Collegiate, across the canal, where she made a friend who had the memorable name of Hendrickje Jurrina de Vos (Hennie for short). Hennie said proudly that she shared her first name with Rembrandt's wife Hendrickje Stoffels, a fact that delighted Norma Joyce, and led her to suggest that they pay a visit to the National Gallery. In those days, it was housed in the east wing of the Victoria Memorial Museum on McLeod Street. Hennie, whose home had many books, to say nothing of thick oriental carpets spread across tables in the living room just as they were in the great Dutch paintings, was delicately unimpressed. You have to go to Europe, she said, to see good art. "Let's go," said Norma Joyce, and on the way home from school they would plan in detail a year in Europe as soon as the allies won.

At Hennie's house on Woodlawn Avenue, Norma Joyce was introduced to chocolate *hagelslag* on buttered bread, a rare treat given the double fact of shortages and rationing. Hennie's father, who worked at the Dutch embassy, was discreet about his source of supply. Hennie confessed that she had the chocolate sprinkles for breakfast.

No porridge?

No porridge.

Does Princess Juliana have them for breakfast too?

That made Hennie laugh. The two of them followed closely the doings of the crown princess who was living out the war in Ottawa. They knew that she pushed her baby pram through Strathcona Park, graciously nodding to everyone and always the first to say hello. One day they actually saw her mother, Queen Wilhelmina, come into Freiman's department store on Rideau Street. She bowed to every person in the store, a hopelessly un-fashionable woman in her big white skirt and white top. Norma Joyce thought she looked like a square envelope – not that she said so to Hennie, who was immensely proud of her unglamorous queen. Juliana's little girls were notoriously chubby and happy. No doubt chocolate sprinkles were the reason.

Hennie came home with Norma Joyce too, though less often. They would do their homework together at the dining room table, then retire to Norma Joyce's bedroom upstairs to draw. One day, lying side by side on the three-quarters bed, they switched from drawing fashionable women to desirable men. Hennie drew the head, Norma Joyce the ears, Hennie the eyes, Norma Joyce the mouth. When it came to the nose, Hennie's attempt threw them into hysterics. They beat both pillows they were laughing so hard.

"I'll show you a nice face," said Norma Joyce. She went into her closet – it was large enough to turn around in – and tugged the pull-string attached to the light bulb on the wall. "Wait a minute," as the closet door swung to behind her. She lowered the suitcase at the back of the closet onto the floor, undid the straps, and opened it. She took out her cigar box, removed the snapshot, replaced the cigar box, turned off the light and came back out of the closet.

"Who is he?" asked Hennie.

Norma Joyce had stretched out beside her friend. "Do you like his face?" she asked.

"I prefer *my* nose," letting go of the picture and rolling over in laughter. Then she turned on her side and leaned on one elbow. "Who is he?" she asked again.

"My cousin."

"He doesn't look like you."

"He's in the air force."

"Let's copy his face," said Hennie, and they set to work copying. Each of them had an unlined notebook she used for drawing. "If he's your cousin," asked Hennie after a while, "why do you have his picture hidden away?"

Norma Joyce erased his mouth and drew it again.

"Because I stole it," she said.

That night, after supper, she took the photo from under her pillow, where she had put it face down when it was time for Hennie to go home and for her to set the table. It was dusk. She sat down on the edge of her bed, turned the photo over in her lap and went perfectly still. Maurice's face was a blank – as if somebody had forgotten to put the pattern on this particular plate.

She turned on the bedside lamp and held the photograph directly underneath the light. His features swam back into place. Her eyes must have played a trick, or else the waning light.

As usual, she was wishing that the photograph were a better likeness – that she could see him in person – that snapshots could be like movies – when his face seemed to break in half. One side of it – the right side – slid down. Now one eye was lower than the other. His whole face was askew.

Mrs. Dove answered the door, and there stood a girl with a wild face – a white face – even white lips – chattering out something about her son. Is he all right? Is Maurice all right?

Calm down, she told her, you're frightening me. *Arthur?* she called over her shoulder.

I'm sorry, said the girl. I'm really so sorry. And then Mrs. Dove realized it was the Hardy girl who lived just below them.

The girl grabbed her hand. Mrs. Dove didn't like having her hand grabbed, and pulled it away. By this time Maurice's father had joined her in the hallway.

Promise me something, said the girl, appealing to both of them. When you hear from him – as soon as you hear *anything* – tell me.

But when the telegram came, Norma Joyce heard thirdhand from Ernest, who had heard from Mrs. Hulder, that Maurice Dove was in a hospital in England. He had crashed his plane and his mother was beside herself.

"When did it happen?" asked Lucinda.

"The Monday before last," said Norma Joyce.

"You've talked to the Doves? Why didn't you tell us?"

Norma Joyce didn't answer. She said slowly, "I wonder what he looks like now."

From then on, Mrs. Dove passed along news about Maurice when the small dark daughter asked, even though the girl made her so uneasy. This was the family Maurice had spoken about. Strange that he should think the older sister such a beauty. Of course some women lose their looks early, especially on a farm, but Lucinda's hair was already going white. As for the younger sister, she was downright alarming. "How did you *know* he'd been hurt?" Mrs. Dove asked her. "I saw him at the foot of my bed," said Norma Joyce. It was the simplest answer, it came out naturally, but as she said it she realized that she hadn't seen her brother Norman for a long time, not since leaving Saskatchewan.

Maurice's recovery was long and slow, but apparently complete. Eight months after the accident he was flying again, though surely the war was almost over and if God had any mercy, his mother said, he would be home soon. By now it was the spring of 1945.

On May 7 the principal at Glebe Collegiate assembled the student body in the graceful auditorium with the stained-glass windows and announced that Germany had surrendered. The war was over, he exulted, and the rest of the day was theirs! Students surged out of school and downtown, Norma Joyce and Hennie among them, where thousands of people were spontaneously marching and yelling and singing on Sparks Street as a blizzard of paper swirled around their heads. Norma Joyce kicked about torn-up tax papers, letterheads, adding-machine paper, ticker tape, confetti. Then a blue-coated massed band came swinging down the street playing one march after another, and the sun shone after days of cold rain.

It was three o'clock before she got home. Lucinda was pulling in the clothes off the line – a Monday and not even the end of a world war could interfere with wash day – and Ernest was listening to the radio.

In the months to come, her sense of anticipation about Maurice's return was balanced by her sorrow at Hennie's departure. Like Princess Juliana, Hennie and her family moved back to Holland. In August the two girls exchanged parting gifts. Hers to Hennie was a copy of *Tess of the d'Urbervilles*. Hennie's gift to her was a book she still has. *The Natural Way to Draw* by Kimon Nicolaïdes. Any object can be drawn, Nicolaïdes wrote, "although those which have been formed by nature or affected by long use will offer the greatest amount of variation, as a flower, a stone, a piece of fruit, or an old shoe."

Lucinda was the one who saw him first. On a cool and cloudy afternoon at the end of the following May, she was walking down Sunnyside Avenue with a bag of groceries in her arms. Inside her bag there was a small sack of potatoes, a dozen onions, a shoulder roast, and a loaf of bread. Half a block from Seneca she saw him come around the corner. His hands were in his pockets, his eyes were on the ground. He was thinner and more real, more physical than she was prepared for. Lucinda slowed her pace and took in the clothes covering his long limbs, the traces of last night's sleep in his mussy hair, the pallor of his skin, the likely smell of cereal on his breath. She felt almost repelled, though she didn't know why.

He looked up and then she could see that one of his eyes was slightly higher than the other and that a scar angled across his right eyebrow. He looked her in the face even as he nodded and passed by without a glimmer of recognition.

In the kitchen she set the groceries on the table and said to Norma Joyce, who had just come home from school, "Maurice Dove is back."

But in answer to every question – When did he get home? Is he coming to see us? Is he all better? – she said she didn't know.

"*Didn't you talk to him?*"

"No." She was putting the loaf of bread into the bread box on the kitchen counter to the left of the sink. "I didn't."

"Why not? Why didn't you talk to him?"

"Because he walked right past me." Now she was taking the roast and potatoes to the sink.

"He didn't see you."

"He saw me." She turned around and looked at Norma Joyce. "He saw me," she said again. "He just didn't recognize me." Then she shrugged, "It's been a long time." On her face was that Prairie look of adapting to an unavoidable truth. So it goes; better luck next time.

The following day was the first of June, another in a long string of cool, grey disappointments if you were waiting for summer to arrive. At eleven in the morning Maurice Dove came down the front steps of his house. He turned left and walked to Aylmer Avenue, turned right and proceeded up to Bank Street where he turned left again – a tall, unhurried man being followed at a distance by a girl in white gloves. He crossed over the Bank Street bridge and continued on to the newspaper shop between Fourth and Fifth Avenues. He went inside.

Norma Joyce waited outside. She hadn't been able to eat anything since the afternoon before. Her stomach hurt and she felt lightheaded.

Maurice came out with a copy of the *Journal* and stood for a moment, uncertain which way to go, until he heard a thud just behind him and to his left.

He knelt on the sidewalk and patted the girl's hands. She was wearing the kind of thin, white cotton gloves girls wore to Sunday school, but it was Saturday. He pulled off the gloves to rub the circulation back into her hands, and saw his ring.

Maurice was accustomed to the various shocks of war but not to surprises from his past. He looked from his ring to the ashen face and felt both fascination and dismay. ("Ever since I've known you," he will tell her one day, "you've aroused more mixed feelings in me than anybody else I know.")

The war had changed him. He was more relaxed in some ways, more arbitrary in others, more determined. He had plans for himself that he had postponed for King George and didn't intend to postpone again; he had a sense of urgency underscored by his narrow brush with death; and a sense of being lucky that was only reinforced by the sight of his long-lost ring.

Norma Joyce opened her eyes and there he was coming out of the snow again: white spots floated in the air.

She whispered by way of introduction, "Norma Joyce."

"I know." The colour was coming back into her face. He put his hand under her head. "Feeling better?"

"You remember then."

"Saskatchewan," he said, "Willow Bend."

As she sat up, Maurice rocked back on his heels.

"I found your ring," she told him, just as she had planned to. "So I see."

He helped her up and, taking her arm, led her into the nearest café, where he asked if she would like some iced tea or some lemonade and she said yes, some lemonade. She peeled off the white adhesive tape from around the underside of the ring, and put the ring on the table in front of him. He picked it up, placed it in his open left palm, turned it over, then slipped it onto the ring finger of his left hand, where it made a loose fit. "My mother's right," he said. "I have lost weight."

"I like how you look," she said firmly, and he smiled.

He said, "You like me rearranged?"

She nodded. "You look more interesting."

"You sound like a painter," he said. He was amused and pleased, and so was she. "I used your watercolours until they were all gone," she said, "but I still have the box." Then she said she wanted to hear all about his life during the war. She wanted him to start at the beginning and tell her everything he had seen and done.

"There's something I want to ask you first," he said, and he held up the hand that wore the ring. "Where was it?"

She reached for her glass of lemonade. "Under the range," she said, taking a sip and not looking at him. "When we moved I found it."

"Sharp eyes," he said.

She gave him a quick look. "Sharp blue eyes," he said. "I remember that." He was smiling at her – an amused, worldly, tender smile that went right through her. She could feel it enter her ribs and come out the other side.

And he had walked right past Lucinda.

"What else do you remember?" she asked, looking at him so intently that he laughed.

"Why? Have I forgotten something I shouldn't have?"

"Do you remember my sister?"

"I remember your sister," he said. "I remember her well." But for the life of him he couldn't recall her name.

Before they parted company – he said he was making his way downtown – she extracted a promise that he would visit them the next afternoon.

Maurice came down the slope for tea. He was bare-headed and
dressed for the heat that still hadn't arrived – in light summer
pants, a soft-collared shirt open at the throat and rolled up at the
sleeves, and sandals. Ernest, watching from the kitchen window,
thought, Here comes the flyer, here comes the glamour boy. He
was worried for Lucinda. All she needed was to have her heart
broken again.

Norma Joyce, watching from the same window, darted to the
back door and opened it before he knocked. She brought him
inside, where Ernest gave him a cordial but reserved welcome,
shaking his hand, congratulating him on his safe return, allowing
his eyes to settle on those sandals. Lucinda had changed into a
freshly ironed white frock with navy blue pockets. She would
throw a white sweater over her shoulders when they went outside. Her father needn't have worried. She was fine. She looked
Maurice in the eye and spoke in a calm, pleasant voice, inviting
him to sit outside under the apple tree if it wasn't too cool for him.

Under the tree were two big Muskoka chairs painted dark
green, and a folding canvas lawn chair. Norma Joyce grabbed a
stool from the back porch and Maurice took it out of her hands.
He carried it to the tree and set it down beside the canvas chair.
Lucinda brought out the tray that held the teapot under its
quilted cozy, the flowered teacups, the creamer of milk, the
spoons, serviettes, and plate of sugar cookies. She set it down on
a small wooden table beside one of the Muskoka chairs. "Don't
you need a sweater?" she said to her sister, but Norma Joyce
hadn't even noticed that the sun had gone behind clouds and a
light wind was stirring.

Once they were seated – Norma Joyce on the stool, Maurice beside her in the canvas chair, Ernest and Lucinda facing them in the Muskoka chairs – Ernest said that he'd never seen anybody but a Catholic priest wear sandals. Maurice just smiled. He explained that a buddy of his had picked them up in North Africa. Another flyer? No, a soldier who was recuperating in the same hospital. Our beds were side by side for two months – unfortunately he didn't pull through. He left you his sandals? In a manner of speaking.

"They're surprisingly comfortable," he added.

"No one wears them over here," Lucinda said mildly, allying herself with her father. She had poured the tea and now she handed her father a cup, then Maurice, then her sister. Norma Joyce moved her stool closer to the canvas chair.

"Jesus wore sandals," she said.

Maurice laughed. "I'm in even better company than I thought." He looked down at her and the twinkle in his eye was amused and teasing, as of old, but different in some way that unsettled her. Lofty? Mocking? Certainly leavened with the sort of experience that no woman, his eyes implied, knew anything about.

"I want to know," she said, "how you crashed your plane."

"*Norma*," Lucinda remonstrated. "My sister hasn't changed."

But Maurice said he didn't mind. It happened when he lost his way in bad weather. He'd been ordered to go up on a practice flight without a radio – there was a shortage of radios, there was a shortage of everything – and when he flew over the North Sea the fog closed in. He made his way back but couldn't get his bearings, so he pushed the plane down and flew low until he saw railway tracks. He followed the tracks between hills until the land flattened out, then he caught sight of a runway but he overshot it, nosed down, and flipped over.

His telling was so straightforward, he wore his mistakes and his courage so easily, that Ernest surrendered without a struggle. They agreed that Neville Chamberlain was a better birdwatcher than a prime minister, they lamented an electorate so fickle that it would toss Churchill out of office, they agreed about the wasteful necessity of war and the pugnacious temperament required to wage it effectively. They agreed on everything – to Norma Joyce's surprise. She listened, but mostly she watched. She had moved her stool again, ostensibly to be beside the cookies, but really to get a better view of Maurice. Now she was positioned on Lucinda's right, diagonally across from him, and could study his changed face. His left cheekbone, she noticed now, was pushed in a little, and he looked older, hungrier, and harder; yet his talk was smoother. His eyes settled on Lucinda for a moment – taking her in from head to foot with one quick, cool glance. He saw Norma Joyce watching him, and winked.

She grinned back. "How long did they keep you in the hospital?" she asked.

"Six months. But then I had to leave because the nurse wanted to marry me."

Everyone laughed, and anyone but Norma Joyce would have let it go. But she kept her eyes trained on his face. "Why didn't you want to marry her?" He just raised his eyebrows and smiled the question away, so she asked something else. "Is it true flyers are big drinkers? We hear they drink gin all the time, even in the air."

This time he winked at Lucinda. "You're right," he said. "Your sister hasn't changed."

It was Ernest who asked about his plans for the future – but Maurice wasn't to be pinned down about that either. He intended to spend the summer lazing around, then who knows? He wanted to travel and to write, but he had to find a way to make money. He was going to take the summer for himself, and then he would get serious about his future.

"Don't you know what you want to do?" asked Norma Joyce.

"I know exactly what I want to do," he said.

Ernest approved. "Take some time," he advised. "Give yourself a change of scene."

And that's when Maurice mentioned Lake Clear. "We have a cabin," he said. "You should come along for a swim and a picnic." His relaxed glance included all three Hardys until he recalled where they were from. "Do you know how to swim?" he asked the two sisters.

"You promised to teach me," said Norma Joyce.

"I did?"

"He had other things to remember," said Lucinda.

Maurice smiled at her, this woman who had let herself go as soft and wide as an old sofa on a back porch.

"Where is Lake Clear?" asked Norma Joyce.

On the back of an envelope he pulled out of his pocket, Maurice drew a map showing the way to Lake Clear, with an X for the cabin.

"Lucinda knows how to drive," said Norma Joyce. "She's teaching me. I'm trying for my licence in three weeks."

"Come next weekend then. Come on Saturday," he urged.

"You should go," said Ernest, looking at Lucinda and forgetting his worries of an hour ago. "I'll pass, but you should go."

"It's too cold for swimming," she said. "What a late spring we've had." The wind had dropped but it was still cool. No bugs though, apart from a bee that hovered around Norma Joyce. "Bees love Norma Joyce," said Lucinda.

Her sister smiled mysteriously and blew on her tea.

"Okay," Maurice said. "Explain."

Norma Joyce smiled again. She said, "I was sitting under this tree in May. I was drying my hair in the sunshine, leaning forward so it fell over my face, and I heard this drone in the distance. It got louder and louder," she said. "Can you guess what it was?", watching his face and gratified by his interest. "A swarm of bees settled on my head."

"The smell of shampoo!" he exclaimed. "They mistook you for a honey source."

The source of honey grinned back at him, and for the first time he appreciated how full and round her breasts were under the pale yellow blouse with two, no, three buttons undone.

"Gerry Hulder got them off." She nodded to the house next door. "He used a long clothes brush and brushed them out of my hair."

"You must have kept very still." How round her breasts and how full her lips, blowing on her tea.

"They lay on the ground," she said, "and then they flew off."

"Gerry's the one with all the freckles?"

"Joe's got more. But it's hard to tell them apart."

His gaze followed hers to the house next door where sheets and pillowslips were hanging from three different lines. Mother H. was still taking in laundry, that hadn't changed.

Then he asked, "Are you happy here?" He had swung around to look at all three of them, struck by how different this setting was from the one they had known in Saskatchewan. "Has Ontario been everything you hoped for?"

Lucinda glanced at her father. It was the sort of personal question that made him uncomfortable, and sure enough he was looking determinedly down at his cup. "Yes," she said quickly. "We are."

"I'm not," protested Norma Joyce. "*I'm* not happy."

There was her sister's embarrassed laughter, which she ignored as she warmed to the serious issue at hand. "I want to live in a big city, or else in the woods. Ottawa is in between, don't you think Maurice? It's not a real city and it's not the country. It's *nowhere*," suddenly more passionate than she intended to be. Intemperate.

"I wouldn't say it's nowhere," he said gently.

"You liked it well enough before," said Lucinda. "I heard you tell Mother Hulder you loved it."

"And you, Lucinda?" He was trying to remember how old she was. The white in her hair was deceptive. She was still beautiful, you just had to look twice. "Do you like it?"

"It's very green," she answered with a smile, "it's very peace-ful. Yes, I like it," and she excused herself to go inside for the lemon meringue pie. It had probably set by now.

And then he only had eyes for the pie. Watch any man, he could be ninety years old and drooling spit, but at the sight of homemade pie every last one of his wits will spring to attention.

"How did you know lemon meringue was my favourite?"

"You told us!" said Norma Joyce.

"Did I?" He was amused by her and by himself. She was still little despite her breasts. Still homely despite her mouth. "You have a memory like an elephant," he said.

"An Indian elephant or an African elephant?"

"Which has the big ears?"

"You think my ears are big?"

Such wounded surprise that he and Lucinda burst out laughing. And then the tables turned. Maurice wanted to know if Lucinda still made her famous sponge cake, and the laughter died away.

"I got tired of it," she said. "You get tired of making the same thing."

"At least revive it for birthdays." He was balancing his plate on his knee. "Who has the next birthday?"

No one answered.

Ernest moved in his chair. "Excellent pie, Lucinda. I hope we're allowed seconds." He caught her eye and she gave him a grateful smile.

"Lucinda has the next birthday," said Norma Joyce. "On June 13th."

"Lucinda *June* Hardy," proud of himself for remembering. "I expect an invitation. I'll bring two presents to make up for the birthday I missed."

This was unexpected. She put down her fork. She said almost to herself her voice was so quiet, "I waited for you."

Under the apple tree. He lifted another forkful of lemon meringue pie. Delicious, he said, truly delicious, you haven't lost your touch, only half listening to her, so intent was he upon his pie.

How could a man be so cheerful, she wondered, so sunny, so unaffected and at the same time so hurtful?

"I waited and you didn't come," she said.

"But you got my letter?"

"Yes," she said. She looked at his puzzled face. "Your letter said you were still hoping to come."

Norma Joyce and her father were very quiet.

"There was a second letter," he said. "Don't you remember? I explained I couldn't make it after all."

And she thought, I didn't get a second letter because you didn't write it. Perhaps you meant to. But there wasn't any letter.

———◦———

Lucinda didn't root around like her sister, she didn't sally forth. She had to overcome reluctance – first that – before taking a second step. The following Saturday Maurice tried to coax her into icy Lake Clear but she wouldn't budge off the warm sand, and then he was too busy defending himself from a volley of waves to think any more about Lucinda.

Later, he and Norma Joyce lay panting on towels in the sun while Lucinda went to the car to get the picnic lunch. His eyes were closed, he was dozing off. She raised herself on one elbow to study every particle of pale, whiskered skin, bright scar, wet lips, glimpse of teeth. Emboldened by love, she grabbed a lock of his hair and yanked, then planted a kiss on his mouth-in-mid-yelp.

Down the beach he raced after her, into the water where they tormented each other until they were blue with cold. He found an old down sleeping bag in the cabin and spread it on the grass. She wriggled into it to warm up, and when she emerged, her body was covered in tiny feathers.

This is always central to old fairy tales, the prince's tendency to forget. But then maybe charm and forgetfulness always go together. Maybe forgetfulness *allows* you to be charming because people don't register enough to be a burden. And so the Prince Charmings forget their true loves until something reminds them, a shoe that fits, or a ring they recognize, or a wave of water in the face. Certainly in those heady days after his return, Norma Joyce did her best to be unforgettable.

The next weekend they went alone. For swimming lessons, she said. Lucinda was ill with the migraine that had arrived on Thursday, rescuing her from the complications of her twenty-sixth birthday; Ernest was off with his apple trees. Maurice borrowed his father's car and they left at noon. It took two hours to get to the lake.

In the car her hand went to his cheek, then to the milkier, softer flesh under his chin that had drawn her eye from the very beginning. She said, "I spy with my little eye something that is blue."

"Is it all blue?" he asked. "Is it edged with black? Is it held easily in the hand?" He still had that relaxed, attentive way of guessing something into existence. "Is it part of the car? Is it the blue sky in the side-view mirror?"

Summer had arrived. It was dark and cool in the cabin and hot and bright outside. There was the small beach, a ten-minute walk away at the end of a dirt road, and there was the granite outcropping close at hand. You could dive off the granite directly into deep blue-green water, or wade out into shallow water at the beach.

Near the cabin the grass, where there *was* grass, was soft, a miniature meadow with pine trees alongside. Closer to the water, large slabs of granite sloped about like banquet tables. Soon Maurice was busy examining patches of lichen on rock through a small magnifying glass at the end of his pocket knife. She knelt beside him. He said that when he wanted a sample he scraped the lichen off with his knife, or poured water over it to make it swell, after which it came off easily. He handed her the magnifying glass and she bent low. She watched the lichen bounce into shape, he watched her breasts push against her blouse. The lichen was ashy green, stiff to the touch. What's it called? she asked. Sunburst lichen, he replied. It looks scrawny, she said. No, laughing, it's flourishing. And this one, this tiny black one? When it grows larger, he told her, it looks like a burnt black rose.

Near the ground it was warmer than a foot above, by five or ten degrees.

This time they swam off the rock. He tied a rope around her waist and in she jumped, reassured by the gentle tugging she felt on the rope. Under his watchful, approving eye she learned within minutes, a natural, he said, a born swimmer. (Since then she has heard true stories of women who marry their swimming instructors. The painter Albert Franck, for instance, who worked at Oakwood Swimming Pool in Toronto, saw his future wife swim by below him; perhaps he fell in love with her beautiful back, this man who painted the backs of old Toronto houses.)

They drove home in the late afternoon. In the car Maurice rested his hand for a moment on her bare knee and she felt electrified. She remembered a girl at school, a bad girl, who said sex was more exciting than going up in a Ferris wheel.

An hour later her knee still tingled. It was enough to make her believe that knees were the very seat of passion.

Such a delicate thief, the sound of rain the next morning when the lilacs were over and the day lilies just beginning. She slipped outside in bare feet, picked a lily from the clump at the foot of his garden and looked up at the bedroom window she knew to be his. She continued up the slope to the back door, always unlocked but guarded by old Sammy, who knew her. She scratched Sammy's ears. Dawn was delayed by the rain. The air was grey-blue.

Not quite placeable stealth, and Mrs. Dove reassured herself it was only the rain and went back to sleep. Up the back stairs she came, and into his room with the west-facing window. She climbed in beside him and he didn't stir.

A sound sleeper, and warm. She inched closer until she touched his large, naked, heat-producing back.

He rolled over and opened his eyes, and she said, "I couldn't sleep."

He had a way of rubbing his face, and he did it now – with flattened fingers he scrubbed his face up and down the way you would if you were washing yourself vigorously first thing in the morning, or if you were trying to keep yourself awake late at night. Then he propped his pillow against the bedstead and, leaning back, he looked at her. In this light she seemed older. In appearance and approach not unlike the little English nurse he had barely escaped.

"Scoot," he said.

She left him the lily and one of her long black hairs. He picked the hair off the pillow and twirled it between his fingers. It could have been a piece of fishing line it was so wiry and coarse. No hook, yet how drawn he felt. When he closed his eyes he saw her lying on his pillow.

She told her father she wanted to sleep outside. There's that old tent in the basement, she said, I know where it is. An hour later she was wrinkling her nose in pleasure at the potent, eye-watering smell of old canvas.

The tent was comfortable for one, large enough for two. A folded blanket came to the aid of the canvas floor; a sheet run through the sewing machine served as a sleeping bag. Lucinda should have noticed how effortlessly she did this; the seams were as straight as arrows shot by Cupid.

Into the tent she climbed, zipping the screen door shut and falling in love with the long, dry, ripping sound that would remain, of all sounds, her favourite. The canvas smell (like crayons) and the papery tone of light, the feeling of suspension and privacy inside what was barely a room, and she had never been happier.

In the morning Maurice looked out and saw, sprung up below him like a mushroom, the white tent.

He took his cup of coffee to the foot of the garden and in the quiet of the morning heard a brush locking horns with thick hair. The sound drew him across the grassy alley and around to the front of the tent, where she was kneeling in the entranceway whacking away at her long, black, resistant hair.

He sank down crosslegged on the grass and offered her a sip of his coffee. "You look like a gypsy," he told her.

"A gypsy?" Giving him a long, steady look. "Not Italian-Japanese?"

"Who said you looked Italian-Japanese?"

"You did. You said Lucinda looked Scandinavian and I looked Italian-Japanese."

"I'm awful," he laughed. "Are you going to forgive me?"

She began to brush her hair again. A cardinal was singing on one of the upper branches of the oak tree next door.

Maurice reached over and circled her wrist with his hand. Wrists and knees. Her heart was beating fast.

"What's the verdict?" he asked.

"I'm thinking," she said, touching the side of his face.

That afternoon, napping on his bed, he dreamt about her. She was arranging flowers in a vase on his mother's dining room table. Except for an apron, she was naked. So was he, standing in the doorway with a most enormous erection. She looked up and smiled at him. Then she ran over and jumped into his arms. She straddled his waist.

Probably it happens fairly often, falling in love in a dream. You wake up with an appetite for someone you might not even like. But in the dream there was sex, and upon waking, the idea of sex, and from then on that person is on your mind in an entirely new way.

That night, when she heard her name called softly, she unzipped the tent door and in he came. "I dreamt about you," he said.

He sucked her nipples, he took them between his teeth, he lowered his penis into her mouth, and in the morning she discovered that though the grass was dry, the tent was dripping with dew. She stood in bare feet on the warm dry grass and swept her hand across the sopping wet surface of the tent. Only the tent and only herself. A wet fleece in a dry field.

That was the third night.

The first night he took her warm hand and put it on his eye-boggling erection. Don't you want to see what you do to me? and his eyes glittered. No, she thought. Not really. Later on he entered her, causing such pain that she wondered why it wasn't broadcast on the news.

The second night she shied away until he worked her with his fingers and tongue. Then all the tautness that had held her in its grip for twenty-four hours flooded out of her.

The third night he lowered his penis into her mouth and in the morning he stood in his window and watched her send dew flying across the grass.

At night there was the tent below glowing from the candle inside, a paper igloo, he thought, eastern and northern coming together in the Prairie girl with the olive skin. His mother said she looked foreign and his mother was right. She was probably reading about the Tartars right now, down there in her tent.

By day the tent was all shadiness, all canvas safety and cleverness, a room fitted out exactly with pockets and screen windows and screen door, private but exposed, and conducive to constant traffic between them.

For the next few weeks he thought she was beautiful. Even during the day he wondered how he had ever thought otherwise, forgetting that this had happened once before, this business of finding her thick lips suddenly full and her odd, oversized head handsome and her olive skin unforgettable. Her skin was the colour of pale burnished walnut, and except for new leaves in early spring, he had never felt anything so smooth.

One day, while he was listening to *Madame Butterfly* on the record player in his parents' living room, he saw Norma Joyce walk by outside with books in her arms. He went to the door and called her name. He waved her inside, and said he wanted her to hear something.

She put her library books on the hallway table, then followed him into the living room, where he stopped the record. "Where are your parents?" she asked him.

"In Montreal for the day."

He sat her down in the armchair beside the fireplace, then, turning back to the cabinet that had a record player on one side and a radio on the other, he said, "All you have to know is that the opera is set in Japan and that Butterfly commits suicide in the end."

"That's not all I have to know. What happened?"

"Okay," with a smile. And from across the room he explained that for three years Butterfly had been waiting for Pinkerton, who was an American officer and her lover, to return to Japan. While he was gone, she had given birth to his son. When he came back, Maurice said, he brought his American wife with him.

Watching Norma Joyce's responsive face, he thought how much he liked her, and that Pinkerton must have liked Butterfly no less. An uncomfortable thought. But Norma Joyce, aggressive, bold, tenacious, curiously experienced, was made of different stuff than Butterfly. If Norma Joyce was anything, thought Maurice, she was resilient.

"Turn it on," she said, gesturing to the record player.

They listened to the second side. Again he watched her, and again he thought how well she listened. Every note registered on her face, but she did not cry. After it finished she said, "*I* wouldn't have killed myself."

"That's good to know," he said with a smile. "I'm glad to hear that."

But he didn't ask her what she would have done.

———◉———

In mid-July the first thread came loose. On a hot, breezy afternoon, while Mother Hulder hung out sheets for the second time that day and her twins Gerry and Joe took turns mowing the lawn, Maurice came down the slope for iced tea. As usual, they sat on chairs under the apple tree. Maurice talked to Ernest; Lucinda busied herself pouring and serving; Norma Joyce watched Mother Hulder. She was thinking of the sheet she had soaked surreptitiously a few weeks before, and the one danger made her forget the other. Lucinda mentioned the stove. It kept blowing a fuse, they would have to call a repairman, and Norma Joyce said, without thinking, "Call Mr. Washburn. He repairs washing machines and stoves."

Lucinda smiled in surprise. "That's an odd thing for you to know."

"Maurice told us."

Maurice raised his hands in ignorance, and Norma Joyce said, "Remember? In your letter."

"There wasn't anything about a Mr. Washburn in Maurice's letter," said Lucinda. She was refilling their glasses, it was a beautiful summer afternoon, and Norma Joyce realized the enormity of her mistake.

"I don't know why I would have," Maurice said. "Mr. Washburn died before the war."

"Not *before* the war," Norma Joyce said, caring more about accuracy than her own well-being, and speaking to the ground. Mother Hulder had told her Mr. Washburn died in 1941.

"Well, it's a perfect name for the job," offered Lucinda. "Like a banker called Coyne or a doctor called Payne."

The allusion to the naming game, and Maurice nodded his head slowly. "I remember now. I *did* mention him."

"No," Lucinda insisted, "There was nothing about a Mr. Washburn in your letter."

"The next letter. You've forgotten."

"I haven't," she said firmly. "I haven't forgotten." This business of a second letter had been on her mind since he mentioned it, and she was glad to have the chance to underscore the truth. "That's not something you forget." She drew in her breath. "Norma Joyce never came home without the mail. It didn't matter what the weather was like, did it?"

She turned to her sister for corroboration, but Norma Joyce was staring hard at her half-empty glass and what did Lucinda finally see? She saw her sister taking letters out of her school bag, and putting them on the kitchen table, and concealing one or two without a word. The post office was at the back of the general store. Groceries were at the front, then dry goods, then the mail counter with the slot for letters and the tiny wicket above. Norma Joyce almost always waited until the mail was sorted between four and five o'clock before coming home.

"Well, the mails are hardly dependable."

It was Ernest, bitter about his unacknowledged letters of advice to the Department of Agriculture. He began to go into detail about his most recent one, thus affording Norma Joyce the chance to go inside and replenish the plate of cookies.

When she came back out, they were talking about new strains of apples.

"Norma?"

She looked up from where she was reading on her bed. Lucinda was standing in the doorway.

"Was there a letter, then?" Lucinda's face was in shadow. She didn't appear to be angry.

"There wasn't a letter."

"No? Please don't lie to me, Norma."

"There were two letters."

"Two letters." She came into the room and sat down on the edge of the bed. Norma Joyce made room for her. "What did they say, these two letters?"

"That he wasn't coming. The first one said he might not be able to come and the second one said he couldn't come."

"And you didn't tell me."

Norma Joyce said nothing. Her book was open in her lap. She turned it over and ran her fingernail down its soft grey spine.

"What were you thinking? I'd like to know."

Norma Joyce didn't look at her. She could imagine the puzzlement, pain, and quiet accusation in her face. The book was *Adam Bede*. She had been reading the part where Dinah Morris gets Hetty to confess.

She said, "I don't remember."

"Of course you remember."

"No, I don't." She looked at Lucinda. "I was only nine."

"Were you?" It was a genuine question. "You always seemed older."

Norma Joyce reached for the bookmark on the bedside table. She turned over her book, inserted the bookmark, and closed it.

"You loved him, didn't you?" Lucinda said. "I told him you did."

Up came the fierce blue eyes. "So did I!"

That was the difference between them, and they both knew it.

It was nearly six o'clock. The smell of potatoes drifted up the stairs. "It's time for supper," Lucinda said. "It's time to set the table." Her voice sounded very tired.

Then Norma Joyce said, "I don't know why. They were in my school bag. I took them out. I wanted to know what they said."

She heard the almost stupid innocence in her reply, but it was the best she could do.

"And you didn't want me to have them. Or did I even cross your mind?"

"I'm sorry."

"So what did he say? I'm curious."

"Not much besides what he was doing and –"

"When you told him you loved him. What did he say?"

"Oh. He said, maybe in nine years."

"It's been seven."

"No," said Norma Joyce. "Eight."

A few days later Lucinda came outside with a jug of lemonade and saw them in the shade of the apple tree, bent towards each other, talking. Not like two people falling in love, but like two people who have been in love for a long time, talking about what to do. Sitting on the grass, one in white, the other in grey, as perfectly known to each other as two animals grazing side by side. She stood with her jug of lemonade and they weren't aware of her, so intent were they upon each other.

The weight of the jug, the ache in her wrist.

———◆———

Mrs. Dove watched her son pay repeated visits to the unsuitable sisters. She made inquiries. Two or three phone calls to his former department head at the Experimental Farm, and she was able to tell him about an opening at the Brooklyn Botanic Gardens. Without a moment's hesitation, he fired off his application.

Unsuitable, because he could do so much better. She knew the tendency of young men – of any man – to settle for the nearest woman, and while Lucinda had been lovely, she had lost her looks, and the younger sister had no looks to lose. What sort of grandchildren would I have? Besides, she didn't want her only son marrying the hairdresser next door.

Norma Joyce saw the change in Maurice, the shift in direction, the alteration in mood, and like Darwin she knew immediately that she was being left behind. Now Maurice made it gently clear that he was busy, either with old colleagues at the Experimental Farm, or in the library, where he was reading and preparing himself for the job interview he would have in New York. What mattered to Maurice was the job. By this time it was early August.

He came back from New York to the feel of fall in the air. A difference in light as much as temperature. His mother had made him a blueberry pie. "My favourite," said the ingratiating son.

The next morning he put on his faded green windbreaker and went down the slope to get it over with. The tent was still up, but surely Norma Joyce was sleeping inside, now that the weather had turned. It was the middle of August.

They were finishing breakfast. Lucinda invited him to sit down for a cup of coffee. Ernest folded his paper. Norma Joyce, who was noticeably pale, watched him avoid her glance. He draped his jacket over the back of a kitchen chair, and then she saw the small black circle on the white shirt pocket over his heart.

"Yes," he said, "I thought I put the top on my pen, and I had, but the wrong end."

"I mentioned it," she said, "because I thought it might be happening now."

"Lemon juice," said Lucinda. "Lemon juice always works."

He sat down beside Ernest. From across the table Norma Joyce asked, "Did you have a good trip?"

"I even use lemon rinds to clean the piano keys," said Lucinda, pouring him a cup of coffee.

"Did you like New York?" she asked again.

Oh, yes. He liked it. He liked it so much he would be moving there in two days and starting his job at the rose garden in a week, "Thank you, Lucinda," smiling at her sister as she refilled his cup, and talking to her father about the Brooklyn Botanic Gardens for what, she realized with perfect clarity, he intended to be the first and last time. On the other side of the window a cool August wind stirred every leaf, on this side of the window

Maurice was already gone – caught up in his new job, his new life, his future. "More?" Lucinda asked her coffee-loving sister, but Norma Joyce shook her head and said she'd gone off coffee. It made her feel sick.

Perhaps if she had been more direct, or less so. Since she was both too direct, and not direct enough.

She followed him up the slope.

"Maurice. Wait."

But when she looked into his face for the old welcoming look, it wasn't there. Rather a measured-out civility that chilled her. "When will I see you again?" was what she managed to say.

He looked down at her intense, pressing face. "We'll see each other," he said. "I'll likely be back for Thanksgiving. We'll stay in touch."

"You don't want me," she said.

It was a raw and miserable statement. To his ears it sounded exaggerated, melodramatic, childish. He smiled.

"I wouldn't say that," and a look of sexual tenderness passed across his face, but she was staring at the ground and missed it. "But I think we need to get on with our lives. You need to get on with your life too."

And now she felt him turning away from her, and still she hadn't told him. "Maurice," she said again.

He waited, but the words wouldn't come. They were heavy stones in the pit of her stomach, and she didn't have the strength to haul them out.

"Wish me luck," he said with a smile. He brushed the hair out of her eyes. "You'll be fine," he told her, and his voice had softened.

"No, I won't."

"You will. I have great faith in you."

Sammy came down the slope, wagging his tail. She patted his head. Maurice's words had soothed her and brought her close to tears. She was biting her lip. Now he said quietly, "You're something special," and he seemed to mean what he was saying, even as he used it to close the conversation. He called Sammy. He and the dog climbed the rest of the slope together, and the back door closed behind them.

Maurice was gone two days later. She knew because the curtains in his bedroom were no longer drawn at night.

August came to an end. For three nights she stayed up late, sewing a dress. "For school," she explained when Lucinda asked her. She would be entering grade thirteen after Labour Day.

But on September 2, when Ernest and Lucinda were in the garden, she slipped out of the house and took the streetcar downtown. It was seven in the evening, and the sun was shining into the storefronts on the east side of Bank Street. Rich golden light. Beside her rode the brown club bag that had belonged to Uncle Dennis, and deep in her purse was the money she had taken from Lucinda's purse and from the narrow uppermost drawer in her father's chest of drawers. Notes left in both places. *I'll pay you back, that's a promise.* A total of $157.93. She took the night train to New York and arrived at Grand Central Station in the early morning.

Like Gretel she felt, putting her head into an oven hot with the aroma of people. Every bit of air seemed cooked. Every bit of space gobbled up by bustle and noise. She carried her bag into the vast marble and cream-coloured interior of Grand Central, and there she raised her eyes to the blue vaulted ceiling full of illuminated stars and was struck by the absence of wind in this sky-inspired hall. She smelled cinnamon, coffee, sweat, perfume, smoke, dusty sunlight, trapped heat, flowers. She heard heels on the marble floor and realized she was in a new world.

The heels approached rapidly. She wheeled around to see bearing down on her a woman in a black linen dress and black pumps who looked up at the last minute and smiled as she hurried by – a warm radiant smile – and Norma Joyce felt a wave of relief. A lucky sign, she thought. She was in a new world, where something as simple as a stranger's smile could transform everything.

With relief came hunger. She found a coffee bar and, standing up with her bag tucked between her feet, consumed a glass of milk and three powdered donuts, sprinkling herself with powdered sugar in the process. Next time she would get a danish. Then she made her way to the circular information kiosk in the centre of the station, where she learned that Morgan Hall on 45th Street between Second and Third Avenues catered to women. It was clean, cheap, respectable, and two blocks away. That's where she would go.

Outside, old heat lay about. She remembers the thick hazy atmosphere, the wide sidewalks, the yellow taxis, her sense of exhilarated dread at being swept along as she found her way. Morgan Hall, when she came to it, looked like a bank. Solid, twelve storeys tall. Her room was on the ninth floor, another lucky sign. A small room with a single bed, a sink, a wardrobe, a dresser. The tufted bedspread was off-white, the walls were hospital green.

She asked downstairs about a post office and the wrinkled blonde at the receiving desk said, "A post office? I'll tell you where there's a post office," and drew her a map on a piece of lined paper. "You'll see the city at the same time," she said. Then Norma Joyce asked her how to get to the Brooklyn Botanic Gardens and she said, "For that you need the subway," and drew her another map. The woman's hands were small, her fingernails painted with a pearly pink polish. Norma Joyce took both maps and said, "You have pretty hands," and the woman's face lit up with the most delighted smile. "You know you can rent an iron," she told Norma Joyce. "Ten cents an hour. Just leave it at the elevator when you're done. There's a little ironing board in your wardrobe."

So first Norma Joyce ironed her dress in her room, then she made the thirty-minute walk across town and down twelve blocks to the New York General Post Office with its two-block sweep of steps and its equally long inscription above many columns. She read it from start to finish, "Neither snow nor rain nor heat nor gloom of night stays these couriers from the swift completion of their appointed rounds," and her sad history followed her as she read the words. Neither snow nor rain nor heat nor gloom of night, but a sister – a sister could interfere with the round of mail.

In the main lobby, decorated with the coats of arms of all the nations you could write to, she found a piece of nearly blank paper in a waste basket, tore off the part that was written on, and wrote on the remainder, "All well. Don't worry. I'll be in touch soon. NJ." But she had no envelope, and so she rifled through the waste basket once again until she felt a touch on her shoulder. "Are you looking for something?" asked a raspy-voiced woman, white-haired and wearing a butterscotch-coloured dress.

"An envelope."

"You say en-velope. I say on-velope." The woman reached into her purse and dug around. "So let's call the whole thing off. Will this do?"

"Thank you."

Norma Joyce had come to a city with personality, a multi-storeyed world. It was the opposite of the prairie, yet there was something childlike about it – so many people in one building, like animal characters in storybook trees. In the books that teach children about opposites – wet and dry, hot and cold, sweet and sour, tall and short – she was on the *tall* page. The *huge* page.

Having rented a room in the morning, she went to the botanical gardens in the afternoon. She saw Maurice at three o'clock, beside the Cardinal de Richelieu roses.

Even before she had entered the subway, streams of sweat were trickling down her sides and gathering around her waist. Her dress was a soft-grey twill with red piping around the collar and cuffs; it had long sleeves and a fitted waist. By the time she was walking along Eastern Parkway looking for the garden gates, her armpits and collar were dark with sweat and her right sleeve was soggy from having been dragged so often across her face. Like Scarlett O'Hara, she had no handkerchief.

The gates to the garden were huge. Black wrought iron worked with vertical rows of leaves, cones, and vines, and with horizontal renditions of wheat, barley, and oats, every one a grass she recognized. On the other side of the gates were trees, open lawns, many shades of green, and a gardener pruning a shrub.

She stepped through and approached the gardener for directions, and then she set off on the pathway he indicated. It was shaded by crabapple trees, lindens, and European hornbeams, then lined farther on with Japanese lilac, cut-leaf beech, and crape myrtle. Reading the labels steadied her as she walked along. The path opened out into a wide area full of light even though the sky was heavy with rain clouds, and then it came to the Cranford Rose Garden. A sign at the entrance said the first roses had been set out in the fall of 1927, then more were added as Mrs. Cranford's memorial to Mr. Cranford.

She walked into the garden through a latticework arcade. On the right, a wedding party was having pictures taken beside a pond, the bride in white, the bridesmaids in lemon yellow. To her left, at the other end of the garden, was Maurice. She saw him in profile, bending over a rose bed.

Her feet took her the rest of the way, past the General Washington rose, the Hugh Dickson rose and the Arnold rose, past the Kathryn Morley, the Felicia, the Bloomfield Courage, the Mrs. Antony Waterer and the MacGregor Damask, right up to the Cardinal de Richelieu, a gallica introduced in 1840, a medium-tall rose with only a few blooms left. Maurice was bareheaded and bare-handed, examining the rose like a young doctor with a perfect bedside manner. She thought, One day he might name a rose after me.

She said, "Who was Cardinal de Richelieu?"

And he could scarcely believe his eyes when he looked up. She was so small, so dark, so oddly foreign-looking.

"Norma Joyce Hardy," he said, as though identifying her from a distance.

She *was* very small, about the size of Jane Eyre, and dressed in sober grey.

"Do you want to sit down?" he asked her.

He walked over to a stone bench under a tree, and sat down. He put his hands on the bench on either side of him. She followed him and sat down too. There was a foot of open space between them. Maurice reached for the handkerchief in his back pocket and wiped his face.

"Is it *always* so hot?" she asked, drawing her sleeve across her forehead. The wedding party was headed their way. She heard a shrill voice raised in objection and she heard Maurice say, "Do you have family here?"

She looked at him.

"Are you visiting somebody?" he asked.

He had the knack of self-possession, of not reacting to someone but staring, instead, just off to the side. It was very powerful, the effect on the person waiting for a certain response, of not getting it.

She said, "I think this baby's going to be a boy." In the awful heat – she had never been so hot – it was a desperate thing to say.

The colour left his face. It was like adding bleach to a wash. White came forward. She could count the beads of perspiration on his upper lip.

"Why am I not surprised?" he said to himself. "Shocked – but not surprised."

He dropped his head into his hands and groaned. She touched his arm. Brushed his white cotton sleeve with her fingertips.

He took his hands away from his face and folded them under his chin, then looked at her sideways. Their faces were level. "What are we going to do?" he asked, and the mix of emotion in his voice – the worry, resentment, and shock – made her feel giddy and numb.

"What are you thinking?" she asked.

"I'll tell you exactly what I'm thinking. I'm thinking, You bought the ticket, you take the ride." It was cruel but she had asked. Then he said, "I'm sorry. That was unfair."

The way he held her off, and then softened. The rhythm of it. To be drawn, and then forestalled.

He looked her in the face. "I have to know what you're going to do."

This was putting the shoe on the other foot.

"That depends on you," she said simply.

"Of course." He stood up and walked over to the nearest rose bed. Shoved his hands into his pockets and kept his back to her. Turned and retraced his steps.

She loved his troubled face. The only thing she couldn't stand, she believed, would be not seeing him again. He resorted to his old gesture of rubbing his face up and down. Then he ran a hand through his hair and pulled it – like Stan Laurel.

She said, "Another fine mess you've gotten me into."

A startled glance at her deadpan face, and he burst out laughing. "Dear Norrie," he said, dropping onto the seat and taking her hand. "We had a good time, didn't we."

They sat in silence for a while. It was much too hot to hold hands, so he put her hand on his knee and distractedly stroked it. The wedding party drifted their way and for the first time they caught his eye. The groom was young and pathetic in his ill-fitting suit. Just a boy. The bride was bossy. Her mother was bossier. He watched them, and Norma Joyce felt his mood change.

He said, "Why did you tell me not to worry? I thought you were safe. You said you were safe."

"I thought I was. I wasn't sure. I hoped I was."

"*Hoped?*" He swung on her bitterly. "What good is *hoped?*" She was in possession of her hand again, and of something more – a new understanding. He said, "You shouldn't have tricked me," and his voice was cold. She understood that you can pass from summer to winter in someone's mind without even leaving the room.

She made things worse. She said, "I asked if you wanted children. You said you did. You said you thought it would be wonderful to have children."

"A general question," he said. "I gave a general answer to a general question, not a blanket invitation."

He was very angry.

She could hear the photographer losing patience too. The members of the wedding party were wilting and fractious in the heat. Cinderella dressed in yella, she thought. Went upstairs to kiss her fella.

"What do you want me to do?" he said.

"Nothing," she said flatly. Then she gave him a small, ironic look. "Everything." And she shrugged.

"Everything I can't do. But I can help."

"I don't want *help*."

Then why did you come, he almost asked. But he knew why, and he wasn't going to ask.

"I don't need *help*." And now it was she who was angry. The anger gave her something to lean her shoulder against. It held her up even while it offered resistance, just like this shifting, retreating, obstinate man beside her.

"Look at me," he said. "I have to know what you're going to do."

She guessed from his impatience that he was asking for peace of mind so that he could get back to his work. "I'll figure something out," she said.

He ran his hand through his hair and Norma Joyce said, "Don't worry. I won't say it was you."

She saw the gratitude and shame on his face. "I wasn't worried about that," he said. But she knew he was. Then he said, "Adoption is the only answer. You know that, don't you."

She looked up at the sky. Any moment it was going to rain. Water in wells was rising, flies were biting more, Maurice was repeating the same point – give the baby to a family that wants it – and she felt more tired than she had ever felt in her life. She wanted to lie down on the grass and sleep.

"Norrie?"

But she refused to answer him.

"When will you be going home?" he asked her.

"In a few days."

"You've got a return ticket?"

She could have weasled into that small opening, made room for herself and more room. She could have appealed to him. *Worked* on him. Said no, I don't have a return ticket. I don't have a plan. I don't have anything.

She said, "I've got a return ticket."

"Good," he said, "that's good."

"You want to get back to work," she said. Her guess was right. In the back of his mind he was already thinking about the report he was in the middle of writing – he had merely stepped outside for a moment to clear his head, to admire the roses. He rubbed his eyes slowly with both hands. He was thinking as well about the trap she had laid for him. He said, "He was the power behind the throne."

"What?"

Maurice pointed across the grass. "Richelieu ran France under some Louis. A real conniver and he came to a bad end."

This last was gratuitous since he didn't know what end Richelieu had come to and didn't care.

She said, "There's a flower named after him. That's not such a bad end."

"You're right," he said. "You're right," and despite himself he softened – enough to stand up and go over to the rose and with his pocket knife cut off a bloom that was neither red nor pink nor yellow nor white, but some colour she had no name for. He came back and gave her the rose.

But really it was too hot to hold anything for long. She let it drop into the grey folds of her grey lap.

"If you need anything, Norrie, you should let me know. Will you?"

"Yes."

"Promise?"

"I will."

"Here," he said, "this is where I live." He took a notepad and pen from his shirt pocket and wrote down his address. He said, "I wish I could show you around the gardens, but I hardly know them myself."

"I can find my way."

"I guess you can," he said. "You found me."

She watched him head back the way she had come. At the latticework walkway he turned and looked at her on her bench. He didn't wave. Maybe it was too hot. Certainly the wedding party looked half-dead. The groom had thrown himself down on the grass, the bride was standing over him, the flower girl was tugging at the bride's sleeve.

Norma Joyce stood up and walked in the opposite direction, carrying her stupid rose.

Wisteria as sinuous and gnarled as willows in the coulee. Then a higher bank of crape myrtle in bloom, the flowers lacier than lilac but similar, and a member of the Loosestrife family, native to China, the label said. She climbed the path under those frilly blooms thinking *Loosestrife for Luce*. She hurt all over. As if she had walked straight into a wall. Whop! Now here she was, jarred back about a foot.

She climbed to the top and looked down. All she could see were the crowns of trees and low cloud. Behind her, there was snipping from a pair of shears, and there were crickets. She climbed the slope a bit more and looked down, without impediment, to the rose garden. Maurice was gone.

It began to rain. All the benches nearby were empty. She stood under a Japanese pagoda tree and thought of Marco Polo and his long travels across the globe through every sort of hardship. Behind her was a pale, imposing building, probably a library or museum. She turned right and walked towards a fountain, scalloped like a cockleshell, with a modest spurt of water. She would have thrown in a penny had anything remotely coherent come to mind.

A gardener was talking to another visitor. "On a day like this," he was saying, "when you only get a quarter-inch of rain, it's smart to put down water because it soaks in real good."

She heard the sprinklers very clearly now. They were set out in two rows the full length of the long garden. At the far end of the garden were the big black gates.

And then she heard her name.

She turned around. Maurice was coming along the path towards her.

Now that was a sight worth seeing. He came up to her breathing hard, his sweat smelling like old canvas. No wonder she loved the smell. He said he had had another thought, there was another possibility. And her heart gave a big knocking lurch.

What possibility? she asked.

Rather than go home to Ottawa she could stay in New York. Yes?

It might be easier for her if she stayed here.

The rain had stopped. The air was still. He would help her with money, he said. There were homes for girls who found themselves in her situation. There was nothing to be ashamed of. It happened a lot.

"Oh." Her knees weren't working, and he caught her arm.

"Sit down over here," he said.

"No, I'm all right." She shook herself free.

"Please sit down."

"I don't want to sit down."

"At least think about it," he was saying.

She couldn't look at him. She found it physically impossible to meet his eyes. She said, "What am I thinking about? That you're so ashamed of me you want to put me in a home?"

He took her face between his hands and turned it towards him, and what he said next would work its way into her and stay, that's how canny it was, how open to interpretation. He said, "Don't ever doubt my feelings for you."

Now her eyes met his. "You've got my address," he said.

She nodded. "Yes." And now she smiled.

Without saying goodbye, she turned and walked towards the gates, then stopped to look back. He was still there, watching her.

As if pulled around by a string she went back to him. She could see the uncertainty – the wariness – well up in his eyes. She pulled his head down and kissed his mouth. He pulled back just perceptibly.

In the subway, having paid her five cents and taken one of the dark green seats, she turned to the man beside her. "What colour would you say this is?" she asked.

"I'd say that's coral."

She looked at him gratefully and he smiled at her. His eyes were shy, intelligent, anxious. In his brown shoes, brown trousers, and brown jacket he was a small mouse of a man with a brown briefcase in his lap. His last name should be Little, she thought. He should marry someone named Less. Or More.

By now the rose had folded in on itself. It was like a small soft snout. It was like a penis, after the event. Very thoughtfully she ate it. Somewhere people ate roses. She had read about it in a book. I wonder why, she thought. It has no flavour at all. But she was so hungry she could have eaten a horse.

Overnight the heat lifted and in the morning, through the open window in her room, she smelled the ocean. Her dress swayed on a hanger in front of the window, where she had hung it to air. Her rinsed out underpants and slip were dry, as were the detachable perspiration pads that snapped into the armpits of her dress. In the drawers of the small chest (painted brown and shoved against the wall) were folded her remaining clothes: two skirts, two blouses, a cardigan, a slip, three pairs of socks, and another set of underpants. She put on the grey dress.

Downstairs the wrinkled blonde said it was a perfect day for the Empire State Building, have you seen it yet?

She went. Her grey dress would come into its own now that fall had arrived. It was loose around her waist. If anything, she was losing weight. Some things she couldn't eat – frankfurters, for instance, or anything in grease – and she stayed away from coffee.

At the top of the Empire State Building she appreciated fully what she already knew: that she was on an island. The east wind blew into her face. Clouds swept by – and she was sailing on a ship to Europe. Maurice was leaning against the railing twenty feet away and she felt his eyes upon her. They were in the same city. At any moment he might appear. But she wouldn't seek him out, she decided, not until she had found a job and a place to live. She wouldn't beg.

Flattering light. It made even the dirtiest smokestack look beautiful. So why not her? It glittered off clock towers and rooftops, off spires and water tanks, off windows. It rippled like water. The shadows were deep.

How small New York was. She could see all of it, and beyond. A man was telling his young son that if you looked far into the distance you could see Canada, and, on the other side, the Gulf of Mexico. From up here the city was child-size. The cars below were toys strewn across the floor. Playthings.

She tilted her head back until she saw nothing but sky. I could be on the Prairies, she thought, but I'm not; how very far away I am.

Once more she looked straight down. This time she saw a shaded valley, at the bottom of which lay a coat of many colours torn into narrow strips. She watched the red and yellow cars move and stop and move again. Joseph's jealous brothers had thrown him into the pit and poor Jacob was at home old and brokenhearted. It served him right for stealing Esau's blessing. She had never liked Jacob.

But she liked New York. Within a month she had found a job, rented a room on West 23rd Street near Eighth Avenue, painted its walls apple green, and bought herself bright-red lipstick.

The job had materialized in the first week. On one of many

long walks she spotted a sign in the basement window of a printer's shop on Seventh Avenue. *Help needed now*. She went down three steps and through a glass door that had *Quality Printing* written across it in gold lettering. Inside, two greying heads were bent over a black printing press.

"Where have you worked before?" they wanted to know. And she answered, "I can start right now, if you like. I'm from Canada."

She started in the bindery, and in a month they gave her a raise.

They were Frank and Hilda McIntyre, members of the old school of worker-employers who were above mass production, easy profit, big wages. As a result, they had been left high and dry by their underpaid former assistant, and here they were with a rush order and no way of filling it, until in walked their guardian angel. A Canadian, they said to each other and anyone who asked. Frank was the talent and Hilda the fluttering helper who regularly at ten in the morning, at half past twelve, and at three in the afternoon made coffee on the hot plate in the back of the shop and produced from a cupboard a tin of her own oatmeal cookies.

The long, narrow cellar shop had two front windows covered with full-bellied wrought-iron grilles, and two back windows protected by horizontal bars. At the front, a window box sat inside each grille. Norma Joyce looked up from the long table at which she collated symphony programs or boxed up business cards, to see red geraniums and feet going by and the flash of fenders. A small animal in her lair, invisible to passersby unless they chanced to look down and catch a glimpse of her dark, glossy head.

The long table stood to the left of the door when you entered; it was part of the bindery, and edged up against the folding machine and stitcher. To the right of the door was the small treadle platen press Frank would teach her how to run, and straight ahead, the massive wooden desk at which Hilda answered the phone and kept nervously careful records of every transaction. Behind Hilda was an aisle, formed on the right side by the Linotype machine she operated and by the counter-high wooden cases containing the drawers with different fonts of type – Goudy, Bodoni, Park Avenue, etc. – and on the left side by three letter presses: the Miller cylinder press, used only for big posters or handbills; the trusty Heidelberg platen press; and the slightly less reliable Gordon platen press. To her, Frank seemed as forthright in his favouritism as any father. The Miller, he said candidly, was next to useless; the Gordon was a good sport; and the Heidelberg was his right arm. The shop printed stationery, handbills ("dodgers," Frank called them), concert programs, voting lists and ballots, milk and bread tickets, business cards, invitations, bookmarks, bereavement cards, menus, receipts. She learned at his side – working under naked light bulbs at the angled make-up top above the drawers of type – setting the type in a composing stick, then making it up in metal galleys that were like cookie sheets, but edged on three sides. It was the sort of small, precise work she was good at.

At the very back of the shop, on the left, was an upright piano at which Frank sometimes sat during a slow moment. On the right ran the low countertop and sink, and the chairs they sat in for their morning and afternoon coffees – or in Norma Joyce's case, hot water. "Whoops, I forgot. No coffee for Norma Jean," became Hilda's annoying refrain.

"Norma *Joyce*," she said.

It wasn't Beatrix Potter. It was a brown-and-black engraving from one of those old children's books that you read at your peril. Fearful Hilda scurried back and forth as if pursued, perfectionist Frank progressed from one dark task to the next, preoccupied Norma Joyce stewed in her own uncertain juices.

She had seen Maurice. A chance sighting, two weeks after the rose garden, and outside Macy's. A Saturday, and having finished work at noon, she had gone home to rest for an hour. She had made herself a soft-boiled egg on her hot plate, eaten it with bread and butter, then gone for a walk on what would become a favourite route – she headed east past the delicate iron balconies of the Hotel Chelsea to Sixth Avenue, then north up through the wholesale flower market, west to the fur district on Seventh Avenue, then up through the garment district. From flowers to furs to garments. From buckets of chrysanthemums on the sidewalk to pelts piled up behind grille-covered windows to trucks unloading bolts of material at the curb. Her final goal was the array of window displays on Fifth Avenue, the perfectly framed dresses, the shoes and jewels, the fresh-cut flowers and furs all safe and out of harm's way.

A long walk. As usual, she had bitten off more than she could chew. She remembers wind-glaze in her eyes, the bounce of reflections off plate glass, the ache in her bladder, the busyness even at knee-level, and the blare all around her as if she were Jericho and the trumpets were sounding. The Public Library beckoned with its bathrooms and benches, and she used to take refuge in that vast marble hall from the squealing press of accidents-in-the-making. The thing to be in New York was a book, she thought.

She wasn't a book, she was a winter coat for her baby. Always too warm, and more attuned to ill-luck than she had ever been in her life. As a child, locked in a running competition with disaster, she had imagined accidents all the time, in the belief that if she got there first in her mind, the bad things wouldn't happen. A faith-in-reverse, if you like, and one that required constant vigilance.

Now she was pregnant in New York City, and dangers had multiplied a hundredfold. Even in the library, at the foot of the wide set of marble steps sweeping up to the second floor, who did she see plunge over the side and hit the floor with a sick, dead thud but Norma Joyce Hardy, lately of Ottawa. Who did she see tripping at the top of the steps and tumbling head over foot to the bottom, but herself. Overstimulated, overtired, and only seventeen.

It was outside Macy's that she saw Maurice step off the curb to hail a cab. He stretched out his arm with the easy gracefulness she would always associate with him. He looked handsome and rumpled and thin, the breeze whipping his shirt and defeating her voice when she called out to him. A good thing too, because he wasn't alone. He was with a young woman who looked just like Lucinda.

The yellow cab stopped. He held open the door for her, and then got in beside her. Before the cab moved out into traffic, Norma Joyce saw him put his arm around Lucinda the Second.

The next day her stubbornness slipped on the banana peel of his address. In the morning, after a sleepless night, she fished it out of the bottom of her purse, and that afternoon she landed on his doorstep.

He lived on West 60th, not far from Columbus Circle, in an old and impressive greystone building. You rang the bell and the occupant came down in an elevator to let you in. "I thought you were someone else," he said with a cautious smile, and she supposed he meant the woman who looked like Lucinda. But he invited her inside. They took the elevator up to the third floor. There was the elevator, its slowness, and their silence. A doll inside a doll inside a doll, and the inside doll was their silence.

He held the door of his apartment open for her, but he didn't put his arm around her shoulders. Nor at first did he offer her anything to eat or drink.

Compared to her place, the apartment was large, light, and tidy. Three rooms, high ceilings, very little furniture. An armchair, a wooden desk, two sets of bookshelves. Through French doors in the living room she saw a double bed, neatly made, in the room beyond. Nervousness made her circle the living room, and curiosity brought her to a stop at his large desk. It was a working desk. His papers were in neat piles, his books stacked up to one side, his pens and pencils confined to a Mason jar. To the right was a typewriter table. There was paper in the typewriter: she had interrupted him. The books were about English and Japanese gardens.

"The botanical garden has a Japanese section," he said, coming to stand beside her. "I wanted to learn more. In a few months I'll be here," picking up the book about Kew Gardens.

"You're going away?"

"In March. It's an exchange," he explained. "I'll be gone for six months."

March, according to her calculations, was the month when this baby was due. "March," she repeated, as if she hadn't quite taken it in.

"This you'd enjoy," putting down the book about Kew and picking up a biography of Marie Curie. "She was a remarkable woman." Their shoulders didn't brush, neither did their hands. But she felt him. Like the heat on an ironing board after you've just finished ironing.

"How was she remarkable?"

"I'll tell you," he said, not hiding his pleasure at being able to take up the facts of someone else's life. They moved into the kitchen – he offered her tea, she asked for a glass of water – and he talked about Madame Curie.

Norma Joyce listened, and as she watched his familiar, expressive face, an old feeling came over her, of subdued excitement, of wanting to know everything there is to know, of wanting a life of study and learning, of application, and of the satisfaction engendered by application. The feeling was triggered by this man she loved, talking so clearly and well about the shape of Marie Curie's life. A student in Poland then a governess, an unhappy love affair, then her meeting with Henri Curie in Paris where, after the most painstaking work, they discovered radium. After he died – a terrible death, his head split open under the wheels of a horse-drawn cart – she was devastated by grief, Maurice said, looking at Norma Joyce, but even so she continued their work. She worked all the time. She was a beautiful woman who worked all the time. Over the years, said Maurice, there's been a tendency to say that without Henri Curie there would have been no Marie Curie, but it isn't true.

What beautiful hands he had. He swept a few crumbs into a pile, then swept them away with the back of his hand. With any luck, their baby would inherit his hands and not hers.

"Norrie?"

She looked up.

"I'm very selfish," he said.

Sounds came in from outside – cars, pigeons, a yapping dog. His windows were open.

"There are certain things I want to do. I've thought about it a lot. Books I want to write, places I want to travel to. I've lost a lot of time already."

She studied the traces of lipstick on her glass. She knew what he meant even before he made it explicit.

He said, "I don't want children."

She took a sip of water. "Ever?"

"Not for a long time."

"Like nine years," a touch of sarcasm in her voice.

"Longer."

Norma Joyce pushed back her chair. She went out into the living room. He thought she was leaving, but she crossed to the French doors. She could see the kitchen doorway reflected in the glass, and the wide bed, covered with a blue and white bedspread, through the glass.

"I don't love you," she said so quietly that he didn't hear.

"I'm sorry?" he said.

She opened the French doors and went into the bedroom. I don't love you, she said to herself as she took off her shoes and lay down on his bed. She should have had a bath before she came.

She could smell her feet. He followed her into the room and sat down beside her.

"I could stay here," she said.

He didn't reply. His eyes were so worried he could have been King George.

"I mean just for tonight," and she closed her eyes.

Seeing the shape of Marie Curie's life – the beginning, the middle, the end, like a piece of art developed step by step, or like a science project mounted on bristol board – had made her feel a deep, restful excitement, and she tried hard to hold onto the feeling. I want to be like that, she thought again. I want to be caught up. I want to be swept up in something that takes me over and leads me on.

Even in the midst of trying to keep her head, she wondered how she looked. It was her best position, this one of lying on a pillow, skin sloping back off her cheekbones. Cary Grant chose this position, she would learn years later, after he got older and the flesh on his face gave way. He always lay back on the bed and had the woman lean over him. She tried to remember what underwear she was wearing, and whether it was clean.

"Did Marie Curie have any children?" Opening her eyes to see if his face showed even a glimmer of desire.

"Two daughters. One of them wrote the biography."

Not a speck. Just coolness and consternation. "What are you thinking?" she asked him.

He was thinking of the camel and the tent. He was seeing the girl who had reached out her hand and staked her claim the very first time he saw her. He was wondering how he had ever let her get this far into his life.

He said, "Nothing."

Then he stood up and went back to the kitchen. She heard him run the tap to wash their few dishes. Then she closed her eyes, and actually slept.

That night she saw how it would be. She put out her hand and touched his shoulder. He rolled away from her.

He slept and she lay awake.

When it got light, she shook him. She had to shake him hard. "I haven't slept all night," she said.

He moved to get out of bed and she grabbed his arm, but he pulled firmly away. She followed him into the kitchen and still he held himself away from her, pouring milk into a saucepan, which he set on the stove.

Then he said, "I'm sorry." He turned around and looked directly at her. "I shouldn't blame you, Norrie. I know it's more my fault than yours."

His quiet admission undid her.

To her horror she began to weep. Her eyes were like Christ's stigmata, the way they gushed. His handkerchief wasn't up to the job; he had to get a towel.

He put a cup of hot milk in front of her.

"I'm not an invalid," she said.

"Just drink it. It'll calm you down."

"What have you got against tea?"

"Just drink it."

Oh, she would think years later, the implacability of mild men.

She drank the milk. She ate the toast he made for her. She borrowed his brush to brush her hair. She said, "I saw you outside Macy's on Saturday. You were getting into a cab."

"Okay," slowly.

"She looks like my sister, the woman you were with."

He considered this a moment. "Lucinda was more beautiful," he said, "until she lost her looks."

His tone was so matter-of-fact that she could only stare at him. What she saw was the steady, scientific gaze of a comfortable man. Maurice Dove would never be his own worst enemy.

"Is she a new friend?"

"I'd say Louise is more than a friend."

More than a friend. "So what am I? Less than a friend?"

That earned her a small smile, but nothing else.

———◆———

Without fail, whenever she left work at the end of the day, Frank took his pipe from between his wet lips – his lips were always wet – and said, "Thanks for your help, Norma Joyce. See you tomorrow." His tobacco smell niggled at some old memory, but she didn't push and the memory of the old fortune teller didn't come.

His mother's people had been printers in Edinburgh, Frank told her. A great-great-uncle, who worked for the printing firm of John Ballantyne, had corrected Sir Walter Scott's spelling. His mother knew long portions of *The Lady of the Lake* by heart, and so did he.

One day during their coffee break, when Norma Joyce looked especially tired, he removed his pipe from his mouth and said in a soft, musing voice:

Soldier, rest. Thy warfare o'er
Sleep the sleep that knows no breaking;
Dream of battled fields no more,
Days of danger, nights of waking.

He was a tender man, was Frank. He knew Burns too, and Milton. He said that his mother used to read poetry to his father when he was setting type. His mother had a beautiful reading voice. Not unlike yours, he said.

Norma Joyce had liked him from the first moment. His kindness, his patience, his various sympathies. And he had liked her. Her quiet company, her Canadian accent, her industrious ways. They were comfortable together. They fit.

By now it was October. The weather had found its balance, and by some miracle it kept it, week after week after week. It happens so seldom, and only in the fall, that the air is at once dry and light, the sun warm and ripening, the winds gusty and bright, the clouds boyish and irrepressible. The heat was gone, her nausea was over. No longer was she in danger of having to run to the toilet to retch. It had happened twice, and she had excused herself by saying it was the smell of the ink, she would get used to it soon. She had written to Ernest and Lucinda, a letter this time, telling them where she was and not to worry. She had work, and a place to live. She would be able to pay them back soon. In reply Lucinda wrote that the money she'd taken was the least of their worries. Didn't she realize how much anxiety she had caused?

She and Ernest were glad to know she was well, but they wanted her to come home. She shouldn't worry. Her father's anger had already passed.

Now her waist began to thicken. She asked Hilda's advice about sewing machines and received on loan a portable Singer that Hilda no longer used. On her next free day Norma Joyce visited Macy's and studied the clothes on the racks. She memorized one dress that was suitably loose-fitting, went home immediately, drew the pattern on an old newspaper, and cut it out. She had an eye for design, a memory for detail, a deft way with a pair of scissors.

Her desk was so small that she sewed on the floor. (Is anything blacker, she wondered, than a sewing machine, or more golden than the word *Singer*?) Seated on the floor and bending over, she sewed until her back gave out. Then she would stretch on her side and rest her eyes on the golden frieze of stylized figure eights and tiny squares-on-end that decorated the edge of Mr. Singer's useful machine.

Her room contained a single bed with a wide bench at its foot, a desk suitable for a child, an armchair, a standing lamp, and a footstool. The kitchen area consisted of a waist-high ice box, the square table that sat across it, a cupboard above with doors too paint-thickened to close. No sink. She washed her dishes in the bathtub.

Her one window gave onto a fire escape. After she washed it, inside and outside were transformed. Now she saw clearly and with pleasure the well of light outside, the pattern of red bricks on the facing wall twenty feet away, the neighbouring fire escape with its potted geraniums and folding chair, and the neighbour who came out at dawn to water the plants. It took very little to make her happy, this girl who wanted so much.

She moved the child's desk over to her window and, in the early morning, before she went to the shop, she drew for an hour. Sometimes she drew the bouquet of flowers she would buy every Saturday, sometimes the basket in which she kept her carefully folded clothes, sometimes the dresses on hangers hooked over the movable arm of her standing lamp, sometimes the pigeons on the fire escape. She pinned her drawings to the apple-green wall.

In the evenings she sought out quieter streets than the one she lived on. She liked to walk past the Theological Seminary on West 20th between Ninth and Tenth Avenues, then cross the street to the red-brick and brownstone buildings with their deeply recessed doorways and wrought-iron fences, which every so often enclosed beds of ivy growing up the trunks of slender city trees. She walked past buildings with brass door knockers shaped like paws or beaks, and sometimes she stopped to see who moved around inside the lit rooms. Across the street there might be a woman bending over a table or a man pouring a drink, and she would wonder what they were having for dinner and picture a roast with gravy; on good days she would imagine being invited to join them and on bad days she would imagine standing here in the dark, looking hungrily in, for the rest of her life.

Sundays, she went to Central Park and walked across lawns and over bridges and past playing fields. She heard mothers scolding children, and young men swearing hard, and once, a Chinese woman whispering an English lesson to another Chinese woman on a bench. When it began to rain she crossed Fifth Avenue at East 70th and entered the Frick Museum, whose inner courtyard, with its benches and greenery and splashing water, was a balm to any weary spirit. Off the courtyard were rooms furnished with velvet sofas and brocade chairs roped off from tired bottoms, and with paintings in carved gilt frames. One wall, covered in green velvet, was home to Rembrandt of the big nose. She studied the worn unlovely face in his self-portrait of 1658 and wondered what sort of man this was who could look at himself so unsparingly. A short, stocky, regal man waiting for the blow to fall, but calm even so, in his hat and cloak and what looked like the robes a disciple might wear: in that dresslike swirl of material, he looked more pregnant than she did. She would learn that 1658 was one of the worst years of Rembrandt's life – just as she would learn that Central Park began in the stress and panic of the depression of 1857 – but having declared bankruptcy, having been forced to sell off his private collection, here was Rembrandt making use of himself. Here he was turning his misery to account.

She stayed in the Frick until closing time at five o'clock, then made her way home. There was something of Rembrandt's darkness about New York. A velvet sootiness, especially underground, where it hovered around the raftered ceilings of the subway and settled into grime as deep as plush, but above ground too, on busy sidewalks, in the shadow of tall, dark, handsome buildings. What she was struggling with then, she realizes, is what she's struggling with still – how to make a life out of very little.

One Saturday morning in early November, calling from the shop, since she had no telephone, she invited Maurice to come for dinner. She heard his hesitation build at the other end, and she broke it by saying, "Don't worry. I won't poison you."

"All right," he said. "I've been wondering how you are."

He arrived an hour late, carrying in one hand a grease-stained paper bag of something, he didn't say what, which he set down on her desk. Then he turned full circle and whistled. "It's like a chuckwagon in here," he said.

"Or a tent," she said.

"You have everything you need."

"I wouldn't say everything."

But he was busy taking in her cozy, rudimentary arrangements, which included a low table set for two: the wide bench pulled into the middle of the floor and covered with a checked cloth. Only after he surveyed the whole room did he look down at her tough, unprotected face. Her cheeks were wider, her eyes brighter, but otherwise he wouldn't have known she was pregnant. Nor would others guess until towards the end; she was naturally small and compact in pregnancy. She was judicious about her clothes, she would use a girdle.

The intensity of her gaze   he felt eaten up   made him uncomfortable, and his discomfort made him overly hearty. He enthused about her tiny desk.

"It comes from a school for dwarfs," she said.

Some people, Lucinda for instance, thought she had no humour at all. But Lucinda was wrong.

Maurice grinned. He sat down on her bed. "You've done well. I'm impressed."

She had used her hard-earned money to buy him a steak. (A mis-steak, she would call it shortly.) A grand notion, but she had never cooked one before. The mashed potatoes were in her one

saucepan, ready to be heated up again on the hot plate; the buttered green beans, room temperature and they would remain so,
were in a bowl.

Her hot plate had two temperatures, high and low. The fry
pan was thin. She set to work.

Maurice watched her. "You're completely self-sufficient. I'm
glad. I was worried about you."

"I don't eat steak every day, you know. I bought it for you."

"What do you eat then?"

"Bones. I get them from the butcher." She was melting
butter in the fry pan. "I make soup. He thinks I have a dog."

In the end, bumping against each other, stepping on each
other's feet, telling each other what to do, they produced a steak
half the size of what she had bought. Maurice cut it in two and
slid the pieces onto their plates, along with the warmed-up potatoes and the room-temperature beans.

They sat down on the floor and crossed their legs. Each took
a bite. Maurice said with a smile, "It's very *je ne sais quoi*."

"Chewable," she said. "It's very chewable."

They were, for half an hour, a merry pair.

"I brought dessert," he told her, and without getting up he
reached for the grease-stained white paper bag on her desk.

She opened the bag to half a dozen crullers. "Crullers," he
said.

"As in duller," she said with delight.

In flavour they reminded her of Mrs. Haaring's fritters. But
Maurice didn't remember Mrs. Haaring. "Willow Bend," she
said. "We sat together in the kitchen while everybody slept. You
asked her what it was like to live on the Prairies."

But he shook his head. No recollection.

She stared at him. Then she reached across their makeshift table and grabbed his collar. She said, "Don't you *dare* forget me!"

He chuckled. He put his hand on the side of her neck. He rested it there for a moment.

"Not a chance," he said.

Before he left she gave him a slip of paper on which she had written down the address and phone number of Quality Printing, but he didn't call her. A week went by, and she called him. But he had pulled away from her again. He would only say that he was busy, he was working hard, yes he was fine. He asked her if she was eating well, and resting. When she said she wanted to see him, he said no, not a good idea, not now. I'll call you, he said.

But he didn't. She called him, several times because she couldn't help herself. The last time, in the background, she heard a woman's voice.

"Who's that?" she asked. "Is that your more-than-a-friend?"

He didn't answer.

"Is it?"

"Her name is Louise," he said.

By now it would have been the end of November, and though she told herself repeatedly that somehow everything would be all right, she couldn't sleep any more. She would lie on her bed taking slow deep breaths to coax herself towards slumber, and she would choke on her own breath. It would jerk and stall in her throat. She would gasp and roll onto her side, then onto her other side, turning and twisting in the narrowness of her bed. I'll die here and what will they put on my gravestone? SHE NEVER HELPED.

Finally she would get out of bed and sitting in her armchair, wrapped in a blanket, read from *An Anthology of World Poetry*, which Frank had given to her. She read repeatedly Christina Rossetti and Emily Dickinson and certain old Spanish and French verses in translation, searching for the moment in a short, precise poem when it began to shake with meaning. Then she would breathe easier, and sometimes after that she would sleep.

She liked knowing that Christina and Emily published so little and lived like nuns. She understood the attraction. During the hours she had to herself for reading and drawing, she lived more fully than at any other time. Privacy, she had always known, offered rich rewards. Privacy, seclusion, concentrated work.

And yet she was lonely. The baby in her belly was literally shunting her to one side, in a city where isolation seemed to come individually wrapped. As the days got colder and shorter, and dark December added an inner lining to the big black glove of Manhattan, she was grateful for the well-lit company of Frank and Hilda. Frank taught her how to print wedding invitations on the small treadle platen press. It was like an old sewing machine: you operated the treadle with your right foot, turned the big wheel on the side with your right hand, and fed in the cards with your left. One day the press closed on her hand. That was a surprise. She turned the wheel to open it, but only closed it tighter. Turned it the other way, and this time released her hand.

"Frank," she said. "Frank?"

Her left hand was flattened and engraved in gold with Dorothy Buckle's wedding invitation. Enlarged knuckles ever after, and a new respect for the old press. Frank put ice on her hand, then used a large, clean rag to make a sling. She went home early, but was back the next day.

Over coffee she asked them how they'd met. Hilda, who looked like she weighed at forty-five what she had weighed at thirteen, blushed and scurried to the cupboard while Frank said they'd met at church, and were married three years later at City Hall. She asked if they'd had a honeymoon, and he said no. He'd had to be back to work by eleven, so they went down the street for coffee and doughnuts.

Norma Joyce's reaction surprised him. "Coffee and doughnuts!" she enthused. "That's what I would do. Where did you sit?"

"The counter."

"That's what I would have done!"

"No fuss," said Frank.

"No ballyhoo," said Norma Joyce.

"No malarkey," said Frank, rising to meet the gleam in her eye.

"No hoopla!"

But Hilda interjected, "I don't know. I *like* a big wedding," and there was something plaintive and girlish in her tone.

Norma Joyce had never seen them touch. Twice she had felt Frank's hand on her own shoulder, but had never seen it on Hilda's, and Hilda herself managed to move through the shop without ever brushing against anyone. She had no hips, and over the years Norma Joyce would come to think of her as Hipless Hilda of the Sweet Smile. A kind and jumpy woman. Once, Norma Joyce kissed her on the cheek and she squeaked in alarm. Another time she asked, "Hilda? What did you want to be when you were growing up?"

"Oh, a mother. Always a mother," said Hilda. Then with a quick smile she added, "But that wasn't to be. Never mind," she said, "I'm busy enough as it is."

Frank said, "She's talking about her quilts."

Hilda said, "I'm on number three-oh-nine."

Frank said, "She'll hit a thousand before she's through."

Hilda, it turned out, sewed quilts for the needy. Members of her church contributed old scraps of material, and she fashioned them into single-bed-sized quilts at the rate of two a month. It wasn't so much that she liked to sew, she explained, as she liked to see how well she could arrange an odd assortment of colours, fabrics, and sizes into a pattern. A habit from childhood, this penchant for making do. In the absence of coins, for instance, she had collected locks of hair and taped them into her scribbler. "Show me," said Norma Joyce. So the next day Hilda brought the old scribbler to work and identified the various locks of hair from her family, from the girls at school, from the music and dance teacher who taught the Highland Fling, the Irish Washerwoman, and the Sailor's Hornpipe, and from various cats, dogs, lambs, and horses. Hilda had grown up on a farm, in upstate New York. She said, pointing to one spot in her scribbler, "All that's left of Ryatt is the grease."

Norma Joyce said, "I knew a Ryatt too. His father committed suicide."

"Well," said Hilda primly, "there's *no* excuse for that."

One day after Hilda had gone home to make supper (she and Frank lived in an apartment a few blocks from the shop), during a moment when Norma Joyce and Frank were cleaning the presses, wiping off the rollers with rags dipped in coal oil then wiping off the oil with rags dipped in naphtha gas, she asked him what he would do if he discovered he had a son.

"I mean, let's say a woman came to you, I mean you'd known her in the past, and she put a baby into your arms and said it was yours. What would you do?"

He took his pipe out of his mouth and scratched behind his ear.

"If she said, Frank. Here's your son."

"To tell you the truth," putting the pipe back between his teeth, "I'd probably jump for joy."

He was dressed, as always, in suspenders and baggy pants and shoes nearly out at the toe, his grey hair thick and rumpled, his rough capable hands stained with ink.

"Any man would," he said. "He might not know it until you put the babe into his arms, but every man wants a son. Or a daughter, for that matter."

"Of course, it might not last," she said. "After the first thrill is over, I mean."

"That's true. Some men don't stick around."

They finished cleaning one press and were about to start on the other when Frank said, "Norma Joyce, why don't you call it a day. I'll finish this."

And from then on he was so solicitous of her health that Hilda turned a startled pink when Frank took three tickets out of his shirt pocket and said to Norma Joyce, "You said you'd never been to the opera." Dear Frank. He knew everything.

A week later, in the Metropolitan Opera House, the lights went down and the great golden curtain rose on the scene Maurice had sketched in so briefly the summer before. Pinkerton was inspecting the little house he intended to share with Butterfly after their

"Japanese" wedding. Pinkerton wore white, Butterfly wore yellow. Other characters came and went bringing warnings, or curses, or bad news, or offers of marriage, but the real story was the love affair between a careless man and a devoted woman.

Three years passed, and here was the boy born to Butterfly after Pinkerton went back to America, here was Sharpless with the letter Butterfly refused to read, here was the cannon salute as the ship entered the harbour carrying Pinkerton and his wife, here was Butterfly waiting all night long for him to come to her. And here was the dawn. And plenty of tears.

Frank pushed his handkerchief into her hand.

"I almost never cry," she said afterwards when Hilda remarked on the state of her face. "I can count the times I've cried on one hand. So when I do the tears gush out, you know, from the build-up. That's how I explain it."

"It happened a lot," said Frank. "Soldiers overseas. Women left behind."

Then, because Norma Joyce was scanning the crowd so intently, Hilda asked, "Are you looking for somebody?" Norma Joyce shook her head, and they headed down the carpeted stairs.

Norma Joyce knew she was no Butterfly, and she wasn't sure that Butterfly herself was Butterfly, that any such person was really possible. She didn't trust the appearance of purity, no matter how much it moved her.

Christmas she spent with Frank and Hilda, and Frank's aunt Joan. Frank and Hilda's apartment was a surprise. It was more spacious and tasteful than she had expected. She was used to the working undersides of their lives, not this bright and comfortable overleaf of cherrywood shelves fitted under and around the living room windows, of facing sofas separated by a low wooden table covered with magazines and books, of a table off to one side reserved for a jigsaw puzzle in progress. She and Hilda and Aunt Joan worked at the puzzle (the *Cutty Sark* in full sail) while Joan told stories about her declining health and the wretched cleaning woman who read her mail. "There's nothing lower," Aunt Joan said, "than reading someone else's private mail." And Norma Joyce felt doubled over with dishonour. Even now she can hear that outraged tone of voice making its good-hearted, rock-firm pronouncement.

The next day was the Feast of Stephen. She set out to bring Maurice a birthday card. It was a watercolour she had made, of meadow grass picked in Central Park. *Poa pratensis*. She had looked it up in the library in Agnes Chase's *First Book of Grasses*. As it turned out, she never gave him the card because her arrival coincided with his departure. She reached the steps of his building just as he and Louise came out the front door. It was early evening. A few flakes of snow were falling. They melted the moment they touched the ground.

He said her name. She said she'd come to wish him a happy birthday. I should have called, she said. I was just passing by.

She was on the sidewalk; he and Louise were on the top step looking down at her. The few snowflakes that landed on Louise's fur hat stayed. Her maroon coat had fur trim. She was wearing stockings and pumps.

"I thought I might see you at the opera," Norma Joyce said brightly, reminding herself of Hilda and understanding in a flash the sorrow that might lie beneath Hilda's cheery façade. "Someone brought me there last week. It was *Madame Butterfly*."

"We didn't go," he said, and now they were coming down the steps and she moved to one side. She heard the *we* but not as much as she would later when the conversation replayed itself in her head. "Maybe I've seen it too often," he said, not weighing his words, the situation was so awkward.

Louise hadn't smiled or nodded in greeting, but then he hadn't introduced them.

"Which way are you going?" he asked.

In confusion Norma Joyce looked to the right. He said, "Then we'll say goodbye. We're going the other way." He touched her arm. "Thanks for the birthday wishes."

———◦———

From then on, she would assemble a kind of composure. Head bowed over the treadle press, belly growing, fingertips turning gold from wedding invitations or black from bereavement cards, she would practise a kind of calm. And it was *practice*. Rehearsal for the time she would have to face Lucinda and her father. She had written to tell them she was coming home, though she hadn't said why, and Lucinda's reply had been almost motherly. "We've missed you," she wrote. But Norma Joyce knew how difficult it was going to be and steeled herself.

In the middle of January she told Frank and Hilda she was going home. You haven't been with us five months, protested Hilda. What are we going to do without you?

She was seven months' pregnant and soon even Hilda would guess, and would she be so kind-hearted then? I'm going back to school, Norma Joyce said. Does school start in January? It does in Ottawa.

A week before leaving, she called Maurice to tell him too. He was silent for a moment. Then he said, "That's probably best. Your father knows, does he?"

"No. Not yet."

"It's going to be hard," he said. "Are you worried?"

"Are *you*?" she asked.

Again he was silent. She said, "I'm not a blabber, Maurice. I know I'm on my own."

He could have taken that moment to disagree, but he didn't. He asked her if she had enough money. She said she had. He wished her luck. She replied, rather dryly, that that was something you can never have enough of. He told her he would be thinking of her, and now, in saying goodbye, his voice had all the warmth so absent before.

She couldn't help admiring him for being so steadfast, so unshakeable, so impervious to her.

On her last night in New York, Frank and Hilda invited her home for dinner and Hilda took her picture. Frank still has this record of her New York transformation. She was wearing a loose dress she had made of rose Viyella bought on sale. Her thick dark hair was piled loosely on her head, her thick dark eyebrows plucked into fine lines, her face ageless and full of life. Her elbow rested on the arm of a chair. A book lay open on the table in front of her.

She finished it on the train before getting into Ottawa. It was Frank's copy of *Jane Eyre*. "Take it," he'd said.

"I'll send it back to you when I'm done."

He opened the book, stroked out his name and wrote hers above it.

She closed the book and looked out the train window at the snowy fields going by – a far cry from the lanes and hedgerows in *Jane Eyre*. What a tough and timid character Jane was. She liked her so very much despite her terror of sexual sin. Eyre-Rochester. From *roche*, no doubt. That was an old game, the one of rock, scissors, and paper. Strength where you least expect it. The dove that's harder than hard.

————◆————

The day she came home would be remembered as the coldest day of the century. February 3, 1947. In Snag, Yukon, the temperature fell to –82.4° Fahrenheit. A man called Wilf Blezard, interviewed in the newspaper, said he threw a pan of water outside and it hissed and fell as wheat-sized kernels of ice. He heard dogs barking in a village more than four miles away. His spit bounced.

Wrapping her scarf around her head, Norma Joyce waited at the war memorial for the B streetcar to take her along Sparks Street to Bank, then south on Bank to Sunnyside and west on Sunnyside to Seneca. From there she walked to her father's house, coming through the back door at nine o'clock at night.

Lucinda and Ernest were expecting her later in the week. Her letter had been deliberately vague: she didn't want them to feel obliged to meet her at the station. They were in the kitchen when she arrived, listening to the radio describe the worst blizzard in Saskatchewan history. Highways were blocked, schools were closed, bread companies had stopped making deliveries. Eaton's and Simpsons had shut their doors. Near Weyburn four locomotives and two snowploughs were buried in a drift half a mile long and eighteen feet high. The man on the radio said it was "utterly fantastic."

In comparison, a runaway daughter was a manageable disaster. Ernest didn't get up, but he said, "Come in and get warm. Put your feet on the register."

Lucinda said, "You must be cold right through," and she filled the kettle for a fresh pot of tea.

They both wondered what she had done to herself. She looked like such a city girl. Almost pretty.

Norma Joyce sat down at the kitchen table. She said she had the money she owed them, and she began to tell them about New York, but Ernest interrupted. "In the morning," he said. "Have your tea now."

Lucinda ran a hot bath for her and put a hot water bottle in the bed. When she wished her good night, Norma Joyce said, "Lucinda?"

"Yes?"

"Thank you."

Over breakfast Norma Joyce told them.

That explained it. That's why she looked so much better than she had ever looked before. The prodigal daughter.

She didn't say who the father was, and they didn't ask. They knew. The whole story went without saying: her months in New York and her return alone.

Lucinda said she hoped she'd been eating well. You'd better make an appointment this morning to see the doctor. She said, "I'm glad you came home. This is where you belong right now."

Ernest did not say a word. He stared straight ahead out the kitchen window and up the slope to the Dove house, sick at heart, he was so ashamed. But grudgingly, over the next few weeks, he came to admire his level-headed daughter. No fuss, no tears, no talk. He admired steadiness in anyone, but especially in women. Their afternoon naps coincided. Norma Joyce always made tea for them both when she came down from her room.

Even then she appreciated how remarkable her father and sister were. They could have shipped her off to a home for unwed mothers, they could have treated her with silence and contempt. They did neither. They took her in, and their attitude set the tone for how things would be. They didn't ask her to apologize or explain, and they didn't apologize or explain either. They knew there'd be plenty of talk – but, like other blights, it would pass in time, and sooner than some.

In their reliance on pride, in their embrace of Prairie reserve, the Hardys might as well have been back on the farm.

From January through March snow fell steadily. Often Norma Joyce found herself lying awake in the middle of the night, though the snowy light in her room suggested it was closer to morning. She would hear slippered feet, the toilet flush, slippered feet again, and the sound of her father's bedroom door. In her mind she would see footprints in the snow. Lucinda's footprints going down the porch steps into the snow then back up the steps out of the snow, only to turn because something had caught her attention.

You could see the whole story just by looking down.

The baby was a week old. Greedy-guts, she liked to call him. Sleep-robber. Thorn-in-my-side. Never had she slept so little.

She lay on her side. Her tiny, ravenous son slept beside her. Beyond him was the window that overlooked the Doves. A path had been shovelled from that house, down the slope to the laneway, just as a shovelled pathway led from her house up to the lane. From her window she could watch new snow cover up old footprints, and prepare the ground for footprints yet to come.

One morning, when she looked outside, she saw what she had been wishing for – fresh tracks, coming from the Dove house, crossing the lane and continuing to her house.

She dressed quickly, her heart pounding. Picked up the baby from his side of the bed, and carried him downstairs.

But it wasn't Maurice. It was his mother.

Mrs. Dove sat at the kitchen table. Her boots were beside the door. She had just slipped down, she said, to bring a gift for the baby.

Norma Joyce stood in the kitchen and felt herself go red with embarrassment and confusion. She didn't understand. Was his mother laying claim to her grandchild? Apparently. She wanted to hold him in her lap. Next, she fell to the job of admiring him, especially his red hair.

"Mrs. Hulder told me he was a redhead," she said with great complacency. "I wonder where that comes from. There's no red hair in your family, is there? Nor in mine. The Hulders, on the other hand. That's a family with red hair."

Now Norma Joyce understood. Not to claim, but to disown. The red-headed Hulder boys were nineteen, and easy scapegoats.

Would she ever, she wondered, protect her son as assiduously as Mrs. Dove protected Maurice?

A baby blanket. And a card.

"That's from Maurice," said Mrs. Dove, pointing to the card.

"Maurice?"

"A flying visit," she said. "He flew in yesterday, and out again this morning. Before he goes to England. But he wouldn't leave without seeing his parents."

The card, in Maurice's writing, said how glad he was to hear that she was well. He wouldn't disturb her. His mother had a gift for her, and would deliver his card. He'd signed it *All the best.*

And Mrs. Dove was all baby, all oohs and ahhs.

After that, only insomnia. The baby nursed every two to three hours around the clock. Between feedings Norma Joyce lay awake. Her face was wide and grey with fatigue.

———◆———

A week later she came downstairs with the baby wrapped in blankets. Lucinda was in the kitchen with a customer. Norma Joyce saw the backs of their heads as she took Ernest's car keys off the round table in the hallway; she called out that she was taking the baby for a ride, maybe that would make him sleep.

"Good luck," Lucinda called after her.

It was the end of March and snow had been falling every day. The streets had been cleared and would be cleared again in a few hours. It wasn't that cold. She started the car, and within minutes the baby was asleep. He was in the back seat in his basket.

She drove to Renfrew, then on to Eganville, taking the route to Lake Clear. She did it automatically, without thinking.

Her head rustled as if it had dried out inside. Even over the sound of the car she heard the inner workings of her sleep-abandoned skull.

But how restful it was. How good to get away, to be moving through the big, soft, white world she had almost forgotten about. Her route wound past billowy fields and bush, up and down snow-softened hills, across a narrow bridge, and eventually sideways when her car slid off the road.

Within minutes snow covered the windshield. She turned around and looked at the baby sleeping soundly. Already it was getting dark.

She got out of the car and locked the doors. Snow blew into her face, and she turned her head to the side. In half an hour she would be back. She would find someone to help her.

What happened after that would be written up in the *Renfrew Mercury*, the *Evening Citizen* and the *Ottawa Journal*. Photographers would come to the house but Ernest turned them away, so only the bare facts were reported, of a car that went off the road in the early evening of March 26. The driver was Miss Norma Joyce Hardy of 99 Fulton Avenue in Ottawa. Miss Hardy went for help, the papers said, and returned with a neighbouring farmer, John Flower Senior, but they failed to find her car because it was completely buried under falling snow. Inside the car was a two-week-old baby.

It seemed to Norma Joyce that she hadn't walked all that far before she bumped into the mailbox painted with flowers. Red tulips, yellow daisies, blue violets: a bouquet shoved into her mittened hands. But it must have been farther than she realized, and she must have taken a turn that she later forgot. Tire ruts in the laneway led her to a farmhouse filled with round and beaming faces. The father who answered the door, the mother who insisted she have tea and something to eat, the nine children who surrounded her – they all beamed at her the way her twin brother Norman used to do.

She thanked them, but could she have the tea later? She needed to get back to her car. Her son was sleeping inside.

John Senior and John Junior put her into their pickup – it had chains around all four tires – and they set off down the rutted laneway to the road. She sat between them. This was the part of Ontario where split-rail fences separate cedar trees from rocky fields in a farm landscape too bloodyminded for any but the very patient. Father and son were unruffled, quiet. John Senior asked how old her son was and was relieved to know he was a baby; he'll be fine, he said, babies can survive more than you think because they sleep so much, and it's not that cold, it's never cold when this kind of snow is falling, and it's supposed to snow all night. She felt oddly calm – as she had right after her mother died. Her breasts began to leak milk. They had more feeling than she did.

After a while John Senior stopped the truck. You said your car was blue? A Hillman? We must have missed it. He turned around, a nice manoeuvre in a tight spot, and backtracked until once again they were at the flowered mailbox at the foot of the lane. Let's try again. He pulled into the lane, backed out and set off again.

No tire marks but their own. The snow will have covered yours, he said, and Norma Joyce nodded, seeing again those footsteps in the snow on a night not unlike this but windier, harsher. She took her hand away, and Maurice had come up the final step.

She still felt stirred by the way his face changed during sex. He gave in to giving in. She did that. She had that effect.

She remembered taking his hand, a miniature woman leading him to a miniature meadow, the grass so hot and the pine needles so pungent and the wild strawberries so profuse that it wasn't surprising they got as good as they gave: they laughed to see their backsides stained red by the berries they had rolled on. Grass devils instead of snow angels, he said, looking down at the shapes they had left behind.

When the truck next stopped it was completely dark except for the headlights, and the light that came off the snow. Someone new to snow would have remarked on the quality of that light, the way it shone upwards, though *shine* is too bright a word for something so delicate and plain.

It would continue to fall all night long, the large, soft flakes of winter-spring.

Phone calls were made. Norma Joyce was fed, then put to bed in one of Mrs. Flower's nightgowns. She asked for a towel and wrapped it around her chest. She slept in the downstairs bedroom off the kitchen, nine hours of deep sleep from which she arose – with heavy, aching, oozing breasts – to hot coffee and thick pancakes and a circle of Flowers around the big kitchen table. Mrs. Flower said, "I'm glad you slept, I thought you might be too worried," and Norma Joyce reddened. "You needed it," Mrs. Flower said. "Anybody could see you were dead tired." Then she said, "Jesus will look after the baby."

Norma Joyce looked at her round, kind face. She thought but didn't say, better Jesus than me.

Later that morning another car followed suit in the same dip between two low hills, a collision so soft it knocked away just enough snow to reveal a blue fender. The driver got out. He heard a small tired cry and looked around for a cat. He wasn't a religious man, he told the police, but when he peered through the car window and saw the baby basket inside, he thought of Moses in the bulrushes, and he hadn't even gone to Sunday school.

Norma Joyce unlocked the car. She leaned in, lifted the blanket away and saw on the baby's cold, tear-stained face a coin of frostbite. Then he stirred and began to cry. She took off her mitten and put her warm hand on his cheek.

It was the echo, the repeat. It sank in as something inescapable, her connection to certain things. She took the baby into her arms and felt a surge of tenderness and relief.

"What's the wee one's name?" the younger of the two policemen asked her.

He didn't have a name.

"Red hair," said the other policeman, "that figures. You can't kill a redhead," he said. "You can't kill an Irishman or a redhead."

John Senior drove mother and nameless baby back to the farmhouse, where his wife made her comfortable in the big rocker in the bedroom she had slept in so well the night before. She nursed the baby and decided his name would be John Francis Hardy.

These coincidences happen. A snowfall had ushered Maurice into their house, another snowfall ushered their son back into her arms. She drove home in the afternoon, feeling rested and hopeful and a part of the world again.

Early morning like the dusty bloom on a purple grape, and beautiful to see after so many months of darkness. On the radio a man said all the rain now would mean lots of strawberries later. The middle of April, and so much was visible it was as if every fence had been taken down. All the fine grey lines and weathered grasses, all the contours of land unobscured by white or green, all the twigs like hair and through the hair the shining scalp of the sky.

In the afternoon, while Johnny napped, Norma Joyce drew at the kitchen table and got more done than she ever had before, soothed as she was, and excited, by the delicate tones of all that had come through this long, long winter.

Everything was spare and in motion towards something out of sight.

Towards colour.

But for now the world was a big silver brooch over her heart.

She had fallen in love with her son, and the love spilled out to include her neighbourhood, this calm cluster of tree-lined streets between river and canal, and her family. Lucinda held Johnny while her sister ate, gave him his bottle when she began to wean him off the breast, took him into her own bed early in the morning so that Norma Joyce could come downstairs to draw or read. Ernest called him "my little man," and in his presence he became almost talkative. Finally, he had the son he had always wanted. He took him in the baby buggy to the park, and in the car to see his orchards on the old Carp Road.

What a difference a grandson made. He was the warm and crackling hearth they gathered round. The oil on troubled waters.

Spring turned into summer. Mrs. Dove came outside in her gardening gloves, and Norma Joyce pretended not to see her. The two women practised avoidance at close quarters. Whenever she sat outside, Norma Joyce kept her back to the house above.

Summer came on fast. By June all the windows in the house were wide open to a city full of gardens, yet the smell seemed sweeter inside than out, as if summer air had activated hidden summer walls, or actually turned the inside of the house over, like a mattress, from its dark winter side to its light summer side. Soon it was so hot that on Hopewell Avenue a line of irises flopped over like horses in a New York heatwave.

Lucinda filled a portable wash basin with water and gave Johnny cool baths under the apple tree while Norma Joyce studied the flowers coming into bloom. She looked into the face of an oriental poppy, unprepared for the shock of its flagrant, all-out beauty: hundreds of purple-black ballet slippers waved in the air, while down below, in a sort of scarlet pit, the poppy's skirts had been thrown back to receive brushstrokes of dark mascara, lavishly applied.

"Lucinda? Mind if I draw for a while?"

"I don't mind," wrapping Johnny in a towel and gathering him into her lap.

Lucinda-as-auntie had come into her own, and of necessity she would keep coming because in September Norma Joyce got a job dressing windows for Freiman's department store on Rideau Street.

If you were to see their house at dawn, if you were standing in Maurice's old window, for instance, and looking down the slope, you would see shades go up in both windows because both sisters rose early. Lucinda took Johnny down into the kitchen or outside; Norma Joyce worked at her desk on the exercises in *The Natural Way to Draw*. At seven-thirty she came downstairs to have breakfast and play with her son, and then she took the streetcar to Freiman's.

Now the hours spent studying display windows in New York would come in handy. Inspired by their bravado, she set the overlooked beside the prized – yesterday's crumpled newspaper, last year's scuffed shoe, last fall's weathered grasses beside a silk dress too expensive to buy. Dogwood from Eganville, long grasses from the Chaudière Falls, birchbark from the old Carp Road – all carefully identified and arranged next to the latest, most expensive fashions.

At the Experimental Farm people commented. Have you seen the windows at Freiman's? Somebody down there must be a naturalist. And in the fall she got written up in the *Ottawa Journal* as the window dresser who spent her weekends rambling about the countryside picking up leaves, twigs, grasses and birds' nests, all of which she arranged with ingenuity and care in her window displays on Rideau Street.

Norma Joyce put the clipping into an envelope and sent it to Maurice at the Brooklyn Botanic Gardens; he would have returned from England months ago. Even though she didn't expect a response, it was a long time before she gave up hope of hearing back.

She would work at Freiman's for the next six years, creating what the newspaper referred to as "fashionscapes." After one especially deep snowfall, she made snowflake cut-outs, working from some of Bentley's forty thousand photographs of snow crystals, numbering them as he did, and hanging them on a backdrop of several black velvet dresses. At Easter, in a small window, she suspended the slender bough of a beech tree, in the fork of which there nestled a hummingbird's nest the size of an egg, then placed beneath it a series of hand-painted egg cups. Off to one side was the real story, the feathery Easter hat for $17.50 and the pale-yellow gloves for $5.29.

Gerry Hulder used to bring Norma Joyce things whenever he came to see his mother. He was raw-boned and quiet, this red-headed twin who had rescued her from the bees. A hornet's nest, a snakeskin, a rusted-out sap pail, oddly shaped pieces of driftwood. He was studying forestry, so he was often in the woods. She liked him. He was kind and shy. He made the baby smile. But he was very young. And his visits always brought chugging in his wake a mother who was as frosty to her as she was friendly to Lucinda.

One morning, after Norma Joyce had been at Freiman's for three years, her sister paid her a visit at work. Lucinda had been to the dentist on Dalhousie Street, and now she walked to Rideau Street, crossed to the south side and proceeded west, wondering if she would see Norma Joyce in one of her windows, and she did. She stopped to watch. A few passing cars interfered with her view, but not for long. Her sister of the olive skin worked quickly and with concentration – putting masks on two mannequins before she adjusted their stumbling feet in a nighttime forest scene of outstretched gloves and clothing caught by branches. People said her windows looked alive, and Birks had tried to steal her away from Freiman's.

A form of magic, those windows. So it seemed to Lucinda. The mannequins were stepping out of torn, dusty overcoats into elegant silk and satin. Even Norma Joyce called them her Cinderella windows, playing on every woman's desire to be more beautiful than she knows.

Lucinda crossed the street. It was a November morning in 1950; Johnny was at home with Ernest; the apple season was over and the season of gloves had begun. Lucinda rapped on the window and Norma Joyce smiled and waved her inside. They headed upstairs to the lunch counter, where they sat side by side stirring their cups of coffee. Norma Joyce was thinking about her window; Lucinda was pondering how best to impart the information she had gained that morning when Mrs. Dove waylaid her in the street.

"Norma? I saw Mrs. Dove this morning." She tried to remove from the telling any of her own feelings, but Norma Joyce heard the lack of surprise, and the quiet note of vindication. "You don't seem upset," Lucinda said. "I thought you'd be upset."

"What do you expect me to do?" With a tired smile. "Muss up my hair?"

Lucinda had to smile too. Sometimes she forgot how tough her sister was. "I forget how strong you are," she said.

"I don't know what that means," more immediately hurt by this facile summation of her character than by the news of Maurice's marriage. Little hurts would often trouble her more than big ones. With emotions no less than with money, she could be penny-wise and pound-foolish.

"Did she tell you his wife's name?"

"Louise."

"Louise. I've seen her. She looks like you."

"Louise Hunt. From Long Island. She's a violinist."

"Louise Hunt. Well, it won't work."

"Why not?"

"Dove and Hunt. A bad combination."

In her mind Norma Joyce shut the door on Maurice. He came to her begging. She shut the door.

She kicked over the flowers on his grave.

She was through.

And that might have been the end of it but for one thing: he wasn't through with her. When Johnny was six years old, Maurice moved back to Ottawa.

Norma Joyce still rose early. She liked to drink her first cup of coffee in the canvas folding-chair on the back porch. The porch was small, with a low roof and a green wooden railing.

Early one morning in September, as she sank into the canvas chair holding her cup in both hands, it began to rain on the pink-mauve cosmos at the foot of the steps, the heliopsis as tall as giraffes along Mother Hulder's fence, the apple trees, the grass in the laneway, and the two Dove lawn chairs caught in the open. Johnny came out and climbed into her lap.

His current treasures were in his hands. A fifty-cent coin, a book about Greek heroes, a rubber ball.

"It's the last day of summer," she told him, and he asked if all the flowers would die tomorrow.

"No," ruffling his thick red hair. "They won't. It just means tomorrow will have twelve hours of light and twelve hours of darkness. Night and day will be even steven." An old riddle came to mind. "What falls but never breaks, and what breaks but never falls?" she asked her son, thinking how soft the rain was and how grateful she would always be to see it. "Give up?"

He gave up.

"Night and day," she said, "which is also the name of a beautiful song."

"I'm hungry," he said.

They went inside. Several of his half-eaten apples were on the kitchen counter – he loved apples, but not after their flesh began to go brown. Her sister would make these leftovers into a compote with plums and slices of lemon.

Lucinda was more indulgent now, but still unable to waste. She scrubbed carrots and potatoes in less than an inch of water and bathed Johnny in not much more. She instructed him to turn off the tap while he brushed his teeth or lathered his hands, to never let the tap run. "Water manners," she called it. She taught him other manners too. *Always, even in summer, leave your shoes at the door. Say hello to everyone you meet so they don't feel overlooked. Never leave a letter unanswered and never read anyone else's mail.* Said with such gravity that Johnny came to see these acts as the height of courtesy.

She also taught him how to chew. Your grandmother choked to death on a piece of meat, remember, and be sure to be extra careful with fish: always keep a piece of bread handy, a glass of water won't do. Lucinda and Ernest chewed their food the way some women brush their hair, a hundred strokes whether it needed it or not.

Lucinda was still sleeping. That was unnatural. That could have been taken as a sign. But Norma Joyce wasn't looking for signs.

She and Johnny returned to the porch with their buttered toast just as Mrs. Dove came out to rescue her chairs, shaking them off before folding them up and lifting them onto the porch. She and Norma Joyce saw each other, but they did not wave.

Mrs. Dove missed her son. He never came to visit, and her friends didn't understand why. Maurice and Louise came to see her and Arthur in Florida every winter, but he avoided Ottawa. She knew why and didn't blame him (not that she believed the boy was his), but she would have liked to show him off – her son who knew everything there was to know about plants and climate – and now she was going to have her chance. He had been invited back to the Experimental Farm to write a new grass manual for North America. An opportunity he couldn't pass up, he told her; he'd be working side by side with his favourite old boss. But I have a favour to ask, he said. Are the Hardys still living in the same house? Then will you tell them I'm moving back.

Her *why* was sharp.

"Because they should know," he said in his reasonable voice.

"They'll know. As soon as you move in, they'll know."

"I won't move in," he said, "unless you tell them."

Such awkwardness.

But here's a piece of luck. Norma Joyce and the boy have gone inside, and Lucinda has come out with a bowl of crumbs for the birds. Mrs. Dove sees her from the kitchen window. The rain has stopped, the sun is coming out, Lucinda scatters crumbs under the apple tree then heads to the raspberry patch, though surely there can't be many left. "Are you still getting raspberries?" Calling out as she comes down the slope. "Look at that. Aren't you lucky."

And aren't we all lucky.

Lucinda smiled and listened, and slowly picked the berries into a cereal bowl as she learned that Maurice Dove was moving back to Ottawa. Sought-after especially, according to his mother, by senior people at the Farm. "They love him over there," she said.

"Everybody loves Maurice," answered Lucinda, quietly and without irony.

A pleased Mrs. Dove rattled on. He would be able to walk to work, it was so close, and he and Louise would have the house to themselves since she and Arthur were moving to Florida for good. "I've been trying to convince Arthur for years."

One of the raspberries happened to be the same pale powder-pink as Mrs. Dove's soft old cheek. Lucinda offered her some.

"Oh no. No thank you, my dear." And she made her way back up the grassy, flowered slope.

Lucinda gave her yellow bowl a shake. It was a quarter full. Not many after this. Then she shaded her eyes against the sun and followed the progress of Mrs. Dove, who navigated the wet grass as daintily as a cat.

It was eight-thirty on the last morning of summer, and an apartment block of emotion had just gone up in her back yard.

Ernest looked at his favourite daughter. At the short white hair and the skin cross-hatched with fine, fine wrinkles, as if she slept on the finest grass, and he had to think hard for a moment to remember how old she was. She was thirty-two. She would never marry, and it still surprised him.

He asked her when. At the end of October, with his wife. But before that, alone, for a few days in early October. "What should we say to Norma Joyce?" she asked.

"Tell her," he said. "She'll know what to do."

"She'll leave, that's what she'll do. She'll move away."

"Probably so."

"She'll move away and we'll lose Johnny."

"Johnny isn't ours to lose," her father said. Then he added with surprising gentleness, "It's not the end of the world, Lucinda."

"It's the end of *my* world," she said.

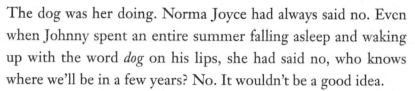

The dog was her doing. Norma Joyce had always said no. Even when Johnny spent an entire summer falling asleep and waking up with the word *dog* on his lips, she had said no, who knows where we'll be in a few years? No. It wouldn't be a good idea.

But when Mother Hulder came to the fence later that morning to say that a cousin of hers had puppies so irresistible she had told him to come to her if he had no luck elsewhere, "and now what am I going to do when poor Raymond knocks on my door, as he's bound to?", Lucinda had an answer for her.

"Tell him to knock on my door."

The knock came at four o'clock, and she made sure Johnny was beside her.

There were three puppies in a basket. Johnny chose the fluffi-est one, a light brown mutt with black circles around his eyes. He looked like a little professor. Chops, the boy called him, because they were having lamb chops for supper.

Norma Joyce came home to a dog plus news of Maurice's return, and it didn't take long to put two and two together.

After supper, over the dishes, the sisters talked. Lucinda washed, using a dishmop and scalding soapy water in a dented white dishpan with a red rim. The dishes were never rinsed. The soap came off when Norma Joyce wiped them dry with a tea towel. She stood on Lucinda's left and imagined living next door to a happily-married Maurice. What hurt her most, what *galled* her, was his evasiveness, his casualness. Not bothering to speak to her. Using his mother as a messenger. Turning her world upside-down and rubbing her face in his charmed life.

She should pitch her tent on his doorstep and howl. Throw rocks through his windows. Aim rotten eggs at his door. That would liven up the neighbourhood.

She said, "We'll move back to New York, that's all. We'll leave before he arrives."

The window above the sink was taller than wide. In the evening light Lucinda's skin looked worked over and tugged at. Blonde skin – Norma Joyce knew from observation – had very little staying power. Her sister's hands were a care, the fingers bubbly with tiny blisters that itched like fury. Stay away from soap, the doctors said. But how could Lucinda stay away from soap?

"Come with us," said Norma Joyce.

The dishmop stopped for a moment. Lucinda looked out the window and her face softened. Johnny and Chops were horsing around on the grass.

"We could go together," said Norma Joyce.

She didn't answer. She was trying to picture herself in New York but all she could see was a round of errands on Norma Joyce's behalf.

"I can't, Norma. But thank you for asking me."

"Dad would be all right."

"He would be. It isn't that."

"What then?" Quietly sorry for her sister's worked-over skin and workaday life. "Why won't you come?"

Outside, boy and dog rolled and tussled on the grass. Lucinda smiled again. Then she said, "I couldn't leave him behind." She looked at Norma Joyce. "Or are you going to take the dog?"

"You know I can't take the dog."

And there it was. The girl who had left her dog behind, the girl who always put herself first, the girl who couldn't be trusted – and her older responsible sister.

The next morning Norma Joyce came downstairs early and met cool air on the seventh step. There were fourteen steps in all. Warm air rises, she thought, and cool air flows in below – thank you for that, Professor Dove. She boiled water in a saucepan, stirred in a few heaping tablespoons of coffee, and watched moodily as the rich, dark brew frothed up and then settled down when she took it off the heat. Hilda's technique.

It wasn't yet six o'clock. Johnny was still sleeping. So was Ernest. Lucinda had been up in the night with a migraine, but now she was quiet too.

Norma Joyce looked around the kitchen and took in every surface – the approach of light as soothing as the glide of small fish in water, or the suggestion of lift on the Prairies, or the gradual movement of leaves towards the sun, which Darwin studied when he was too ill to attempt anything else. Maybe if I saw him, she thought. Maybe if he saw Johnny . . .

Outside, dew soaked through her shoes on the first day of fall. It was the time of beautiful skies, and colour on the ground.

Of yellow leaves, purple flowers, bruised air. Of gardens crowded with asters so tall Mother Hulder had tied hers up like pigtails stiffened with sugar water.

The door opened behind her and out came boy and dog. Shhhh, said Norma Joyce, pointing up to Lucinda's drawn shade. Shhhh.

They went back inside and put a box of crackers, a bottle of water, and the book about Greek heroes into a knapsack, slung it over Johnny's shoulders and headed to the Rideau River, several short blocks away. Barely a cloud in the sky and crickets non-stop and the sun warm on their backs. Vines the colour of someone choking.

New York, she told herself. Give your notice at Freiman's and call Frank to see if he can use you. Get out of here before you weaken. Be away when he comes in early October, and gone by the end of the month. Already she could feel her resolve giving way to curiosity. Soon the dreaded eagerness would arrive, and she'd be lost.

Johnny and Chops played beside the river until they were tuckered out. Then Chops fell asleep over her shoe, and she read aloud to her son.

After twenty years Odysseus had finally come home, but what awaited him? Those awful suitors. (That's what *I* was, she thought, an awful suitor.) So what did he do? He disguised himself as a beggar and set off for the palace. Not a soul knew who he was until he passed a dung heap where an old dog lay asleep and forgotten. The dog pricked up his ears and slowly wagged his tail and Norma Joyce stopped reading out loud. Her eyes leapt ahead to the rest of the paragraph: "Odysseus would have liked to pat poor Argus, but he would have betrayed himself. So he went on into the palace and

Argus died. His weak, faithful heart could not withstand the emotion of seeing his beloved master again." Tears spurted into her eyes. "I can't read this," she told her son, setting the book down on the grass. "It's too sad. You'll have to read this part yourself."

She was both awful suitor and loyal dog.

She was also a sucker for scenes of family devotion, as only the black sheep of a family can be. For her they were like wealth to the poor – infinitely desirable, absolutely unattainable – certainly not meant for the likes of her.

The boy picked up the book. He studied the picture and she studied her boy. How was she going to tell him that they couldn't take his dog to New York? What had possessed Lucinda to say yes to Mother Hulder?

She thought back to scruffy old Darwin – Mrs. Gallot would have taken good care of him, she knew, just as Lucinda and Ernest will take good care of Chops. There had been no choice; though she could have spoken up on Darwin's behalf.

And now she has to leave another dog behind. Lucinda, in her irreproachable way, has gotten even.

———◆———

Lucinda gathered tomatoes against a predicted frost. Early October, and a cold snap preceded what would be a long Indian summer. She was aware of them moving through their garden, but she didn't look up until she heard her name. She set down her tomatoes and stepped across the lane to meet his wife.

Maurice hadn't come alone, after all.

He asked after Ernest. Ernest was very well. We are *all* very well.

And then, because she had a yielding nature, she said her sister was away for a few days, looking for an apartment, and her father and nephew were at the apple orchards on the old Carp Road, and Maurice relaxed.

She looked again at Louise Dove and the resemblance was so striking surely they must see it too. Or had she changed so much? She felt herself step forward into her younger body while the old husk of herself remained behind, with hands smelling of tomatoes.

Lucinda asked if the house would be big enough for all of them.

"The house," said Maurice, "is plenty big for the two of us if we decide to live in it."

No children then.

———◆———

By a miracle of good timing Frank's aunt Joan was leaving her rent-controlled apartment on West 20th to live with a cousin in New Jersey; she would sublet the apartment to Norma Joyce. Frank and Hilda were delighted to have her back and eager to help in any way.

"It's all perfect," Norma Joyce said to Lucinda.

They were packing up things in her bedroom while Johnny napped down the hall on Lucinda's bed.

"So did you see him?" Norma Joyce asked.

"I saw *them*. His wife was here too."

"Your twin," said Norma Joyce.

Lucinda was taking things from Norma Joyce's closet. She

had laid her clothes on the bed, and now she was pulling a suit-case out and undoing its straps.

Norma Joyce was occupied with dusting off books and putting them into boxes. She wasn't watching her sister. She said, "He ended up marrying you, Lucinda."

She shouldn't have said that.

Neither one spoke as they continued to pack. Then:

"Norma?"

Lucinda was on her knees with the suitcase open in front of her, the cigar box open in her lap. She was gazing at two letters. "You kept them?" She said it so quietly she could have been a pin dropping. "All this time?"

She had the unpardonable in her hands.

There, upstairs, on a warm October afternoon, Lucinda looked at Norma Joyce with a long, slow look that became part of the uncanny atmosphere of one of the longest Indian summers on record. Outside, the treetops were full of warm wind. White curtains moved in the breeze. The small white envelopes lay still in Lucinda's lap.

Then she examined them – stamp, address, return address. Norma Joyce watched her, and nothing was quite real except the desire – the wish – for this old trouble to go away. But the sight of Lucinda looking gave her Lucinda's eyes, and she felt sorry and sick.

A moment later, however, laughter rose in her throat. She had to turn away and swallow hard. It felt like an emotional stroke – half of her caving in, while the other half chuckled – and she remembered Maurice's face sliding in two directions when his plane crashed.

"I would have given them to you," she said finally. "You never asked."

"I never imagined you still had them. I didn't think . . ." Lucinda stopped.

"You didn't think I was such a magpie," supplying a nicer word than thief. She steadied her hand on the suitcase, but rather than cool, hard leather, she felt the spongy numbness of her fingertips, and even that feeling was far from clear.

And what was Lucinda thinking as she looked at the letters in her lap? That the past was rolling up behind her like an old carpet waiting for her to get out of the way so it could roll up some more.

She said, "Shall I put them in your suitcase?" It was her one moment of sarcasm.

"They're yours."

"They *are* mine."

Lucinda June Hardy, Willow Bend, Saskatchewan.

After Lucinda went to her room and closed the door, the little Tartar stopped packing. She pictured Lucinda on her bed reading the letters, and she gripped her face with her hands and gave her head a shake. Then, after a moment, she veered back to the task at hand.

Every so often she would stop, stricken and thinking of all the consequences, one after another. And then she would veer away.

Lucinda hadn't opened the letters. She had perched on the edge of her bed so as not to disturb Johnny. She studied his face. How like Maurice he was around the mouth and nose and eyes, but how like her sister in his high wide forehead, and in the wilfulness that would serve him well at everybody else's expense.

Lucinda had fallen into the habit of touching men's hands – the baker's, the streetcar driver's, the librarian's. The baker's hand was surprisingly cool, even damp, but not unpleasant; he had very large muscles, short-cropped hair, very white skin. The streetcar driver's hand was warm and dry, and the lines of his undershirt visible through his carefully ironed shirt. The librarian's hand was cool and rough, the underside of his forefinger cracked-red and worried-looking, like her own. She touched his hand when she paid the fine.

The book Lucinda returned late by one day was something her sister had borrowed. Lucinda found it on the kitchen table one night when she couldn't sleep. It was about Constable and Turner, and related the scene in the National Gallery when Constable, with great care, was adding the last touches to his newly hung painting. Turner came into the room. He walked up to his own painting, hanging on the wall beside Constable's, and with one stroke added a single flash of red to the centre of his canvas. Then he left. "He has been here," Constable said to another painter, "and fired a gun."

Lucinda saw a small hand go up to a frostbitten cheek and remain there until the skin turned pink. She saw in her sister the same remarkable confidence that filled Constable with awe.

Lucinda has stopped sleeping. From this point on, night gums away at her like spring sunshine on old snow. Soon nothing is left but a thin bright bone.

In the morning she goes to her bedroom window and opens the curtains. October 11? Already? Wasn't it only yesterday that she bent low over a clump of forget-me-nots, unsure whether they were the source of the sweetness in the air, and they were? Only yesterday that the lilacs were past their prime but still in bloom, turning to rust along their edges. Only yesterday, and now it's today, and soon it's night. She lies down at midnight, and panic skitters across her chest like mice – panic panic panic – until again she gets up. She finds paper and a pen and begins to write.

Her handwriting has changed. It's bigger and sloppier, as if she's writing in the dark, and she is. Now she sits on the top porch step in the moments before dawn, adding a few more thoughts to the long, ongoing letter that she never delivers.

After it gets light she comes back inside and upstairs into all the retained warmth of the previous day: day-old heat like day-old bread, a little stale but still welcome.

She writes: *Don't you remember the day I waited for him to come? You could have rescued me. You could have spared me all that trouble if you hadn't been so selfish.*

She writes: *I always suspected something, I even suspected this, so why is everything so hard?*

She runs her hand through her short white hair. She says to her sister, "I can't sleep."

Norma Joyce says too easily, "You'll be fine."

The day before they move away, Lucinda hears her reading aloud to Johnny about Hercules going without arms. "Without arms," shouts the boy, raising his arms in the air.

"Without arms," continues his mother, "or ears or a nose," and the boy shrieks with laughter.

They are seated together in the big Muskoka chair under the apple tree, Maurice's son and her sister of the tar-hair and tar-gums who insinuates her way into the lives of dogs and boys and certain men.

"You'll be fine," her sister says again when she waves good-bye at the train station and takes Johnny away – stealing him just as she stole the letters – a boy as much hers as Norma Joyce's. Who looked after him all these years?

She writes: *My devious sister who destroys everything she touches.*

At two in the morning, Lucinda sees in the bathroom, left behind like a calling card in the white sink, one of her sister's long black hairs. It continues to move after she tries to rinse it down the drain, to move after she unsuccessfully grabs at its soft body with a piece of toilet paper. Move, and send out its serpentine life.

Her hands are an open book. Everything she touches stains her skin. Apples, carrots, potatoes, beets, all leave behind a wash of colour on tormented fingers. Shampoos and chemicals have been her undoing. No more hairdressing, the doctors say. You must find another occupation.

She lies in bed and feels herself going crazy with clawing itchiness and sleepless panic.

Mother H. has promised her a healing lotion, and on the late afternoon of October 25 she comes over smelling of the talcum powder sprinkled copiously under every fold of bountiful flesh. Beeswax, she says of her concoction, and olive oil.

That night Lucinda draws white cotton gloves over her beeswaxy hands, and for the first night in weeks she sleeps till morning. She dreams that she visits Mother H. and they begin to dance. In the fat woman's arms she becomes a good dancer, supported and propelled by her know-how and bulk. Then Mother H. confesses what she really wants. Lucinda goes home and comes back with money distributed around her body in several pockets and other hidden places. The fat woman must find the money. Lucinda lies down on the bed. Mother H., humming with excitement, caressing with exquisitely light touches, finds the money by undressing her, little by little. Her fingers locate seams and stroke them, discover pockets and penetrate them. She applies her tongue to the juicy pocket between Lucinda's legs then bends to her breasts, tongues and flicks and fingers her breasts, sucks and kneads and rolls them between her fingers, flicks and flicks with her tongue. Then she takes Lucinda's hand and puts it on her cheek, lowers it to her neck, then to her bosom, then lower still, until Lucinda pulls her hand away and wakes up to an October day so warm it's as if someone's wish has been granted. Summer has come back.

It is a boisterous, beautifully lit day. The sky spills over with dark cloud and bright light. All the colours and late berries, the thickening vines and wild grapes are held like some big purple jewel of mourning in a hot gold setting.

For once Lucinda knows her sense of well-being for what it is, and decides to go for a drive before the migraine hits. On the afternoon of October 26, after cleaning the house from top to bottom, she steps out into the driveway and whistles for Chops. Whistles again. He can't be far.

She goes around to the back and there he is with Ernest. *Chops.* But he won't leave her father. (This is something Ernest will remember afterwards. She called for the dog twice. She wanted to take him along. She wanted to give him a run in the woods. Of course she meant to come back.)

Lucinda gets into her black convertible. She ties a paisley kerchief around her head, takes from her pocket the letters digging into her thigh, the two from Maurice, the one she's been writing to her sister, and puts them into the glove compartment of her car. It's almost three o'clock, and only Mother Hulder sees her pull away.

Very soon she's passing split-rail fences with scarlet sumac on one side and scrubby fields stretching into the distance on the other. In the ditches, bouquets of field asters stand on their own two feet. Everywhere the trees have a silvery cast, as does the sky, because the day is so strangely warm. She isn't going fast. The road is like water it's so shiny. The light blinds her from time to time, but she isn't going fast. Carleton Place, Lanark, McDonald's Corners. Then a sign for Snow Road.

Had she been thinking more clearly, she would have turned back, but she wasn't thinking clearly, and soon she wouldn't be seeing clearly either. Scintillating, pulsing light always made it happen faster, the darkening on either side as her peripheral vision grew dim and the pain took over.

It's the time of year when all the remaining yellows are at their most vivid. Lemon yellows, tawny yellows, coppery yellows. The cool pearl opalescence of yellowy black birch. The dull rich yellow of old, old maple. All of them, all of the yellows, vibrate in the air.

She turns on the radio and someone is singing "Autumn Leaves."

Lovely song.

A memory pricks at her, something triggered by the name Snow Road and by the song. Some unnameable affinity she feels on this very warm day when two seasons are in the air at the same time.

The road winds up a hill. Bunched cedars on the right, golden maples on the left. At the top you can see the road winding its way down to a lake at the bottom. The lake is shallow. Close to shore are tall weeds and old stumps. Between the lake and the road stands the most beautiful tree for miles around. From here, at the top of the hill, the road seems to be one long easy slope, but first it dips down, then it levels out, then it dips down again in a long incline to the bottom, where it bends left, skirting the tree and hugging the curve of shoreline for a thousand yards or so before it winds up another slope and out of sight.

Lucinda's car comes drifting down the hill. It makes the first dip and the levelling-out, and then it follows the long slope down to the bottom and into the great golden tree.

III

"Air also expands from increase of heat, that subtle
and mysterious agent which acts mechanically, and in an
unexplained manner – a manner which is felt through
the very densest as well as the lightest matter, yet no more
explicable, to the general senses, than sight, or the electric
touch, or the moral emotion in one human being caused
by a look or a word from another."

ROBERT FITZROY, *Weather Book*

What she remembers most about Lucinda's funeral is her father standing in her bedroom doorway the night before, and the letters on the kitchen table the morning after. It must have been just before dawn when she opened her eyes and saw him looking at her as he had when she was a child, though then she had pretended to be asleep. The same feeling, of ill will flowing towards her.

This time she spoke from her pillow. "What is it?" she asked. "What's the matter?"

But Ernest didn't answer. He turned around and headed back to his room, leaving her to lie awake.

At breakfast she said, "Why were you staring at me in bed?"

He was spreading peanut butter on his toast and didn't look up.

"Ernest?" And she made her voice light. "What were you up to? Were you giving me the evil eye?"

He smoothed out the peanut butter. "That's your department," he said.

He would blame her for Lucinda's death just as he had blamed her for Norman's. He said nothing more, but in his attitude towards his youngest daughter there was a hardening-off. She had seen him give failed crops the same cold shoulder.

All her information had come from him. The terse phone call to the print shop, the brief explanation about the funeral when he picked her and Johnny up at the train station, the description of the accident (after Johnny had been tucked into bed), the finger pointed at the letters on the kitchen table the morning after the funeral.

It had been a short service at the Williamson Funeral Chapel on Powell Avenue. Everyone whose hair Lucinda had ever cut was there to say what a fine woman she was, and what a tragic death. Norma Joyce had thought Maurice might come, but the only Dove who showed up was his mother. Mrs. Dove passed along his condolences, though, as well as the information that he and his wife wouldn't be arriving in Ottawa until the first day of November.

"The very day we're leaving," said Norma Joyce.

"Such a tragedy," said Mrs. Dove. "I've always said you can't be too careful when it comes to cars."

"Cars," said Norma Joyce, "and men."

Later, when she pressed her father for more information, he would only say, "She was very tired. She missed Johnny."

He could have said a lot more. He could have repeated Lucinda's words: it's the end of *my* world. He could have described how she wandered the house all night long. How her younger sister had spoiled her chances for happiness a long time ago. But he was a man of few words who admired self-restraint, especially his own.

He could have also said that the day she died Lucinda looked happy for the first time in weeks. That she whistled for the dog to come with her. That sadness might not be the only reason for her death. But that would have let his other daughter off the hook.

The police had found the letters in the glove compartment of the crumpled-up convertible, and given them to Ernest. "One of them's for you," he told her, pointing to them on the table. Two old letters with King George hanging on in the corner, and a new one addressed simply to Norma Joyce. She picked it up. It wasn't sealed.

"Have you read it?" she asked.

"I don't read other people's mail," her father said, and he took the newspaper and his cup of tea into the living room. Norma Joyce didn't believe him.

She read the letter through, then looked at the other two letters and saw that Lucinda had annotated them like a schoolteacher correcting an essay. *Not to be trusted* was written in one margin. *She undermined my life from the very beginning* was written across the top. *Honesty is the best policy* appeared pathetically at the end.

She put the letters into her pocket and went outside. By now, the last day of October, nearly all the leaves were down. They lay around her feet as she stood lost in thought for a moment, before shoving her hands into her pockets and setting off. She walked for a long time, until she found herself on the Chaudière Bridge, barely knowing how she'd got there. The wind stirred her hair. The Ottawa River was turbulent and close. Had she turned her head to the right she would have seen

another sad crisis underway: winter was coming to the Gatineau
Hills, the trees were nearly stripped of leaves. But she only had
eyes for the awfulness under her nose: the Chaudière Falls trun-
cated and twisted into the squat productivity of the Eddy Paper
Company. E.B. Eddy had put these magnificent falls to work.
E.B. Eddy hadn't been hampered by second thoughts.

"I'm sorry," and she said it aloud. "But you were the one who
wasted your life."

She stared at the foam and bark and sticks sweeping by before
raising her eyes again to the factory-barracks made of stone.
Beautiful buildings. She thought they were. Interesting, beautiful, baleful. Like a mean white bull that won't let anybody by.

What melodrama, she thought. What an easy way out. And
she pictured what her father had described: Lucinda under a
blanket of leaves so deep they had to sweep them off the hood of
the car to find her neck going one way, and her body another.

But how effective. To leave behind a letter she couldn't
answer, and to deliver it in a way she couldn't forget. A grisly sort
of mailbox, the glove compartment of a crashed convertible.
Especially since inside, like figures in some operatic love pact, lay
the companion letters from Maurice. The letters had joined
hands to make their howling last exit together.

You've never admitted that you ruined my life, went one scalding
paragraph, *because you've never thought about it. Even when you were
little you took what you wanted. Well, you'll go far. You're the kind of
person who does.*

It would have been easy to toss the letters over the side of the
bridge, but she didn't.

It was a very long walk home.

Something went out of her after that. Hers had always been the amorality of the overshadowed sister, but now her sister was gone, and how was she to live her life?

Eighteen years would go by before she came back to look after an ailing father on a cane, and what is she to make of those eighteen years? If she closes her eyes, particular scenes float to the surface. She sees herself standing in Johnny's doorway, watching him sleep, and understanding what it means to be disappointed in your child. She sees in almost photographic detail a summer's afternoon so perfect that for a few hours everything seemed possible again. She sees in rapid succession – her hand coming down over Maurice's mouth; the moment when lamplight gave her a better view of sexual betrayal; the evening when she absorbed the details of Hilda's face: the pale, rather dry skin, so much like Lucinda's, the thin lips, the nostrils cut high to expose the inside of her nose, delicately red like skin held up to a lamp. The clear eyes, unaccusing, accepting, and hurt.

———

In New York she worked for Frank and Hilda six days a week, from nine until five, with an interruption at three to pick up Johnny from his public school a few blocks away. They formed a family, Frank and Hilda, Johnny and herself. Perhaps, in the spirit of "more than a friend," she should say "more than a family," though that wasn't the case at first. At first it was simple. The four of them celebrated Johnny's birthdays together and passed every Christmas and Thanksgiving in each other's company. Frank took him fishing in the Hudson River and taught him how to play cards; Hilda knit him socks and became his official babysitter.

Johnny would give them exactly what he had given Ernest, the opportunity to have a son. It was Frank who taught him how to play "Home on the Range," saying it was Franklin Delano Roosevelt's favourite song, but it was Hilda who gave him piano lessons on Saturday mornings, then took him home with her for the afternoon.

Norma Joyce and Johnny lived on West 20th now, in the ground-floor rent-controlled apartment they had sublet from Frank's accommodating aunt. From the sidewalk, if you peered through the window, you could see its full length, from long bedroom through living room into kitchen and postage-stamp garden. A smaller bedroom, off the kitchen on the left, was out of sight. That was Johnny's room. The living room had a working fireplace; the bathroom didn't have a tub – that fixture, which occupied a corner of the kitchen, Norma Joyce called Saskatchewan. Time to visit Saskatchewan, she would say to Johnny on Saturday night. Time to soak in the slough.

He was the apple of her eye, this loud, shy, energetic boy who loved to tell jokes. Bursting into the kitchen, he would say, "What do you do with a blue banana?"

"What?"

"You cheer it up!"

"What's the longest pencil in the world?"

"What?"

"Pennsylvania!"

They liked the same books. Sherlock Holmes, *Treasure Island*, *The Tale of Samuel Whiskers or the Roly-Poly Pudding*, and all the bloodcurdling stories in the Old Testament. Johnny had a tolerance for any movie under the sun and Norma Joyce took him to everything from *Brigadoon* to *The Bridge on the River Kwai*. Nearly every Sunday they went to Central Park, emerging from the subway into Columbus Circle and making their way through Merchant's Gate to the playground or the pond. Though later he would lose his free and easy ways, she can still see her son peeling off his shirt on a hot summer's day and pretending to be an Indian. (Her handkerchief served as a headband, any convenient feather on the ground became an eagle's plume.) She would take out her watercolours, fill the Thermos cup with water from the pond, and paint a white horse galloping across his chest, a blue crescent moon on his forehead and ochre streaks under his cheekbones. Together they came home with pockets full of stones, dead insects, seed husks, bits of bark.

Norma Joyce made a place for him at the work table in her bedroom, kept him in watercolours and ink, hung his paintings beside her own in a room that contained a single bed, two long tables, and many shelves that had been fitted into place by Frank. She still got up early to draw or paint. Working with pencil, India ink, watercolours, and oils, she made detailed studies of twigs picked up in Central Park, of shells seen at the Museum of Natural History, of printing presses and Frank's pipes. She took pains to duplicate the chipped and faded colours of old fire escapes: the lamp black, yellow ochre, cinnamon and iron oxide orange, and, wherever dust was lying on top of black, the soft ash-grey. A painter of tiny landscapes and tinier still lifes in wild, gargantuan, abstract-expressionist New York.

Some years, Norma Joyce was able to convince Ernest to come for Christmas. She would suggest the visit when she wrote to him in the summer, then extend the invitation again when she wrote in the fall. Four times a year she corresponded with her father, one letter per season, and he replied to each one. But only once did he write to her without being written to first.

At Christmas he stayed three days, no more, no less, sleeping in Johnny's bed while Johnny slept on the sofa. In their small apartment he was on his best behaviour, helping with the dishes, setting the table, entertaining his grandson by teaching him how to whittle, or helping him assemble a model airplane, or instructing him on how to hammer together a set of shelves. But he was still her father. Still reserved to the point of gruffness whenever she tried to draw him into conversation. Christmas day they would spend at Frank and Hilda's, where Ernest enjoyed the company of a man who wasn't "a stranger to work," as he put it, and of a woman who was "first-rate."

These visits cost him something, she knew. Yet whenever she offered to make the trip to Ottawa, he shrugged. "Look," she said finally, "I'm going to leave it up to you. When you want us to come, we will."

Four years would pass before this relatively calm period in her life ended. News came in the unexpected letter from her father. Penned almost as an afterthought, though clearly it was why he had written, the final paragraph let her know that Maurice Dove and his wife were moving back to New York. Some high-up job at the botanical gardens. A For Sale sign in front of their house.

She found it perverse. Even when she tried to leave him behind he wouldn't be left behind. Surely Maurice was dogging her as much as she had ever dogged him.

The news upset her more than she could have imagined. The idea of their being in the same city, the possibility of their crossing paths – of his seeing her and stopping to speak, or seeing her and passing her by. She didn't know which would be worse.

Why did it disturb her so deeply? Because it revealed her life to be what it was. A making-do, a getting-by. A personal drought she hadn't been aware of, until she came upon the well.

———◆———

She was working at the small treadle press when he came through the door. Six months had gone by since her father's letter, but it was still a shock to see him, and to see him looking older and more dapper. He was wearing a grey tweed jacket and grey trousers, and carrying a soft black briefcase. A man at ease in his clothes, at home in the world. He went straight to Hilda, who was bent over her account books, and worked the same old magic, judging by the look on her face. Norma Joyce was on his right but behind him, almost hidden by the press; he didn't see her, and from his relaxed, assured manner it was obvious that the name Quality Printing meant nothing to him. He left, whistling.

She stood fixed in place, then grabbed her coat and ran after him. Being passed by, she realized, was worse than being seen. Let Lucinda be overlooked, she thought, not me.

It was late fall. The time of long coats and short days when the city turns into a cold, unfurnished black-and-white interior that everyone walks through briskly.

She wasn't fast enough. When she got to the corner, he was gone.

"Everything all right?" asked Frank when she came back.

"What is it?" fluttered Hilda. "What's wrong?"

"Nothing's wrong. Someone I used to know, that's all. Nothing's wrong."

"Mr. Dove?" asked Hilda, in one of those leaps of observation that took Norma Joyce by surprise.

Later, after Hilda left for the day, Norma Joyce went through the job-ledger on her desk and found his address. He was having business cards made. They would be ready for him in a week.

The next day was Saturday. She worked until three, then asked Frank if she could leave to do a few errands. She would pick up Johnny from Hilda at five-thirty, as usual.

His address took her to the Park Slope section of Brooklyn. A row of brownstones, old and attractive, with potted flowers on the steps. White mums. She could never see mums without thinking of Mrs. Haaring in Holland carrying her bouquet onto the train and arriving two months later to a world where blowing snow seeped under the window and drifted over the foot of her bed.

From across the street, she studied the handsome façade and the long windows, the pale granite stoop, the wrought-iron railing. A car pulled up in front of his building, and a moment later her eyes widened because the front door opened and Louise Dove, looking as well groomed as Norma Joyce remembered, came down the steps. Even from across the street she could see that her shoes were suede. Louise got into the passenger seat beside a woman in a fur coat, and Norma Joyce stuffed her ink-stained hands into her pockets. Once the car had pulled away, she crossed the street and walked up the steps to the carved and varnished oak door.

Three buzzers to the left of the door: DOVE was #1, the first floor. She ran her finger across his name, written in big block letters, and felt herself go weak. Why do they say it brings out the best in us? she wonders. She was about to ruin one love with another.

On a cold fall day, standing on a stoop in Brooklyn, she thought, If I leaned over the railing, I'd be able to see in.

And there he was. On the other side of the floor-to-ceiling window, about eight feet away. He was at his desk, sitting easily, as tall men do, utterly at home with pen and paper, utterly absorbed in his work. His left arm rested on the desk, hand flat and relaxed, his right hand she couldn't see, but it would have been moving steadily back and forth across the paper.

This was what she wanted for herself, this sort of concentration. She wanted to work in the same self-forgetting way. Looking in at Maurice – seeing him for the first time since his light touch on her sleeve and murmured "thanks for the birthday wishes" had sent her into exile – she realized that she wanted it even more than she wanted him.

In that moment, he turned his head to look out the window, and saw her.

Oh my. Of such moments are long humiliations made.

She watched his face skip wariness and go directly to alarm. Then he stood up and gestured that he would come to the door.

A short wait with the wind lifting up the hem of her dark green coat. She had been snooping again, and this time she'd been caught.

The door swung open and they were face to face. She was on the stoop, he was in the doorway dressed in a blue flannel shirt and the same grey pants as yesterday. But he wasn't whistling any more.

"Norma Joyce," he said, and she thought his voice couldn't have been any flatter.

"Hi." She managed a smile. "I tried to catch up to you yesterday. You came into Quality Printing."

"You were there too?" And now he at least sounded curious.

"I work there. For Frank and Hilda. Same as before." She watched to see if he would remember. "You don't remember," she said, taking a kind of strength from this desolate truth.

"Sorry," opening the door wider, "do you want to come in?"

"That's what I thought." She worked her lower lip with her teeth. "I won't come in. But I have a question."

He waited in the doorway, and she studied his hand resting on the door frame. The ring she knew so well was the only ring he was wearing. Marlon Brando's hand, she thought. *Guys and Dolls*. It was much quieter here than in Manhattan. Quieter, lighter, leafier, but no less cold. She shivered.

"At least come in out of the wind."

So then they were standing in a small lobby with four brass mailboxes and wood-panelled walls; the interior glass door was wedged open. Her question was hard to phrase until it formed itself into a blunt statement. She said, "You've never come to see your son, and he's almost eleven."

He leaned back against the mailboxes and folded his arms. "*Is* he my son?"

"You know he is, Maurice. Anyone would know. It's obvious."

To his credit, he didn't look away. He held her glance, his face pensive, sober, affected by her. The way she liked his face to be. He was silent, and she tossed him a bone. "Your business cards are going to say *writer*."

Unable to repress a smile, he said, "My first book comes out this spring." He would have said more, but a phone began to ring.

"Sorry." He pushed the wedged door open a bit more, kicked out the wedge, and motioned her through. His apartment door was on the right, and ajar. "I'll just be a minute." He waved her into the living room, then headed down the narrow hallway into the kitchen.

Norma Joyce sat down on a long sofa upholstered in light-green velvet. Clearly they had no children, and no intention of having children. Velvet! She stroked it with the flat of her hand. The room was big, well furnished, bright. On the right, next to the tall window she had looked through, was his desk, the same one he had had on West 60th. Beside it were shelves filled with books and records.

She sat listening to his light resonant voice and realized after a moment that he must be talking to his wife. There was a tone of intimate irritation that no one else could have inspired.

Maurice kept talking. "Yes, yes. I'll remember."

Norma Joyce stood up and walked over to the shelves. The records were mostly jazz and opera. *Tosca*, *The Barber of Seville*, and here was Butterfly with her powdered white face and yellow silk kimono. Butterfly wouldn't have followed Pinkerton home. She wouldn't be snooping around looking at things that didn't belong to her. Butterfly was an honourable woman. But Butterfly was also dead.

She went to his desk. The last words he had written were: "the vicissitudes of a life without brilliance."

Picking up his pen, she wrote directly below, "Through all the mist and the fog I love you."

Then she let herself out, and took the subway back to Frank and Hilda's apartment to get her son.

The following Saturday morning Maurice came to pick up his business cards, and to see her. She and Johnny were boxing up basketball flyers at the long table in the bindery just to the left of the door. And so he saw his son for the first time.

Same light blue eyes, same mouth, same smile, same long clever fingers. Even their hair, though a different colour, had the same floppy thickness. Father studied son, and Norma Joyce had the satisfaction of watching his face slowly yield to the evidence in front of him. He sat down at their table, and she noticed Frank looking curiously in their direction and felt a rush of pride. Vanity, she thinks now. Look at the handsome man I bedded.

Maurice asked her where they lived, his tone chastened – concerned – and she could feel her world opening up: the world of a woman whose son turns out to be the ace up her sleeve. She told him where, then asked if he would like to visit.

He didn't answer right away. Then he said, maybe, yes.

That night, what came into her mind was the word *leniency*. Life was showing that it could be lenient towards her.

———•———

And so the Sunday visits began. Maurice would arrive at two in the afternoon, and depending on the weather they would head to a museum or a park, usually Central Park because Johnny liked to sail his wooden sailboat on the pond no matter how cold it got. Frank had spent hours on its construction, using the *Bluenose* as

his model, and Maurice was properly impressed. The park had
more than enough to keep them occupied. Slick, bewhiskered sea
lions at the zoo; haughty llamas with yellow piano keys for teeth;
a shaggy yak, an aoudad with large curved horns, a long-furred
tahr; an orangutan in a cage. There were hills for sledding; a
carousel to disdain as being just for little kids; the chance to out-
skate everyone else at the Wollman Memorial Rink (Johnny
would copy Maurice's technique, perfected, Maurice assured
him, only after he moved from Florida to Ottawa and learned to
play hockey "when I was older than you are, and not nearly so
co-ordinated"); ice-cream vendors on hot summer afternoons;
rowboats for rent on the lake.

On these excursions, there was something about Maurice's
calm, detached, but interested presence – reassuring yet remote –
that deboned her. She was nothing but workable, expectant flesh,
aware of every inch of him beside her.

In the wintertime he wore the rumpled tweed jacket she liked
so much. "Louise says I need a new one," he said. "Louise is
wrong," she countered. In the summertime a light cotton shirt
and pants, and not shoes but sandals – resulting, by summer's
end, in a cross hatching of light and shadow on his feet, the skull
and crossbones of an interrupted tan. Once, he reached too far
for something, and she had a chance to come to his aid.

But now she's getting ahead of herself. This is the day she still
likes to relive in her mind because it has the feel of a continued
story, because it happened before the next complications began,
because of the way it ended. And it always works best if she leads
up to it slowly.

Their first outing was in November. A cold afternoon when
snatches of carousel music came on the wind and she tucked her

hands into her sleeves to keep them warm. Johnny was sailing his boat on the pond. "Here comes the *Hispaniola*," another boy cried, because it was so fast and well made.

Maurice was watching Johnny, but asking questions of her. Did she like her job at the print shop? "Surprisingly, I do. I'm good at it." Was she finding opportunities to paint? "Yes, a little every day." Did she have enough money? He could be sending her something every month. He *should* be. "We're all right, but that would help. Yes."

"Are you very angry?" he asked, turning to look at her.

She shook her head. "I don't know why. I could be, and I used to be, but I'm not."

She paused, then said, "Have you told your wife about Johnny?"

"Not yet."

"Johnny doesn't know either," she said. "I've never told him. I've never told anyone. Some people," she said, "some people choose to believe he isn't your son because of his red hair. You believed that too."

"There was a question in my mind. I'm sorry."

"You sent me that card. After he was born. Through your mother."

He flashed her a look, his eyes strained and ashamed, then looked away, and she pressed her advantage. "Are you going to talk to him?" she asked. "I think it should come from you – now that you're a part of his life. You're going to have to tell Louise too."

"I know," he said. And yes, he was going to do both. "In time."

Then he left her side and joined Johnny. With long sticks they sent the boat out across the pond, running alongside the edge to keep up. Maurice would be as relaxed with her son as he had been with her as a child. A confident, easy, transitory presence.

Only once in the months that followed would he frown with annoyance. She had asked him what Louise thought of his Sunday visits. "She's getting used to them," he said tersely.

"Are you happy together? You and Louise?"

"Louise and I are *married*," he said, wanting to forestall any more questions of that kind. But he said *married* as if he were saying *cement*; and she formed her own hopeful conclusions.

As a child, she remembers, she was drawn to anything that was closed off. She liked stones because they remained intact, as did buttons and bones. Wood was less resistant. Fabrics were weak. She was drawn to the way Maurice closed himself off too. Nothing broke his concentration in that drifting dustbowl world where inside and outside were mutually permeable. Attracted from the very first, in other words, as much to his lack of attention as to his attention; when he was absorbed in something else, she could watch him. His concentration provided room for hers.

It was an afternoon in early July when they took a picnic for three to Central Park. She remembers the clouds because they lay on their backs and watched them, she remembers his back because he peeled off his shirt, she remembers his eyes because they held that soft, easy-over slide towards desire.

White clouds were heaped up in the clean blue sky. The wind was from the east, and fresh, providing a respite between the last heat wave of June and the first heat wave of July. Johnny had his softball, and he and Maurice were throwing it back and forth. She had a blue cloth bag, which contained a blanket and their food: a Thermos of lemonade, buttered bread, cheese, and apples. They were on their way to the lake and the Ramble beyond, and Maurice as usual was pointing things out – an Osage orange tree, or a diamond pattern in the stonework of a bridge, or a curving bench that was also a sun dial. He knew the answer when they read the plaque to Balto the Alaskan sled dog, and she asked, Why? Why was the dog team transporting medicine to Nome in the winter of 1925? An outbreak of diphtheria, answered Maurice. He told them that Cleopatra's Needle, the obelisk quarried 3,500 years ago by Thothmes III, had been brought over by ship in 1880, towed on pontoons up the Hudson, then set into a great cradle and rolled on cannon balls to this very spot. Walking beside him was like walking beside a book, the word made flesh, and her pleasure equal to what it had been at Lake Clear when, on a walk through the strawberry meadow he was carefully tending to be wild and productive, he identified as cleavers the prickly stems that stuck to her legs like Cellophane, the ajuga growing around the berries, the climbing cow vetch, horsetails, Joe-pye weed, yellow wands of agrimony, fleabane, cinquefoil, frogs' bellies, jewelweed, yarrow, butter-and-eggs, moneywort, curly dock, tansy. Occasionally he bent to pull a weed, which responded to his sharp tug like a dog heeling on a leash (far more cooperative than the tangles he later tried to brush out of her hair).

The two days blended together in her mind, the afternoon in Central Park a continuation of their happiest time together. They even found some wild strawberries at their feet, growing in clusters beneath the dense shade of their thick leaves. She spread the leaves apart and here were red jewels hanging on a dark bosom, and soft air, and the sun beating down on the berries and filling the air with their smell. Remember, she said, remember the berries at Lake Clear. Wherever we walked, she said, we smelled them.

A flood of red over the course of that day – from berries, to berry-stained fingers, berry-stained clothes, berry-stained skin. She said, I remember you called it a bumper crop.

He smiled and said he couldn't keep up with her memory.

The berries were pendulous, perfect, firm but ripe. She picked some and gave them to Johnny. "And me?" Maurice asked.

"You can get your own," she teased.

They found a grassy, secluded spot in the Ramble and spread out their food on the blanket. Nearby grew some butter-and-eggs. "*Linaria vulgaris*," he said, reaching too far for a stem and crying out in pain, but proceeding to tell her anyway about the orange tip, "which acts as a honey guide for insects looking for the nectar inside."

"Turn over," she instructed.

She knelt beside him and rubbed the kink out of his back. She rubbed for a good long while. Johnny was sprawled on Maurice's other side, deep in his book. He alternated between surliness and excitability, sometimes disappearing into an adventure story, sometimes shutting himself in his bedroom for hours, sometimes clamouring for Maurice's attention and claiming him all to himself, the split in his personality between loud and shy having become a split between needy and withdrawn, and it worried her.

"It would be easier," she said to Maurice, "if you took off your shirt," and he did.

"Your neck is swarthy," she said, which made him laugh. She was thinking about the lovely glide of brown to white from thigh to buttock. She knew how easily he tanned.

When she was finished, Maurice rolled over onto his back and asked, "Where did you learn these things?" His eyes like Cary Grant's, when the woman finally registers. She was aware of Johnny, propped up on his elbows, reading a Hardy Boys book, she remembers now, because it elicited from Maurice the amused comment, "I don't know the Hardy Boys, I just know the Hardy girls."

"I used to do it for Lucinda. She had headaches. She said it helped."

Maurice said, "You must miss her."

She didn't answer right away. Mention of her sister had tugged her down a different path, and broken her concentration.

"Yes and no. We didn't have much in common, but you know that."

"I thought you were alike in a lot of ways."

Her look of surprise, and he added, "I didn't think so at first, but later on . . . the way you talked. I mean your inflections, and the long pauses." He went on. "You were both Hardys. You liked to play your cards close to your chest. Neither one of you laughed much. And your skin smelled just like hers."

Now she just stared at him.

"You weren't sisters for nothing," he said, to underscore his point.

"What do you mean, our skin smelled alike?"

"It smelled alike."

He stretched out his legs comfortably, and put his hands behind his head. "I should know. I kissed you both."

"So you did."

"Hello and goodbye. Several times, you remember."

Had the afternoon ended on this note of wounding lightness, she would have remembered it less fondly. But he reached out his hand. "Help me up," he said. She took his hand and threaded her fingers through his. She made no move to get up, and heard Maurice say, "You've changed."

"You have," he insisted when she raised a quizzical eyebrow. "You're not so intense. Not so desperate."

"*Desperate?*"

"You used to scare me half to death," he laughed. "I like you better this way."

"My new technique," she said with a droll smile.

He smiled too, but she was only speaking the truth. She had toned herself down, hoping to work upon his affections more subtly than she had in the past. She said, "You change when you're a mother," and this was also true. "I'm a lot more cautious," she said. "About everything."

"You're older."

"That's not it. It's being a mother."

He squeezed her hand. "Help me up," he said again, and Norma Joyce stood up and tugged on his arm. Once he had his shirt back on, they folded the blanket together, packed up the cloth bag. Johnny, having returned from the world of his book, was pestering Maurice to play catch.

Watching them together, Maurice and her son, it came over her that Johnny was "a wheat child," a perfect cross between herself and Maurice, just as Marquis wheat combined all the good qualities of Red Fife and Hard Red Calcutta, and none of the bad. They threw the ball back and forth, and Johnny caught it every time.

Johnny had taken the news about his father very gravely, too gravely, she knows now. Once again they had been in the park, and she had thought how handsome they were, how well they conducted themselves, how serious, with their open faces and few words on that day in late March when all but the dirtiest snow had melted away. Maurice had taken the *Hispaniola* from Johnny and set it on the bench; Johnny had leaned into his knee and listened. With Maurice, at moments like that, you could be forgiven for thinking you were in good hands. And with Johnny, when he grew up, a woman might think the same.

Her son had listened to his father, then turned to her and asked, "Is it true?"

"Yes, it's true."

He had held her eyes for a moment, but she couldn't tell what he was thinking. Then, turning back to Maurice, he wanted to know what he should call him.

"Maurice is fine. That's what we're used to."

She should have remembered herself at eleven, an age when words move out of reach. When they shut themselves behind big gates and taunt you, demanding the passport you've left behind. All Johnny would say, when she questioned him at home, was yes, he was glad Maurice was his father, "but why doesn't he live with us?"

"He told you that," she said gently. "He's married to someone else, and he lives with her."

"Why didn't he marry you?"

And here she made a mistake. She looked into her son's assessing eyes and said, as a joke, what she thought he was on the verge of thinking. "Who would want to marry *me*?" But that pair of Maurice-blue eyes looked back at her without a hint of humour.

She tried to recover. "Look. It's his bad luck that he doesn't live with us."

But all Johnny would say was, "I wish he did."

And on that perfect summer's afternoon in Central Park, she thought it still might happen: that with waiting and patience things might come right.

They were retracing their steps back to the subway and passed again the little pocket of wild strawberries – she couldn't resist bending down to pick some more. This time she said, "Open your hand," and she gave the few she'd found to Maurice. He took them from her with such a chortle of private pleasure that she asked him what he was thinking about. He shook his head. "Tell me," she insisted. And so, while Johnny tossed his ball high in the air, running forwards and backwards to catch it, Maurice told her the Indian tale about the time Old Man Coyote spied a group of women picking wild strawberries, and buried himself in the earth among some strawberry plants so that only the tip of his penis was showing. The women came along, said Maurice with a wicked smile. One of them said, "There's a big berry here, but it's different. It has deep roots." All the others came over and tried to pick it too. Some pulled at it, said Maurice, some nibbled at it. "Oh my," said one, "this berry weeps."

They were both laughing now, and he took her hand. "Another woman disagreed. She said no, it's not weeping, it has milk in it."

Johnny came over to them, wanting to know what the joke was, and Maurice ruffled his hair. The breeze picked up, the summer clouds were sweeping across the late-afternoon sky, and Maurice was holding Johnny's hand, and hers.

There would be times when she would forget his face, when she would find it hard to bring the exact details of mouth and eyes to mind, but she has never forgotten his touch. It was deft and sure, and then it was gone.

Norma Joyce didn't see him again until August because his summer vacation intervened. After that, when they got together, he was more distant and more forgetful. One day in the fall they were having an end-of-afternoon snack, the three of them, in a Schrafft's, sitting at one of the tables, even though Johnny preferred the swivel stools at the ice-cream counter. Maurice handed Norma Joyce the cream jug for her coffee, but she shook her head.

"No?" he said.

"Black. I always take my coffee black."

"I thought you took cream."

"How long have you known me?" Offended, because for nearly a year they had been rounding off their Sunday visits with danishes and coffee.

Maurice had cleared space on the table, and he and Johnny were playing poker discreetly. Their game went on while Maurice talked – in pointed detail, she realized later – about the book on roses he had written that was doing so well, and another book on the natural history of New York that he was finishing up. He said he wanted to capitalize on his knowledge of plants and climate and expand on them, creating a niche for himself as a roving nature writer with a wide appeal.

"Darwin the Second," she said dryly.

"No," correcting her even though he knew she wasn't serious. "I wouldn't write scientific treatises, even if I could. There are too many academic books that nobody reads. I want to be read. There's nothing wrong with that, is there?"

"You should write adventures," Johnny advised. "That's what I like to read. You'd be good at it."

"Scientific adventures," Maurice said. "Exactly."

"Where do you get your confidence?" she asked. "It seems boundless."

"Life is short," he said simply, "and you have to think big."

And then he dropped the first shoe. Norma Joyce wasn't sure she'd heard him properly, the restaurant was so busy. Every stool at the counter was occupied, and people were actually pressing up against a few slow eaters, encouraging them to finish. She was aware of the line-up for tables, but it didn't bother Maurice. He repeated himself. He had received a Fulbright scholarship to Oxford. Post-doctorate work. He would have time to do research, renew his contacts at Kew Gardens, find an English publisher. A marvellous opportunity. How could he say no?

"Easy," she said. "The way you said no to me."

He studied her while he chewed. Then picked up his cards with his left hand and studied them.

Johnny said, "You're going away?"

"Not for good," Maurice reassured him. "Don't worry."

She looked away, to families eating blintzes or cheesecake, to mothers and fathers, brothers and sisters, aunts and uncles, all bright and bossy and well fed. She looked back at Maurice, and disregarding Johnny, said quietly, "So you're leaving us in the lurch again."

He put down his danish. He wiped his fingers. He said, "Maybe this time I can make it up to you."

And there was the surge of hope. It shot up inside her so suddenly that her hands trembled and she spilled her coffee.

"How?"

"Give me a little more time," he said, looking searchingly into her face. "I'm working on it."

How carefully she dressed during that period of a year when she saw him every Sunday. How thoroughly she scrubbed her inky hands, plucked her eyebrows, shaved her legs, tried out new shades of lipstick – always feeling the sort of anticipation that makes the air crackle around you.

(Why *my* shop? she asked him once. Why didn't you go to some print shop in Brooklyn? And he explained that it was accidental, he'd been on his way to his publisher's, he'd had a few minutes to spare. And so it would always be: she was on his unconscious route.)

Seated across from her a few weeks later, before she had even had time to adjust to the news of his departure, he dropped the other shoe. He said he wanted to adopt Johnny.

Lunchtime, and just the two of them, and he began to talk about schools in England and all the advantages Johnny would have. "It would be a wonderful opportunity," he said, "and besides, it's my turn to shoulder some responsibility. You've been doing it on your own for too long."

She sat stunned, but if he realized he pretended not to. "You've been a tower of strength," he said. "Johnny's a great kid, and you've been wonderful with him."

This was too much. "So everything's wonderful. To coin a word." Her voice was full of bile.

Maurice leaned back in his chair, putting a bit more distance between them. Then he rubbed the back of his neck with his hand. "You're angry."

"For a smart man," she said, "you're not too bright."

He looked offended, then foolish, then a bit sullen. "We both want the best for Johnny. I don't mean to interfere, but I'm thinking of his long-term interests. You have to admit –"

As she watched his face and listened to his reasonable voice, a sense of loss so painful welled up inside her that she reached across the table and pressed her hand over his mouth, hard enough that he pushed her arm away.

She tugged her jacket off the back of her chair and put it on. An elderly man bumped into her on his way out and she grabbed the table to steady herself.

"Norrie?" said Maurice, half standing. "Don't go. Stay and talk. Are you all right?"

"No," she said. "I'm not."

He didn't follow her. She walked back to work, down the three steps and through the glass door into the print shop in the cellar.

———◦———

Now when she looks back she has the sense of having succumbed, even as she carried on. Of having let herself become small in that huge city. She was a badger scurrying along, nose to the ground, intent on avoiding the wealth of possibilities that loomed above. The Hardy crouch, Maurice once joked when she sprang at a nickel on the sidewalk.

In New York City there was nothing sustaining – what was it Maurice had said of Maria Chapdelaine? She'll have moments of happiness but no sustained happiness? – there was nothing sustaining in her life. She darted back and forth between apartment and work, raising her son singlehandedly (though with the help of Maurice's cheques), staying with her job out of need and loyalty and something else: some undercurrent between herself and Frank that consoled her, especially after Maurice went away.

But nothing else, she thinks now, except her prairie talent for isolation, a sort of self-ostracism that grew naturally out of her childhood.

In bookstores she saw his face. She didn't buy his books (soon there were two), out of some wounded, deep-down resistance; but she read the titles: *Following the Scent*, his history of old roses that traced their progress around the world, and *A Naturalist in Manhattan*, his urban guide to natural history. She looked at the dedications: to his parents, to Louise. She studied the photographs of the author on the back. In his flannel shirt, in one case, and his tweed jacket in the other, he looked younger than he was, his expression more studied than she liked: on view again, in a way she found most unsatisfactory. But then she had always liked him least in the company of others – when his smiles had a way of going in too many directions – when he nodded and said,

Indeed, indeed – when he lost his concentration and scattered into pleasantness, into nothing but surface.

Once, leafing through a book about writers, Norma Joyce saw a picture of someone else she recognized. The same unassuming but interested eyes, the same small moustache and large ears, the same tie. This little man, who had identified the colour of her coral rose in the subway so many years ago, was E.B. White. His *Charlotte's Web* a book she had read to Johnny more than once.

Strange, the way paths cross and keep crossing. An old friend from the Prairies has resurfaced on her father's street, in a coincidence as startling as the one years ago, when another echo from their Prairie past came crackling over the kitchen radio. It was that unforgettable New Brunswick honk. *Dad! Norma! Listen!* Northrop Frye, the young preacher who had travelled on horseback in the early thirties, was talking about William Blake.

Afterwards, her sister had bought a copy of Frye's *Fearful Symmetry*, only to fall asleep over it night after night until it became a joke. Where's my soporific? Lucinda would ask. Johnny would have been about two.

Now he was nearly thirteen, taller, and as gloomy as his grandfather since Maurice had gone away. When he wasn't at school, he was inside, reading. He lacked a circle of friends, just as she did, and might easily be on his way to becoming a recluse, like herself. On Saturdays he still came to the shop. Frank was teaching him the trade and paying him an hourly wage. With Frank and Hilda he was his old self, but with her he had become moody and unreachable.

And he was haunting the mailbox in the vestibule down the hall.

One day, after seeing him go out into the hallway like a puppy and come back like a whipped dog, she tried to sit down beside him on the sofa. "Make room for me," she said, and then he moved his feet. He was already two inches taller than she was and his feet were enormous. They hit the floor with a clunk.

"You miss him," she said with a sigh.

"I don't know why he had to go," he muttered. He was rolling his upper lip under so that it rested on his top teeth, over and over again. "What's in England anyway."

"Don't," she said, and he stopped. "The queen," she joked, but he didn't smile. She said, "Maurice has never been one to turn down an opportunity." But that hardly cheered her son. She tried again. "It isn't that he doesn't care about you."

His face was stony.

"He does care about you."

"No, he doesn't." In a tone of disgust.

"He wanted to take you with him. That's how much he cares about you."

Those twelve-year-old eyes swung up and caught her in their harsh high beams, and she realized she should have asked him if he wanted to go. Oh Lord, she thought. He would have said yes.

"Johnny?"

And then she had the pain of watching him turn away completely, like a young plant towards a more interesting sun, knowing that she was the one who had put him in the window.

After that, he was barely civil to her. She didn't know how often he wrote to Maurice, but the replies came steadily, about twice a month. He squirreled them away.

She made one barefaced attempt to win him back. She suggested they do something together again, the way they used to.

"We never did anything together."

"Yes we did," she said patiently. "We used to make things. Remember? Remember the Plasticine figures we made? A whole set of cowboys and Indians. We had battles on the kitchen table."

But he said no, he didn't remember any of that.

She stared at him, dumbfounded. But he seemed to mean exactly what he said.

One night, some months later, she found herself standing in his bedroom doorway, watching him sleep. They were in the middle of a heat wave. Johnny lay naked on his bed except for his underwear – such a long drink of water, this son of hers – and she could sense her love for him – the shape of it, the gist of it, even its place in her life – but the love itself wouldn't come, except in the scraping, chafing, unhappy way of a particular word that refuses to surface.

She doesn't understand how memory works, and she's not looking for an explanation. She *is* interested, though, in what happens when something nearly gets forgotten, only to raise its hand and pull itself back up into the light.

Maurice had two more surprises for her. The first arrived after he had been in England for more than a year, his stay extended, as it would be again. Sky-blue, tissue-paper thin, sealed up the sides and addressed, this time, to Norma Joyce Hardy.

She opened it and read,

> *Green rushes with red shoots,*
> *Long leaves bending to the wind –*
> *You and I in the same boat*
> *Plucking rushes at the Five Lakes.*

We started at dawn from the orchid-island:
We rested under the elms till noon.
You and I plucking rushes
Had not plucked a handful when night came!

Nothing else, except her name at the top and his at the bottom, and the source of the poem in brackets after his name. (An anonymous Chinese poem translated by Arthur Waley.) He was still wooing by Waley.

She had received her first poem.

Her pleasure was so profound that it actually changed the way she looked. Hilda said, "Somebody's had a good night's sleep. Or have you cut your hair? You've cut your hair!"

"I didn't cut my hair," laughing and giving Hilda a kiss on the cheek. "I shaved off my beard." And it was wonderful to hear Hilda's giggle of delight.

Norma Joyce caught Frank looking at her, and when she smiled back, he ducked his head – befuddled, embarrassed, exposed, and somehow pleased.

Maybe she should have replied to Maurice with Elizabeth Barrett Browning instead of letting her feelings rip, but for ten pages she poured out her heart, reminding him of everything there was between them, from the first moment, when she removed her mitten and put her hand on his cheek, to the last. "Johnny misses you so much," she wrote, "and so do I." She told him how often he appeared in her dreams, and how erotic the dreams were. She reminded him of her warm and supple hands, and worked herself into quite a pleasant froth detailing the round of delights that awaited him.

When he didn't answer, she wrote again. And then again, not

realizing that men often cast back to the previous woman before casting forward to the next.

Then once again.

Until a quiet letter from him, a few months later, put an end to all of that.

It was her habit in those days to venture out into the city. One day she ended up in Riverside Park, where she stared across the Hudson River at New Jersey on the opposite shore, before clambering down among the rocks that lined the riverbank. Men and boys liked to spend hours fishing in one spot, half-hidden by raspberry bushes and wild roses. Here, unbroken by the vertical thrust of steel and glass, the sky was larger and she could watch the weather come in from the west.

Maurice had told her years ago that the world would not exist if it hadn't been for bad weather: an initial storm, followed by subsequent storms, that threw up different forms of life.

Bad weather, she thought, and the forbidden. That's what gets things started. And what brings them to an end? Car crashes and quiet letters.

His was dated May 10, 1961. He missed Johnny too, he wrote, but "soon we'll be able to see each other again on a regular basis." (Nasty phrase. Bills appeared on a regular basis. Examinations got written on a regular basis.) "I'll be moving back to New York next year," he wrote, "and bringing with me someone I want him to meet. You must have guessed that Louise and I weren't happy. Now she's met someone else, and so have I."

A stunning reversal, had she been Napoleon.

She felt like her father during the 1930s, cursed with the blessing of persistence. Like her father she had been ploughing a dry field, and like him, she had known better.

It couldn't have been long after that when Frank invited her to come with him to *Turandot*. It would do her good, he said. Hilda and Johnny can handle the shop for an afternoon, you're looking pale. We've been worried about you.

On a Saturday, after lunch, they walked together to the yellow-brick opera house on 39th Street, entering through one of the side-street vestibules and climbing the stairs to the Family Circle at the top. Once they had found their places, she went to the edge of the balcony to revel in the elegance of the hall. The five rising tiers of seats, the maroon-and-gold walls, the baroque ceiling and sunburst chandelier, the proscenium arch with its curved shoulders, the great gold curtain. Using Frank's field glasses, she read the names of the composers written on the gilded plaques set into the proscenium arch: Gluck, Mozart, Verdi, Wagner, Gounod, Beethoven. Then she turned the glasses on the audience, to see what they were wearing. It was a game, to count up minks and sables the way Johnny used to count up pips in his grapefruit.

Her seat was on Frank's left. Having read the program, she was thinking uncharitably about icy Princess Turandot and her use of riddles to avoid love, when Frank surprised her by lifting her hand off her lap and examining not the palm but the back of her hand.

"Cats?"

"Raspberries," she said. "I found some bushes along the Hudson River."

"It's too late for raspberries."

"I was after one dark red stem."

Then he did something even more unexpected. He raised her hand to his lips and kissed the scratches. His lips – those wet-looking lips – were warm and dry. Then he put her hand back into her lap, but nothing was the same after that. Something very soft had turned over inside her.

She was the one who took things further. She invited him to come home with her, and when he turned off the bedside lamp she turned it back on. "I want to see you," she said.

She saw: ropey, loose-skinned whiteness. His penis semi-erect and gently turned at the tip, rather like a Jack pinecone. The patches of thin hair on his chest and thighs, the hairless calves. His eyes defenceless without his glasses.

His penis had such an odd sad turn at the end, like a shepherd's crook, or the beginning of a question mark. Their hands were of a matching inkiness.

Frank turned off the light, and that helped. He ran his hand from her shoulder across her breasts over her stomach and between her thighs, and that helped even more. He marvelled at the smoothness of her skin. He said she was beautiful. "Say that again," she said. He stroked her everywhere. Then he put his hand under her buttocks and lifted her on top of him. And later he entered her, exquisitely, from behind.

"You remind me of Darwin," she said when she was lying very close beside him on the narrow bed.

"No beard."

"My dog." She grinned at him. "It's a compliment. He was a wonderful dog."

They were always careful. Hilda could have guessed only from an increase in Frank's patience, a lessening of Norma Joyce's irritability. Johnny, locked into his teenage thoughts, his teenage doings, wasn't paying attention to his mother. He had made a friend in ninth grade who lived a block away, and now he spent as much time at Tom's place as at his own.

Frank was sixty. Twenty-eight years older than she was. They saw each other every day, but had to manufacture opportunities to be alone. This was reason enough, had she not wanted a change from painting and drawing anyway, to begin making her small assemblages. They required Frank's help. He made the open-faced shoebox-sized cabinets in his workshop at home, then brought them over on Sunday afternoons. She called them her window boxes because they were miniature versions of display windows, homes for things she had picked up off the street, or found in the park, or made. Frank said they were doll's houses without the dolls or the furniture. Doll's houses invaded by nature: by the tattered leaves, dead bees and shiny beetles, birds' nests and bark she had been saving for years. She furnished her window-box rooms with the leftovers of the natural world.

Maybe having sex greased her creative wheels. In any case, she entered a period of considerable productivity, finding again, as she had on the Prairies, salvation in small things.

She painted as well. Laundry hanging outside; flowerpots; old shoes; a coffee pot full of peonies beside a wood stove of equal size; interiors brightened by bits of real wallpaper or cloth; coal-oil lamps; tabletops littered with domestic debris; polar bears at the zoo; trees in bud; view after view of Central Park. In some of her paintings she used chips of crockery, bits of bone, feathers, hair: touches that appealed to her literal mind. She found the twigs she picked up and set on her windowsill as interesting as anything she could imagine, the variation in line simple but endless.

A few years later she would look at her little pieces on the wall and say to Johnny, "If I were a man, I'd paint huge canvases. The smaller the man, the bigger the canvases. Have you noticed that? But I'm not a man."

"You're a monk," said Johnny.

She found this very funny, and Johnny grinned too. He was sixteen now, and not nearly so disgusted with his dull wren of a mother since Maurice had come back and taken him under his dazzling wing. He was spending every Sunday in Brooklyn with his father and stepmother. On Saturdays, he continued to work for Frank and Hilda.

What a tableau we must have made, she thinks, picturing the Saturday afternoons in the shop and the suppers they had afterwards. Years of meals eaten at the nearest Howard Johnson's, because Hilda liked their chicken pot pie and Johnny their vanilla shakes. By the time Johnny was eighteen, Hilda had finished her seven hundred and fiftieth quilt, and Frank, out of who knows what desire for atonement, had given her a mink coat. Hilda would sit in the orange booth with her fur draped loosely over her shoulders until the food arrived, and then she would get up, fold the coat very carefully, and put it at the far end of the booth, out of harm's way. "If I saved it for special I'd never wear it period," she said.

One evening, after Norma Joyce said Howard Johnson's never looked so classy as when she was in it, Hilda replied, "You know, you can borrow it if you're ever stepping out."

"You know me, Hilda. I don't step out."

"No? Well, you should." And there was something in her tone that made Norma Joyce take a second look at this motherly wisp of a woman. She saw the tilt of her head, the unforced calmness, the expression in those hurt, unsuspicious eyes, and a week later, as they were lying side by side, she said to Frank, "Let's not do this any more."

She heard him let out a big sigh.

There was a long silence. Then he said, "I remember the first day you walked into the shop."

"Me too."

"You had on a grey dress. I thought you were some kind of orphan."

She laughed and propped herself up on one elbow to look at him. "Such a beauty. Johnny calls me a monk. You call me an orphan."

"You're beautiful to me," he said.

What a warm, sad, amused smile she gave him.

He reached for his trousers, took out his wallet, and showed her the snapshot he'd been carrying around all these years, taken when she had been seven months' pregnant and about to go back to Ottawa – his recklessness tempered by the snapshots of Johnny and Hilda that followed.

Dear Frank.

But she couldn't help saying, "Aren't you afraid Hilda will see that picture?"

"She's not the sort who snoops."

"I am."

"No, you're not."

"I am, Frank. I'm the kind who reads other people's private mail. I'm the kind who sleeps with other women's husbands."

He stroked her hair, then her face.

"I'm a disloyal sneak."

"You're as loyal as they come."

———◆———

The last time her father drove down to see them was the Christmas when Johnny was twenty, and already living on his own. This was in 1967, the year the city of Ottawa gave away crabapple trees to commemorate dear old Canada's one-hundredth birthday. Ernest told them he had planted one in the front yard and one in the back over Chops's grave, an old dog by the time he died under Ernest's bed, taking refuge from the thunderous fireworks on Queen Victoria's birthday. Norma Joyce imagined the trees flourishing, year after year, adding their blossoms to those of the other apple trees, whose bouquet was already so abundant that when you went upstairs in the month of May you walked into Abraham's fiery bush, so completely were the walls bathed in reddish-pink.

She knew, from what Ernest said when he wrote to her, that Mother Hulder was the one who kept an eye on things, bringing over casseroles and talking his ear off while he ate in silence. Her father had no patience for Mother H.'s endless talk, for the soft mud of her questions and answers, the unclipped long grass of her drawn-out directionless murmurings. No doubt he was skilled at cutting her off. "Thank you for supper, must be off," she could hear him saying as he headed for the bathroom.

It was Mother Hulder who phoned to tell her about his heart attack. The call came in August of 1971, when Ernest was eighty-one years old; he would need full-time care. Norma Joyce would have to go home, whether Ernest wanted her or not.

Johnny helped her pack. They had what she called a grand hoeing-out, a cleaning so thorough that even Lucinda would have been impressed. She felt her sister in every flick of the dustcloth, as bare surfaces appeared and box after box got carted into the hall.

Johnny would stay in the apartment while she was gone. For several years he had been sharing a place with two other anthropology students at Columbia University. He wasn't unhappy to leave their joint mess behind.

They went through her stacks of watercolours and drawings, small studies, still lifes, oils. The figures made out of clay and papier mâché. The window boxes. What a lot there was, when you got down to it.

"When did you do so much stuff?" Johnny asked.

"When you weren't looking," she said.

"No, I mean it. You could open up a store. You could sell them. Or take them to a gallery. Why don't you take them to a gallery?"

"What gallery? I don't know anybody. You need to know people."

"You're like Frank," he said. He meant that Frank liked things the way they were. People came to him every so often suggesting he expand the shop or combine efforts with another firm, but Frank was content to work steadily and unheralded at what he did well.

"I wish I were like Frank," she said, "but I'm not."

She didn't really understand her deep reluctance to put herself on display – to search out a gallery and market her work. It's true that for a while she didn't have time. Johnny regulated her days and nights, as children do. But after that? Perhaps there was the desire to prove Lucinda wrong. If she were as self-serving and cut-throat as Lucinda believed, she wouldn't be living like this. Or maybe she needed that old rivalry to whip her along. Maybe, for all she wanted to believe otherwise, she wasn't anything unless she had a sister to rub the wrong way, an opposite to butt up against.

"I like them," Johnny was saying of a stack of watercolours he'd taken down from a shelf.

"Don't sound so surprised."

"I'm impressed," he said, and she leaned over and kissed him on the head.

"Take one," she said. "Take as many as you want."

"You need an agent," he said.

"I do it to keep myself company. An agent is not what I need."

"I know what your problem is," he said. He gave her a long look with his light blue eyes. "You're a landscape painter."

"What's wrong with being a landscape painter?"

"Don't get touchy. I just mean it's hard to be a landscape painter if you're living in New York."

"My son the genius," she said, and she meant it.

Later, Johnny pulled several boxes of papers and pho-tographs out from under her bed, and soon he was asking, "What about this? And this?"

Then, "What about these?"

Each time, she looked up and made a quick decision about whether to toss or to keep, but this time her face underwent a change. She stretched out her hand and he gave her the letters.

They were small, off-white, time-softened. As serene as a jack-in-the-box. A visual kick in the teeth.

"Do you remember Lucinda?" she asked him.

"A little. She used to give me a nickel for sweeping up the hair clippings on the floor."

Norma Joyce smiled. Then she looked thoughtfully at her son. "Has Maurice ever mentioned her?"

He shook his head. "He asks about you, though. He always wants to know how you are."

"Does he now?" And despite herself, her voice was eager.

"He told me once he thought you were remarkable."

Astonishingly, she felt her heart lighten and a smile come unbidden to her lips. She could live on crumbs, it seemed.

Who was it – Matonabbee? – who boasted that his women could survive on the food they licked off the spoon that stirred his pot? A remark she'd come across in a book about the far north, and never forgotten. A fantastic statement; no less so when applied to love.

Norma Joyce returned to Ottawa in September, thinking it would be easy. But returning is never easy, and nor is September. There's something in the air, some deep disturbance from which October with its colour and unexpected warmth provides a reprieve, but to which September is all open. All falling towards. The light is different, and the crickets never cease.

Emerging from a taxi at about three in the afternoon, to stand on the sidewalk in front of her father's house, she felt caught in the molten dusty chalklight of school. In the foolscap glare of one of Mrs. Graviston's sprung tests. It got her in the eye, the high nervous forehead, the murky heart. It sliced her open, and oh the shock, to be seen so clearly by the light.

From dark New York to this.

She shielded her eyes, and there was Mother H., bigger than ever despite her little-girl voice, filling her father's doorway. All dressed up in a pleated frock and white pumps as if going out for tea.

"Welcome back to the thirties," sang out Mother H., and Norma Joyce didn't have a clue what the old dame meant. But now she does. Now the words seem uncanny, as if Mother Hulder knew all along what lay in store.

In the hallway, setting down her bags, she heard her father's cane. Was he coming to meet her?

No. He was headed to the kitchen. There she found him, seated at the table, waiting for his tea.

"Hello, Dad," bending to kiss a cheek as smooth as warm glass. He smelled like muffins. "How are you feeling?"

"Old," he said.

Mother H., busy with the kettle, and talking in that floaty, roundabout way of hers, told her that someone named Vera cleaned and shopped for Ernest twice a week, that the squirrels were eating all the bulbs, shame on them, and that someone else whose name she could never remember came twice a week.

"Doris," said Ernest. "Three times a week." He hadn't looked her in the eye, or bid her welcome, and she could guess what he was thinking. That she should have stayed in New York and minded her own business.

She had come back to look after her father, a man she had never much cared for. And why? It seems obvious now. As if every move she made through fall, winter, and spring led here, to a day in late May when cleaning house has produced not merely a sense of virtue but actual booty: something to open and gaze at in wonder, as a shared past floods her eyes.

But in September she thought her only reward would be the more limited one of proving herself capable of at least one act of loyalty.

Her father's bedroom was the dining room, made over. In

one corner a toilet and sink had been installed. "This makes sense," she said to Mrs. Hulder.

"It had to be," came the reply.

A single bed with a bedside table, an armchair with a footstool and a standing lamp, a low dresser, and, on the dresser, the silver oval frame that used to contain the photograph of her mother, but now held a picture of Lucinda.

"Where did it go? The picture of my mother?"

It was evening. Ernest had settled into the armchair in his room with a mug of tea beside him, milk, no sugar, and Norma Joyce was examining the photograph on the dresser.

She had already investigated her sister's room upstairs, half expecting a shrine, but the closet was empty. A few books were on the shelves. The surface of the dresser was bare; its drawers were empty too. She felt her sister in the room, though, as a reproach: a headache coming on, a page that refuses to turn, a story that needs a different ending.

Ernest pointed with his chin. "In behind."

She turned over the frame. The blue velvet backing had worn thin. She undid the tiny metal hinge, then with the edge of her finger raised up the back – its blue silk underside was still unfaded – and eased her mother out from behind Lucinda. She looked at both pictures: Lucinda in the frame, her mother in her hand. A similar age, she thought. Late twenties, early thirties.

In her mother's face there was a sense of purpose and repose. In Lucinda's face something given over, something weak, or off balance, unless all she was seeing was her own lack of sympathy.

Two beautiful women.

She sat down on her father's bed and continued to study their faces.

"What was she like? My mother?"

He shifted away from her in his chair, and his lips tightened. Oh, how he hated to be questioned, this proud, taciturn, deeply conservative man so used to giving orders, first on his farm, where others did his bidding, and then in his orchards, recently sold, where again he was in command.

"Am I anything like her?"

Now that Ernest had one question he could pointedly ignore, he was willing to address the other. Everything on his terms, she thought.

He said, "Your mother was unlucky too."

He picked up his mug. His swallows were loud but his sips were louder. He sucked in tea like a vacuum cleaner, his neck the pleated hose. She could have circled it with her two small hands, so thin and scrawny had it become.

Then, in a change of tone that surprised and beguiled her, he mused, "Maybe I got in your mother's way. She would have been happier in the city."

Norma Joyce had always thought so.

"I don't suppose you got in her way. Circumstances did. Back then everybody's luck was rotten."

"You make your luck," Ernest said.

"You don't really believe that, do you?"

But it was the wrong question asked in the wrong way. A challenging question asked too aggressively. He wouldn't dignify it with an answer.

In the morning, before breakfast, she went for a short walk under high sunlight so rich and golden it set the treetops shimmering. Looking around her at the houses, the gardens, the graceful trees and large sky, she realized how starved she was for the natural world. How hungry she was for leaves, grass, laneway, the slope of a low roof, the angle of a hedge, the sag of a wooden fence. Not just the natural world, but a simpler world.

She walked on. Then stopped again to look. If she tilted her head way back, she could see straight up through tall shade into an umbrella of pure light.

But then it clouded over, and later began to rain.

When she opened the curtains in Ernest's room, he said, "Gloomy."

She helped him dress. He had trouble getting his right arm into his sleeve, and each button was a chore. When he tucked in his shirt, he held his fingers flat, thumbs folded into his palms, a habit formed from his days on the farm when his thumbs split open in the cold, dry air.

In the kitchen he stood looking out at the rain. She stood beside him and said, "I can't see rain without feeling grateful," and he snorted, "We're not in Saskatchewan any more."

Surely she had fallen in love with Maurice because he was so different from Ernest. The one, a merciful, unstrained presence who had the rare gift of never trying too hard, of letting people be themselves, of winning without appearing to compete. The other, an overbearing, critical, despondent man who took everything personally. Who relished disappointments, because they proved him right.

"You and I are so alike," she said.

He turned away from the window and came to the table where she was sitting. "I don't see how," he said, pulling back his chair and sitting down.

"Impatience," she said. "Self-disgust."

"I always thought your sister and I were alike," accepting the plate of toast with a mild glance in her direction. "But maybe you're right."

How little it took. Just that. Just that slight bending tone – that widening-out of thought – and she was willing to do just about anything for him.

Then, as if thinking about Maurice had conjured him up, an hour later she saw him.

What a strange shock. In the middle of the entertainment page, and next to a brisk review of a local art show, a picture of Maurice Dove looking half his age: shirt open at the throat, disarmingly lit-up boy-smile. Her eyes devoured the picture and then the article. His fifth book, apparently, and over the next few months he'd be promoting it, a popular history of the grasslands of North America based on years of travel and research.

An old paper, September 10. She had spread it open on the kitchen table to catch the apple peelings, because what was she doing? She was making her father an apple pie. A bid for approval so naked that even now – though it's only eight months later – she shakes her head in disbelief.

Ernest was paring the fruit just as he had always done for Lucinda, taking pride in producing from each apple one long unbroken peel.

"Look," she pointed with her knife. "Maurice Dove."

He looked. "Now there's a man who's done well for himself," he pronounced. "I always thought he would," paring steadily, slowly, perfectly on, despite his shaky hands.

She sliced, and sliced her finger. A drop of blood fell on the apple's white flesh. Garnet red on pure white. And she thought of Maurice's lips, which turned red whenever he ate an apple – a susceptibility to anything tart, she thought – anything, she thought tartly, except for me. And she found herself wishing that she could see him.

———◆———

The landscape was the same. Beyond the back porch, the ancient slope led up to the old Dove house, which was built on the shore of a glacial lake, *while your house*, Maurice had told her once, *is in the vanished water*. Through the old Dove windows, enlarged but still uncurtained, she saw a slender mother at the sink, a father who arrived home at six, a curly-headed girl at the kitchen table, and a dark-haired boy.

Especially in the first weeks, she would go down the porch steps into the garden and run her hand over sturdy geraniums (releasing their strong, eager scent), over feathery cosmos, tough parsley, scratchy brown-eyed Susans. She liked to feel the uneven lawn underfoot, the give and take of stone pathway, leaf-strewn flowerbed, patched-up sidewalk. To watch the leaves and clouds for colour and movement. To follow the lane-way to the street and the street to the river, where everything was so much the same, and yet so different, that she felt both relieved and confused.

September, she remembers, turned cold and stayed cold until the last day. Then there were several warm days in a row. On one of them, she was sitting outside in the green Muskoka chair, still delighted at being able to move so easily between inside and outside, whether it was early or late, and without having to run a gauntlet of locks, when Mrs. Hulder leaned over the fence and said, "For one second, I thought you were Lucinda. Poor Lucinda. The Lord always takes the good ones. I don't know why."

Norma Joyce didn't know either. But she felt her small, dark child of a mistake climb up on her back.

You come home and fall away from yourself. The recent past disappears and the distant past comes forward. Her son was six years old again and the last few years were a blur. It felt like a form of senility, in which life was both in and out of focus: a pair of glasses so new they gave her a headache. And, aching, she surveyed the years in New York – unable to account for the waste – while her childhood reared its vivid head. An early adolescence so strong and defining that she had never really left it behind.

Mother H. liked to arrive mid-morning, unannounced, and with "a little something for the larder," like butter tarts so sweet they made your teeth ache. Or fudge.

"We'll send her our dental bills," Norma Joyce said to her father.

Their sweet-toothed neighbour appeared in the garden the same way, when you weren't expecting her, and had the same unwelcome effect.

One afternoon Norma Joyce was picking apples under a most dramatic sky. All of it – the high banner of light blue, the pelting black clouds, the low, slanting light – all of it was suffused with radiance, dusty gold or beaten gold or both. The earth had tipped like a plate, and was spilling colour and light from gorgeous ceiling to gorgeous floor.

For a moment, rain fell while the sun shone, and Mother H. materialized beside the fence. She said, "An old woman is getting married."

"You're getting married?"

Out came her little-girl laugh. "When the sun shines and it's raining, an old woman is getting married, that's what they say."

"So is it going to be you or me?" asked Norma Joyce.

"Oh, it's not going to be *you*," said Mother Hulder.

Ridiculous, hurtful old woman.

But it was Mother H. who told her about the old friend living in one of the rowhouses on Carlyle Avenue, just two houses down from "the old Dove place," as everyone still called it, since Maurice Dove was the neighbourhood's most famous son. Mother Hulder was unveiling her butterscotch squares and Norma Joyce was saying, "Now listen to me. You're eating too much sugar," and in reply she heard, "That's what Mrs. Gallot says too."

"Mrs. Gallot?"

"She claims to know you."

Norma Joyce swung around on her father. "Why didn't you tell me?"

"Her daughter lives here," said Mrs. Hulder, "and one of her sons. That's why she came."

So that afternoon Norma Joyce picked more apples, selecting the best ones to take to Mrs. Gallot's back door, where she received a resounding welcome from a small dumpling of a woman in a full black skirt and floral sweater, with curly grey hair, glasses hanging on a black cord around her neck, hands busy expressing delight.

"New York has been good to you! Look at you. New York–French. Your hair, your shoes. I'm so happy to see you, my dear," kissing her again on both cheeks.

"Audrey Hepburn shoes," laughed Norma Joyce, raising her foot in its flat, narrow, black leather shoe.

"Yes, *yes*," said Mrs. Gallot with delight. "And a dancer's chignon," admiring the dark hair parted in the middle and pulled back into a bun at the nape of Norma Joyce's neck. At forty-two Norma Joyce's face was round, her forehead as high as ever, her neck surprisingly long. Silver earrings in the shape of shells covered most of her soft, oversized earlobes.

They sat down at a kitchen table spread with a hand-embroidered cloth (blue cross-stitch on white), and Norma Joyce said, "This is the sort of thing my sister could do in her sleep."

"She was a lovely girl," said Mrs. Gallot. "We never know, do we, what's in store."

"No," said Norma Joyce, "we don't." She asked about Ginny, and learned that she was living in Toronto after a second bout of cancer, but she seemed to be fine, "touch wood and God bless her because she is the sweetest, purest human being on the face of the earth." She asked about Darwin, and learned that he had lived to a ripe old age. One night he failed to come in to be fed, and the next day they found him under a pile of straw in a corner of the barn.

She was apprised of Mrs. Gallot's other children: her young-est daughter Natalie lived in Ottawa, with three children, as did

Mickey with his two, "which is why I moved here ten years ago. To be useful.

"Now," folding her hands and putting them on the table, "tell me about you, Norma Joyce. Are you painting?"

"I paint. Yes. When I have time. I don't sell anything though. I seem to paint for the closet."

"But it makes you happy."

"It used to make me happier."

Mrs. Gallot looked at her with sharp, kind eyes. "Ginny's taken up ceramics since being sick. Not that she has your talent for that kind of thing."

"You're the only one who ever thought I had talent, and I love you for it."

When Norma Joyce stood up to leave, Mrs. Gallot offered to show her the rest of the house, and she noticed the game of Scrabble underway on the dining room table. "Bella and I like to play," said Mrs. Gallot. Her boarder Bella Pugg, from Winnipeg. A real live wire who was studying at Carleton University, and managed to write for the *Citizen* too. "You have to meet her." And, as it happened, she did.

"We accept words in English *or* French. This one is both," pointing to *vestiges*.

"A good word," said Norma Joyce.

"Bella's, not mine."

They proceeded into the living room, where Norma Joyce recognized the black walnut furniture her father had sold along with the farm, but what she felt drawn to was something else. A watercolour on the wall, of wildflowers arranged in a silver vase against a pale green wash. Every line perfectly placed. The colours most delicately applied.

"Who did this?" she asked. "It's beautiful."

"Your mother did that."

Mrs. Gallot was standing beside her.

My mother. She looked at Mrs. Gallot in wonder.

"In the attic I found a chest *full*," she said. "*Full* of her sketches and watercolours. He never told you?" Norma Joyce shook her head and turned back to her mother's watercolour. *My mother.*

"I kept this one, and shipped the rest to your father."

"Were they all this good?"

"I thought they were. I thought they were very good. There were some of you – reading. Well, maybe not reading. You were sitting with a book. There was a drawing of you and your brother. How old was he when he died?"

"Almost two." She scrutinized Mrs. Gallot. "They were in the attic?"

"I thought he must have forgotten them. I wrote to him. Twice. A letter, then a Christmas card. Then I just packed them up and sent them. You never saw them?"

"I don't think they exist. Maybe they never arrived."

"There were some nudes," Mrs. Gallot said. "Completely innocent. We had no models. Your mother drew herself in front of a mirror." Then she lifted the watercolour off the wall. "You should have this," she said. "I've enjoyed it for a long time. Now it's your turn."

After Norma Joyce left Mrs. Gallot's house, and came down the steps to the street, she stood for a moment gazing around at a neighbourhood her mother had never seen.

Carlyle Avenue formed a T with Pansy Street, so named for its previous life as a flower-lined laneway leading to the old brick farmhouse, behind her, but hemmed in now by other houses. Looking to the end of the leafy street, the trees entering their period of fullest beauty, her mother's picture tucked under her arm, she felt like a berth into which a boat has just slipped. The telling nudge as two things, which have been apart, come together.

Later, after they sat down to a supper of meatloaf and baked potatoes, she said, "Mrs. Gallot gave me one of my mother's pictures."

Ernest raised his old, watery eyes from his plate. They were the last gasp of blue. She reached across the table and dropped a small pat of butter onto his baked potato. "What happened to all the rest?" she asked.

He began to eat.

"Mrs. Gallot said she sent a trunkful of them to you. Where are they?"

"Your sister handled that," he said. "I don't know what she did with them."

"So the trunk arrived."

"Your sister dealt with that."

"Ernest." She leaned towards him. "This is important."

"There wasn't much," he said. "Your mother didn't do much. A few drawings. They weren't anything special. She said so herself."

"You threw them out." Her voice was very quiet.

"It wasn't a trunk," and he kept on eating.

She pushed her plate to one side. She stood up but her head throbbed. She sat down again.

"You and Lucinda threw them out."

Her father ate slowly, steadily, thoroughly on. The King of Chewers. She listened to him, and her eyes filled with tears.

So she shook her head to stop the flow, and squinted hard at the yellow-and-orange papered walls, the cupboards painted white, the yellow countertop speckled with grey flecks, the window above the sink in which the old dishpan with the red rim still sat.

She tried another tack.

"Why did you cover my mother's picture with Lucinda's?" She gestured to the oval frame in his room, and repeated her question. "Why did you cover her up with Lucinda?"

Ernest had finished eating. He lined up his knife and fork on his plate and pushed the plate a fraction of an inch away. "Your mother reminded me of your brother," he said quite simply.

"Norman," breathed Norma Joyce.

"She never recovered from that. She blamed herself. She shouldn't have left you two alone."

Her father was smoothing the tablecloth on either side of his plate, and she thought, If a photograph of my mother reminds him of Norman, then what about me?

Her father was asleep in his chair, mouth slightly open, head tilted to the left, body slack and frail. She took the folded blanket off the foot of the bed and spread it over his knees. How delicate – flaky-white – his hands had become. Bumping a knuckle was sufficient to make it bleed. Two Band-Aids were on his right hand, one on his left.

The evening lay ahead. In the living room she turned on the lamp and began to read one of the dozens of pamphlets her father had written over the years, this one about apple trees so old their branches lay along the ground and you had to bend down to pick the fruit. Duchess, Wealthy, Grimes Golden, Ben Davis, Ontario Snow, Thomas Sweet, Maiden's Blush, Sheep's Snow, King, Blenheim Orange – names that had gone the way of all flesh. She thought of other names – voile, organdie, chambray, moss crepe, figured silk, chintz, taffeta, glazed piqué, slipper satin – as exotic now as the names Cathay and Golden Coin and Mint, restaurants that once proliferated so oddly all across the Prairies.

When she was little, she used to call to her mother to come outside and lie on the prairie. They would lie flat on their backs and look up at the huge night sky. Those were the days when she believed that stars were holes in the floor of heaven. Around them rose the spicy smell of grass and sage. Even in the grass the wind found them. She held her mother's hand.

She remembers the room she shared with her sister. It was papered with a pattern of blue roses and spiky leaves on an ivory background, "as if they've taken a chill," Lucinda said once as they lay side by side before she blew out the lamp. She remembers the border of leaves around her sister's silver thimble, the scroll-pattern on the treadle of the old sewing machine, the frost medallions that formed in the dead of winter on nail heads in the back porch. She remembers the farmwife whose hus-band committed suicide. Everyone went to help, taking food into the pathetic kitchen, and you could see the woman's face all goose-pimply with shock, and her children's poverty-stricken wrists – sleeves too short, mittens too small – adorned with weather bracelets of chapped, reddened skin. A week later they were gone. They took the money collected on their behalf and bought train tickets to British Columbia, leaving behind a poorly furnished farmhouse, unlocked, and one half-starved cow in the barn.

Her mother's watercolour was on her bed, where she had put it when she came home. She found a hammer and nails in the basement, and soon the picture was hanging above her work table (a square table also found in the basement and carried up with the help of Vera on a day when she came to clean). Her banging didn't seem to disturb her father in his chair. Downstairs everything was quiet.

At least this much of you has been saved, she thought, standing back to make sure the picture was level.

On the table below was her mother's photograph. Norma Joyce had found another frame in a cupboard, this one metal, not silver, a backing of velveteen, not velvet, butterscotch-coloured, not royal blue. It occurred to her that, again, she was reconstructing her childhood corner. Already she had a jar of purple asters, goldenrod, coloured leaves. A bird's nest. The hornet's nest reclaimed from a corner shelf in the basement, where it had been sitting ever since Gerry Hulder gave it to her: large, globular, papery to the touch and ash-grey: exquisite. The day she had brought it upstairs her father had said, "What are you going to do with *that*?"

Lucinda and her father had put no value on her mother's art. That must be it. Some of it they'd found off-putting. The rest not good enough to keep.

But she couldn't understand it. She could only picture Lucinda caught up in the full lust of house-cleaning, laying waste to her mother's drawings, just as several years before she had destroyed her little weather room. Some misdirected or well-directed fit of energetic savagery. Either careless and unthinking. Embarrassed and hidebound. Or vindictive, dismissive, small-minded and mean.

But the next morning Ernest said, "You might like to have this." He set her mother's pale-green recipe book down at her place at the table.

Its spine was like a loose flap of skin, the glue having dried out and given way. And inside: Date Loaf, Cry Baby Cookies, Crisp Rolled Oat Cookies, Lemon Squares, Rhubarb Jam, Black Currant Jam, Hot Pot, Hot Potato Salad, Hot Cross Buns, the handwriting a twin to the delicate, precise strokes in the water-colour, all the letters tiny except when an *f* or *g* reached up or dropped down, or when she crossed her *t*'s with a stroke several letters wide. At the back: a recipe for Rhubarb Brandy, a pattern for knitting a dress, another pattern for a cardigan; and then the drawings of arrowheads, skulls, shells, fish bones, several pages of fossils, the face of an owl.

She looked up from her father's peace offering, and said, "I *am* glad to have it. You know, I found her old fur coat hanging in a closet downstairs."

"I don't remember a fur coat. That wouldn't be your mother's."

"Persian lamb."

"Maybe."

That afternoon Homecare Doris arrived, a bottom-heavy woman with large hands and thick wrists who read thrillers in her spare time. Norma Joyce made use of her presence to escape.

Outside, the colours were tawny, even the reds were yellow reds, and she thought of the shades and warmth of women's hair, and remembered the calluses on Lucinda's fingers that came from holding the scissors too tight.

She was in a neighbourhood of back alleys and thickening vines that produced the occasional whiff of something nutty and fermenting. The leaves of the Virginia creeper were livid, neither blue enough for a bruise nor red enough for a burn. She heard the yellow leaves of the box elder brush against the brick of Mrs. Gallot's house.

She knocked. The door opened and she said, "They threw them out."

Mrs. Gallot drew her into the kitchen, sat her down at the table, then took hold of the glasses on her bosom and repeatedly opened and closed their metal arms.

"Why?" wailed Norma Joyce. Then, "I *know* why. Her things weren't important, that's all. They didn't matter. They didn't count."

"Bella had something like this happen," sighed Mrs. Gallot. "She lost a whole book she'd written. She left it on the train when she came here from Winnipeg."

"That's just careless."

"Well, people *are* careless, even with things that matter to them. Sometimes *most* careless with the things that matter most. I don't know why." She was still working the arms of her glasses.

Norma Joyce rubbed her face with her hands, then looked out the window. "Do you suppose he loved my mother?" Her troubled eyes swung back to focus on Mrs. Gallot. "You knew them both. You saw them together."

"Yes." Mrs. Gallot was firm. "I saw them together. He was a devoted man, your father."

"Well," said Norma Joyce, "so much for being devoted."

———◆———

Ernest turned pages in his room. She told him through his half-open door that she was going to the art gallery, she would be back before Doris left for the day.

On Bank Street she caught the number 7 bus downtown. No streetcars any more, and the gallery in a new location: an office building on Elgin Street. She had an hour, and she didn't expect much.

But somebody had been acquiring art since she and Hennie used to visit after school. On the second floor she came face to face with Rembrandt's *Esther* of 1633, plump and serene in her sumptuous, embroidered velvets. Then Simone Martini's *St. Catherine* of 1320, so sad and brave, with only a hint of the torment to come in the heavily jewelled neckline that dug into her shoulders. Then, in a short corridor, two tiny paintings by Chardin from 1738: *The Return from the Market* and *The Governess* side by side above a wooden chest.

"They're marvellous, aren't they?"

A young woman in a wheelchair had come up beside her. Dark hair, lively face, red lipstick, lime-green scarf. She had a notepad in her lap, and a drawing pad. "I come in at least twice a week to see them and I'm never bored."

"You're an artist?"

"Art student. But you're an artist. I can always tell."

Norma Joyce felt flattered, and foolish to feel flattered. "How do you tell?"

"You look envious," the girl laughed, and so did Norma Joyce, who said, "But you're the one with the drawing pad."

"I see them better if I draw them. It also keeps me alert to each one." She opened her pad and showed a partly diagrammed *Governess*. "I draw all the curved lines in blue, the vertical lines in red, the diagonals in pencil. I was diagramming the Rubens. Have you seen it? Then I'll show you," and she wheeled into a long narrow gallery, Norma Joyce following in her wake, and stopped at *The Entombment of Christ* by Rubens.

For a moment the two of them looked at the body of Christ, marble white and heavy, being lifted by two men, while three women gazed down in sorrow.

Norma Joyce said, "What a scene of crowded grief."

The girl in the lime-green scarf nodded. "It's after Caravaggio's picture where everybody's arms are in the air. But this is different," she said. "It's all curves."

"I was diagramming it one day," she went on, "when a little girl came up to me, she was with her class from school and obviously bored, and she said, 'What are you doing?' So I pointed out the curves, the verticals, the diagonals. 'Well, you missed one!' she said. 'Where?' And she showed me the hand of Mary Magdalene. You see?" To Norma Joyce, who looked and nodded. "See how she's resting her cheek on her hand. The hand is a diagonal but the wrist is a vertical. '*Well, you missed one!*' I loved that," and out came another wonderful belly-laugh. The girl was bewitchingly happy, ardently enthusiastic. A tonic. "Have you seen the Lippi?" she asked. "And the Hans Memling? They're on this floor too. Well worth a look."

Norma Joyce followed her directions to the Memling, a Virgin and Child from 1472 in which the infant's face looked much graver than his mother's; then the painting by Filippino Lippi from the same period. Another Esther, but this one was altogether different from Rembrandt's. This Esther was Lucinda in her prime. A tall, willowy, fair-haired beauty clad in a flowing pink dress and all alone as she approached a castle. Such long fingers. Such hesitation.

Later that afternoon Norma Joyce played cribbage with her father. The light had almost gone. They sat in the gathering dusk beside the living room window, the fading sunset so rich in colour that she hadn't turned on a lamp.

"You deal," said Ernest.

While she dealt, she saw something out of the corner of her eye: it was what you would see in the fall if you were driving up a hill and had almost reached the crest: nothing but blue sky ahead and a filigree of golden leaves on either side. The image flitted by whenever she turned her head, and each time she felt strangely comforted.

"I think she fell asleep," she said. "Dad? I'm sure Lucinda fell asleep at the wheel – Ernest?"

He was studying his cards, and she had to guess what he was thinking. Probably that all the people most precious to him had been dead for a long time. He had never talked about any of their deaths, and he wasn't going to start now.

"Lead on, Macduff," he commanded.

"*Lay* on, Macduff," she said.

"*Lead on.*"

"Lay on, Macduff, And damned be him that first cries, 'Hold, enough!'"

She could have let him win, but then she wouldn't have been her father's daughter. Fifteen-two, fifteen-four, fifteen-six and two pairs for ten. No more capable of keeping the exultation out of her voice than he the disgust off his face, either then, or later on, when various forms of cold precipitation began to fall. Day after day there was snow, rain, and a thick mixture of the two like gruel. Ernest stared out the window. "Awful," he muttered. "Awful weather."

One morning, when Norma Joyce was scrubbing the day-lights out of the kitchen floor, she heard a visitor come in.

"What are you doing down there, my girl?"

"Getting my exercise," she said, grinning up at Mrs. Gallot. "Some women golf, I clean floors," and she stood up into a fond and laughing embrace. Drying her hands, she said, "I can't get warm," and made a face at the day outside.

"Try hot baths," said Mrs. Gallot. "Hot tea, and two hot baths a day."

"Are *you* ready for winter?"

"If there's plenty of snow," said Mrs. Gallot, "then I won't complain."

And there was. By mid-November light snow was falling so steadily that soon very little became a lot, and since there was no wind, it built up on every surface. Children came outside to make elaborate snowforts of several little rooms furnished with snow-beds and snowtables. At suppertime they went back inside with snow-encrusted hair.

Norma Joyce measured the accumulation on Ernest's Chevrolet, which sat week after week in the driveway, since she walked everywhere and he didn't go outside. She used a long ruler and heard the question, "How much?" asked in a high, reedy voice.

It was the dark-haired boy from above. The one she had seen so often through the old Dove windows.

"More than eighteen inches," she told him.

He was standing in the middle of her yard, holding his toboggan by its rope, having overshot not only his property but the laneway. She made her way through the snow to where he was standing. "You can come all the way into my yard," she said, "I don't mind."

He stared at his feet, suddenly shy just as Johnny would have been at the same age.

"Do you know where that is?" Norma Joyce pointed to *Siberia* written in red across the front of his toboggan.

"Russia."

His name was Max. He had freckles, and crooked teeth, and a good sense of geography because a big map of the world hung on his kitchen wall. Day-Glo Vermeer, she would think, looking up the slope after dark to the domestic tableau of mother and two children seated at a table with the map of the world behind them. The father had dropped out of the picture, it seemed. Though it was lovelier than Day-Glo, those various shades and levels of blues in the distance.

No children in Vermeer. No weather either. Just the suggestion of both in the luxurious solitude of women alone with their letters and pearls, beside windows free of frost and dust.

The next day, buying milk and bread at the corner store on Sunny-side, she saw the girl in the lime-green scarf, in living illustration of the rule that the person you notice is the one you'll see again. This time the girl was standing on her own two feet, buying a newspaper.

"Where's your wheelchair?"

The girl's laughter filled the store. "I only use one when I'm looking at pictures. Much more comfortable than a stool. I can sit with my notebook for hours."

"What a good idea!"

"They have them on the first floor, as you go in."

The girl paid for her newspaper. Norma Joyce had her milk and bread. "You must live around here too," said Norma Joyce.

"On Carlyle."

"Then you're Bella Pugg!"

"And you're Watson," said Bella Pugg.

"You mean I'm wrong?"

"I mean you're right. You're absolutely right!" And laughter pealed out of Bella, such uninhibited, infectious laughter that Norma Joyce thought, *This* is what I need.

"*I'm* Watson, you're Holmes," said Bella. "How did you know?"

"We're neighbours. I've seen your double word scores on Mrs. Gallot's Scrabble board."

"But she always wins," lamented Bella.

They left the store together and headed down Seneca Street. Norma Joyce asked Bella what else she should see at the gallery, and Bella mentioned Joyce Wieland. "She'll try her hand at any-thing. Quilts, cakes, films, perfume. I guess it was living in New York that stirred her up."

"I lived in New York. I'm still trying to figure out what it did to me."

Bella looked at her and chuckled. "Not everything she does is big and splashy. The piece I liked best was something simple. She took the letters that General Wolfe and General Montcalm wrote just before they died on the Plains of Abraham in 1759, and had them embroidered on linen, and then she framed them side by side."

"*Letters*," said Norma Joyce, as if speaking to herself. "*Embroidered* letters."

"So you have history, drawing, writing, and embroidery all in one."

"Yes."

By now they were at Woodbine Place and Carlyle Avenue, which was where they'd part company. Norma Joyce stared down the remaining length of Woodbine to Bronson Avenue and the fields and hills shining beyond under the white winter sun. "I wish I'd thought of it," she said. "I've always wondered how to use letters." She felt ecstatic and despairing. To find an idea that fit her perfectly, used by someone else.

"Don't worry," said Bella. "There are a million ways. Ideas don't run out."

"Yes. You're the one who lost a manuscript and lived to tell the tale."

Bella groaned. "Don't talk to me about that."

"I lost a baby once. In the snow."

"But you *found* him," looking at her with startled eyes.

Norma Joyce nodded. "My son. And then I lost him again, to his father. In a manner of speaking."

Bella said, "I tell myself if I lost it, it couldn't be very important. But I don't really believe that."

"No," said Norma Joyce.

Max was drilling pucks into a snowbank. His mother was on the porch calling to him, but he wasn't listening.

"Do you know Ida?" asked Bella.

"Just through the window."

"Her husband moved out a month ago. I'll introduce you."

And so "Norma Joyce Hardy, painter" got introduced to "Ida Berns, translator, and mother of Max and Rose."

"Nervous wreck, more like," said Ida, a tissue balled up in her hand and her voice husky with a cold.

Max, they learned, wanted his mother to take him to the library and she wouldn't. She had supper to make, he had his room to clean. "I don't have time to go to the library," her voice rising in pitch as she spoke.

"I'll take him," said Norma Joyce. "I've been meaning to go anyway."

"You're sure?"

"I can be away another half hour. Mrs. Hulder is sitting with my father. I'll leave my groceries with you?"

Somewhat to her surprise, Max agreed to go with her, though after a block he was whimpering from the cold. "Don't you have a car?" he moaned.

"It's the east wind, we're walking right into it."

He stopped dead.

"Do you think a polar bear is stalking us from behind?" she said. And he began to walk forward again.

Eight years old.

On the way back, Max carried the bag of books over his shoulder, happy now that he had his three adventures, and willing to carry her books as well – two about art, and two by Maurice Dove.

A small test. To see if she could read Maurice's books without causing herself pain, and to see if they were any good.

The following week she took Max to the library again. On the way there he barely said a word. On the way back he asked, "How do you get a thought out of your head?"

"You have a thought you want to get rid of?"

"Yes."

"Well, sometimes it just goes away on its own after a while."

"What if it doesn't?"

"Sometimes talking about it makes it go away."

"I don't want to talk about it."

She looked down at him as they walked along. His scarf was blowing about in the wind. "Wait," she said, "let me fix it."

But he didn't have the patience to stand still.

"Are you cold?"

"No."

She had glimpsed his father hurrying up the walk the other day. A prosperous-looking man whose dark moustache was white in the middle as though he had dipped his mouth in a bowl of milk. A boyish face, though tired and preoccupied.

Max's face was more like his mother's. The dark hair and olive complexion. At first, just seeing him through the window, he had reminded her of the boys she used to see in the Eaton's catalogue, so fresh-faced and healthy. But now he seemed very pale.

As did his sad-eyed mother, whose head was burdened by endless detail. Ida translated books from French into English, reading her translations aloud to herself "like Flaubert," she said to Norma Joyce. "You know Flaubert?"

Norma Joyce brought Max home for cocoa and cookies since both seemed to be in short supply in his intellectual, troubled household. Her father was at the kitchen table playing solitaire. Max leaned over the cards, not in the least bit squeamish about this shaky old man, and before she knew it Ernest was teaching him how to play. He learned fast.

It gave her an odd sort of pleasure to watch her father relax with the boy as he could not relax with her. She shaved Ernest every morning, trimmed his eyebrows and the hair in his ears, mended his underwear, washed his sheets. She made the apple pies he loved, she read to him in the evenings, she continued to clobber him at cards, but nothing she did made his face light up the way it lit up for this dark-haired boy.

December arrived, as dark and close and welcome as her mother's old black Persian-lamb coat which taxed the shoulders of the strongest hanger in her closet. At night she spread it across her bed, comforted by its weight, and in the morning she looked out at her childhood idea of Ontario: the gentle never-ceasing snow on sloping rooftops, the peacefulness of winter gardens holding safe the memory of apples and every kind of berry, the dimensions of a world protecting you from fierce accidents of every sort.

Against her will, but not to her surprise, she liked Maurice's books. His writing was sure, intimate, unafraid of its subject matter. Anyone would want to know this person, anyone would be drawn to him. No wonder he had such a following – she and Johnny were just two of many seduced by the unapologetic charm he had harnessed and put to work. Neither of the books she had borrowed was his most recent: the history of the grasslands, on loan to another reader. Rather, they were his *Life of Darwin* and his equally praised weather book, *Floods and Famines*. In both, he had tapped into the same sweet groundwater, the same informed, companionable tone. "Before a storm," he wrote, "animals become less wary knowing they might not feed again for several days. Birds lose their caution, children become insufferable. Nothing is more responsive to the fluctuations of weather than children, unless it's willows and grasses."

She remembers closing the book and looking outside at falling snow. An elderly couple, arm in arm, were walking down the middle of the street, their progress recorded in the tracks they left behind. They could have turned around to see the quiet effect they had had, but they didn't. Nor did the mailman, who came striding along a few minutes later.

She liked the quiet then, and she likes it now, the muffled quality of December having extended through to May – to a house rendered even quieter by death, and the hush of discovery.

She sat looking out at the snow, first with Maurice's book in her lap, and then, after the mailman came, with Christmas cards. One was from Johnny (he would be spending the holiday with Maurice, but he missed her and would try to visit soon), and one from Frank and Hilda (apologizing for not having answered her letters, but they were busier than they wanted to be, and very tired. Hilda was the writer. At the end Frank added in his spiky hand, "We miss you." His remark she believed more than Johnny's, but she was grateful for both). Red poinsettias and a golden pear. A sheet of music surrounded by a wide red border.

The blast of red, the way it suffused a wintry month, totally disarmed her. She was back with her mother, learning to associate colour in December with the delirium of mail.

And still the house was quiet. She could count up the sounds: the creak of floors even when no one was moving about, the skitter of something in the walls, her father's cough, the tick of the kitchen clock, the dry-on-dry raspiness of her knuckle rubbing back and forth across her lower lip: a delicate sound, that one, like something heard through a keyhole. Then the lullaby of soft humming when the furnace came on. And then the hard thump of her father's cane.

Thump, thump, thump. Until it stopped right beside her chair.

So she turned and looked up at her glowering dad, who had wanted his lunch fifteen minutes ago.

"What time is it?" she asked, a little surprised by her mildness, and understanding that it would only infuriate him more.

"It's time to stir your stumps."

"All right," she laughed. "You're a hard man, Ernest Hardy, but I guess you're right."

She got up then, and went into the kitchen. Ernest followed. What a pair we are, she thought. The only survivors of a family of five, but unfit for each other's company. Explain that one, Darwin.

Not just a quiet house, but a city in which things happen quietly. From January on, keeping pace with the lengthening days, there unfolded a simple image that contained all the events that would follow: a frostbitten ear blossomed into "a touch of spring," then a voice she recognized, then words she could barely hear, and finally the sound of someone calling her name.

It was early January when she borrowed Ida's skates and tried out the canal, several miles of which had been cleared of snow then flooded for skating. Wiping away the frost moustache and beard that kept forming on her face, she skated all the way downtown (it took forty-five minutes), where she bought hot chocolate and rested on a bench for a few minutes before skating home. On the way back, just past Pretoria Bridge, she saw blood on the canal. It spilled out like a body lying flat and vividly red, not the dull shade of spilled hot chocolate but a brighter, thinner shade of red. She looked down and thought, *That's what happens when you get too cocky.* And she skated more carefully after that.

She was sitting on a wooden bench, bent over and unlacing her skates, when she felt someone settle down beside her, and then a warm hand cover her ear. It was Bella Pugg.

"Your earrings," by way of explanation. "Your other ear's frostbitten too, but it doesn't look to be so bad. Metal conducts the cold."

Norma Joyce put her own hand over her left earlobe, then removed her silver hoops.

"I always take mine out before I go skating. At least I try to remember," said Bella.

"Thank you, neighbour. I didn't know you were back. How was Winnipeg?"

Bella bent over her own skates, and struggled with the laces. "Shit, it's cold." She wiped her nose with the back of her hand. "My mother's sick and my father's useless. That's how Winnipeg was. How's the painting?"

"What painting?"

"Ah." She reached into her canvas bag for a rag to wipe off her blades. "Mrs. Gallot told me I needed to boost your ego."

Norma Joyce laughed. "I love her like a mother," she said.

The two women took the wooden steps up to the street, then started for home, with Bella doing most of the talking. She wanted to see more of Norma Joyce's work. "I *like* the drawing you gave Mrs. Gallot. Max and your father playing cards. It's *good*. You know why?"

"How's your mother?" asked Norma Joyce.

Bella fished in her pocket and pulled out her pack of Player's Light. She was not to be put off. "I write about art for the paper," she said. "I could interview you. I do it all the time, interviews with local artists. Ottawa painter comes home, after how many years in New York? We'd talk about what you did there. What you learned. What you think of Ottawa."

"Don't ask me those questions. Those are awful questions."

"People need to know you're here. You need to get out and about."

"No, I don't."

"Why don't we visit the gallery together, that would be easy. Do a sort of walking interview about the paintings you like and why."

"You are a pest, Bella Pugg."

"I know, but that's why you love me," laughing her warm easy laugh.

By nightfall Norma Joyce's earlobes had puffed up and turned fire-engine red. Fire-engine red, she thought when she looked in the bathroom mirror, and softer than anything she had ever touched before.

As the days got longer, Ernest got more frail. He had to sit down to pee and found it hard to get back up again. He couldn't wipe himself. And he wouldn't call for help. Norma Joyce kept an eye on his whereabouts and went in without any comment except, "I'll do this."

Some nights, when she heard him thumping around, she joined him downstairs and made cocoa in a saucepan on the stove. "Here," handing her father a cup so hot it had a layer of thick froth on top, "burn your tongue." Ernest's lips would twitch into a smile. She liked to believe that at caustic, near-affectionate moments such as that, they understood each other.

He still perked up whenever Max came over. They played poker now, as well as cribbage.

"Don't forget to chew," she would caution Max when she put a plate of sliced apples, or carrots, or cookies in front of them.

In the meantime, her earlobes itched, dried out, and shed their skin, and notes began to appear in her mailbox. One of them said, " 'The artist must go at his own speed. His whole life is a painful effort to turn himself inside out.' – Sir Kenneth Clark himself." Another said, "What did the Buddhist say to the hotdog vendor? 'Make me one with everything.'"

The irrepressible Bella Pugg.

In February the light turned golden. It was October light, really, slanting between the powder-blue sky and the suede-blue shadows inside her small deep footprints.

"A touch of spring," said Mrs. Gallot, when she arrived with a pot of hyacinths and daffodils. She brought the flowers into the kitchen, where they had tea. Ernest joined them at the table, and then Mrs. Hulder dropped in too, as faithful as ever with her casseroles and squares. Bella, according to Mrs. Gallot, had flown back to Winnipeg for the week. "Her mother's in a bad way. Did she tell you?"

"She's still sick?"

Mrs. Gallot tapped her forehead.

"Oh, dear," said Norma Joyce.

"It's been going on for a long time."

"I'm sorry." And the image of Bella the merry, the capable, the indefatigable broke open, and a new reason appeared for her headlong run at life. Something besides intellectual curiosity was nipping at her heels.

So this was why Bella took such an interest in middle-aged women who had lost their way. Norma Joyce felt oddly touched – for herself, as well as for Bella.

After Mrs. Gallot and Mrs. Hulder left, she moved the spring flowers into the middle of the kitchen table. Then pulled over the newspaper. Folded it open to the coloured comics, and propped it up beside the flowers, thus creating two good diagonals. The window frame provided a strong vertical and horizontal. Then she dunked her watercolour tray in the basin in the sink to soften up the colours, filled two glasses with water, found a clean rag, paper, a good pencil, and got started. With the pencil she began to mark on her twelve by sixteen inch paper enough detail to provide a guide when it came to drawing with the paintbrush. Minutes later she stood up and paced around the kitchen. Sat down again, irritable and jumpy, and pencilled in more carefully the comics and a few of the flowers. Took a deep breath, wet her brush, and rapidly started to apply a very light yellow. Ten minutes went by and she was actually getting somewhere – having washed out her brush and moved to a warmer yellow and now a yellow-orange – when a crash in Ernest's room brought her to a furious halt. Her father had upended his glass of water onto the floor.

Interruptions. Timidity. Bad temper. Loss of nerve.

After two weeks the flowers were dead, and several water-colours, all unfinished, lay on the table in her bedroom. They rebuked her as effectively as an unwalked dog.

But nothing could stop the advance of light. A natural, spiritual increase conferred equally upon everyone. At the time, she thought she had come to a near halt, her movements tailored to fit her father's life. But something was working on her. After New York, what she needed was stillness.

By the middle of March, it was bright at seven in the morning, the light warmer, less metallic than in February, almost petalled, the way it softened the branches of the apple trees rather than striking against them. The snow was warm too, and packed, and when more snow fell it was like lotion on a lotioned face: it drove the old snow farther into the ground.

One night she woke up to the sound of beating wings around the gutters, and the patter of small feet on the roof. She listened. It took a moment, but she identified the angelic sound of melting, of snow moving about and water starting to trickle.

March 29 was her birthday. She was forty-three. Ernest didn't remember and she didn't tell him. To her surprise, Johnny phoned, and so did Frank, who never phoned anyone. "When are you coming back?" Frank asked her, and she told him she didn't know.

"Don't think you aren't missed," he said.

Outside, the air was raw, the sky grey and low. She went for a walk anyway, heading up the alley past the house with the purple African violet blooming so lavishly in a high small window that, once again, she stood there trying to figure out if the plant was artificial or real, and while she was doing that it began to hail. Tiny granular pellets.

"Graupel," said Ernest when she got back.

"How do you know that word?"

"Did you think you were the only reader?"

Made bad-tempered by memories of perfect crops destroyed in six minutes flat. What was his name? The man of forty who lost everything, while on every side of his flattened fields, the sun kept shining. Perkins. John Perkins. He turned grey overnight.

Stories like that were common currency then. You would hear phrases: *he turned grey practically under my eyes*, *the cattle died on their feet*, *emotion gripped her senses*, and the whole story would fall into place.

It was the day after her birthday. She called Bella, on the off chance that she might be free, but Mrs. Gallot said she wasn't home.

"I'm off to the gallery," Norma Joyce explained. "Just looking for company."

"Maybe you'll find her there," said Mrs. Gallot.

By the time Norma Joyce got downtown, it was the middle of the afternoon. In less than an hour, she would have to head back to Ernest. First she spent some time with the two paintings by Chardin, then she walked to the French room, a small, round room with walls of grey-green watered silk on which all the French paintings were displayed. In the doorway she saw Maurice Dove.

His back was turned, which was lucky; it gave her a moment to recover. His hair was completely grey. He was wearing a brown tweed jacket and dark brown trousers, and standing between a large woman in a rose tweed suit, and a slender, younger man. He was saying how clever they were – his two companions – how clever they were to position Canova's graceful dancer in the centre of the room so that she could keep an eye on handsome Paris on the facing wall. He sounded well pleased with himself, very amused, very cultured.

Then the three of them turned to leave and she was directly in their path, although she didn't seem to register except as an obstacle to skirt.

She stuck out her foot, and Maurice stopped short in surprise.

"Maurice Dove," she said. "Don't you dare pass me by."

"Norrie?"

And with that one word, her heart slid open.

It didn't hurt to air it out. To have that soft, warty intricacy of feeling exposed and moved over by the air.

Norrie.

Who would have thought it would be so easy?

He introduced her to the woman in rose tweed and the slender young man, both of whom worked for the gallery. They were heading up to the cafeteria, and he assured them that he'd be along in a few minutes.

And now she and Maurice were alone with the sassy dancer and Paris as a nude shepherd and the painting of little peaches and the one of the Italian woods.

"It's good to see you, Norrie."

He seemed to mean it too. Her passionate letters of ten years ago had left no ill effects. Seeing the expression in his eyes – welcoming yet complacent – made her realize two things. That he liked having her in love with him, one. And two, that as far as he was concerned it would never go beyond that. Later, she would feel like the pasta salad at every potluck supper. The table would be empty without it, but he had no intention of putting any on his plate.

The old familiar bitterness. She would not say that she had been reading his books, and admiring them. Only, "I saw your name in the paper. Congratulations. You've done well, Maurice."

He smiled. "Life is good," he said. His face had widened and his voice was huskier. "Johnny told me you were here looking after Ernest. How's it going?"

So casual, so breezy, this rival for her son's affections. This old lover who stirred up her insides every time she saw him. His neck and the underside of his chin had the old appealing milkiness, and it would have been pleasant to reach out and touch them.

"Where are you staying?" she asked.

"The Lord Elgin."

"How long?"

"Leaving tomorrow, I'm afraid. I fly to Toronto at five o'clock."

"Then you'll have time to take me to lunch before you leave."
He laughed.

"I mean it. It's the least you can do."

"All right." Though the answer was slow in coming. "Where?"

"Murray's," she said. "At noon. You won't even have to leave your hotel."

"Not noon. One o'clock."

"Fine. Just don't be late. I have things to say."

"Say them," he said. "I'm here."

She closed her eyes and thought for a moment. Then she shrugged. "Where do I begin?"

"At the beginning," Maurice answered with a smile. "Always begin at the beginning."

"Then I'd have to begin with you."

Her simple words had the desired effect. He looked at her long and intently and she returned his look – her expression bemused, weary, searching – until she was jostled by school-children. A breathless teacher arrived a moment later, only to take one look at the sexy dancer and march her pupils right back out again. Norma Joyce and Maurice smiled at each other. Still smiling, she said, "And you, I'm afraid, turned into a dead end."

Maurice gave her a quizzical look, then cleared his throat and glanced away.

"You don't like being called a dead end."

He didn't answer. A few more pokes, and he'd not show up for lunch.

"Anyway," she said, "what I wanted to say was something else. You told me once that I should never doubt your feelings about me. Do you remember that? You don't remember."

"Go on."

"I should have asked you what they were."

"Ah," closing his eyes and rubbing them with his left hand. "The girl with the good questions."

A plump, bespectacled docent was taking a group of well-dressed women from picture to picture. Norma Joyce heard her say very crisply, "Your eye follows moment to moment through to the central focus," and she and Maurice moved to one side as the women trooped by.

"To tell you the truth," he said, running his hand through his hair, "I've always had mixed feelings about you." His smile was rueful. "I think you've aroused more mixed feelings in me than anybody else I know."

"Well," she said dryly, "that's something."

Then he said he had to join his companions upstairs, they were waiting for him. And he walked her to the circular staircase that led to the lobby below.

"Tomorrow," she said. "One o'clock. You can order mixed salad to go with your mixed feelings."

"Okay." He smiled, somewhat warily, she thought.

"Don't stand me up."

Then she headed down the stairs, carefully, to avoid falling flat in front of him. But at the bottom, when she looked up to wave goodbye, he wasn't there.

Nor was he there the next day when she got to Murray's. She took a window table overlooking Elgin Street (having phoned to reserve, knowing they'd be busy at one o'clock), and waited. The window had a buildup of frost melted and refrozen countless times. Her hands were folded on the paper placemat in front of her. The waitress, who filled both glasses with water, wore a maroon uniform and said she'd come back later. Norma Joyce checked her watch.

Another ten minutes, and she was still waiting. It would be too bad if she didn't get a chance to unburden herself.

Then a tap on her shoulder. "I'm sorry. Have you been waiting long?"

"Punctuality is the courtesy of kings," she retorted. "As Paul Newman said to Robert Redford."

"Sorry," pulling out the chair and dropping into it with a groan. "I was being interviewed. Couldn't get away. I tried." He unbuttoned his tweed jacket, ran his hands through his grey hair and smiled at her. "Tell me what you've been up to besides looking after Ernest. Still painting?"

She shook her head. "Not much. All but stopped, to be honest."

"Then you'll start again," he said simply.

"Why?"

"That's your fate, isn't it?" He took a drink from his glass of water. "Your life will stop and then it will start again. That's what the old fortune teller said."

She stared at him. "You remembered that."

"Who could forget?"

"*I* forgot." It stunned her, she who prided herself on remembering everything. The brimming eyes came back to her, the worn-out suitcoat, the smell of tobacco and peppermint, the kiss on her cheek. "He was a strange old man, wasn't he?"

"I liked him."

"So did I." She rested her head on her hand. "He said I would have one child and his life would stop, then start again. Well, that certainly happened. You knew that? I lost Johnny in the snow for twelve hours."

"He told me it was one of your favourite stories."

"Quite a beginning."

The waitress returned, and this time Norma Joyce noticed her orthopedic shoes and large, red knuckles. They ordered hot turkey sandwiches, and withstood the waitress's supplications on behalf of the whipped turnip. "The kitchen must be after you to push it," said Maurice with a wink. The waitress giggled, and confessed that yes, all the girls were supposed to talk it up.

"I have a confession too," said Norma Joyce after the waitress had left.

But Maurice was looking around him at the restaurant. It was crowded at this time of day, a haven for the elderly and the single: ballet dancers staying at the hotel, tourists, ladies in lavender suits, old gentlemen.

"You're not listening," she said.

"You have a confession." He smiled at her. "I'm all ears."

"It's not that important."

"I like confessions," he said. "Confessions and secrets."

"This is both." Then she took a deep breath and said, "The letters you wrote to my sister before the war. You remember?"

"You mean, the ones she never received."

"You guessed!"

"No."

He didn't go on, and she opened her hands wide in impatience. "What then?"

"Lucinda told me."

Again, he didn't go on. But this time she sat very still. Her eyes were fixed on his face. Then her shoulders sagged, and she looked down.

"Norrie?" he said.

She was staring at the table. The corner of her placemat was folded over. She began to run her fingertip back and forth on the fold. Finally she said, "So? When? What did she say?"

"Right after Johnny was born. When I was visiting my folks."

"She told you I stole her letters?"

"She didn't use that word, but yes."

Their plates of food arrived, and now she was speaking to him across the tops of the waitress's wide arms. "How did she put it?"

"All this was a long time ago. Are you sure you want to hear it?"

"Yes."

"Why don't you eat," and he picked up his knife and fork, and for a few moments she watched him chew. Her own utensils stayed put.

Then she reached over and took hold of his wrist, so that he couldn't lift his fork to his mouth.

"Okay." He leaned back in his chair. "It was in the afternoon. She knocked on the door, my mother and I were both at home, and she came in with something she'd baked. One of her specialties. Cake? She said she had something to say. Not unlike you yesterday," and he let this sink in. "The word she used was 'trustworthy.'"

Norma Joyce stirred in her chair. "*Un*trustworthy. I was *un*trustworthy."

"She said you'd lied about the letters. You might lie about other things too."

Norma Joyce didn't speak for a while. When she did, her voice was flat and bitter. "Like who the father was."

"It was years ago, Norrie."

"My sister," she said, and she turned her head to stare out at the street, but it was the earlier scene that rose before her eyes. Lucinda walking up the slope to Maurice's door – maybe she stopped to look back – then carrying on, bearing her item of baking, and her message. She would have apologized for her sister who had always been "a care." A care, and a sneak.

Lucinda. Keeping the peace. Making it possible for the Hardys and the Doves to go on as neighbours.

Good Lucinda. Wily, punitive, good Lucinda, who had made her wash every dish in the house. Who had turned her weather room upside-down. Who had thrown out her mother's drawings. Who had always known how to get even.

"And you didn't defend me." She looked at him, and could see that the idea had never entered his head.

"Why didn't you tell me?" she asked.

"What would have been the point?"

"But you're telling me now."

"You *asked*." He studied her for a moment. "She was thinking of you too. Your welfare. She wanted to keep it in the family. She said it would be better for you if I stayed out of the picture. I think she was right. I was never very good for you, Norrie."

"Who has been good for me? What on earth are you talking about?"

Her ferocity startled him. For a moment he looked confused, even a little stupid. She had bumped up against the edge of his understanding. But then he had never thought her predicament through, for the simple reason that it had never been a big part of his life.

"You make a good pair," she said. "You and Lucinda. You should have married her."

"I didn't want to marry her," he said evenly.

"Or me. For that matter."

And then someone recognized him. An old gentleman passing their table stopped, and said he was sorry to intrude but aren't you Maurice Dove? I've seen you on television. I just want to say how much I've enjoyed every one of your books. Maurice was gracious, at ease, in his element. But after the old man left, he rolled his eyes at her.

So this was how he operated. He dispensed affability while remaining in cahoots with *you*. It's called having your cake and eating it.

Knowledge is always useful, she thought as she stood outside waiting for the bus. Knowledge is always surprising and always useful. It never wears out.

Who was it who said revenge is best eaten cold? Revenge, like porridge, is best eaten cold.

In April Ernest took to his bed and refused to eat. This was new. Her father refusing food, a man as punctual in his eating habits as the blue jays who arrived at the bird feeder every morning at ten after eight.

Evenings, she read to him and he didn't tell her to stop. "Is there anything you *want* me to read?" she asked one day.

"You're doing fine," he said.

Thomas Hardy's *Under the Greenwood Tree*. She had picked it up off the shelf in the living room, never having read it before, and it seemed better, simpler, more interesting to her than any of his later, grander novels. No doubt there was a lesson in that, she thought, for people who were interested in lessons.

Homecare Doris reassured her. It often happens this way. "They decide they've had enough. We'll see. He's not in pain. Just worn out."

They bathed him together now, and somehow Ernest retained his dignity even as they lifted him in and out of the bath. In bed he looked more and more like a little grey mouse, his gravity like the child's in Hans Memling's Virgin and Child, old age and infancy coming together in his shrunken features.

Towards the end of April, she phoned Johnny and told him to come. He flew up the same week, and she met him at the airport in Ernest's Chevrolet. Miraculously, the car started. Even more miraculously, she didn't drive it off the road, a woman who hadn't been behind the wheel of a car in years. Who drives in New York? she said to Johnny, squinting through the windshield as they made their way home to roast chicken and apple pie.

Johnny in Ottawa was different from Johnny in New York. Undistracted by his studies and regular life, he had time for her. They worked together in the kitchen, preparing the salad, setting the table, washing the dishes. He rattled on about his courses, took an interest in her drawings of Ernest and Max that covered the kitchen wall, took an interest in Max when he came over to show them a card trick he'd learned, kept asking what he could do to help. She saw Maurice in his face, especially in the concerned blue eyes that were concerned only up to a point. He was a young man with his life ahead of him.

As for Ernest, it was as if all he'd been waiting for was a visit from his grandson. For the duration of Johnny's stay he came alive, winning three cribbage games in a row and sitting at the table for every meal. But once Johnny left, he stopped eating altogether.

The end of April was cold. Not a leaf in sight. Every twig and branch looked as if it had been set with silver. Laid carefully like a table.

One day she followed Echo Drive to Pretoria Bridge, where the sudden openness of the canal, the long curving line of its banks, the parallel lines of snow-dusted pathway and dark road, the plantings of willows, spruce, oaks, and bushes under burlap offered a view so satisfying that for a moment, standing on the bridge, there was nothing else she wanted and nothing about the wanting that bothered her.

Another day, walking in the arboretum, she came upon a smoke tree sprawled low and wide with tufts of what could have been an old woman's hairnet on its bare scalp, and four pendulous berries hanging like rubies off a twig. One glance, and she was back at Lake Clear: the ground a strawberry woods, and herself another Gulliver on hands and knees, parting the treetops and gobbling the perfect fruit. Those were the days, that summer after the war, when she followed the weather every morning in the paper. Smoke in the Mackenzie Valley, showers in Saskatchewan, thunderstorms in Ontario, fog along the Bay of Fundy.

Scattered showers in the parched landscape where they'd met, and rain now, where they were.

She climbed the pathway through labelled trees to the area where the arboretum levelled off, then followed a slushy road to the lip of the sliding hill gone to springtime rack-and-ruin. No more dogs milling about. No more sledders on their silver saucers making reckless descents and plodding returns.

On her way home she saw: Siberian larches as bumpy as grape stems after the grapes have been pulled off, a squirrel high in a tree sawing open a nut like a tiny woodcutter, a big woman scolding her little dog Peaches, and a young woman, leash in hand, chasing after long, loping Vince.

"Good Lord, where is your sister?"

Her father, standing in the bedroom door. Agitated. Lost. "Wait," she said, getting out of bed and reaching for her dressing gown on the back of the chair.

She took him by the arm and led him downstairs. "She's not here. She hasn't been for a long time. I'll make us some tea."

It was four-thirty in the morning. They sat across from each other at the kitchen table with their cups of tea, and she asked him if there was anything else he would like. Yes. He wanted to see the farm again. The farm? She'd been thinking of toast.

"I thought you hated it."

"Why would you think that? I loved the work."

He had. He had loved the hard grinding work of it. So had Lucinda. It was their calling. Brute labour had located their impressive backbones.

"But it broke your heart," she said. "All that work for nothing."

"It wasn't for nothing."

"I'm sorry. I don't mean it was all a waste."

"It was hard work, but I wasn't afraid of hard work."

"I know," she said, and that morning she called a travel agent about tickets. When Doris arrived, she told her that Ernest had rallied. He had eaten a good breakfast, seated at the table. He even seemed bent on going back to Saskatchewan one last time.

"Let's just wait and see," Doris said. "Don't buy the tickets yet."

It was the middle of May, rainy and cool. The tulips should have been in their prime, but too much rain had bent them low. Norma Joyce went for short walks, stopping to scrutinize the different reds. Chinese red, she remembers thinking, before revising it to Mountie red.

Once, it was snowing lightly when she got up in the morning, and she said to Ernest, "I'm not going to say it's snowing. I'm just going to say there's snow in the air."

Upstairs, her bedroom window was turning pink. In a week it would be vivid, in three weeks every petal would be on the ground. That night Mother H. covered her flowers with plastic bags, some white, some black.

Again, before dawn, she heard something and went downstairs. When she entered his room, his head relaxed on the pillow. She filled his glass with fresh water and raised him up so that he could take a sip. He made a face.

"Tea? I'll make you some tea."

She went into the kitchen, turned on the light and plugged in the kettle. She stood in one spot until the kettle boiled. It was twenty-five minutes to five. Her father had always made her mother a cup of tea at five in the morning.

Again, she cradled him with her left arm so that he could sip his tea. She bent close. "What did you say?"

He said it again.

"You're a good . . . daughter."

It's always beautiful, the way things come to you in the early morning. Light touches one thing at a time. There seems to be plenty of time. The narrow bed, the bedside table, the white cloth crocheted around the edges, the glass of water, the little clock, the box of tissues, *Right Ho, Jeeves* in big print. Ernest said he liked it, but she hadn't heard him laugh.

The room was clean and neat. His breaths were shallow and far apart. She took his hand and an old image came into her mind from the worried months when she was pregnant, years ago. She used to close her eyes and imagine walking on the prairie in the late summer, the air clear as water, the wind slipping around her, and a hand slipping into hers.

Her father's hand was as cool as a flower. His body was like a frail blue tulip. His arms were like drooping stems.

He opened his eyes. She had to lean nearer.

He said it slowly, unmistakeably, in a hoarse whisper, "Good . . . night . . . . Lucinda."

Then he closed his eyes, and they stayed closed.

After a while she said, "And good night to you. Irene."

The blessing conferred and then withdrawn. In the short time between the two events her brow had finally been smoothed. No wonder Jacob went to such lengths to get his father's blessing.

Noses and tear ducts become more capacious as we age. Sad but true. She was in that position of old, on her bed, lying on her side, with her knees pulled up.

She had never thought she cared. Had always thought she was grateful to her sister for occupying her father, and grateful to her father for addressing everything he said to Lucinda.

He had been a man to whom courtesy mattered. Indeed he had been almost courtly in his manners, the sort who stood up when a woman stood up and always walked nearest the road when he walked beside her. He had even done this for her. Putting his hands on her shoulders and shifting her to his inside. Later, she would do the same for her small son.

No, she hadn't minded her father's unabashed favouritism. She hadn't thought she cared.

IV

"For most of our lives the days pass waywardly, without meaning, without particular happiness or unhappiness. Then, like turning over a tapestry when you have only known the back of it, there is spread the pattern."

JANE GARDAM, *Crusoe's Daughter*

The quiet is broken when someone calls her name. Late morning has turned into afternoon without her knowing, so absorbed has she been by her discovery. It's as if her father's death has brought her mother back to life, but on his own grudging, hurtful terms.

She goes to the back door and steps outside. It's the end of May. Hanging on the clothesline, and already dry in the hot sunshine, are the pants, shirts, socks, and dressing gown destined to be picked up in a few days by a local charity. Two weeks have passed since her father's death. Johnny has come and gone, and she has fallen heir to a house, a new kind of solitude, and the sudden onset of summer.

Max and Ida are waiting by the porch steps.

"We got you something to read," Max announces, climbing up to her with his arms full of library books. At the top, a few slip out of his grasp.

"Oh, Max!" chides Ida, and Norma Joyce bends down to pick up *Adam Bede* and *The Godfather*.

"I just didn't know what you'd be in the mood for," Ida says from the bottom step, amused and semi-aggrieved. "So finally the librarian picked one, and I picked the other."

And something else. A children's book about the weather. A little book with transparent sheets that change a sunny day into a rainy day, a clear day into a foggy day, a fall day into winter. The scene stays the same but its expression changes.

"I love this kind of book!" Norma Joyce sits down on the top step and turns the pages, and for the second time today her lap is swimming with images. "My son used to have a book like this."

What would it be like to paint on this sort of transparent material? she wonders. Like painting on film, but more manageable perhaps. What is it called? Mylar?

"You can keep it for a while," says Max.

"Max," she says, "you're a prince."

Max and Ida leave it with her, and she doesn't tire of watching each page settle perfectly over the previous scene, point for point, altering it slightly but significantly.

Now it's evening, and she's at the foot of her garden. She sees Mrs. Gallot bending over her bed of columbines and calls to her. They meet in the grassy laneway between the houses.

"I found something wonderful today," Norma Joyce says. "You have to come and look."

They follow the stone pathway down the slope and go up the back steps into the kitchen. The light inside is dim. Norma Joyce switches on the lamp hanging above the kitchen table and Mrs. Gallot sucks in her breath.

The table is covered with drawings, watercolours, oils.

"Where did you find them?"

"In the basement. The little room behind the oil tank. They were packed up in that," pointing to a flat wooden box leaning against the table. "I found a few cartons of Lucinda's things, then that box, wedged between them and the wall. I never bothered to go in there. Somehow I thought they were in a trunk."

"No, this is how we sent them." Mrs. Gallot puts on her glasses and begins to go through them, pausing to look at each one with delight.

There are several watercolours of flowers, some pencil drawings of family, sketches of the farm, a series of ink drawings of blades of grass, several nudes: Florida May from the waist up, the face sometimes blank, sometimes sketched in, and these almost too hard to look at, being such bald reminders of her isolation and sudden, early death, but so skilfully done that Norma Joyce feels both pleasure and pride. There are several oils too. Executed before Norma Joyce was born, or she would have remembered the smells of paint and turpentine. One is a portrait of Lucinda seated on a stool, bent in rapt concentration over a book.

"I was wrong. They didn't throw them out, after all."

"Thank goodness," says Mrs. Gallot, sitting down with a weighty sigh. "I was sorry to think they had."

"I misjudged them both." She picks up the oil painting of her sister. "How do you know, though? I mean at the time."

"You never know."

"Anyway, now there's a thought I can't get out of my head. I keep asking myself: Did Ernest forget, or did he choose not to tell me out of spite?" Norma Joyce shakes her head. "You know what he said to me? He said she didn't do much. I don't know whether I should be angrier for my mother, or for myself."

"Here." Mrs. Gallot pulls out the chair next to her. "Sit down beside me."

She sits down, and finds herself smiling as Mrs. Gallot reaches over and brushes a loose strand of hair off her forehead, a crumb off her lower lip. "Did I ever tell you," says Mrs. Gallot, "that my father went to bed for two years. He gave up. I don't know why. He lay on the sofa, reading magazines, and my mother and my brothers and I ran the farm."

Norma Joyce looks at her with interest. "What made him recover?"

"Oranges. It was a belief in those days. The efficacy of oranges."

Oranges. They come into view like a still life: peeled and fragrant on a plate.

"Your father wasn't spiteful," says Mrs. Gallot. "He was proud. And he was the first to help anybody in trouble. More than once he told us to take water from his well."

"He wasn't *just* spiteful," says Norma Joyce. Then she turns her eyes to the window. "It's too nice to be indoors. I'll walk you home."

Ottawa has taken her by surprise, so rapidly has it turned into a garden. The air is warm and lush, the grass thick, the foliage dense. In the laneway they meet Bella, who looks tired and admits that she hasn't been sleeping. Norma Joyce tells her that Mike the barber grows a white trumpet flower whose sweet scent is supposed to give you good dreams.

Bella shrugs. "The only flowers I know are nasturtiums. They like bad soil and hate fertilizer, so my poor mother never managed to kill them."

"It's true," agrees Mrs. Gallot. "They were the one flower you could grow in the Dust Bowl."

"I've got my ticket," Norma Joyce tells her. "June 10th to the 16th. A week is long enough, I think."

"It would be for me."

"Where are you off to?" asks Bella.

"She's going back to the scene of the crime. Dear old Saskatchewan."

"You'll be painting?"

Norma Joyce smiles at Mrs. Gallot and says, "My agent, Bella Pugg."

"There's only one thing I miss," says Mrs. Gallot. "The smell of the Prairie grasses."

"Yes."

"I used to have some tucked inside a book. When I came across it a few years ago and opened it up, they'd all turned to dust."

"I'll bring you some."

"The perfume was still there, though, as spicy as ever."

"I'll bring you some," says Norma Joyce.

On the morning before her trip, she walks down the laneway to the corner store, wondering as she looks around her if anything could be any greener. In the night, the heavy sky had emptied itself for an hour. Now the world has risen several inches in greenness. Jack's beanstalk is, in spirit, everywhere.

On the way back, carrying milk under her arm, she sees Max on the sidewalk in front of his house.

"Did you hear the big news?" he asks her, his hair standing up and out, his slender figure clad in shorts and a red-and-blue shirt. "I swallowed a quarter."

"No," she says. "No, you didn't."

They laugh, the two of them. But he means it. He says, "It stuck in my throat."

"How did you get it out?" she asks.

"With tweezers," he says.

The front door opens and Ida comes down the steps pushing her limp, dark hair behind her ears. A woman in need of a shower and a holiday. Yes, she confirms with a moan, "Can you believe it? As if I didn't have enough troubles." They had to spend four hours in Emergency, she says. Max was on oxygen and a heart monitor. Then they put him under, and removed the coin with a long pair of tweezers.

"How did it happen?" Norma Joyce asks Max.

He ducks his head. "I forget," he says. "It happened yesterday. I don't remember."

"He was flipping it," interposes Ida. "Lying back on the sofa as usual and flipping it in the air, and somehow – I was in the kitchen, I didn't see this – it fell down his throat and lodged behind his windpipe. Our little moneybags," shaking her weary head.

Max rubs his throat and observes, "It still feels sore." His voice is thoughtful. He has been the scene, the repository, of a big event, and now he no longer wants – or needs – to draw attention to himself. He looks subdued, almost burnished by the incident.

"Did the doctor give you back your quarter?"

"I threw it away," he says. "I never want to see it again."

"I don't blame you."

There's rain in southern Saskatchewan. Here, the air is dark and the ground is covered with petals.

In the kitchen she removes the last white tulip from the vase on the table and all its remaining petals fall off. She picks them up. In weight and appearance they're just like pieces of dead skin pulled off a lip.

She still feels punished by the cold water of her father's last words. It will take discipline, she knows, not to fall into self-pity, but to work, to get things done, to shoulder the rest of her life and not let it go to waste.

Upstairs, as she packs for her trip, she thinks of Ernest. The image of his grey, still, peaceful face alternates in her mind with the image of the coin falling into Max's fascinated mouth. She's not going to Saskatchewan *for* Ernest, or even for her mother, whose drawings of the farm are pinned to her bedroom walls. That is, she's not going for them alone. Something else is pulling her, though what it is she can't say.

She packs a raincoat, and games of cribbage come back to mind. Her father had been a childish loser until the very end. A grimly determined and regretful man. Brooding about the past while ploughing ahead. Full of complexity, yet simplistic about other people. "Lucinda," he loved to say, "gave of herself completely."

How they had hurt each other with their lack of mutual admiration.

Everything is in her bag now, but for one thing. She goes over to her dresser, where she has set aside a small white envelope. She hesitates, then picks it up and slides it into her bag.

Just outside Regina, Norma Joyce stops her rented green two-door sedan for an historic point of interest (as the sign says). It's early afternoon, the flight was easy, but now, unfortunately, she's the one behind the wheel. In her nervousness she imagines a green rental car piled up on the side of a deserted Prairie road. Either she will be dead, or she will owe a great deal of money.

There is hot bright wind and yellow flowers in the fields, a dead deer by the roadside. One glance at the deer and a piece of venison sticks in her throat.

Here everything is green too. Not a trace of what made for so many desperate lives and desperate deaths. The sign says she's standing on the bed of a glacial lake that emptied to the southeast fourteen thousand years ago, making way for a vast prairie of western porcupine grass, wheat grass, June grass, and blue grama grass to flourish on soil forty metres deep. She turns around in a circle, one hand shading her eyes, the other holding a map that flaps in the wind. On the green-and-white highway marker, one arrow points to Moose Jaw, the other to Winnipeg. Straight roads for anxious drivers.

She's even more anxious than she knows. Once back in the car and heading west, she looks in the side mirror and nearly jumps out of her skin because a green car is right on her tail. But then she sees it's her own car. Watch out, she thinks. The great adventurer is on the loose.

She calms herself by pretending she's her father. Ernest had been one of those tireless, competent men who could sit behind the wheel for hours. She remembers the long overnight drives he made to New York, fortified by the bag of seedless grapes on the seat beside him.

Just past Swift Current, low hills rise in the middle distance and moving at their base, and at her pace, is a long, dark freight train forming a necklace of beads around the soft-green hills. After a time the hills peter out, but still there's a roll to the land that invites anyone to reach out and smooth it. A line from *Adam Bede*: ". . . where the trees are few, so that a child might count them."

So this is why I came, she thinks. To see with my own eyes this wide, loping grassland. Whenever her glance shifts from road to landscape, her eyes relax.

All afternoon she drives. In the early evening, she reaches Tom's Guest House, southwest of Willow Bend. A big frame house painted white, with old Ontario lines inside and out, and she wonders how it came to be here, in this watered coulee beneath the lip of the far-reaching prairie, a fine old shoe dropped by some princess in a hurry.

Her room is on the second floor. The window faces west and jiggles in the everlasting wind. In the morning she comes downstairs and a small brown nut of a woman, lively and wrinkled, extends her hand, saying, "I'm Terry, Tom's wife. Who are *you*?" And, "Why are you here?"

The other guests come soon after. The tall young German, the small journalist with the notebook, the quiet librarian who loves Prairie history. They sit together at a long table in the dining room while Terry fills their cups with weak coffee and rolls her smokes from Player's Extra Light and Zig-Zag Kut Korners.

The journalist is writing an article about the Cypress Hills, "and anything else that takes my fancy," he says. Within minutes he has Terry remembering a yard sculpted down to bone-pavement by the wind, caterpillars coming in a straight line up the walls and over the roof, dust gathering against snow fences until it was so deep it was wonderful to play in. Her parents were burned out three times by prairie fires, and the fear of fire "just hung on them."

After breakfast, Norma Joyce climbs the steep driveway to the prairie bench above the coulee, where not a single tree inter-feres with the lines of low grassy hills in one direction and wheat fields in the other. Our place was near here, she had explained to Terry, but on the other side of Willow Bend, and she had given its location.

Terry said, "I wonder. I expect the Hutterites have it now."
"The Hutterites?"
"They've bought up a lot of land. You'd be surprised."

First, she drives to Willow Bend. It's smaller, quieter, emptier. The dairy is gone and the hardware store might as well be. It's no longer a tall, dark, narrow place of ceiling-high shelves, crammed and mysterious and male, and certainly her favourite place after the post office; now it's a wide-open floor full of bright plastic.

How eerie to come back to a place you know and not know it. How wide the gap between then and now, and how fast it fills with sadness unless you're careful. The town is familiar in outline but not in particulars. Two towns really, not unlike two sisters, whose connection only underscores the enormous distance between them.

The Chinese restaurants are gone, the Mint and the Gem, where sometimes her father would have a plate of ham and eggs while she and Lucinda ordered fried egg sandwiches with HP sauce. There's a place called Jim's Café now. She goes inside, sits by the window, orders a chicken sandwich, and hears someone behind her say *Daisy*.

She turns around and recognizes, one table over, Daisy Thompson. The girl who loved horses. Until she got pregnant at fifteen, she used to be great friends with Lucinda.

"Daisy?" Norma Joyce leans towards her table. "I wonder if you'll remember me."

Daisy looks up. She's wearing a soiled white blouse with short sleeves. Her skin is a mottled brown. Her eyes are china-plate blue. Her short, bushy hair is yellowy white.

"It's such a long time ago, but I'm Lucinda Hardy's sister. We used to live near here."

"I remember Lucinda Hardy. Roald? Don't you remember Lucinda Hardy?"

Daisy's big, affable companion stands up and pulls out a chair for Norma Joyce, who joins them and learns that they live together now, easygoing Roald of the graceful manners, and weatherbeaten Daisy of the intense-blue eyes. Daisy has her father's ranch. She spends her days there and her nights in town with Roald. A happy woman, thinks Norma Joyce. A happy pair.

They ask her about Lucinda and Ernest. They want to know where she's staying, and if she's been back to the farm yet.

"Well," says Roald. "There's no hurry."

"I imagine it's different."

"You won't recognize it," he says.

"Come to the ranch," Daisy urges. "Come any afternoon."

From the café Norma Joyce walks through the rest of Willow Bend and finds it in full decline. Stores boarded up, streets nearly empty. But it's noon and the church bells are ringing. She walks towards the bells, passing the high school she never attended, now turned into a museum open seven days a week, according to the wooden sign next to the sidewalk. She makes her way through an open space in a blossoming caragana hedge (the shrub imported from the Russian steppes in the 1890s, as Maurice once told her unimpressed father) and up the walkway to the museum steps. A piece of paper taped to the door has the names of two people who promise to open the place for you at any time. She writes down their names, and at the grocery store the woman behind the counter telephones for her. If she is willing to wait, someone will come by in half an hour.

She waits in the shade under a willow tree until the museum gent comes along. A healthy-looking old man in Bermuda shorts and sneakers. One of those coarsely genial men who loves to be listened to by any woman younger than himself. But Norma Joyce can be pushy too. He wants to show her all his railway memorabilia, she doesn't want to see it. He wants to show her all his war memorabilia, she doesn't want to see that either. She insists they move right past the glass cases full of faded uniforms and medals and flags, into a large room turned into a pioneer kitchen and sitting room at one end, and an archive of old books and newspapers at the other. She lets him show her the Zenith stove with its warming closet and water tank, the one-hundred-pound bags of flour and sugar, the fruit jars they used for canning meat, the horsehair furniture and handmade quilts, and then she buries her nose in a copy of *The Family Herald* from 1938.

How cozy newspapers were then, how they wrapped you round with a sense of many connected lives: toughminded Dorothy Dix, the continued stories, the recipes and lists of old superstitions, the ads from people looking for lost relatives, the ailments and accidents and cures, the advice about growing crops and living your life, the radio programs, the hymns, the long read. I miss the past, she thinks, raising her eyes and looking around her. *Welcome back to the thirties.* She suddenly remembers Mother Hulder's words.

Her guide in the Bermuda shorts doesn't leave her alone for long. He wants to know where she comes from, and some stubborn streak of privacy – or whatever it is that makes her choose difficulty – moves her to say that she's living in Ottawa, "at the moment."

"Ontario!" he spits. "The only place I hate more than Quebec is Ontario! Quebec for the language, Ontario for the money!" He says he grew up thinking Ontario had everything. Wealth, fine clothes, no hardships. A utopia. "This is into us yet today. We were the milk cow and Ontario had it all. Big boats, tall buildings. They had McIntosh apples, Mother talked about it. It was all a mystery, something you read about in books."

They're alone in the museum. It's large, filling all four rooms of the old school, as well as the hallway and the basement. Norma Joyce finds herself being taken through every room. It's almost three o'clock before she gets out the door. Even then he keeps talking. He wants to know what people in Ontario think of "us in Saskatchewan."

"What did you think?" he asks her. "When you were waiting for me to open the museum – did you think some old hick was going to show up? Does everybody in Ontario think Saskatchewan is full of hicks?"

Norma Joyce shakes her head. The sun is pouring down, the air is sweet with the smell of caragana in yellow blossom, and it occurs to her for the first time that her own unrequited love affair has always been nestled inside the larger one between Saskatchewan and Ontario. Saskatchewan so bitter, tenacious, aware. Ontario so careless and immune. An affair between two landscapes and two histories no less real, and no less ongoing than are certain romances between people.

She finds her mother's grave in the small cemetery outside town, and Norman's beside it. A lark bunting, small and black with white on its wings and a repertoire of the most musical whistles, flies straight up then settles down either on caragana bushes or on the ground. Many plots have been covered with long slabs of white cement, a recent clean-up, she imagines, by more prosperous descendants who let themselves be sucked in by some crackerjack cement salesman. Only a few old stones remain. *Florida May. Beloved wife of Ernest Rupert Hardy. 1896–1934.* And beside it, a smaller stone: *Norman Ernest Hardy. 1929–1931. Too good for this world.*

She sits down on the grass between the two graves and listens to the bird whistle its heart out. Lilacs are in blossom at the edge of the cemetery, planted no doubt by homesick settlers from the east. For a while she just sits here, thinking that we don't recover from things, and then we think we do. Look at the land. Completely green as though it was never touched by drought. But anyone who knows it, knows differently.

She has outlived them all, mother, brother, sister, father. She was the smallest, the darkest, the most difficult. But she's still here and they're not, and it would be wrong to miss a certain crowing of her inner voice. She is still the younger, competitive sister. A dwarf after gold. So there is the crowing and there is the tenderness as she looks east to Ontario, where her father and sister are buried, then back to these two grassy graves side by side.

And now she pulls over to the edge of the road to look at the farm. The house is gone. What's here is more industrial plant than family farm, a collection of pre-fab granaries, quonset huts, barracks-like buildings. No architectural beauty of any kind. No effort at trees or orchards. A few petunias in the way of flowers. A Hutterite farm now, and a blessing Ernest didn't come. He would have seen all his labour turned to account by a bunch of farmers being smart – she can hear his words – in the stupidest way.

The sight of their old farm being worked to death; the contrast between her father's dream of a watered, varied, fertile expanse and the reality, fifty years later, of farm as factory; the weight of his sense of failure; the overwhelming loss of the landscape – all these things make her rest her head on the steering wheel for some time, before she pulls away.

Then, in the rear-view mirror, as the farm disappears from sight, she catches a glimpse of her father's face – a certain look he sometimes had, and so rare that it always caught her off guard. She had seen it at her mother's funeral, and again when one of their outbuildings went up in smoke, and then on the day she took Johnny away to New York. It was almost a look of acquiescence – surprisingly mild – to a fate beyond his control.

On a back road west of Willow Bend, she pulls over to the side and stops next to a stretch of land "that's never been broke," as they say around here; virgin prairie, and her father's voice one of the few that had been raised in favour of its protection. She gets out of the car. In her pocket is the small white envelope she had packed at the last minute, as suspicious then as she is now of her motives. She takes it out of her pocket and opens it up. Then she shakes its contents into the everpresent wind (a hundred kinds of wind on the Prairie), and watches the wisp of her father's hair, white and fine, float over the long grass until it's out of sight. "Good night," she says, "old buzzard."

One evening Tom takes her for a long walk to the end of the coulee she's been exploring every morning; the young German comes along too. They meet behind the house, and off they go: slender Tom in his cowboy boots; tall, striding, big-boned Horst; and Norma Joyce, keeping up. We'll walk out on the bottom, says Tom, and come back on the top. Out through the watered valley, in other words, and back on the windswept plain. She likes having the two landscapes separated out this way, intricate tangle down below, bare prairie up above. One flavour at a time.

It's eight o'clock when they set out, and the sun is shining as it has been all day. Where the lawn ends, the path begins. It leads through long grass and over a crick into a stand of trembling aspen, past banks of wolf willow not yet in blossom ("but soon," says Tom), back to the same meandering stream and out to the hills at the far end of the coulee.

Right away she bends down and takes a blossom between her fingers to slow the rapid progress Tom means to make. He is a quick man, and agitated. She doesn't know why.

"What is it?"

"Wood violet," he says, also bending down over the small white flower, a crowd of them on the green floor. It seems to calm him, the act of stopping to identify the flower. They go more slowly after that.

Some things she remembers before he names them, but it's easier to pretend she knows nothing. "Field chickweed," he says of the tiny white flowers everywhere. "Hawthorns," of the silvery trees in white bloom. "We used to put a sheet on the ground and beat the trees to release the fruit." Saskatoon berries in white blossom. Blue larkspur. Snowberry bushes. A towering balm of Gilead in which a red-tailed hawk has its nest.

"That's a hymn," she says. "You don't know it?"

"No."

"Paul Robeson made it famous. I could sing it, but I'll spare you."

He smiles for the first time.

Three-flowered avens with their heavy, reddish-pink heads drooping down as if they *could* blossom more, but won't. That lowered-head resistance. *It happened yesterday. I forget.*

It's nearly dark when they get back. Tom lends her his local history of the area. She takes it to her room and reads into the night, coming back repeatedly to a photograph of two sisters who stand with their arms around each other, in short summer dresses, short dark hair, and bangs. The younger one clutches a black-and-white cat, the older clutches a black purse as if it were a cat. They look devoted to each other and intent on life, the younger more determined, the older more easily hurt; neither one smiles. They are Molly and Jean Perkins, daughters of the man who turned grey overnight, and what became of them? The older one married first, she reads, had two sons and died when she was thirty. The younger married the same man a year later, and they are both still alive.

That night, after falling asleep, she dreams that she's teaching a class of drawing students who are gathered in a circle. She leaves them for a moment to go to the bathroom and brush her hair, but the brush is full of Lucinda's hair. When she comes back, she notices a long snake sliding across the wall above their heads. They're unaware of it, and she isn't frightened. With a stick she reaches up, thinking to knock the snake down. To her surprise, it wraps itself around her wrist so firmly that the pressure wakes her up.

She opens her eyes, still unfrightened, and her brother Norman is at the foot of the bed, as clear as can be. The little-boy features, the grey woollen clothes hand-knit by their mother, the solid stance. He has one hand on the bedpost, and is gazing at her with thoughtful, calm, affectionate eyes. A most consoling presence.

The moment her feet touch the floor, he's gone.

She dresses, and very quietly goes down the stairs and outside. First light has just begun to nudge aside the darkness. She hears a horse moving through low willows beyond the edge of the lawn. A rooster crows. Then a wren starts up with its long song. She looks down at grasses the colour of winter knees. As pale as a boy's knees.

It gets lighter. Colour returns. And what she always hopes for when she looks at a painting happens now: a sense of relief as her eye moves from foreground to middle distance to horizon, from grass to bushes to low, bare hills and sky. She sees everything she's been overlooking for so long. The simple steady movement into the distance of landscape and light.

After breakfast, she gets out her drawing pad. Using a pencil with a very fine point, sharpened, as Nicolaïdes instructs, on sandpaper, she places the point of her pencil on the paper and imagines that the point is touching not the paper but the line of hills she is about to draw. Her pencil moves across the landscape like weather.

She draws all morning.

In the afternoon she finds Daisy surrounded by animals and sky, her eyes like turquoise beads (beautiful against her yellow-white hair and tanned skin). Daisy takes her into the kitchen, where they talk so intently that she overbakes the bread.

"We used to love to play house," Daisy says of herself and Lucinda. "Each of us took a slope and that was our farm. We rode wooden stick-horses. We were always outside. But that changed after your brother died." She could have said after your mother died, and that would have been true too. But this was truer. Everything changed after Norman died. She remembers her father staring at her with open dislike, her mother taking her into her lap, and her sister – this is the keenest memory – making room for her in her bed and putting an arm around her. She has touched a toothache of affection, and the pain stuns her.

Into her mind steals that long summer when Lucinda lay in bed week after week. *He could have written. It doesn't take much to write a simple letter.* Then, afterwards, how convenient it was to believe her sister was fine. She looked fine. She put on weight, she filled out, she didn't complain. And how easy to act accordingly. To overlook her once again and go after what she herself wanted. To underestimate what Lucinda was capable of feeling, to underestimate what those feelings could make her do.

"Never mind," says Roald when he joins them. "I *like* crusty bread."

After they have tea and the hot, buttered bread, Daisy shows her the house, room after room a decorative bedlam of fake flowers, photographs, newspaper clippings, wooden plaques, and flies. Lazy, lazy flies bounce against the windows. And here is Maurice's book about the grasslands on a table beside the saggy chesterfield.

"I'm in there, you know," says Daisy when Norma Joyce picks up the book. "He came here and interviewed me."

"Did he? I haven't read this one."

"I just read the part about me. Roald's the reader."

"What did you think of him? Maurice Dove?" Aware, and a little amused, that she still can't pass up a chance to say his name, or to talk about him.

"Oh, he's a fine figure of a man. See what he wrote inside?"

Norma Joyce opens the book and reads, *For Daisy Thompson, who gave me such a pleasant afternoon inside and out.* And a still-legible signature, despite his success.

"He mailed it to me," says Daisy. "He said he would, but I didn't expect it."

Such a charmer, thinks Norma Joyce, looking at the photograph on the back and remembering the first time she saw him, standing there at the foot of the steps. She was eight, and he was twenty-three.

A child falls in love with a man, and the man is seduced by the intensity he has generated. Then his attention shifts to something else. End of story.

She and Daisy step outside into a burst of liquid birdsong. Then walk through deep, crested wheat grass and broom, past a rabbit hutch, and into the shade created by a tall hedge of caraganas, which had been planted in a double row like a miniature boulevard, so that you could, if you chose, walk from end to end under the feathery leaves.

Norma Joyce says, "Wait." Hunching over, she makes her way down the leafy tunnel. At the far end she turns too quickly and a twig jabs her in the cheek.

"Foolishness," she says, rubbing her cheek with her hand and laughing as she emerges from the hedge. "I'm bigger than I thought."

Flush with the caragana runs a fence with a gate. They squeeze through the gate, checked by grass as in winter it would be checked by snow, and see, surrounded by meadow, the remains of the original log house built by Daisy's father sixty years ago.

It's nearly five o'clock when she leaves. The sun slants across prairie towards shadow-lengthened hills that invite walking, though no one seems to walk. She sees two men on horseback and a few cars, that's all.

The lift of the land, like a shirt on a man's back, and she feels her loins stir. She can't look enough, and she can't look without emotion.

Early the next morning, she comes back from sketching, her feet wet from the heavy dew, and closes the window in her room because it's surprisingly cold. Then she opens the big red book of local history. In 1903 it started snowing on the 20th of May. It was calm on the 21st, but stormed again on the 22nd and 23rd. "It would be difficult to say how much snow fell. All the cattle south of the river drifted." In the early fall of 1913, a prairie fire blackened the country. The snow, when it came, was too dirty to drink, and homesteaders had to carry water by pail and tea-kettle three miles from a neighbouring farm. On January 18, 1915, there was a blizzarding chinook and a rainbow. That was a wet year. It rained all summer and there was a fine crop. There was no rain the summer of 1917. "No rain saw the money fast disappearing from under the rock in the cellar where it was kept."

Now on a Thursday in June, 1972, it starts to rain. Oh, long-awaited, precious rain. It doesn't let up all morning. In her room, seated beside the wet window, Norma Joyce reads on. "Work as he would, he couldn't tire himself out," an Englishman who came to Canada because of ill health, and here became robust. His large map of the heavens was worn and tattered "from his sitting outside on winter nights holding it above his head so he could identify the stars and planets."

In the early afternoon the rain stops. Then she heads across the lawn. She takes the little wooden bridge over the crick and follows the path. Soon she's walking between banks of wolf willow. They form an aisle of silver leaves as luminous as the reflectors on a child's bike. They brush against her shoulders and she stops, takes a sprig between her fingers, and sees what she's been hoping to see all week – tiny, yellow-green, one, no, two of what will be many, and a smell like jasmine – just as strong but not as sweet because some wild-leaf smell cuts through the jasmine-sweetness. Under her eyes the wolf willow blooms. The prairie cinquefoil blooms. A lupin blooms. She raises her head and sees, eight feet away on a hawthorn branch, a large olive-coloured bird with bandit eyes and a Mohawk haircut. The name *cedar waxwing* drops into her mind. What a thrill.

Travel is medicine, says big-boned Horst over supper. "How do you say? I had love-pain," thinking of the German word and translating literally. He had gone to Morocco, broken-hearted and twenty-one, "and when I finished with the new problems, the old problems are not so big any more."

"What were you curing this time?" she asks him, but he only shakes his head and smiles.

Norma Joyce slings her leather satchel over her shoulder and heads to the car. There's a place she wants to draw before she leaves, a stretch of grassland a few miles away that leads to a bluff overlooking the Frenchman River.

She turns off the highway onto a dirt road the width of one car and proceeds for a mile or so before she parks. As usual, there's not another soul in sight.

It's seven o'clock in the evening. The sun is shining. The air is warm. She sets off through the long grass towards the bluff, her eyes on the view ahead. All around her, the place is jumping

with meadowlarks and lark buntings, and then it's jumping with
Norma Joyce Hardy. Directly at her feet a rattlesnake has reared
up, rattling and hissing like a maniac. She looks down at its
furious head and the coil it surges up out of; she looks straight
down its wide-open throat and then she's leaning against the car
door, out of breath and her heart pounding.

Standing close to the car, she makes a rapid sketch of this
fiercely guarded place. Then, working quickly and gingerly, she
gathers grasses to take home to Mrs. Gallot. Prairie wool, they
call it, because it's so coarse and matted.

Behind the wheel again, and out on the main road, she rolls
her window all the way down and drives for a time, zooming up
to the crest of a low hill, then dropping down into a valley full of
wolf willow, its smell so intoxicating that she breaks into song –
"Do Not Forsake Me Oh My Darlin'" – and there is no one,
absolutely no one on this patched and bumpy road in this nearly
empty province, to say HUSH.

The sun comes down in a final blaze of glory, the rattler rises
up in fury at her feet, and terror and joy press through her until
the accelerator is almost to the floor.

She arrives back to young Max under the linden tree. A Sunday afternoon, and he's beside himself with excitement because tomorrow is the day of his class picnic. Not once, he tells her, in all the years that his teacher's been having them, has it been anything but sunny on the day of the class picnic. That's what Miss Patterson says.

"Lucky you!" calls Ida in greeting. She has just come outside with a trowel in her hand. "You've been away! How was it?"

"Almost as good as a picnic," smiling at Max.

"But it's going to rain tomorrow," blurts Ida. "I just heard it on the radio."

Her son gives her a bitter look, then swings away from them both. He heads down the laneway, kicking at stones as he goes.

"He'll be so disappointed," says Ida. "Nobody gets more disappointed. Not even me."

"Maybe he'll be lucky. Maybe the weather will hold."

Mrs. Gallot has caught sight of her and is waving from the foot of her garden. So she leaves her suitcase on the back porch, and from her satchel takes the plastic bag of grasses and makes her way up the laneway.

"Smell this," opening the bag and raising it to Mrs. Gallot's nose.

Mrs. Gallot buries her head inside, then re-emerges. "*This* is what I wanted. I wish Bella could have smelled them."

"Could have?"

"She had to go home yesterday. Her mother. I guess they're worried she'll do herself harm."

"Oh dear. I'm sorry."

Mrs. Gallot looks at her face and says, "I don't mean to take the wind out of your sails. Come inside and tell me about your trip. Did you meet anybody we know?"

"Mr. Rattler."

"Who?"

Norma Joyce laughs, and puts her arm around Mrs. Gallot. "Don't you go moving away," she says.

A door bangs shut. In the darkness she reaches for her bedside clock, but can't make out the time. The wind has changed. Poor Max.

An hour later she's on the back porch in her dressing gown, seated on the top step, drinking coffee and waiting for the rain to arrive.

From two blocks away comes the low roar of Bronson Avenue, but worked into that awful background is this sort of birdsong, this sort of garden, this sort of boy coming down the slope in his pyjamas, crestfallen, angry, passionate about his picnic.

"No picnic," he says.

"I know. It's a shame."

He stares at the ominous sky, then kicks the step, miserable with anger and disgust.

"It's a big disappointment," she says. "Maybe you should have your own cup of coffee."

Wonderful, how such a small luxury cheers him. He sits on the step below her, drinking a cup of *café au lait*, as she called it with a flourish. "This wind," she tells him, "is number three on the Beaufort Scale. I was reading about it last night. See the leaves? How they move all the time? See that tea towel on Mrs. Hulder's line? Blowing out like that? The rain will be here soon. Maybe you'd better skedaddle."

But Max stays put.

The sky gets darker.

That you can know the speed of wind by the look of things under its influence, know the power of something by its effect on something else – these are simple truths that Beaufort put to use. At one, smoke moves but wind vanes do not; at two, leaves move a little and you feel wind on your face; at three, leaves move continuously and flags blow straight out; and so on, all the way up to twelve.

She looks down at the dark-haired boy. She says, "I know how to get a thought out of your head."

"How?" He looks at her curiously.

"You draw it."

"Or you can read a book."

"Yes. That's good too."

Then he points at her face. "What's that?"

"What?"

"That," and his finger pokes the spot where the caragana twig jabbed her.

"Ah," she says, "that's Saskatchewan," rubbing it slowly. There must be a bruise.

The first big fat drop lands on Max's head. "Hey!"

"You'd better be off," she says, and she watches him scamper up the slope and home. The screen door slams shut behind his bare feet.

Then the sky lets go. But she doesn't move off the step, not even when the rain pounds down so hard it spatters up onto her legs.

She has worked her way into the heaven of her childhood. Ontario, and all it means. This is where it took so long to "make the land" – three generations to clear two hundred acres of trees and stumps and stones. This is where weary listeners fell for those mythical tales about the Canadian west – how you could plough a furrow a mile long without ever striking a stone, how the feet of oxen were stained red by all the wild strawberries, how the light, dry, spicy air restored the feeblest person to health. This is the place they returned to, some of them, after drought and dust did them in.

She cups her cheek in her hand, aware of the smudge of colour she received when the landscape reached out to claim her and to push her away. I can use this, she thinks to herself. I can begin with the bruise.

ACKNOWLEDGEMENTS

For shepherding me through this novel, I must first thank Ellen Seligman; under her guidance, half a book became a whole book. I'm deeply grateful, as well, to Mark Fried, Lisan Jutras, and Bella Pomer.

Many people have shared information and anecdotes with me, and I thank them all. Let me name, in particular, Gladys Arnold, Nan Sussman, Peigi MacMillan, Rhoda and Roslyn Barrett, Sheila, Edith, and Katherine McCook, Stephen Darbyshire, Nina Phillips, Marian Devries, Ann and Jim Saville, Pansy White, and Norman Malmberg. Members of my own family have been constant sources of information, especially my mother-in-law Ruth Fried, and my parents, Jean and Gordon Hay.

I have relied on many books in my research, and would like to acknowledge several of them. *Between and Beyond the Benches*, edited by the Ravenscrag History Book Society, from which I drew the quotes on page 358; the two books by James Gray about the Prairies in the 1930s: *The Winter Years* and *Men Against the Desert*; Barry Broadfoot's *Ten Lost Years*; Pierre Berton's *The Great Depression 1929–1939*; H.H. Lamb's *Climate, History and the Modern World*; *The Third Radfords* by Joan Key; and two books that have been the best possible company: Wallace Stegner's *Wolf Willow* and Ian Frazier's *Great Plains*.

Finally, I am most grateful to the Canada Council, the Ontario Arts Council, and the Regional Municipality of Ottawa-Carleton for their generous support.